Praise for the Novels of Brad Taylor

The Polaris Protocol

"A great premise, nonstop action, and one of the baddest villains in the genre . . . make this a winner."
—*Publishers Weekly*

"Admirers of the late Tom Clancy will enjoy this and other works in the series." —*Kirkus Reviews*

"Taylor continues to tell exciting action stories with the authenticity of someone who knows the world of special ops. He also has the chops to create terrific characters whom readers will root for. This series just gets better and better." —*Booklist*

"With *The Polaris Protocol*, fans of military and espionage thrillers have a new reason to rejoice." —Bookreporter

"Brad Taylor knows all the ins and outs of the world of special ops. . . . A double dose of daunting bad guys . . . and nonstop action." —*Fort Worth Star-Telegram*

"There's no shortage of excitement in this fifth Pike Logan Thriller, so strap in; it's going to be a ride you won't soon forget." —The Big Thrill

The Widow's Strike

"Clever plotting and solid prose set this above many similar military action novels." —*Publishers Weekly*

"Don your hazmat suit, prop up your feet, and enjoy a good yarn." —*Kirkus Reviews*

"Taylor, whose background in Special Forces gives his work undeniable authenticity, delivers another exciting thriller that the covert-ops crowd will relish. Get this one into the hands of Vince Flynn fans." —*Booklist*

continued . . .

Enemy of Mine

"The story moves along at a rapid clip . . . satisfies from start to finish." —*Kirkus Reviews* (starred review)

"Few authors write about espionage, terrorism, and clandestine hit squads as well as Taylor does, and with good reason: He spent more than twenty years in the army before retiring as a Special Forces lieutenant colonel. His boots-on-the-ground insight into the situation in the Middle East and special skills in 'irregular warfare' and 'asymmetric threats' give his writing a realistic, graphic tone." —*Houston Press*

"Taylor gets exponentially better with each book, and if someone is hunting for a literary franchise to turn into a film, they need to be looking at this series."
—Bookreporter

"Action-packed. . . . Those who prize authentic military action will be rewarded." —*Publishers Weekly*

"Pike Logan returns in another stellar effort from Taylor, a retired Delta Force commander. . . . Readers of novels set in the world of Special Forces have many choices, but Taylor is one of the best." —*Booklist*

All Necessary Force

"Fresh plot, great action, and Taylor clearly knows what he is writing about. . . . When it comes to tactics and hardware, he is spot-on."
—#1 *New York Times* bestselling author Vince Flynn

"The first few pages alone . . . should come with a Surgeon General's warning if you have a weak heart."
—Bookreporter

"The high violence level and authentic military action put Taylor, a retired Delta Force officer, solidly in the ranks of such authors as Brad Thor and Vince Flynn."
—*Publishers Weekly*

ALSO BY BRAD TAYLOR

THE
POLARIS
PROTOCOL

A PIKE LOGAN THRILLER

BRAD TAYLOR

DUTTON

DUTTON

An imprint of Penguin Random House LLC
375 Hudson Street
New York, New York 10014

Previously published as a Dutton hardcover and a
Signet mass market paperback

First Dutton paperback printing: January 2018

Copyright © 2014 by Brad Taylor
Excerpt from *Operator Down* copyright © 2018 by Brad Taylor
Penguin supports copyright. Copyright fuels creativity, encourages diverse voices,
promotes free speech, and creates a vibrant culture. Thank you for buying an
authorized edition of this book and for complying with copyright laws by not
reproducing, scanning, or distributing any part of it in any form without permission. You are supporting writers and allowing Penguin to continue to publish
books for every reader.

DUTTON and the D colophon are registered trademarks of
Penguin Random House LLC.

ISBN 978-0-451-46767-6

Printed in the United States of America
10 9 8 7 6 5 4

To Skeeter and Allan, my biggest cheerleaders

Civil GPS receivers are built deeply into our national infrastructure: from our smartphones to our cars to the Internet to the power grid to our banking and finance institutions. Some call GPS the invisible utility: it works silently, and for the most part perfectly reliably, in devices all around us—devices of which we are scarcely aware.

Dr. Todd Humphreys, statement to the
House Committee on Homeland Security

His story is about power, but he is never really in control. . . . His world is not as imagined in novels and films. He is always the man who comes and takes you and tortures you and kills you. But still, he is always worried, because his work stands on a floor of uncertainty. Alliances shift, colleagues vanish—sometimes because he murders them—and he seldom knows what is really going on. He catches only glimpses from the battlefield.

Molly Molloy and Charles Bowden, *El Sicario:
The Autobiography of a Mexican Assassin*

1

December 2011

Sergeant Ronald Blackmar never heard the round be-fore it hit, but registered the whine of a ricochet right next to his head and felt the sliver of rock slice into his cheek. He slammed lower behind the outcropping and felt his face, seeing blood on his assault gloves. His pla-toon leader, First Lieutenant Blake Alberty, threw himself into the prone and said with black humor, "You get our asses out of here, and I'll get you another Purple Heart."

Blackmar said, "I've got nothing else to work with. The eighty-ones won't reach and the Apaches are dry."

Another stream of incoming machine-gun rounds raked their position, and Alberty returned fire, saying, "We're in trouble. And I'm not going to be the next COP Keating."

Both from the Twenty-fifth Infantry Division, they were part of a string of combat outposts in the Kunar province of Afghanistan. Ostensibly designed to prevent the infiltration of Taliban fighters from the nearby border of Pakistan, in reality they were a giant bull's-eye for anyone wanting a scalp. Attacked at the COP on a daily basis, they still followed orders, continuing their patrols to the nearby villages in an effort to get the locals on the government's side.

The mountains of the Kunar province were extreme and afforded the Taliban an edge simply by putting the Americans on equal terms. Everything was done on foot, and the mountains negated artillery, leaving the troops reliant on helicopter gunship support. The same thing COP Keating had relied on when it was overrun two years before.

The incoming fire grew in strength, and Alberty began receiving reports of casualties. They were on their own and about to be overrun. A trophy for the Taliban. Blackmar heard the platoon's designated marksmen firing, their rifles' individual cracks distinctive among the rattle of automatic fire, and felt impotent.

As the forward observer, he knew the purpose of his entire career had been to provide steel on target for the infantry he supported. He was the man they turned to when they wanted American firepower, and now he had nothing to provide, his radio silent.

Alberty shouted, "They're flanking! They're flanking! We need the gunships."

Blackmar was about to reply when his radio squawked. "Kilo Seven-Nine, this is Texas Thirteen. You have targets?"

He said, "Yes, yes. What's your ordnance?"

"Five-hundred-pound GBU."

GBU? A fast mover with JDAMs?

He said, "What's your heading?"

The pilot said, "Don't worry about it. I'm a BUFF. Way above you."

Blackmar heard the words and couldn't believe it. He'd called in everything from eighty-one-millimeter mortars to F-15 strike aircraft, but he'd never called fire from a B-52 Stratofortress. Not that it mattered, as the five-hundred-pound JDAM was guided by GPS.

He lased the Taliban position for range, shacked up his coordinates, and sent the fire request. The pilot reported bombs out, asking for a splash. He kept his eyes on the enemy, waiting. Nothing happened.

Alberty screamed, "You hit the village! You hit the village! Shift, shift!"

The village? That damn thing is seven hundred meters away.

He checked his location and lased again, now plotting the impact danger close as the enemy advanced. He repeated the call with the new coordinates and waited for the splash.

Alberty shouted again, "You're pounding the fucking village! Get the rounds on target, damn it!"

Blackmar frantically checked his map and his range, shouting back, "I'm right! I'm on target. The bombs aren't tracking."

The volume of enemy fire increased, and Alberty began maneuvering his forces, forgetting about the firepower circling at thirty thousand feet. Blackmar called for another salvo, recalculating yet again. No ordnance impacted the enemy. Thirty minutes later, the Americans' superior firepower meant nothing, as the fight went hand-to-hand.

CAPTAIN "TINY" SHACKLEFORD noticed the first glitch when the coordinates on his screen showed the RQ-107 unmanned aerial vehicle a hundred miles away from the designated flight path. Which, given his target area over Iran's nuclear facilities, was a significant problem.

Flying the drone from inside Tonopah airbase, Nevada, he felt a rush of adrenaline, as if he were still in the cockpit of an F-16 over enemy airspace and his early-warning sensors had triggered a threat. He called an alert, saying he had an issue, then realized he'd lost the link with the UAV. He began working the problem, trying to prevent the drone from going into autopilot and landing, while the CIA owners went into overdrive.

The RQ-107 was a new stealth UAV, the latest and greatest evolution of unmanned reconnaissance, and as such, it was used out of Afghanistan to probe the nuclear ambitions of Iran. It had the proven ability to fly above the Persian state with impunity and was a major link to the intelligence community on Iranian intentions. Losing one inside Iranian airspace would be a disaster. An army of technicians went to work, a modern-day version of *Apollo 13*.

They failed.

*   *   *

MARK OGLETHORPE, THE United States secretary of defense, said, "We've had forty-two confirmed GPS failures. We've identified the glitch, and it's repaired, but we lost a UAV inside Iran because of it."

Alexander Palmer, the national security adviser, said, "Glitch? I'd say it's more than a glitch. What happened?"

"The new AEP system of the GPS constellation had a software-hardware mating problem. It's something that the contractor couldn't see beforehand."

"Bullshit. It's something they *failed* to see. Did it affect the civilian systems? Am I going to hear about this from Transportation?"

"No. Only the military signal, but you're definitely going to hear about it from the Iranians. They're already claiming they brought our bird down."

Palmer rubbed his forehead, thinking about what to brief the president. "I don't give a damn about that. They got the drone, and that's going to be a fact on tomorrow's news. Let 'em crow."

"You want to allow them the propaganda of saying they can capture our most sophisticated UAV? We'll look like idiots."

"Someone *is* an idiot. But I'd rather the world wonder about the Iranian statements."

"As opposed to what?"

"The fucking truth, that's what."

2

Joshua Bryant saw the seat belt light flash and knew they had just broken through ten thousand feet. Time to shut off his iPod, but more important, it was his turn in the window seat.

Only fifteen years old, his passion in life was airplanes and his singular goal was to become a pilot—unlike his younger sister, who only wanted the window to aggravate him. She'd complained as they had boarded, and his mother had split the difference. She got the window for takeoff, and he got it for landing.

"Mom, we're coming into final approach and it's my turn."

His sister immediately responded, "No we're not! He's just talking like he knows what's going on."

Joshua started to reply when the pilot came over the intercom, telling them they had about ten more minutes before parking at their gate in Denver. Joshua smiled instead, just to annoy her. She grouched a little more but gave up her seat.

After buckling up, he pressed his face against the glass, looking toward the wing jutting out three rows up, watching the flaps getting manipulated by the pilot. The aircraft continued its approach and he saw the distinctive swastika shape of Denver International Airport.

A flight attendant came by checking seat belts at a leisurely pace, then another rushed up and whispered in her ear. They both speed-walked in the direction of the cockpit, the original flight attendant's face pale.

Joshua didn't give it much thought, returning his attention to the window. He placed his hands on either side of his face to block the glare and began scanning. On the ground below he saw a small private plane taxiing. With as much conscious thought as someone recognizing a vegetable, he knew it was a Cessna 182.

The Boeing 757 continued to descend and began to overtake the Cessna. Strangely, the Cessna continued taxiing. With a start, Joshua realized it had taken off, directly underneath them. He watched it rise in slow motion, closing the distance to their fragile airship.

He turned from the window and screamed, "Plane! An airplane!"

His mother said, "What?"

The Cessna collided with the left wing just outside the engine, a jarring bump as if the 757 had hit a pocket of turbulent air. Passengers began to whip their heads left and right, looking for someone to explain what had happened.

Twenty feet of wing sheared off as the Cessna chewed through the metal like a buzz saw, exploding in a spectacular spray of aluminum confetti, followed by a fuel-air ball of fire.

Joshua knew the wing would no longer provide lift. Knew they were all dead.

He was the first to scream.

The aircraft yawed to the left, seeming to hang in the air for the briefest of moments, then began to plummet to earth sideways. The rest of the passengers joined Joshua, screaming maniacally, as if that would have any effect on the outcome.

The fuselage picked up speed and began to spin, the centrifugal force slapping the passengers about, one minute right side up, the next upside down, filling the cabin with flying debris.

Four seconds later, the screams of all one hundred and eighty-seven souls ceased at the exact same moment.

3

Three Days Ago

"They're here. I just heard the door open and close."

Even though the door in question was to the adjacent hotel room, the man whispered as if they could hear him as clearly as he could them.

"Jack, for the last time, as your editor, this is crazy."

"You didn't say that when I began."

"That was before you started playing G. Gordon Liddy at the Watergate!"

Jack heard voices out of the small speaker on the desk and said, "I gotta go. Stay near your phone in case I need help."

He heard "Jack—" but ended the call without responding.

He checked to make sure the digital recorder was working, then leaned in, waiting on someone to appear on the small screen. The thin spy camera had slipped out of position just a bit, making the room look tilted.

A hefty Caucasian sat down in view, wearing jeans and a polo shirt that was a size too small. *The contact.*

Another man began speaking off camera, in flawless English with a slight Spanish accent, which, given what Jack was investigating, was to be expected. The words, however, were not. Nothing the man said had anything to do with the drug cartels or America. It was all about technology.

Eventually, the contact spoke. Jack leaned in, willing him to say what he wanted to hear. Wanting to believe his insane risk had been worth it.

He, also, said not a word about drugs, but blathered on about the right of the masses to digital technology and the developed-world governments' undying interest in monopolizing information.

Jack rubbed his eyes. *What the hell is this all about? Who gives a shit about information flow?*

The guy sounded like an anarchist, not a connection for the expansion of the Sinaloa drug cartel into America. The contact droned on about his ability to free up information, then said something that caused Jack to perk up. He mentioned the US Air Force in Colorado Springs.

Now we're getting somewhere.

Colorado Springs was just outside Denver and was the American crossroads for the Interstate 10 drug corridor leading out of El Paso, which passed right by the hotel he was now in. Running straight up until it connected with US Interstate 25, the corridor branched left and right at Colorado Springs, into the heartland of the United States. The future battleground he was trying to prove was coming.

Jack leaned in, straining to catch every word, but most had nothing to do with drugs, or Mexico, or anything else he was investigating. He sat back, disgusted and angry that he'd paid the informant who led him to this meeting. Angry at the risk he had taken. Something bad was going on, but it wasn't anything he cared about.

Wasted money. Wasted time.

Through the speaker, he heard the door open again, not really listening anymore, cataloging how he could reconnect with his sources and informants. Trying to figure out how he could get back on the pulse of his story.

A voice in Spanish splayed out, begging for mercy. The sound punctured his thoughts, not because of the words, but because of the terror, the cheap acoustics doing nothing to mask the dread. Jack stared at the screen, but the man remained outside the scope of the lens. He begged for his life, the fear seeping through like blood from a wound. On camera, the American contact had his hands in the air, his mouth slack, clearly unsure what was going on. Jack heard his own name and felt terror wash over him like an acid bath.

Jesus Christ. It's the desk clerk. He's sold me out.

He slammed the lid to the digital recorder closed and shoved it under the bed, then grabbed the speaker and yanked it out of its connection to the wireless receiver. He threw it in the bathroom, then fumbled for his phone, his hands shaking, looking for a way out that wasn't the door. He realized there was none. Realized he'd made a catastrophic mistake.

He pulled up speed dial and hit a button. The phone went straight to voice mail. He shouted, "Andy, Andy, I'm in trouble. I'm in big trouble. Where the fuck are you?"

The door burst open and he remained standing, the phone trembling in his hand. Two men entered, both pointing pistols at him. He shouted, "No, no, no!" throwing his arms into the air. One snarled in Spanish, and he feigned ignorance. The other said in English, "Get on your knees. Now."

He did so, the fear so great he thought he would pass out. He'd studied the Mexican drug cartels for over four years, seeing the savagery they would inflict on those who attempted to thwart them, and in no way did he want to provoke their ire any more than he had.

They handcuffed him with efficiency, no outward abuse, no punches or smacking just because they could, which did nothing but raise his alarm. They weren't local thugs. They were trained and had done this many times before. He began calculating what he could do. How long he had. He knew they wouldn't kill him here, in El Paso. The drug trade was vicious, violent beyond the average human's comprehension, but it still wasn't here. They'd move him, which meant some time. At least a day while they tried to get him across the border, to Ciudad Juárez, where they could torture him freely.

One day. Twenty-four hours. He looked at his watch and saw the seconds begin to disappear.

4

I opened the door and felt like I needed an oxygen mask from the smoke spilling out, the nightclub so full of fumes from cigarettes that I was having a hard time seeing five feet.

Guess this place hasn't heard of the secondhand dangers.

I felt Jennifer recoil and pulled her inside. Sometimes you get to play baccarat at Monte Carlo in a tuxedo, sometimes you have to belly up to a smoke-infested bar in Turkmenistan. *Story of my life.*

The room reminded me of the bar at the beginning of *Raiders of the Lost Ark,* where Indiana Jones met up with his ex-girlfriend. A bunch of burly men and raunchy women yelling and shouting at one another. All I needed to do was get Jennifer to challenge some big-ass bear of a man to a vodka-drinking contest, and the image would be complete.

Sotto voce, Jennifer said, "This place looks like the cantina in *Star Wars.*"

I chuckled and said, "Wrong movie. Come on. We've got thirty minutes before the meet. Let's see if we can blend in that long."

We found a table in the corner, and I checked my phone, seeing I had lost service yet again. The cellular infrastructure inside Ashgabat, the capital of Turkmenistan, was pathetic to say the least. It was making our surveillance effort very difficult, but in truth no harder than it had been for our commando forefathers who worked through the Cold War. It just meant we had to go old-school.

I keyed the radio strapped to my leg and leaned into Jennifer, as if I were talking to her. "Knuckles, you staged?"

"Yes. We got a box. You send the photo and trigger, and we'll do the rest."

"Roger all."

Jennifer glanced at her watch and said, "This guy is cutting it close."

"I know. He's not stupid. He's aware of the curfew, and he's going to use it."

Nobody was allowed to walk around after eleven at night in the capital, but really that was a crapshoot. A lot of people did, and the police then usually picked on the westerners to fleece for bribes. Or other unsavory things. There had been reports of them arresting women, taking them to jail, then extorting sexual favors. It would make a surveillance effort after the witching hour very, very hard.

"What if he doesn't show? Are we going to push it and try again tomorrow or head to Gonur?"

"We still have forty-eight hours. One more night. If he doesn't show then, we're leaving for Gonur. We can't blow off the contract. This was just a freebie anyway."

Gonur was a four-thousand-year-old archeological site set in the middle of the Karakum desert, and we, as the proud owners of a company called Grolier Recovery Services, had been hired to help a team of experts take a look at the dig. Well, at least that's what the government of Turkmenistan thought.

In reality, we were a cover corporation using counterterrorist operators as employees, all working for an organization so removed from the traditional US defense and intelligence infrastructure it didn't even have a real name. We simply called it the Taskforce, and it had sent us to Turkmenistan to identify a wealthy Saudi Arabian who was funding the Islamic Movement of Uzbekistan. Unfortunately, our cover took precedence over the mission, so if we didn't locate the contact, we were looking at spending a few days sweating in the desert. Something Jennifer would love. She enjoyed anything and everything dealing with old crap.

She waved her hand in front of her face, trying to clear the smoke, while she surveyed the bar, looking for our linkage target. She said, "I can't believe Pedro would meet a rich Saudi in this dump. Why not in a mosque? Or any number of coffee shops? The intel seems off to me."

Pedro was our nickname for a terrorist affiliated with the IMU. He was all set to be removed from the playing field in Uzbekistan when the Taskforce learned he was meeting a contact in Ashgabat. They decided to see if we could identify the contact, implant a collection device in his personal effects, and try to swim upstream to the

Kingdom of Saudi Arabia with the end state being identification of the money man.

I said, "The mosques here are all owned by the government. In fact, the government monitors everything here, like it's still part of the Soviet Union. He'd need someplace noisy. Someplace that self-defeats the bugs all over this damn country."

Which was why we wouldn't be doing anything overt against Pedro. Much easier to take him down when he returned to Uzbekistan. Our mission was pure snoop and poop. No high adventure.

I went to the bar, happy to see a smattering of Europeans, including one old couple clearly forcing themselves to enjoy the "culture." Jennifer and I wouldn't stand out. I got a couple of glasses of hot tea, and by the time I had returned to the table, Jennifer said, "Pedro's at the door."

I casually glanced that way and saw him, our linkage target. He was swarthy, with a full head of chestnut hair and a red beard that looked like a briar patch. Dressed in a striped shirt, the sleeves rolled up to the elbows and the tails hanging out over a pair of black slacks made of rough cloth, he looked like every other regular. He glanced around, locked on something, then began walking toward our three o'clock. I followed his line of march and saw a single man sitting at a table smoking a cigarette. *Bingo*.

"Jennifer, you see where he's headed?"

"Yeah, yeah, I got him."

"It'll be your camera."

We each had a covert digital setup embedded in our clothing—me in the upper shoulder of my jacket, and Jennifer in a brooch on her chest, the battery pack, brains, and Bluetooth transmitter hidden in our clothing. We'd purposely sat at ninety degrees to each other to give us complete coverage of the room. If he had gone toward the nine o'clock, I'd have been getting the picture.

The cameras were digital marvels controlled by our smartphones. They had limited optical zoom but a very, very good digital zoom complete with digital stabilization. The hard part had been getting the things to line up naturally to what we wanted to see, as my jacket kept shifting when I sat down, and Jennifer, believe it or not, couldn't get the thing to aim level because of the swell of her breast. After screwing around with them for a while, we'd managed to figure it out.

Jennifer brought out her phone and began working it, the image from the camera fed to it via Bluetooth. I waited to confirm the man was Pedro's contact, then began relaying to Knuckles as a backup to the photo.

"Knuckles, Pike. Zulu One located. Prepare to copy description."

After a few seconds, I heard, "Send it."

"Dark top, black, possibly blue. Long sleeve, button front. No jacket. Sleeves rolled completely down. Youngish, twenty-five to thirty. Hawklike face, long nose. Swarthy—looks Saudi. Long hair down to his collar, but well kept. Looks long on purpose, not because he can't afford a barber. Small mustache but clean chin. No outstanding identifying marks. Sort of looks like Jake Gyllenhaal in *Prince of Persia*."

Jennifer, working the digital zoom, looked up and said, "He doesn't look anything like Jake Gyllenhaal. What an insult."

I keyed my radio. "Correction. Apparently Jake is much, much more attractive. Stand by for photo."

Jennifer fiddled with her phone for a second longer, then nodded at me.

My radio crackled to life and I heard, "This guy doesn't look a damn thing like Jake Gyllenhaal, except for the hair."

Jennifer grinned, and I said, "Sue me. You guys collapse in?"

"Yeah, we're set."

I saw Jennifer scrunch her eyebrows, still looking at her phone. I glanced at Jake and Pedro, but they weren't doing anything suspicious.

"What's up?"

"My phone just picked up a signal. I have a missed call and a voice mail."

"Who in the world is calling you in Turkmenistan?"

"Jack. My brother Jack."

5

The desk clerk, a trembling, rail-thin man of about sixty, was brought in and slammed into the wall next to Jack. Behind him a dapper man in a business suit entered, taking a seat. The original hard-asses both remained standing. All four were of Hispanic origin.

The gunslingers stayed mute. In Spanish, the dapper man said, "Who do you work for?"

Jack feigned ignorance again, saying, "I don't speak Spanish."

In English, the dapper man said, "You may call me Carlos. Please, tell me why you are here."

Holding nothing back, knowing it might help him survive, Jack said, "I'm a reporter for the *Dallas Morning Star*. My editor knows where I am and will be looking for me. It does you more harm than good to hurt a reporter inside America, and I swear I didn't hear anything incriminating."

Carlos turned to one of the gunslingers. "His phone?"

The man passed it over, and Carlos checked the call

log. "What did you tell the man on the other end of this phone?"

"Nothing," Jack said. "It went to voice mail. All I said was I was in trouble. I swear I haven't *heard* anything."

Looking at the number, Carlos said, "Then why would you feel you were in trouble?"

"Because of who you are. What you represent."

Carlos squinted at the phone, then said, "This isn't a Dallas area code. Who did you call?"

Confused, Jack said nothing, unsure whether Carlos was trying to trick him. Carlos held out the phone, allowing Jack to read the number. His heart sank deeper into the void. *Andy isn't going to do anything.*

He said, "It's nobody. I misdialed."

"Misdialed the entire area code? Who is it?"

Jack struggled to come up with an answer. Anything to deflect attention from the true answer. "It's just a friend I have on speed dial. Someone I went to school with. His speed-dial number is next to my editor's."

Carlos brought up the menu, checked the speed dial, then chuckled and pulled out his own phone, saying, "Not exactly Woodward and Bernstein, are you?"

He dialed a number and stood, moving to the bathroom and letting a gunslinger close in on Jack. Carlos began speaking in Spanish, laying out what had occurred up to this point. Fairly fluent, Jack learned he had interrupted something much more sinister than the expansion of drugs into the United States.

"No, Señor Fawkes still believes we're computer people like him. Hacktivists. He does not know the reasons behind our meeting. He's paranoid but not stupid. He just about fainted when my men came in with pistols. He'll realize something else is afoot if I don't give him some misdirection."

The man on the other end spoke, and Carlos answered, "Yes, I think he can do it. He works at the air force base in Colorado, the one that controls the navigation satellites. The ones that tell the drones where to fly. I think it's worth continuing. We take out their eyes, and we can go back to the old days. The old ways. We'll be the only ones who can do it. Los Zetas will still get caught by them, and the plaza will be ours."

Carlos listened a few seconds longer, then turned his eyes on the desk clerk, saying, "We have paid him handsomely many times in the past. He deserves death for his treachery, but I think we can use him to deflect attention if anyone comes around asking. Keep him alive a little bit longer. I'll pay him before I leave and remind him that I know where his family lives. What about the man himself? The reporter?"

Jack saw the desk clerk's eyes widen and strained to keep his face neutral, waiting on his own fate. What he heard caused his heart to stutter.

"I can't do that here, in America. I'll need a car that can get across the border. Send someone with a SENTRI Pass. I'll be staying at house four."

They're going to take me to Juárez. Kill me using our own trusted-traveler program.

Carlos hung up and said, "Watch him."

CARLOS REENTERED THE original hotel room and saw Mr. Guy Fawkes sitting in a chair, pasty and sweating. *Guy Fawkes. Cute little alias name. Playing me for a stupid cabrón.* An obese Caucasian with greasy hair and a three-day growth of beard, he was clearly out of his depth.

"Mr. Fawkes, sorry for the interruption. My men thought someone had followed you, but apparently they are just overeager."

"Carlos, I don't do violence. I do computers. I'm about transparent information. I was told you could use my information. Let it out inside Mexico."

"I understand completely. I'm sorry, but where I'm from violence is a way of life. I apologize, but tell me, why didn't you send this to someone here? Someone you trust in the networks in the United States?"

Fawkes licked his lips and rubbed the sweat off his brow. "With my job I can't afford it getting back to me. I want it nowhere near me. You saw what happened to Bradley Manning? The WikiLeaks soldier? Or Edward Snowden? The NSA whistle-blower? The damn US government is all over this stuff. They have tendrils everywhere in America. But not in Mexico."

Carlos nodded. "I see. So it has nothing to do with the money I'm willing to pay you?"

Fawkes looked flustered for a moment, then said, "Hey, don't question why I'm doing this. I want it out. *Everyone* wants it out. Fuck this, man, I didn't ask for some *Miami Vice* shit. I'll go somewhere else."

Carlos said, "Calm down. I just have to make sure. If you want it out so badly, I'll take it for free. Because I'm in Mexico, and as you say, I can get it into the world."

Fawkes shuffled in his chair a bit, then wiped his nose like a fifth grader. "I have what you want, but it's not free. Understand?"

Carlos remained silent for a moment, watching the man twitch and knowing he could get whatever he wanted without paying a dime. But he needed something more. He needed the man's skills. He said, "Do me a favor. Run this number for me. Tell me who it belongs to."

Fawkes said, "A test?"

"Perhaps. I, too, have to make sure you are who you say you are."

Fawkes opened up a laptop and got online. Carlos passed him the number, then waited, Fawkes's sausage fingers racing over the keyboard. Eventually, he looked up and said, "It's an archeological firm in Charleston, South Carolina. Not a whole lot of information tied to it. I got a Dun and Bradstreet number, some credit stuff. What in particular did you want?"

Carlos thought about it, wondering what the hell Jack's call could have been about. *Maybe it really was just a friend. Or maybe he's working for the Federales.*

Carlos smiled. "I'd like you to take a closer look when

you get back home. Just poke around and see if you can find anything strange."

Fawkes pulled his head back like a turtle, exposing the folds of his double chin. "You think this is someone after me?"

Not after you. "No, no. I'm just curious. Consider it a favor. How long before your product is ready?"

"I'm not sure. It depends on a lot of different factors. They've just turned on the new control system, and it has some glitches. I have to wait for an aberration, and then when they call me to patch it, I can build the bridge. Shouldn't be more than a week, though."

Carlos passed across a cell phone. "Call me on this when you're ready. Don't use it for anything else."

Mr. Fawkes rose unsteadily, his face glowing with a rancid glean of sweat. He skipped past Carlos, giving him a wide berth on the way out, his body odor lingering long after he closed the door.

A few minutes later, Jack was brought in and thrown onto the floor, the gunslinger passing Jack's wallet across.

Carlos flipped through it and said, "Well, Mr. Jack Cahill, as I'm sure you are much more self-aware than that one wrong phone call would indicate, I'm really going to need everything you heard. I have to know what I envision is still safe."

"I swear to God, I thought I was investigating a drug deal. I have no idea what is going on here. I didn't tell anyone a thing."

"You found this meeting somehow. Someone talked. I need to know who."

When Jack said nothing, Carlos motioned to one of the gunmen, who pulled him to his feet.

Carlos said, "Don't worry, we have plenty of time."

6

I could tell the voice mail was eating at Jennifer. She couldn't listen to it because of the crappy signal and desperately wanted to go back outside where it was stronger. Unfortunately, the mission took priority.

"He probably just wanted to say hello."

She brushed a hair out of her face, saying, "That's not it. I talked to him before I left, like I always do. He knew I was out of town. He wouldn't call unless it was important."

Jennifer was very close with her family, calling both of her brothers and her mother once a week just to chat. Her father was the only one she had no time for.

I said, "Well, whatever it is, you can't do anything immediately from seven thousand miles away, even if you could hear the voice mail. It's close to eleven. These guys will be leaving soon."

She leaned back, and I saw the fear in her eyes. "I hope nothing's happened to Mom. I don't know what else it could be."

I knew the unique dread she felt because it was baggage we all carried on deployment—that a tragedy would befall our family while we were gone—but it rarely came true. I had a little special sympathy, though, because in my case it had.

I said, "Useless worry. Whatever it is, we'll handle it. Together."

She squeezed my hand and said, "Thanks." Her eyes shifted over my shoulder, and she squeezed again. "Pedro just passed Jake a compact disc. They're preparing to leave."

I didn't want to whip my head around, knowing she had the targets in sight. I said, "Go ahead."

She keyed her radio. "Knuckles, this is Koko. Trigger. Jake is leaving first. Pedro is paying the bill."

"Roger. How long?"

"He'll break the plane of the door in five seconds."

"Roger all. We got the ball."

We waited an additional ten minutes, and I saw we were going to be cutting the curfew very, very close. Our hotel wasn't far away, but there weren't very many cabs in this weird city, and we'd need to hoof it or be in danger of getting picked up.

We hit the streets and Jennifer immediately shoved her phone in the air, looking at the signal bar. She began walking down the road like a beagle sniffing a scent, holding her phone this way and that.

I followed behind her, saying, "Jennifer, it's the witching hour. Let's do this from our hotel."

She cut into an alley, saying, "We don't have a signal at the hotel. Let me just check as we go."

She was headed in the right direction, so I let her continue. The narrow space of the alley was lined on both sides with four-story apartment buildings, turning it dark enough that her face was illuminated only by the screen of her phone. She said, "Somebody's got a repeater around here. Signal's getting stronger."

Exasperated, I said, "Jennifer, it's past eleven. Come on."

She stopped, read the signal bar one more time, and dialed her voice mail. I looked past her, toward the end of the alley, and saw two forms leaving the glow of a streetlight. Coming our way. *Great.*

They keyed on the light of her phone. One shouted in Russian. I said hello in English. They picked up their pace and reached us in seconds, wearing uniforms of some kind. I had no idea who or what they were but knew this wasn't going to end well. I couldn't allow them to check our credentials or run our names. We had met all the official requirements to be in Turkmenistan, but with only one more night to accomplish the mission, I couldn't afford to have any kind of spike, any kind of surveillance effort mounted against us again.

This country was a strange place, to say the least. It was a cult of personality, not unlike North Korea, with giant monuments to the "dear leader" all over the place and the police conducting a healthy bit of civilian control, which included watching all foreigners. We'd already lulled them once and gotten them off of us. A spike like this would get them back on. The documents we carried would link Jennifer and me to the entire team, which meant we'd have a blanket on us by tomorrow afternoon.

Traditionally, they'd keep the effort going only long enough to prove that we were who we said we were. Two days from now it wouldn't matter. They could follow us all the way to Gonur. Tomorrow it would prevent us from executing.

Please take a bribe.

If they didn't, the mission was blown. Not to mention Jennifer and I would probably spend the night in some dump prison. *Damn, Pedro, couldn't you have left an hour earlier?*

I played stupid, saying, "Hello. My friend is trying to get her phone to work."

In broken English, the taller of the two said, "It is not permitted to be on street."

I feigned surprise, saying, "Sorry, we didn't know."

The shorter one said, "Papers."

Must have learned English watching old World War II movies.

Jennifer watched the exchange with wary eyes, listening to her voice mail. The taller one tapped her on the shoulder and said, "Stop phone."

She complied, shrinking behind me, saying nothing. I pulled out my wallet, letting them see the crisp twenty-dollar bills they could exchange on the black market. I withdrew one and said, "This paper?"

He took it, glancing at his partner, saying again, "Papers."

Perfect.

His partner tapped Jennifer and said, "Give phone."

She looked at me, and I held out another twenty, saying, "Here's more 'paper.'"

The shorter one took it while the taller one said, "Give phone. Not allowed."

What the hell is he talking about? I knew the cellular rules, and we were meeting them. We were on their network and paying their taxes. More than likely, he wanted the iPhone lookalike just because he thought he could hold us up. Since it was working in Turkmenistan, he thought it was unlocked and something he could now use for himself. Unfortunately, it was actually a special piece of Taskforce equipment, and I wasn't going to allow him to have it.

I pulled out another twenty, looking at the smaller man and saying, "Here, go buy your own." The tall one grabbed Jennifer's arm that held the phone. She jerked it away and took a step back.

The shorter one took the twenty. The taller one pulled out a baton like he was drawing a sword.

Oh shit.

Jennifer saw the weapon and raised her arms in a defensive stance. She did it out of instinct, but the move amped up everything.

I said, "Whoa, whoa, there's no need for this. Here, take everything we've got."

The smaller one snatched the money out of my hand while the taller one said, "Give me phone."

Jennifer said nothing, waiting to see what the taller one would do.

He raised the baton, and I stepped forward. The shorter one shouted and jumped back, pulling his own baton. I held up both hands to him, saying, "Stop, stop."

The taller one cracked me on the shoulder, and that was it. A perfect little bribery now in the toilet. I knelt down from the blow as if it had really hurt, then went in low on the shorter man, knowing the tall one was no longer a threat.

I used a single-leg takedown, throwing him onto his back, then scrambled on top, pinning his arms and crossing my hands into the collar of his wool uniform. I scissored my hands out, the collar cutting the blood flow to his brain. He was out in seconds. His partner wasn't as lucky.

I turned around to find Jennifer holding his head low and pistoning her knee into his face, his arms flailing uselessly in the air, the baton long gone. His head snapped back after the contact and he collapsed unnaturally onto the ground.

I was on him immediately, hissing, "Jesus Christ, Jennifer. You might have killed him."

I checked his pulse and relaxed when I found it strong. His face was a mess, though. I left the twenties on the ground and stood up.

"Can we get to the damn hotel now?"

She was breathing hard, her hair askew, but her eyes were clear. Not even caring about what had just occurred. "Pike, Jack's in trouble."

"You mean like a car wreck or something?"

"No, I mean like bad-guy life-or-death trouble."

7

The *sicario* watched the mechanics of his work with detached indifference. The suffering of his chosen target didn't faze him at all. Like a butcher at the slaughterhouse, he had killed so many living things that it no longer registered as a repulsive task. It was simply work. Unlike the butcher, who killed cleanly and with the ultimate goal of creating food, the *sicario* drew out the death, with no other goal than that which was dictated by his capo. And he could make it last days if he was told to. A bullet to the head was preferable in his mind, as it was much less messy, but that wasn't his call. Sometimes, the capo wanted to make a point.

Like today.

He listened to the man beg and plead through the gag strapped to his mouth and reflected on how the times were rapidly changing. As early as a year ago, he could have done this work without any fear of interruption—the violence in Ciudad Juárez was so extreme that nobody would even investigate the screams. The battle that raged for control of the Juárez *plaza,* as the crossing points into the US were called, had been horrific, giving Ciudad Juárez the unenviable title of the most dangerous city on earth. A year ago there had officially been three thousand screams such as this. He knew there had been many, many more that nobody had heard. Bodies that were yet to be found and tabulated.

But that was then. Now it was prudent to prevent the target from alerting anyone, be it the hated Sinaloa cartel, the authorities, or even some splinter from his employer, the fragmented Zetas cartel. So he used the gag as a precaution.

The *sicario* watched his wild eyes and the drool from his sobs, believing the man could take one more dip before passing out. To his front was a fifty-five-gallon drum sawed in half and filled with water that raged and bubbled like a mountain river, but not from the force of racing downhill. From the propane stove underneath. His target was hung above it on a winch and had already tasted the pain, his feet burned into a mess of molten plasticlike flesh extending to just above the ankles.

The *sicario* spoke to the man next to him, a doctor who was paid to keep the targets alive. "One more, and he'll need to be treated."

"Yes, yes. He is strong. I can treat him. He won't die."

The man was obsequious and obviously afraid. The *sicario* had seen the doctor glance at him repeatedly, then look away, and had noticed how he trembled when they were close together. The *sicario* understood why. For one, it was simply the job and his reputation for brutality.

Coming from the killing fields of Guatemala, he had taught Los Zetas the art of psychological warfare. Had brought the techniques of beheadings and other public displays of death, instilling fear in the enemy. He had achieved a mythical status among all who had heard of him, but more than that, he knew his real-life visage lived up to the legend.

During a battle in the civil war he had been touched by the volcanic flame of a white phosphorous grenade—a grenade thrown by a fellow Kaibil—and had been burned on his head, losing his eyebrows and leaving his forehead looking like melted wax. They had shaved him in the hospital, and he'd kept that discipline ever since, meticulously shaving every bit of hair off his head. The effect was disconcerting, and he liked it that way. Fewer people to test him.

The *sicario* watched the target violently shake his head left and right, the spittle from his screams dripping down the cloth of the gag onto his chest. Ignoring the pleading, he lowered the man and the sweet/sour odor of boiling meat permeated the room again, reminding him of his mother's kitchen, of dinners long ago in Guatemala when he was a child. Before he had joined the Guatemalan Kaibiles Special Forces unit. Before he'd had his humanity sucked out of him like life-giving oxygen from a hole in a space suit.

He intently studied the target's face, and when his eyes rolled back in his head, he hoisted the man up. It did no good to punish him if he couldn't feel the effects. As two other men lowered the target to the floor, avoiding the destroyed flesh of his lower legs, the doctor went to work, inserting an IV and treating the burns. The back-and-forth of treatment and pain would go on until the heart stopped. Some men lasted longer than others. The record had been three days, but the *sicario* didn't feel this one had that sort of stamina. Two days at the most.

He went into the other room for a drink of water and felt his phone vibrate. He looked at the number and answered immediately.

"Yes, El Comandante."

"Pelón, I have a task for you. It needs to be done immediately."

"Yes. Of course."

"Sinaloa has something big in motion. I don't know what it is, but there is a man who does. He's an American, and I've just found out they mean to bring him here to Juárez."

"You want me to kill him?"

"No, no. That's what *they're* trying to do. He's apparently a reporter who knows of their plans. I want you to snatch him from them. Find out what he knows. Find out how he can help us."

That was a tall order. Ciudad Juárez was huge, as big as El Paso, and absolutely flooded with drug cartel safe houses much like the one he was in. Getting to the man and getting out alive would mean a fight, and with the balance of power between Sinaloa and Los Zetas, it would more than likely mean a running gun battle. He wouldn't get to pick the time and place of capture, like he ordinarily did. Sinaloa would be waiting, and Los Zetas no longer had the monopoly on violence they'd once possessed.

Initially formed in the late nineties as an enforcement arm of the Gulf Cartel, the core of Los Zetas was defectors from the GAFE—Mexican Special Forces—who took their name from the code letter *Z* given to them when they were working with the federal police trying to halt the flow of drugs. The government couldn't offer nearly as much money as the Gulf cartel, and the men had simply switched allegiances. Before they defected, the GAFE had done many cross-training events with the Kaibiles in Guatemala, and the connection still lingered, pulling in defectors from that Special Forces element as well, including the *sicario*.

By 2007, Los Zetas were doing much, much more than simply enforcing for the Gulf cartel. Their tendrils extended all the way into Central America, and their brutality became legendary. They split from their Gulf masters, forming their own cartel, and the blood began to flow, with Los Zetas proving to be more ferocious than any other cartel. The guard dog had turned on the master.

In recent years almost all of the original Special Forces leaders had been killed, leading to infighting for control and less restraint as the violence spiraled upward. Los Zetas had turned feral, killing one another as much as anyone else. Like a bonfire, they were consuming themselves in a spectacular spasm of destruction and running out of fuel. Now, with the Gulf cartel in alliance with the Sinaloa cartel, the Juárez *plaza* was in danger of being lost forever, and Los Zetas would do anything to prevent it.

The *sicario* knew that refusal of the mission would simply mean his death. There was no form of loyalty anymore. It wasn't like the early days, when accomplishment counted and the Special Forces bond meant something. Now it was a day-to-day fight for existence.

He said, "You know where he will be taken? What area of the city?"

"No. Not here. But I know where in El Paso. It's why you have been chosen."

"I don't work in America. I *can't* work in America. If I'm caught there, I won't be deported."

"So don't get caught, Pelón. It's just across the border, in an area nobody controls. It will be easy."

Despite his fearsome reputation, the *sicario* still worked for a boss, was still subservient to the Zetas chain of command, and he knew exactly why he was being given the task. Someone would need to penetrate the border into El Paso, capture the guy, then return. Someone who had the ability to avoid a majority of the scrutiny at the bridge. Someone who knew how to get around in America.

The *sicario* didn't fit the last requirement. He hadn't been across to El Paso in over thirty-five years and had no idea what the city was like. But he did have the ability to get back and forth, since he had an American passport.

Because he'd been born there.

8

The *sicario* puttered in the northbound traffic on the Paso del Norte Bridge, seeing the line of cars snaking out before him. He'd done his research and knew it would be at least a two-hour wait. While the bridge operated twenty-four hours a day, he'd decided to cross when traffic was heaviest, giving the men working border control less of an incentive to focus on him.

Inching forward every few minutes, surrounded by all manner of cars, some seemingly held together by duct tape, he reflected on his future. Or more precisely, his lack of one.

From the beginning, the cartels had led a Darwinian existence of dog-eat-dog, with only the strong surviving. Even Osiel Cárdenas, the man who had created the original Zetas enforcement arm, had the nickname El Mata Amigos—the Friend Killer—because he had executed his partner to seize control of the Gulf cartel. Back then, though, there were lines. Reasons for the violence, with a degree of logic, because random killing was counterproductive for business. The *sicario* had seen that change.

The leadership of Los Zetas had become paranoid. Or maybe they were simply crazy, with the calculated thinking of the original members lost to the savagery of the animals who took over from below. It really didn't matter why. In the past the *sicario* had killed for a purpose. Sending a signal to the authorities, getting revenge for transgressions, or simply showing the consequences should someone interfere with cartel business—it had all been designed to retain control. The killings were thought out before they were ordered, with potential repercussions discussed at least as much as the operation itself. Now Los Zetas butchered anyone suspected of working against them based on rumor alone, with no thought given to the fallout.

The man the *sicario* had boiled was one such target. Two days ago, he'd been a valued member of Los Zetas. Yesterday, he had become a target, simply because his boss, El Comandante, had heard he might be turning informant.

The *sicario* was sure El Comandante was crazy. He was like a dog that had been whipped, beaten, and thrown into fights to the death for so long he had lost all sense of what constituted reality. Sooner or later, it would be the *sicario*'s turn. Of that he was absolutely positive. The only reason it hadn't happened yet was because he had never once shown anything but loyalty and had never indicated an interest in greater riches or power.

That, and because the *sicario* had been Los Zetas far longer than anyone else. Longer even than El Comandante. He was one of the few members of Los Zetas still alive from when they were the pipe swingers for the Gulf cartel. One of the original *sicarios*—and that fact, along with his reputation for brutality, held some importance.

He wondered if he himself was crazy. He thought he could discern it in others but wasn't sure about himself. He didn't believe he was, but in his heart he couldn't see how anyone who executed such heinous deeds couldn't be. He should have been eaten up with remorse or fearful of the afterlife. But he wasn't. The acts, like the one earlier today, never bothered him. Didn't that make him loco?

There was only one action that haunted him. Made him worry about where he would spend eternity. During the latter stages of the Guatemalan civil war, his Kaibil unit had been sent to "pacify" a village. They had slaughtered every man, woman, and child. After everything he had done since in the name of Los Zetas, this was the one event that haunted his dreams. Made him sweat when the memories surfaced. The *campesinos* running left and right like rabbits. The machetes falling. The blood. The stench of spilled intestines and chopped meat. It all returned at night while he slept.

The aftereffects of that operation had driven him into the arms of Los Zetas. He told himself it was because they paid infinitely more than the Guatemalan army, but in reality, he had decided that if he was going to kill, he wanted to kill someone who wasn't innocent. As if Los Zetas knew the difference.

Loco thoughts. He rubbed the little statue of La Santa Muerte on his seat, saying a small prayer for his soul. Wondering if the man he had boiled had also prayed to the patron saint of death. And whether that made them both insane.

DRIVING INTO THE El Paso neighborhood known as Eagle, the *sicario* reflected that it didn't look a whole lot different from Juárez. Very few trees, cinder-block houses with yards full of rock and dirt, and adobe dwellings interspersed with seedy automotive repair shops and convenience stores. Situated along the Chavez Border Highway, it was literally a stone's throw from Mexico, butting right up against the Rio Grande River. The thought brought him some comfort that perhaps he could get away with what he'd been tasked.

He'd had no trouble crossing over and was glad he'd kept his passport up to date. He'd never used it to come into the United States but had always treasured it as a final out, a wild card that might come in handy should he be picked up by Mexican authorities—or should he need to run from other, less forgiving types.

The Paso del Norte crossing was northbound only, but he was sure the southbound crossing at Stanton Street would, if anything, be easier, since he would be headed into Mexico instead of the United States.

He turned left off of the Border Highway onto Park Street and began looking for the skate park. He crossed three intersections and started to wonder if the intelligence was wrong. At the fourth, he saw the corner of the park. He turned left again, now scanning for atmospherics. *So far, so good.* The Eagle neighborhood had a very high crime rate, but he wasn't looking for police. He was searching for the street gang that owned this barrio and would be acting as lookouts for the Sinaloa cartel.

He took a left on South Hill Street, boxing his route in, and saw a tattooed hood wearing a dingy white wifebeater and jeans. He was lounging against the front wall of a meat market and talking to another street thug sitting on an overturned plastic bucket. The conversation stopped when his car came into view. They both eyeballed him as he turned, and the *sicario* wondered if this neighborhood was so close-knit that they'd know he didn't have any business here. He ignored them, getting a quick glance at their side of the street, then driving past and looking to the left, away from their eyes so they couldn't see his face. Giving them only a view of the wig and hat he wore.

Seventy-five meters down and he saw the safe house. It was a one-story brick structure with two windows, one on either side of a single door. Small, maybe three rooms total, butting right up to the sidewalk. No yard to speak of, which meant no chain-link fences to contend with. All in all, a plus for the *sicario*.

It was getting to be late afternoon, and while the *sicario* would have liked to wait until darkness, he wasn't sure when the Sinaloa transporter would arrive. Once the reporter was loaded, there would be no chance of taking him. He drove around the block, passing the skate park again. This time, instead of continuing on, he stopped at the alley that ran behind the safe house, a dirty, narrow strip littered with trash. He backed up to the skate park and wedged his car in between two pickup trucks, getting it out of view.

He walked toward Hill Street, scanning left and right. When he reached the alley, having seen nothing alarming, he shifted left and went down it at a rapid pace, walking all the way to the next block. When he passed the safe house, he saw a back door, but it was heavily barred with a wrought-iron grate. Not an entrance, but it would work as an exit.

He circled back to his car, coming up with a plan. It would have to be quick and dirty, but with only one look-out position, they weren't expecting trouble. At most, there would be three men inside to contend with. None would be expecting a threat, but that would change when he knocked on the door. They would arm themselves out of reflex. Unless . . .

9

The *sicario* picked up his pace and reached the skate park and his car. He drove it to the mouth of the alley, backing the vehicle just inside and off the street, but not close enough for the safe house to hear the engine. He threw his wig and hat into the backseat, lifted up a special compartment in the right rear door panel, and pulled out a suppressed Sig Sauer P226 nine-millimeter pistol. The weapon was bigger than he would have liked, made larger still by the five-inch suppressor, but it was necessary. He donned a specially made shoulder rig, seated the pistol, then put on a cheap nylon windbreaker to cover it.

He exited the car and began walking back around the block, toward South Hill Street and the meat market. He knew that the lookouts would focus on his bald skull and scorched forehead, and the image would preclude their brains from making any connection to the man who had just driven past. Which would cost them.

He turned the corner and walked with purpose straight toward the meat market, both gang members staring at him intently. He ignored them, stopping short of the building proper and veering toward a gate in the wooden fence that ensconced the market's property. He opened it like he belonged and went through a six-foot-tall barricade that would preclude anyone from seeing what he was about to do. He searched the area with his eyes and saw nothing but old washing machines and beer cans. No windows on the building or witnesses in the yard. He knelt and called out in Spanish.

"Help me. Please come help."

He waited, then repeated the call. Eventually, the one he'd seen on the bucket came through the gate, saying, "What do you want, *cabrón*?"

He jammed the suppressor into the thug's throat and said, "Call your friend."

The man splayed his hands out in a gesture of surrender.

The *sicario* waited a beat for compliance. When it didn't occur, he twisted the barrel, pushing it deeper into the soft folds of flesh. "Call. Your. Friend."

The man did, bleating like a goat. The *sicario* shot him from under the chin, the bullet going through the brain and taking out a section of skull as it exited the top. The body hitting the ground made more noise than the suppressed 226. He waited.

The wife-beater rounded the corner cursing, walking with a swagger. He saw the body a split second before he felt the suppressor at the base of his jaw, just below his ear. He, too, held his arms out.

The *sicario* said, "Do not talk. Just nod yes. You know the house you are protecting?"

A nod.

"We're going over there, and you're going to knock on the door. Get them to open it without alerting them something is wrong. If you fail, you will die. If you succeed, you can run away down the street. I'll do the rest. Do you understand?"

Another nod, but this time with a snarl on his face.

Trouble.

"Put your arms down. Look at me."

The man/boy did so, glaring at him with a challenge, showing he wasn't concerned.

"I know whose house that is, and they are of no help to you. I am a Los Zetas *sicario*. Do you know what this means?"

The toughness cracked and the thug tentatively nodded.

He jammed the barrel deep into the soft fold of flesh beneath the jaw. "Do you *understand* what this means? For you?"

The gang member became visibly scared, staring at the molten scars on the *sicario*'s forehead.

"I have made many men such as you cry for death. Weeping and begging for their mothers. Your next few minutes will decide if you do the same. Let's go."

This time the gang member nodded vigorously. He'd heard the stories. Maybe even seen the pictures. He'd played at being tough in his own little fishbowl, had dealt out his own version of justice in the barrio, but understood the man with the gun operated in a whole different universe of pain.

They crossed the street, the wife-beater walking in front. When they reached the brick of the house, the *sicario* stopped just outside the left window, his pistol down and hidden between the wall and his left leg.

Wife-beater looked at him once, a mixture of fear and resignation on his face, then knocked on the door. When someone answered from the other side, he stated he was making another run and wondered if the *jefe* wanted anything from the store.

The *sicario* admired his courage. It was the perfect story but was predicated on an answer. If the man behind the door said yes, he would have accomplished the mission. If he said no, the door wouldn't open, and he would be dead.

The man said yes.

The *sicario* had counted the locks earlier and seen three. The gang member glanced at him, holding his position in front of the peephole and waiting on permission to run. The *sicario* strained to hear the locks. When he heard the second one click open, he shot wife-beater in the temple, the man crumpling to the concrete without a sound. By the time the third lock had turned he was standing over the body. When the door cracked an inch, he kicked it hard, throwing the man back.

The *sicario* stepped inside and drilled the guard twice

in the face, causing him to slam against the wall and fling the wallet in his hand into the hallway. The *sicario* moved forward, training the Sig on every crevice. He saw doors to the right and left before the hallway spilled into an open den. He heard someone say something behind the door to the right. He kicked it open and found a man sitting on a toilet, his pants around his ankles. The man uttered something unintelligible, pure astonishment on his face, a newspaper in his hands. He tried to stand and the *sicario* put two rounds above his nose.

He raced to the den and found it empty but identified the back door in the center of the wall. He went to the cubby used as a kitchen and found it empty as well. He shuffled back to the final door, readied his pistol, and kicked it open.

On the floor was a Caucasian man, bound up like a calf at a rodeo. He held his hands out in front, shouting, "Don't shoot! Don't shoot!"

When the *sicario* holstered his weapon, the man's demeanor changed, and tears formed in his eyes. He began to chant, "Thank God . . . thank God . . . thank you . . . they were going to take me to Mexico . . . thank you."

10

I rolled the dice and moved my backgammon piece, surprised that I was beating Knuckles, since he'd taught me how to play the game earlier that morning. I'd figured he was an old hand at backgammon and thus a better player, but then again, we *were* in the middle of a mission. Maybe he couldn't multitask like a master such as myself.

Or maybe he was still pissed at me. Hard to tell. He'd been plenty mad last night, and I wasn't sure which piece of anger had lingered: the fact that I'd let Jennifer go home or the fact that he'd figured out where she and I stood with each other.

The team had tracked Jake to a hotel called the President, a gaudy, giant monument of white marble that looked like it belonged more in Las Vegas than it did in Turkmenistan. Of course, it was owned by the president of the country. It was billed as a five-star resort used for dignitaries and diplomats, complete with indoor-outdoor pools, tennis courts, a spa, and a bar on the sixteenth floor, but, like everything else in this strange country, it gave a vibe that was a little off-kilter. Nothing overt. Just small things, like getting your hand shocked when you used the shower, or the maids rolling the dice about whether they'd show up to clean your room on a given day, or seeing the typed piece of paper in a document protector taped to the window telling the occupant not to open the window between certain hours. Strange all the way around.

Because the hotel was located far outside the city center and because of our little altercation last night, we'd decided to jump TOC to its location, reestablishing our operations at the new hotel. We would have had to do it anyway, since it was out all by itself and not within walking distance of anything, precluding conducting operations from our original hotel, but the police fight made it imperative that we get out of the area. It had been too dark in that alley for them to have gleaned any viable description, so they'd fall back on the only thing they had—hotels within walking distance of the scene—and that would have put us in the net.

As I was checking out, Knuckles came into the lobby. He'd already completed reconnaissance of Jake's room and built a plan of attack. He'd "borrowed" a maid's uniform and determined the room-cleaning schedule—which is to say there wasn't one—meaning Jennifer could access it at any time of the day and not look out of place. He wasn't too happy when I told him that Jennifer was headed to the airport instead of the new hotel. All the flights left at two or three in the morning, and I figured it was better to fly her home in the same cycle of darkness. The police would be looking for a couple, and getting her out would throw off their search. Of course, Knuckles didn't see it that way.

"What do you mean, she's leaving? We're in the middle of a fucking mission."

"Her brother's in trouble. He left a voice mail that's not something to mess around with."

"So call him and tell him she'll be home in a day or two. How bad could it be?"

"He won't answer his phone. It goes straight to voice mail. Look, her brother's a reporter in Dallas, and she thinks he was working on a story about the drug cartels."

That gave him pause. We'd both kept up on what was going on in Mexico because of the potential nexus of the cartels and terrorists out to harm the United States.

I continued. "I heard the voice mail, and he was really in fear for his life. It sounded like someone was about to jerk the phone out of his hand."

He took that in, then said, "You really think this is some type of *Sopranos* bullshit?"

"I don't know, but Jennifer's freaking out about it, and rightly so. She needs to get home."

He tried to maintain his anger, but it was a losing battle. He knew the decision was correct, and he would have made it himself if it were someone under his command. He just didn't like the fact that he had no control over our little civilian company. And I understood that. We were still slogging through how such things worked and who was ultimately in charge, because my company was unique. It wasn't established by the government, but by

Jennifer and me through our own seed money, and yet we got a Taskforce paycheck for missions such as this.

On the one hand, we could be kicked to the curb as too much trouble, but on the other, our company allowed penetration of just about any place on earth—like it had here—and it was run by operators. Confusing, but that's what the world was when you were working outside the traditional intelligence and defense architecture.

With diminishing aggravation, he said, "This damn mission won't work without her. I've already got a maid's uniform and a plan for entry."

I smiled at that. A year ago he wouldn't have used Jennifer at all if he could help it, instead giving her some menial task that wouldn't affect the outcome of the mission. Now he was building operations that revolved around her participation.

"That's not true," I said. "The hard part is gaining entry to the room, and you've already cracked that. The rest is just cover development."

The locks at the President Hotel were made by a company called Onity. They used key-cards just like hotel locks all over the world. The difference was that the Onity lock had a fairly well-publicized hack utilizing the DC barrel connector at the base of the casement, whereby a simple tool could trick it into opening. Onity had done nothing about the vulnerability until a rash of robberies in Houston, Texas, prompted an outcry. They'd created a patch, but they had over ten thousand locks in use around the world, and Knuckles figured this backwater country wasn't high on the list for getting fixed. The hack would still work here.

Knuckles said, "It's not that simple. We're going to have to come up with another solution now."

Jennifer came down to the lobby with her luggage, and he said nothing else about the mission. When she reached us, he said, "Hey, your brother's going to be okay. It's probably just a miscommunication."

She said, "I sure hope so."

I said, "I called your cab. It's outside."

I led her out, carrying her luggage and giving her a little pep talk. Before she entered the cab I admonished her about not doing anything stupid.

"Hey, I know you're worried about Jack, but don't go hot-rodding to Mexico, no matter what you find. It's probably just bad communication, and I don't want you jumping to conclusions. I'll be back in three days. Four at the most. Promise me you won't run off like the Lone Ranger."

Her eyes held nothing but pain and dread. She said, "Pike, I'm sorry I'm leaving. I know I'm hurting the mission. I . . . I know I'm letting you down. Letting the team down. It's just not like him to call like that. Something's really wrong."

I squared her to me, hands on both arms. "Screw that. Let me handle the team. Nothing here we can't accomplish without you." I poked her in the eye to lighten the mood. "Contrary to what you might think, we aren't all wondering how the hell we're going to execute if you leave. Just don't do anything stupid. I'll contact the Task-force. Get them to track his phone and send you a grid."

She said, "You can't do that. For one, it's illegal. For another, it's personal. Don't get in any trouble over this. It's not their problem."

"Yeah, yeah. Don't worry about it. You've given enough to the Taskforce to earn a little payback. Just promise you won't go off half-cocked. The trace will probably show up in Dallas."

She shook her head and said, "You never listen to anything I say." She put her arms around my waist and stood on tiptoe. "You're a good man. I won't do anything stupid. I'm looking forward to seeing you away from the team. These separate rooms suck."

Then she kissed me full on the lips. I returned it at first, bringing her close and savoring the connection. Then I remembered where we were. Who was watching. I broke it off and said, "Get out of here."

I watched her drive away, praying Knuckles wasn't in the lobby. When I turned around, he was still standing there.

Maybe he didn't see anything.

When I got inside he said, "What. The. Fuck. Was. That?"

Damn it.

"What?" I asked.

"That kiss . . . what was that?"

"Nothing . . . that was just a peck on the cheek. She'd have done the same to you."

"I've never had a peck that involved my tongue." He squinted his eyes at me and asked, "Are you *sleeping* with Jennifer?" I felt my face flush like I was a teenager caught in the backseat of a car, and he exclaimed, "Holy shit. You *are* sleeping with her, you damn liar!"

The anger was real, because he thought I'd broken the trust of a teammate. We'd had long talks about the loss of my family, my life, and how I felt about Jennifer, but the conversations were all the same: I was torn apart by their death; I wasn't ready for a relationship; Jennifer was a teammate, period; nobody could replace my wife, Heather; yada, yada, yada.

All of that was true, except for the last part. While Heather's death had left a hole that would never be filled, Jennifer had covered it over long ago, hiding the scar tissue and burying the rage that Heather's loss had engendered. I had realized the connection, but I had been too afraid to admit it. Afraid of rejection. I'd finally worked up the courage, and because of my incredible charm, my fear of rejection had ended up being misplaced anxiety, but that had been only recently.

I said, "Knuckles, it's not like that. I swear it just started."

He stared at me, saying nothing. Wondering what else I'd lied about, because at the same time I was baring my soul to him about my family, he'd reciprocated with other very personal things, and now he felt betrayed.

He said, "You can't sleep with her. She's a damn teammate. Jesus, Pike, you know better."

I was taken aback. This was the first time Knuckles had said she was an equal inside the Taskforce. "She's still a teammate. Nothing's changed."

"*Everything's* changed. This is exactly what's wrong with females in combat arms positions. You'll start favoring her. Doing things to protect her, like you did here by sending her home."

That poked the wrong sore. "Bullshit," I snarled. "I've felt the same about her since we met, I was just too screwed up to realize it. Nothing's changed. Six months ago I let her free-climb off a sixty-story building because *you* said it was a good idea. Then I put her in a position to contract a lethal virus to prevent a pandemic. I thought she was going to die, and I could have pulled her back. Could have protected her. *Nothing* has changed. Let it go."

He said, "That time in Lebanon, when she was inside Hezbollah headquarters. You triggered the reaction force. . . ."

In a low voice I said, "That was because of *me,* not her. It was my mistake alone. I would have done the same if it had been you inside. Let it *go.*"

He searched my face, his mind calculating the ramifications. Eventually, he shook his head, coming to grips with the situation, as I knew he would. Knuckles had always been more liberal than most in the Taskforce, down to the hippie haircut he had worn since I'd known him.

I said, "And I need you to keep this between us. I can't have the entire team second-guessing my decision making."

He rolled his eyes and said, "Why can't you ever do anything the easy way?"

That had been eighteen hours ago, and now I was thinking about losing this game of backgammon as an olive branch, or at least to keep him from getting more aggravated than he already was. I kept my eye on the hallway and waited on the call from the other team. Begging to hear anything, since Knuckles was giving me the silent treatment.

Finally, my radio crackled to life. "Jake's out. Room's clear."

11

Since Jake had passed the secondary team it meant he was headed either to the gym or to the stairs—not to the elevators near us. Given the target, I found it hard to believe he'd use either one, but he did.

"Just entered the gym."

I said, "Roger. Retro, your ball game. No more than thirty minutes."

I heard, "Roger. Coming down now."

After Jennifer left, Knuckles had washed his hands of developing the new course of action, leaving it to me to come up with a plan. I'd basically used the same one he had created, only substituting Retro for Jennifer. With his black hair and seventies porn-star bushy mustache, Retro looked the most like someone from this neck of the woods. He also spoke Russian from his time in the 10th Special Forces Group. Not like a native, but it would be enough of an edge to fool someone who didn't speak it, like our Saudi Arabian target.

We'd found a suit that fit reasonably well and "borrowed" a hotel name tag with some moniker that was impossible to pronounce, and he looked reasonably enough like hotel security. Actually, he looked a hell of a lot better in the suit than in the dated clothes he usually wore.

The target room was on the third floor, and the hallway had two alcoves, one on either side of it, complete with table, chair, and backgammon game. Neither position could see the room itself, but that was irrelevant, since Jake couldn't get out without going by one of them. Decoy and Blood, the ones who had triggered, were at the other position on the far end of the hallway.

The biggest risk was Retro being found in the room. Jennifer, as a maid, could easily have talked her way out, but Retro would have some serious splainin' to do, which is why I had given him a time limit.

Retro came by our position carrying a clipboard and a radio, looking like an important member of the hotel staff. He ignored us, and I waited on a SITREP of entry.

The seconds ticked by, then finally I heard, "Pike, I'm in and we have a problem. There are five CDs here. What do you want me to do?"

Retro had entered with a specially constructed portable compact-disc ripper, intending on working with a single CD. While getting whatever information was on the CD was great, what we really wanted to do was identify the guy's boss. In addition to copying the CD, the ripper would implant a small Trojan horse. Whenever the CD was booted, the virus would reach out to the Internet and contact the Taskforce. From there, the hacking cell would exploit whatever they could find and hopefully identify the moneyman. After that, it was a US government call as to what would happen with the information. Maybe another Taskforce team would get Omega authority for the guy, but more than likely the information would be passed to the CIA for them to leverage with the Saudi liaison services. The problem here was that the ripper took fifteen minutes. With five CDs, Retro didn't have time to complete the mission in the room.

I said, "Do they look like the blank CDs we have in the TOC?"

"Yeah, the CDs do, but the cases are different."

I looked at Knuckles and said, "I'm sending Knuckles up to get them. Meet him in the elevator. Switch out the CDs and rip all of them in the TOC."

Knuckles stood, finally with a grin on his face, a perverse sense of pleasure coming from the curveball, like it had happened because I'd sent Jennifer home.

Retro said, "But what if he comes back while I'm upstairs?"

"Is there a laptop in the room?"

"Not that I can see."

"Don't worry about it, then. He won't check the CDs for information. It's just eye candy so you can rip them."

"Pike, I'll still have to get back in here to replace the real CDs."

"One step at a time."

Retro passed by me moving at a good clip, was gone for a minute or two, then came back holding the blank CDs and disappeared down the hall. Knuckles returned in time to see him scurry by again with the target CDs in his hands, headed to the TOC on the twelfth floor.

Knuckles said, "There's no way Jake's going to work out for an hour and a half. What are you going to do if he returns?"

I said, "Let's cross that bridge when we come to it."

Ten minutes later, the cursed bridge appeared. Decoy came on. "Jake's headed back. He's out of the gym."

What? Who works out for twenty minutes?

With a bemused look, Knuckles said, "Maybe he forgot his iPod."

I said, "Those CDs ended up being a blessing in disguise. If there had only been one, Retro would have been caught."

We waited, and Jake didn't reappear. *So much for the iPod*.

I said, "What do you think?"

"Fire alarm. Trip that and get him to the lobby. That'll be enough time."

"Yeah . . . but we don't know what their procedures are. They could come knocking on every door. Or simply reset it after five seconds."

"Phone call? From the lobby using an internal landline?"

"What'll we say?"

"Tell 'em that he has a package waiting. All we need is a few minutes to get back in the room. The elevator ride itself will be enough."

I thought about the pros and cons. Tripping the fire

alarm would garner a lot of attention and would force us to vacate our surveillance positions. But the biggest problem was that we just didn't know what the official reaction would be. On the other hand, the phone call would make Jake suspicious because he wasn't expecting a package, then grow more so when there was nothing waiting on him. Especially when the desk claimed they'd never called.

In the end, I decided it didn't matter. He could get as suspicious as he wanted, because we were headed to Gonur tomorrow and the mission would be done. The fire alarm option was flirting with contact with official authorities I didn't want to engage.

I said, "Okay, you get in the lobby and make the call on my trigger." I keyed my radio. "Retro, this is Pike, what's your status?"

"It's going quicker than I expected. I'm on disc four right now. Maybe another ten minutes."

I relayed the plan over the radio, then said, "Retro, come down the stairs to Decoy's position. I want you close, but I don't want you to pass Jake on his way out."

He said, "Roger all."

Twelve minutes later, he was done with the CDs and set. I got an up from Knuckles and said, "Execute."

I waited for three more minutes, then Jake passed me, all sweaty from his manly workout. I let him get thirty feet away and stood, saying over the net, "Room's clear. I say again, room's clear."

I began following Jake and heard, "Moving."

I hoped the elevators would be slow getting to our floor, thus giving Retro that much more time. The bank came in view and I saw that wasn't going to happen. One opened and a man in a bellboy uniform came out carrying a box with an address on it and an envelope of legal size.

Oh shit. They deliver packages to the rooms.

Jake spoke to him and the bellboy used a small radio to talk to someone else, then he shook his head at Jake. Our target turned and began heading back to his room.

I passed him and entered the elevator. When the doors closed, I said, "Abort, abort. Jake's headed back."

Retro said, "I'm not done replacing them. He'll know someone's been in the room."

I said, "If he opens the door and sees you I don't think there will be any doubt. Abort."

I reached the bottom and immediately went back up. I turned the corner to the backgammon alcove and saw Knuckles had beaten me back. He shook his head.

I keyed my radio. "Decoy, you got a status on Retro?"

"Negative. He hasn't come back this way."

I paused, then keyed the radio again, "Ahh . . . Retro, status?"

I heard two clicks, and Knuckles realized what had happened at the same time I did. *He's hiding in the room.*

I said, "What do you think?"

"I think if Jennifer were here she could have walked right out holding some towels."

"That's not an answer."

"Fire alarm. That's the only thing that will work. Another phone call's asking for compromise."

I nodded my head and was looking for an alarm to trigger when Retro appeared around the corner, pulling off his name tag.

We both stared at him, and he grinned.

"Well," I said, "what the hell happened?"

"I swear, Pike, he would have figured out the CDs had been tampered with if I had aborted. I had to stay, but I knew he'd been to the gym. What do you do after working out?"

Knuckles said, "Take a shower."

"Yep, and that's exactly what he did. I hid under the bed until the water came on."

Gutsy. But very switched-on thinking.

"You also gave us a heart attack."

He said, "You? When I dove down I remembered I hadn't checked to see if the bed had one of those boxes around it to prevent people from leaving things. *That* would have been embarrassing."

We all chuckled at the near miss, the adrenaline subsiding and the camaraderie beginning to flow. I broke down the surveillance box, saying, "Meet at the bar on the sixteenth floor. Retro's buying. Last chance before we head out to the desert tomorrow."

Up top, in the restaurant bar, we poked fun at Retro and fended off the working girls out looking for a mate. Well, most of us did. I noticed Decoy sizing the women up when he went for another beer, plying his Tennessee charm. *Man whore.* I was in a pretty good mood, lubricated with the beer and happy at the successful outcome, when my phone signaled a voice mail from Jennifer, the intermittent cell service working on the top floor of the hotel. All my humor left when I listened to it. The Taskforce had located Jennifer's brother's phone.

In Mexico.

12

Jennifer pulled into the parking lot, wondering if she should put on surgical gloves before going inside. The place was called the Traveler's Inn, but it looked more like the Motel That Stayed in Business Because of Seedy People. Just off of I-10, on the northern outskirts of El Paso, it looked like it sold rooms by the hour. An L-shaped building, it was a one-story dilapidated structure, with a neon sign that she was sure no longer worked. There was a smattering of cars in the lot facing the motel, most rusted, with dents and dings. A family was loading a pickup, three small kids and a mother and father, all of Hispanic heritage. The sight gave her a little hope. They didn't look like criminals. More like people who simply needed a cheap place to stay. She sat in the car for a moment, wondering what Jack had been doing here.

She'd flown into Dallas the day before, the jet lag tearing her down but the anxiety about her brother's fate driving her forward. Her mother was waiting for her outside of baggage claim, and there was no mistaking the relationship. They had always looked like sisters, and the similarities still lingered, although her mother now colored her hair to keep it the same dirty blond it had always been. The one difference was the eyes. Her mother's were chestnut brown to Jennifer's gray. The single genetic vestige within her from her deadbeat father. Many men had told her they were beautiful, but in truth she didn't think so. The color reminded her of betrayal and loss. She would have traded them for her mother's eyes without hesitation. Make the familial similarities with the person who had raised her complete. Get rid of the genetic flaw given by the person who had deserted them.

Her mother had smiled upon seeing her, and Jennifer saw the wrinkles. Lines where there had been none before. It dawned on her that her mother was getting old. Right before her eyes. She wondered how much was the strain of Jack's disappearance and how much was the march of time.

They hugged and Jennifer said, "Anything new since I left Germany?"

"No. I've got a meeting set up with Andy Cochrane. He's Jack's editor at the paper and knew what Jack was working on. He's the one Jack was calling when he misdialed you. Andy wouldn't talk on the phone."

"What about the police? Has anyone alerted them?"

"Andy did as soon as I called him about your voice mail. They won't do anything for forty-eight hours."

"Even when his damn phone doesn't get answered? And Andy tells them what he was working on?"

Her mother grimaced and said, "Even then. We're on our own, but we've been there before."

"Where's Scott?"

"He's still overseas. He wanted to come home and I told him to stay."

Jennifer's eyes narrowed and her mother said, "Jenn, he's a tour guide. He can't do anything here. He'll want to start raising hell just to raise hell, but it won't help."

Jennifer knew she was right, as she had been all of their lives. Her other brother had been a hellion as a child—much like Jennifer herself—but unlike her, he'd never managed to focus on a set path. He ran off at the next big thing every few months and was now conducting guided tours in the mountains of Croatia for college students. He made no money, but he enjoyed it. Even so, she would have liked to have him here. If anyone could handle Mexico, it would be Scott. He'd traveled all over the world, living out of a backpack and facing down countless obstacles. Because of it, he had an antenna for this sort of thing.

Then again, he's no match for Pike.

Who was a half a world away.

They'd gone to the newspaper office and met Andy, a balding, pensive man now wringing his hands about the danger he'd placed Jack in. He told them that Jack had been building an exposé on the infiltration of drug cartels into America and that he'd warned Jack about the risks. In fact, he hadn't paid for any of the investigation because the paper simply couldn't afford it and the topic was too volatile. Jack had done it all freelance.

Andy had cracked at one point, saying it was all his fault because the story would have put the paper on the national scene, would have guaranteed its solvency, and yet he'd done nothing to protect Jack from retribution.

Jennifer had calmed him down and gleaned the specifics of the hotel in El Paso. Jack had been meticulous in letting Andy know what he was doing, and that trail had led here. The sleazy Traveler's Inn.

On the way down from Dallas she'd received the trace of Jack's phone in Ciudad Juárez. Jennifer had no idea how Pike had managed the track, but the location did nothing to make her feel better. Like a sailor clinging to a sinking ship, creating hope where none should exist, she found excuses in her mind for the trace. The phone had been lost. Or stolen. Or the trace was wrong. Anything to contradict the reality that the boat was going down and she was about to be floating in the ocean by herself.

Jennifer exited the car and surveyed the dilapidated motel, finding room twelve. Her brother's room. She went to the front desk, the door tinkling a small bell like it was still the 1950s. The office was clean but clearly old, a utilitarian check-in counter taking up most of the room. A Hispanic man of about sixty entered from a back door.

"Can I help you?"

She smiled, trying to disarm him, unsure of how to proceed. "Yes, I'm looking for someone who stayed here a few days ago. His name is Jack Cahill, but I'm not sure what he called himself when he checked in. He's Caucasian, about five ten with brown hair—"

He cut her off. "Are you the police?"

She pulled a picture out of her purse and said, "No, no. I—"

"Then I can't give you any information. Would you like a room?"

"No. I don't want a room. I just want to know if you've seen Jack Cahill." She held out the photo and said, "This is what he looks like. He would have checked out two days ago."

She saw a flash of recognition in his eyes, but he said, "Never seen him. He never came here."

"Can you at least tell me if he checked in? Maybe he came when you weren't on duty. Can you look? Please?"

He held her eyes for a moment, then went to an ancient computer and tapped a few keys. After a minute, still scrolling on the screen, he said, "Nobody by that name checked in or out." He turned back to her and said, "That's all I can do. No Jack Cahill came or went. Now, if you want a room, I've got plenty. If not, I don't know what else to tell you."

She said nothing, simply staring, and his eyes slid away. He fidgeted from one foot to the other. Seeing all she needed to, she put away the photo and said, "Thank you for your time."

He waved a hand, then returned to the back room, closing the door. She exited and saw a maid pushing a cart along the sidewalk. Jennifer glanced back through the office window, seeing the counter still empty. She walked up to the maid and said, "Excuse me, I've locked myself out of my room. Room twelve. Can you let me in?"

The wizened old woman, barely scratching five feet in height, said, *"No hablo inglés."*

Jennifer pulled two twenty-dollar bills out of her purse and said, *"Habitación doce."*

The woman glanced back at the office, then snatched the money and scurried to room twelve, unlocking the door. She returned to her cart, eyes downcast, ignoring Jennifer.

Jennifer entered the room and found it made up, ready for a new guest. Her heart sank. Anything left by Jack would be long gone. She searched it anyway, going through the closet and bathroom. Growing frustrated, she knelt down and peered underneath the bed. And saw something metal, hidden in the shadow. She lay down and stretched her arm out, batting the object until she could reach it from the side. She pulled it out, recognizing the device as a battery-operated digital recorder.

She stared at it for a good five seconds, afraid to hit the "play" button. Afraid it would display a disgusting amateur sex video. Or worse, a snuff film of her brother. She worked up her courage, opened the lid, and turned it on. What played was neither raunchy nor ghastly. A Caucasian man talking about information sharing with someone off the screen. She let it continue, confused as to why her brother would have made the recording—if he did. The men weren't discussing drugs or anything about the cartels. It wasn't until the end, when a new man's voice came on, begging for his life, that she was sure. Whatever had happened here, it hadn't been innocent. The man's pleas testified to that. The screen went blank, and she considered her options.

Pike had admonished her about going to Mexico alone—in fact, had forbidden it—but the phone trace was all she had left. She'd talked to the police, aggravated to receive the same answer as her mother. No amount of pleading did any good. The police would do nothing for forty-eight hours, until Jack was considered truly missing. Forty-eight hours she could not afford to let slip. She found the answer idiotic.

There's a damn TV show called The First 48, *done by murder investigators who know that if they don't solve a crime in forty-eight hours, they never will.*

And now, with the hotel a dead end, she'd have to wait forty-eight hours to even begin.

She'd researched Ciudad Juárez, and all indications were that current conditions belied its nickname of *Murder City*. Drug violence was a third of what it had been only a year ago, and investors were returning. Surely she could drive over there in the daytime. Pinpoint the location of the phone. Just for atmospherics. Something she could use when the police were engaged.

At least that's what she told herself.

13

Carlos waited for Eduardo to turn back from the window, wishing he had more information to provide. As the *plaza* boss for the Sinaloa cartel in Juárez, Eduardo had a very low tolerance for failure. It wasn't that he was overtly sadistic, looking for something or someone to lash out at. In fact, he was more intellectual than most. It was simply a function of the job. Failure implied weakness, and weakness bred insurrection. To prevent any moves on his position or his terrain, he would show strength. Carlos knew it didn't matter if the reaction had any bearing on the failure. It was the show that was important. The perception that the boss hadn't grown weak, but that instead the men below him had, and thus were dealt with.

Luckily, Carlos had shown his own strength on numerous occasions and had rarely failed. He couldn't easily be replaced, and he knew it. He also knew that Eduardo wasn't prone to outbursts of violence, unlike the crazies who had preceded him. Eduardo preferred to analyze before striking, but that only went so far, and Carlos knew that his head was possibly on the block.

Eduardo said, "So do you think it was American Federales or someone else?"

"It's too early to tell. All I know for sure is that he was taken. I don't know if he's even alive."

"But who would have taken him in El Paso if not the Americans?"

"You could be right." Carlos held up a smartphone. "He placed one call on this right before we got to him. The number is some random American company, but it could be a cover for an American agency. I have our contact checking it out, but the evidence from the hit doesn't feel like American authorities. Everyone was killed, including the two watchers outside. If it was the Americans, they would have simply rolled up and surrounded the place. Instead, everyone was slaughtered. No lights, no badges, nothing like that."

Eduardo turned from the window. "*Was* he a reporter?"

"He had the credentials."

Eduardo scoffed. "I can make those in my basement. You don't think the American Drug Enforcement Agency can do the same?"

Carlos said, "Yes, but he also had no weapon of any sort and was working alone. If you were an agent, would you get so close to the flame without a weapon? Would you do it alone?"

Eduardo shook his head. "You know this looks bad. Not only were we penetrated, but the very man who did it was snatched from our grasp before we could figure out why. It is bad. Very, very bad. Something needs to be done."

Carlos tensed, knowing they had reached the decision point. Knowing what "something" meant.

Eduardo continued. "I want the motel clerk to pay, and I want it done in El Paso. A lesson across the border. He let the man place the cameras and microphones in the room. If he hadn't given out Mr. Fawkes's room number, none of this would be happening."

Carlos visibly relaxed and said, "I agree, but I think we should wait on that a little bit. He's our only alarm if anyone comes sniffing around the motel. There's too much loose right now that we don't know. Too many holes we cannot fill. He can help."

Eduardo leaned onto the table, his face inches from Carlos. He raised his voice for the first time, the anger underneath spilling out into the room. "Then who should I punish right now? I look like a fucking fool. Perhaps I should punish the man who set up the meeting in the first place."

Carlos leaned back, his hands in the air, saying, "*Jefe,* please. We need to find the informant. Yes, I set up the meeting, but someone told the reporter about it. Someone let him know it was happening."

Carlos saw a vein begin to throb on Eduardo's temple. He knew that in Eduardo's eyes nothing was worse than disloyalty and he wanted to use that to deflect blame. The results were not as he hoped.

In a quiet voice, Eduardo said, "Why waste time trying to root out an informant? Maybe I should just kill everyone who had knowledge of the meeting. Starting with you."

His face growing pale, realizing he was losing control of the meeting, Carlos played his last card. "Don't make a bad situation worse. The greater issue here is accomplishing what I intended to do when I set up the meeting in the first place. *I'm* the one who found the contact. I'm the only one he will call when he's ready. The only one he trusts."

The tinge of a mirthless smile crept onto Eduardo's face. "Yes, you are the one, but why should I even care? You keep driving forward like Don Quixote on something I'm not sure will even work. You think that makes you indispensable? I have a greater problem with this, beyond what I will gain a month from now. People who will smell the blood in the water. Will see weakness where there is none. I need to prevent that, whether your plan works or not." The smile turned sour and he said, "As you know."

Carlos felt his stomach dropping as if he'd misread his cards, turning over a deuce instead of an ace. And he'd placed his life in the pot as a bet. "*Jefe*, it *will* work. We can keep the American drones away from us. The Americans are using them completely to cover the border. They trust technology over men, and this is the way to defeat them. We can be the undisputed controller of the Juárez *plaza*. This isn't something that is worth a blood-letting show of strength. I *know* what is needed. I've been here. Someone has to be sacrificed, but don't give up the goal."

"You had better hope it works. For your sake." He turned back to the window, thinking. Carlos waited on the verdict. When it came, he let out his pent-up breath.

"Deal with the motel clerk. Make it public. Do it in such a manner that everyone knows why he was killed. Everyone knows our reach."

Carlos felt his cell vibrate and glanced at it. Seeing who it was, he answered, holding his finger in the air to Eduardo, begging him to let the call go through. He talked for a minute, then hung up.

"That was the clerk. A woman came around asking about the reporter. Asking direct questions. He had his son follow her because he thought we would want the information of where she's staying."

"Who is she? Why was she searching? Did he say?"

"No, but we can find out ourselves. She didn't go to a hotel. She's coming across into Juárez."

14

Waiting to cross the border, Jennifer spent the time pinpointing the last location of Jack's phone. It was just across the Rio Grande, in the northwestern section of Ciudad Juárez. Googling further on her tablet, she saw the area was called Delicias and had the highest murder rate in the city. An indicator of why the phone was there, and a not-so-subtle reminder of the danger Jack was in. If he was still alive.

She plotted the location in the cheap GPS that came with the rental car and was dismayed to see the Mexican side of the border had no fidelity. The only streets listed in Juárez were the main north-south and east-west corridors. Something she should have expected, since the rental agreement forbade her from taking the car across the border in the first place. The plot appeared in a blank gray field, no roads listed. She would have to navigate there by blind driving.

She crossed the Stanton Street Bridge and passed through the customs facilities without issue, drawing a stare on the US side but nothing on the Mexican side. She felt her gut tighten as she entered Juárez, expecting to see *narcos* walking the streets with AK-47s proudly displayed or hear the popping of gunfire. Instead, it looked much like the city she had just left. A town of Mexican middle-class people trying to make their way. Families walked with their children, vendors on the street sold vegetables and fruit, and a healthy amount of traffic clogged the roads. It didn't look like Murder City, but she knew the history of the bloody ground, including the serial killing of women like her over the past decade.

Still on guard, but somewhat relieved, she pulled over and booted up Google Maps on her tablet, happy to see a 3G connection south of the border. She brought up the city and now at least had a map for reference, although it wasn't tied to the GPS and wouldn't move as she did.

She started driving east on David Herrera Avenue, keeping an eye on every vehicle around her but seeing nothing suspicious. Mostly old pickup trucks and a few motorcycles. Nothing like the late-model SUVs the *narcos* supposedly drove.

She penetrated farther east, the buildings becoming more run-down and the town starting to fulfill its nickname. As she left behind the hotels and restaurants, the area became full of utilitarian concrete structures advertising car repair or dollar sales intermixed with one-story cinder-block houses, all unashamedly tinged with graffiti and fenced off from the street. She tried to look at her tablet as she drove but found it impossible without pulling over. The neighborhood was a compact mass of crisscrossing streets, and she lost her orientation. She threw the tablet on the passenger seat and decided to just vector in by the GPS. She glanced into her rearview and caught a glimpse of the same motorcycle she had seen right after she'd crossed the border, the man in the saddle wearing a lime-green full-face helmet from the 1970s.

She turned left blindly, and the motorcycle followed. She felt a trickle of alarm and studied the bike rider. He showed nothing overtly threatening. The bike was an old Honda with a milk crate bungee-corded to the back, holding bags of some sort. She turned right, and the bike continued straight. She relaxed.

Getting paranoid.

She looked at the GPS and saw she was within a quarter mile of the marking. She continued on, following the blind little GPS tag, weaving left and right, at one point backtracking because of the nature of the roads. Eventually, she reached the grid on the GPS, seeing three houses on a slight rise from the street, all of them protected with a healthy amount of fencing that was a cut above the chain-link and makeshift iron of the neighboring houses. Fencing that was custom built, which gave some indication of who owned the houses.

She slowed and used her smartphone for pictures, wishing she had the Taskforce's ability to rig the car with three-hundred-and-sixty-degree cameras like she had done in the past. She wanted to provide the assault force the greatest fidelity possible when they came to break out her brother. Wanted to believe in the lie that someone was coming to help.

She passed the houses and picked up her pace, now thinking about how to get back to the border crossing. She took a right and stopped at an intersection. She pulled forward and saw the lime-green helmet to her left, sitting fifty feet down the road. Waiting on her.

She felt a bump in her heart rate but did nothing overt. She continued straight, heading east to the Paso del Norte Bridge. She glanced in her rearview mirror and saw the motorcycle fall in behind her.

She took another right to be sure. He remained with her. At the next stop, she studied her tablet but couldn't pinpoint her position with any certainty. When the bike pulled up behind her, she moved forward, going faster than was allowed on the narrow road.

Continue east. Eventually you'll hit the bridge road.

She was forced to slow down behind a battered pickup truck and was thinking about passing when the motorcycle broke off, taking a right and driving out of view. She exhaled and slumped in the seat, releasing the tension in her body. The pickup put on its brake lights and stopped. She turned the wheel to pass and glanced into her blind spot, seeing an SUV flying forward. She jerked back to the right to avoid being hit, but it didn't pass. Instead, she heard tires scream as it skidded to a halt abreast of her car.

The sight collapsed her world like a black hole, causing all thought other than survival to be sucked in. Two years ago she might have panicked, frozen in place as the drama unfolded, but that girl was long gone. Destroyed in a cauldron not of her making.

She had the car in reverse before the SUV had even fully stopped, the engine of her little rental whining in protest as she floored the pedal. She traveled barely five feet before slamming into a dented sedan that had pulled up behind her. She saw the driver fling forward against the steering wheel, and time slowed.

Trapped.

To her front the pickup's passenger door had opened, and a man was exiting. The rear hatch of the SUV began to rise; then she saw the motorcycle coming down the sidewalk toward her, the lime-helmeted rider holding a MAC-10 machine pistol in his left hand. He began firing as he came abreast of the pickup, shattering her windshield in a shower of glass.

She flung herself flat in the seat, Pike's instructions from two years ago on surviving just such an ambush penetrating the chaos. *Your vehicle is a weapon.*

Still lying flat, she jammed the car into drive, jerked the wheel to the right and floored the gas pedal. She hit the curb and rocketed forward, colliding with brick and ricocheting to the left, the bullets still tearing the air above her head.

She crunched something to her front, the car grinding as the object was flung aside. The lime-helmeted rider appeared on her hood, bouncing in the air, the weapon gone. She jerked upright and slammed on her brakes, rolling him onto the sidewalk. As soon as he had cleared the hood, she hit the gas again. He made it to a knee and saw her coming. He held his arms out and screamed, his mouth open through the clear faceplate of his helmet. The bumper caught him just above the waist, slapping him back on the hood. But only for a second. He clawed, trying to maintain his position, the friction of his legs against the ground sucking him under. She rolled over the top of him, the car bucking as if she'd hit an asphalt speed bump. She jerked the wheel to her left and slammed into the street, the pickup and SUV directly behind her.

She kept the pedal jammed to the floor, but the SUV began to gain, its horsepower much greater than that of her rental. She desperately tried to recall her training.

Negate his advantage. Make him drive.

She flew through another intersection, taking a right at a high rate of speed and forcing the SUV to slow or roll over. She worked the car through turn after turn, steam now coming out of the hood of the rental, but gaining distance from the SUV with each one.

Finally, she completed a turn out of view of the SUV. She took an immediate right, completely lost. She kept her speed and continued turning, striving to maintain an easterly heading by watching the GPS. A light came on in the dash and she saw the temperature gauge buried to the right.

Jesus. It's going to quit on me.

She considered the dilemma of driving on blindly. There were at least three cars chasing her, and she could run into any one of them at any time. If that happened, she wasn't sure if her rental would hold up for another race. She wasn't even sure if it would hold up just to get to the bridge—if she could even find it. Given enough time, they would locate her again, of that she was positive. It was their terrain, and they were probably calling in reinforcements right now. The longer she drove, the greater the odds of discovery. When they spotted her they would drive her like cattle until the car died, and she would be caught.

But you might be a block away from the bridge right now. A block away from US border agents.

She pushed the car forward, debating, knowing the decision would determine her fate. She saw a concrete wall adjacent to an open field littered with cans and slid in behind it. She shoved her tablet and Jack's video recorder into her purse and opened the door, her hand trembling at the decision, her conscious mind screaming at her to remain in the vehicle. To make a run at getting to the bridge. She paused for a moment, then committed, leaping out and racing in a crouch down the wall. She reached the street and peeked around the concrete, seeing it deserted. She ran across and disappeared between two houses.

She sat with her back against the rough brick and stared at her Google Maps display, trying to locate where she was. She glanced back the way she had come and studied the building shadows, determining which way was east. She found her brother's phone trace on the map and estimated where she had driven since the attack. Worst case, she figured she had about a mile as the crow flies.

A mile on foot in hostile terrain.

15

The lights blazed on and Jack scurried to his corner, as he'd been instructed to do. He placed his hands over a steel eyebolt in the floor and waited to get shackled, his body shaking as if he were in a meat locker. Not because of any drop in temperature. Because he'd seen what these animals were capable of and knew sooner or later it would be his turn.

After his "rescue" in El Paso, he'd been unceremoniously thrown into the trunk of a car, his legs, arms, and mouth bound with heavy duct tape. He was allowed to keep his watch, and he'd had the sense to check it. They'd driven for about nine hours, whereupon Jack had been taken from the trunk and placed onto the floor of a light airplane, his head covered in burlap. He had no idea how long they'd flown but would have guessed no more than an hour before they landed and he was transferred to the trunk of yet another vehicle. They'd driven for maybe two more hours and stopped. He'd heard the car doors slam; then he'd sat in the trunk forever, the claustrophobia and darkness starting to eat into him.

Finally, his hood had been removed, and the bald man who had captured him in El Paso had pulled him out, his face showing no emotion whatsoever. He'd simply said, "Disobey and you will die. Do you understand?"

Jack nodded, having no illusions about the man's sincerity, his disfigured forehead leaving an impression that the emotion did not. Another man cut off the tape on his legs, hooded him again, and led him into a building. He walked down a flight of stairs until he found himself in what he called the "dungeon": a room forty feet square with fourteen eyebolts along the walls and a small half bath consisting of a sink and toilet. Nothing else.

When they'd pulled his hood off he saw two other men crouching down, handcuffed to an eyebolt. After they stripped the remaining tape from his arms and mouth, they unshackled the two men and left them alone. Gathering his courage, he asked them who they were, but they didn't speak English. He debated giving up his Spanish card and decided it was worth it.

"Who are you? Why are you here?"

The men said nothing, staring at him. One was older, about fifty, and the other looked to be cresting over his twenties.

He tried again. "Where are we?"

The older man finally spoke. "It doesn't matter where. It matters who."

Jack said, "Who? What do you mean?"

"Los Zetas."

The words caused Jack to momentarily lose his senses.

His ears refused to believe their meaning. Thirty hours ago he'd been an intrepid reporter in Dallas, Texas. Now he'd been captured by not one but two Mexican drug cartels and had ended up with the worst. Los Zetas were beyond cruel. Beyond barbaric. Through his research he'd seen the videos. Seen the men getting decapitated with chain saws. Seen the pictures of the mass graves. He began gulping air.

The man said, "You must be very important. I've never heard of them taking a gringo."

Jack said, "Why are you here? What is this place?"

Jack learned that he'd been transferred to a kidnapping safe house. Both men with him were Mexicans in the upper echelons of the corporate executive ladder, members of the tiny minority in Mexico that tasted the good life, and were now desperately trying to get their companies or families to pay a small fortune for their release.

Jack knew all about the kidnapping industry in Mexico. Knew the fates of those unlucky enough to be taken. Los Zetas had little sympathy for people who didn't pay and routinely killed their captives whether a ransom was met or not. But they *had* released people in the past. A small hope. All the two men had.

Twelve hours into his captivity, he saw how minuscule that hope was in two separate instances. Without fanfare, the lights had blazed on. A man came down the stairs carrying a suppressed pistol. He walked over to the younger captive, now cowering on the floor, holding his hands up, begging. The man said not a word, placed the bulbous suppressor against the captive's forehead, and pulled the trigger. Then walked away.

Fifteen minutes later, a crew dragged the body out, still not saying a single word. Jack sat in his corner in shock, literally unable to assimilate the loss of control or the violence being perpetrated. He'd begun rocking back and forth, trying to find something to anchor against, when the room blazed into light again.

Another man had been led down, duct-taped and cowed. They'd released him and explained the rules, then left. This man, younger still than the one killed, maybe twenty-one or -two, scooted to a wall and warily looked at both Jack and the older man. Before they could even begin to talk, the overhead lights blazed on again, signaling someone coming.

A *narco* with a full beard marched down the stairs, carrying a fillet knife and a machete. He stomped over to the young kid and said, "Which arm?"

The kid collapsed, crying and wailing in Spanish.

The man said, "Tell me which arm, and I'll use the knife. Say nothing, and I'll use the machete."

The boy wailed again, then held out his right arm. The *narco* handcuffed his left wrist to the eyebolt, then clamped the right under his own arm. He took the fillet knife, traced the bicep, and began digging.

The screams were horrific, but Jack couldn't turn away. Couldn't stop watching the macabre scene. Eventually, using the knife like a shovel, the man dug out something the size of a large pill. He held it to the light, then dropped it on the floor and crushed it with a boot heel.

That had been over six hours ago, and when the lights blazed on again, Jack was almost catatonic in fear, praying he'd simply be locked into his eyebolt, the punishment going to someone else.

It didn't work out that way. The bearded *narco* appeared and walked over to him. He said in Spanish, "Stand up."

Jack pretended not to understand, and the man slapped his head hard enough to knock it into the wall.

He repeated, "Stand up."

Jack did so.

The man cinched his arms in handcuffs and led him to the stairs. They broke out onto the second level, and Jack entered an ostentatious display of wealth, ornate statues and artwork competing with the gold leaf on the walls. They passed through a den, the far wall made of glass, and he glimpsed a pool surrounded by foliage resembling a rain forest. Before being led into another room, he saw a tiger walking amid the greenery. A live tiger.

The *narco* saw his expression and said, "We keep him hungry for a reason. If you're lucky, we'll only feed your body to him. Make El Comandante mad and you'll be staked to a tree." The man grinned and said, "It is not a pretty thing to see."

Jack was still assimilating the words when he was jerked into a chair in front of a huge desk, looking like it had been made in the eighteenth century. He waited, taking shallow breaths.

The door opened and the bald man with the scar entered, taking a seat in the corner. The man said not a word, simply staring at him, his eyes burning with a weird glow. He perched on his chair like a bird, as if he would take flight at the slightest provocation. He rested his hands on his thighs and sat still, but his eyes were vibrating. Hypnotic. Jack turned away when the door opened again.

A short Latino with a protruding gut and a full mustache entered. He pulled a cigar out of a humidor on the giant desk and sat down, saying nothing. He clipped the end, then made a production out of lighting the cigar. He puffed a few times, getting the glow right, then turned his attention to Jack.

"Mr. Cahill, I've seen your reporting in Dallas. I've done my research. Enough to know that you have done the same. You know who I am?"

Jack shook his head. "I have no idea."

The man scowled, obviously slighted, but said, "Yes, of course. That's why I'm still alive. You do, however, know who I represent?"

Jack nodded vigorously, attempting to make up for his insult. "Yes. Los Zetas. I had no interest in you. I focus on Sinaloa. I've never done anything against you or your cartel. I've never reported against you. Please, killing an American reporter is suicide. Like Kiki Camarena."

The man puffed, then smiled. "Oh, come on. You exaggerate your own importance. Don't compare yourself to Mr. Camarena. He was a DEA agent. A man tied to the United States government. Someone they had to avenge. You are nothing but a reporter. Nobody will care. But why are we talking about death? I am the one who rescued you from that very fate."

Jack waited, unsure of where the conversation was going.

"You were investigating the Sinaloa cartel and attended a meeting in El Paso. The Sinaloa men were creating a plan. Something worthy of killing an American reporter. As you state, those are high stakes. What were they doing? What is the plan?"

Confused, Jack said, "I have no idea. Please. They didn't talk about Los Zetas. There was no discussion about you. I can't help with any plans against your business."

The man leaned back, saying nothing, the cigar smoke coiling around his head. When he spoke again, Jack knew his life was in the balance.

"You heard something that was important. Tell me what it was. Surely they weren't going to kill you over a kilo of cocaine. Were they? Tell me there's a reason I went to so much trouble to bring you here."

Jack vomited everything he knew, detailing how the conversation involved information sharing and satellite GPS technology, but nothing to do with Sinaloa or drugs, begging the man to understand that he was telling the truth. Doing whatever he could to remain alive.

The *narco*'s eyes squinted, and he turned to the window, thinking. He said, "You know who this gringo contact is? What he looks like?"

Seeing a light flicker in the darkness, Jack said, "I

don't know who he is, but I can recognize him. I know what he looks like. I can help if I'm alive."

The man considered his words, then said, "Pelón, what do you think?"

The bald man leaned forward and said, "I think you have brought more aggravation than it's worth. He's an American journalist. Not a peasant to shoot in the head. This will be trouble."

The man laughed, a tinge of rabid hysteria slipping through. When the heaves subsided he said, "Pelón, my dear friend, you are paranoid. Who said anything about shooting Mr. Cahill in the head? What Sinaloa wants is what I want. Control of the Juárez *plaza*. If he helps, he will live. If he doesn't, he will die."

He focused his eyes on Jack. "The search for this man ends at the border. There is nobody in the United States coming for him."

16

Jennifer held her breath, hearing the soft rustle of men jogging by. Her phone vibrated and she saw it was Pike. She ignored the call and sent a text.

Can't talk.

She waited until she was sure the men had gone, then dialed him back.

He answered on the first ring. "Hey, I'm in Atlanta. Should I catch a flight to Dallas or El Paso?"

She kept her voice low. "Pike, I'm in Mexico, and I'm in trouble."

She expected an outburst, but he was all business. "What's the situation?"

She heard a noise outside and hung up.

She held her breath again, afraid to make any sound, not for the last time wishing she had paid attention to Pike and stayed in El Paso. The scuffling faded and she leaned back against the refuse, the stench of the Dumpster she was hiding within nearly overpowering.

A text came in. *I'm coming.*

It was of little use, since even if Pike was texting from

inside an aircraft on the runway, he was still a good five or six hours away, but it gave her a needed boost in confidence, something that had faded after she'd left her car.

Once she'd decided on a direction, she'd gone only about five blocks, running between the concrete buildings, when two cars stopped at a house about seventy meters away—one of them a police vehicle. Two uniformed officers exited and split up, knocking on the doors to houses. She sprang out at the sight, almost giddy with relief. She was jogging toward the police car when a man came out of one of the houses and pointed in her direction. The policeman saw her and bellowed at the other car. The civilian vehicle spilled out men and she began sprinting in the other direction.

She had run blindly through the dilapidated neighborhoods, jumping over fences and zigzagging across lots, her speed much greater than that of the men chasing her. She'd eventually lost them inside a vulcanizing business, the back lot covered with stacks of old tires, some reaching ten feet in the air. She'd cut straight through, but the men chasing were forced to search, giving her breathing room. Jogging through an alley, she'd found a Dumpster behind a grocery store and decided to risk discovery by hiding rather than moving.

Pike's call had been a long five hours ago, way before the sun began sinking below the horizon. She continued waiting until she saw the glow of a halogen security light on the corner of the store, wanting the darkness to cloak her heritage from anyone who saw her.

She raised the lid of the Dumpster and cautiously scanned through the crack but saw no one. She hoped the searchers had given up but didn't think they would.

The bridge had become a long-term goal. Something out of reach. Her short-term objective was now a business area. Someplace with restaurants and hotels, away from the claustrophobic poverty of the graffiti-covered concrete she was now in. Someplace where the people might help her, or at least prevent the men chasing her from doing anything that would draw attention to themselves.

She exited and softly lowered the lid, then began moving down the alley, continuing her trek east. She reached the next road and surveyed the far side for a crossing point, a waxing moon providing enough illumination to show the buildings were all connected in one way or another. No alleys.

She caught movement to her right and saw two figures coming down the sidewalk about seventy meters away. A car turned the corner, its headlights sweeping across her alley and causing her to fall back. It stopped adjacent to the men and she heard muffled conversation carry across the still night air.

Didn't quit looking for me.

She waited until the car rolled on, then studied the men. When she was sure they were moving away and not toward her, she scuttled across the street. She stopped under an awning, the darkness cloaking her, waiting to see if she'd alerted any searchers. She had not. She slid down the wall, putting distance between her and the men, and reached a wrought-iron fence with a gate leading into a small yard. She was leaning forward, straining to see if there was a way through, when a dog hit the fence full force, barking uncontrollably and causing her to leap back. It was a pit bull, literally frothing at the mouth, trying mightily to reach her and rend her flesh, snarling and snapping a foot away.

She scrambled to her feet, the adrenaline firing, and saw the men down the street now running toward her position, no more than fifty meters away, one of them shouting into a radio. She looked at the gate, seeing a cheap lock and handle, the dog alone the real protection for the house. She grabbed the handle, testing the strength. Deciding.

She turned and waited, seeing the men closing the distance, the dog in a frenzy at her back, her arms trembling, her mind begging her to run. When they were twenty feet away she yanked the gate handle with all of her might, breaking it open and freeing the beast.

She swung the gate wide, slamming it against her body as a shield against the dog. It made one attempt to get at her, then shot at the men like a bullet, leaping up and clamping its jaws around the nearest one's arm. Jennifer heard a scream but was already moving through the gate and into the yard. A vicious fight broke out behind her as she sprinted across the open space, the dog holding his own against both men.

She leapt up and toe-kipped off of a cinder-block wall,

gaining another foot while turning in midair and snagging a beam that ran the length of the eave of the building. She swung her legs back and forth twice, generating momentum, then whipped them up and over her head, onto the roof.

She pushed herself the final stretch onto the rough shingles, hearing a gunshot and the scream of the dog. She took off across the building, looking for a way out. She jumped the small gap to the next roof, a tin one, making an enormous racket before reaching the edge next to the street. She squatted down and studied, seeing an abandoned industrial park across the way, the moonlight illuminating the broken windows and graffiti, the small manufacturing plant an unintended victim of the past violence. Beyond it, she saw the lights of Ciudad Juárez. Close. Very, very close.

Get there. Get some help. Get into the light. Get to people outside this ghetto.

She was scrambling off the roof, hanging on the edge with her hands, when two cars pulled to the left and right corners of her block. Men spilled out on both sides, placing her in the middle. She dropped and sprinted across the street, her goal now shrinking even further.

Lose them. Get out of their search grid.

They didn't notice her until she hit the fence of the industrial park, the noise alerting them to her escape. She flipped to the far side and sprinted into the abandoned manufacturing facility, full of machinery, pulleys, and conveyor belts. The men followed, and her goal shrank yet again.

Separate them. Take them out one at a time.

She ran six feet in and crouched behind a generator, the moon illuminating the ground through the skylights above. She heard the men coming and debated her position, knowing she was wasting precious time. Run, or fight? She might be able to outdistance the men and reach the lights on the far side. But she couldn't outrun a radio, and she'd seen a man using one. Stay here and fight, and she could remove them one by one as they searched. Getting a weapon in the process.

The decision was made for her as shadows broke the light. She counted five and dashed back, waiting on them to spread out.

17

She heard muffled talking, then noises from the men moving in different directions. She backed up slowly and crouched behind some piece of machinery she couldn't have identified in the daylight, her primary concern to always leave herself an out. Leave a means of escape.

Don't get cornered. Hit them one at a time, and move on.

She heard one man approaching, walking slowly in the darkness, and waited. She caught a glow behind her and whirled around, seeing nothing, then felt the vibration in her purse.

Christ.

She'd slung her purse across her back and it was her smartphone, coming to life, the glow spilling out. The buzz of the vibration sounding like a bullhorn. She frantically swung the purse around and silenced the buzzing, seeing it was Pike. She powered down the phone completely, listening for a reaction.

The man had paused. She waited, breathing through an open mouth. She heard him shuffle forward and got ready to fight.

She considered what she would do. What technique she would use when he arrived. She wanted to subdue him and grab his weapon. To knock him out. In truth, she wanted to give him the chance to surrender. Other foolish thoughts flitted through her head before she realized she couldn't do any of them. Not if she wanted to live.

He broke the plane of the machine she was hiding behind, and she struck to kill, launching forward like a rattlesnake behind a rock.

She drove a palm strike into the bridge of his nose with her full weight behind it, then circled her right arm around his neck as he staggered back, breaking his balance. She swept his legs out from under him and facilitated the fall, dropping to a knee and slamming the back of his neck onto her thigh. Snapping it cleanly.

She searched him rapidly, finding no weapon whatsoever.

Shit.

She heard the men calling, shouting among themselves from the commotion, then heard them begin to move her way. She slid along the floor, using her feet to check for debris, not wanting to make any noise that would give away her position. She stopped in the shadows of a giant press, sick at what she'd been forced to do, the adrenaline flooding through her body.

Go away. Please, please go away.

She heard two men find the kill, both screaming in Spanish about what they would do to her, as if that would make her surrender.

Four more.

She found another ambush position and waited, needing them to split up again. She felt around the ground, her hand closing on a piece of lumber. She heard the men separate, one moving deeper into the warehouse and the other coming her way, but at an angle that would cause him to pass her position about ten feet away. She needed him close. She rapped her knuckles against the steel of an empty tank, the noise sounding like a subdued gong.

The man hissed and began jogging in a stutter-step, slowed by the darkness. She saw the shadows, the flickering of movement, and waited. He broke into her line of sight, and she struck, cracking him in the head with the length of wood. He screamed, whirling his own club full force, catching her in the shoulder and slamming her into the metal she was hiding behind. The pain snapped through her like an electric shock, bouncing the two-by-four out of her hand.

She rolled on the ground, and he struck again. She writhed, and the club missed, hitting the concrete. She lashed out with her leg and caught his knee, breaking his stance and opening him up. She rose into a crouch as he brought the club high. He swung and she darted inside. She popped his chin back with her left hand, then speared his throat, driving her knife hand as if she were trying to hit something behind him. She sprang back, and he fell to his knees, choking out phlegm. His throat swelled, and he collapsed face forward.

Three more.

She heard the men reacting to the noise and moved away in a crouch. She saw a shadow pass to her left and began backpedaling, looking for a new position that allowed escape. She saw a shadow to the right and froze, needing the man to continue on. Needing one-on-one combat.

The shadow moved down a section of Conex containers, then disappeared. She strained her ears and heard a gasp, followed by the meaty thump of something striking metal.

What the hell?

She remained still and heard the man begin moving again, searching away from her.

She circled back the way she'd come, slipping into a block of conveyor belts. She went twenty feet and realized her mistake. The equipment was pinning her in, giving no escape, leaving a single lane to advance. She turned to get back into the facility proper, among the machines, when she saw another shadow. She crouched, staring into the darkness, praying it was her imagination.

The shadow became a man, coming toward her. She slowly started slinking the other way when she heard a noise. Coming from the other end.

She stopped, trying to focus through the overwhelming fear.

Two on one. Two on one. Need to kill the first immediately.

She knew it would do no good. She couldn't take them both on and win, and they were too close to separate.

The man to her left shouted something in Spanish, and the one to the right answered. They continued on, both with their arms up, one with another club.

They know I'm close.

She crouched and scuttled backward, the belt above her head. Panting, she swiveled left and right, watching them advance, the one on the left much closer. He reached her position, unsure of her exact location. She struck, swinging her leg from underneath the conveyor, whipping it just above his ankles and sweeping him off of his feet.

His head cracked the ground and she fell on top of him, forgetting her skills, instead attacking like a thing possessed. She grabbed his hair and thumped his head into the concrete as hard as she could. Once, twice, three times, until she saw a growing pool of fluid.

She jumped to her feet, hearing the second man closing the distance. Behind him she saw a third, sprinting toward her.

Lord help me, I don't want to die.

She crouched into a fighting stance, snapping her head left and right for a piece of machinery to separate them. Anything to keep her one-on-one, where she stood a chance of survival. And seeing nothing.

The third man closed the gap, assuring a two-on-one fight, both men less than ten feet away. She growled like an animal and raised her fists. He slapped his hands into the hair of the man up front and yanked him off his feet, slamming him into the ground. He rotated around onto the man's chest, pinning him and clamping the head in a vise with both arms. He twisted violently, then stood up, facing her.

"You think you could answer your fucking phone?"

Pike. She sagged to the floor.

18

Crossing the border in Pike's rental, the danger behind them, Jennifer felt the tension begin to fade, leaving her drained. She said, "How'd you find me?"

"Taskforce phone. Did you forget they're interconnected? I was tracking you the minute I hit El Paso. I was scared shitless when I saw it had been stationary for my entire flight, then I picked up your movement to the industrial park. I couldn't believe it when you shut it down. The one thing that I could use, and you turned the damn thing off."

She felt her face flush, only now realizing the phone had saved her life. She snaked her hand into his and said, "I couldn't talk. It was giving me away. . . . I thought I was on my own. . . ."

Pike glared at her. "I *told* you that you weren't on your own. I said we'd figure this out together. I still can't believe you did this. Did it help your brother? I broke a shit-ton of rules getting here, tracking phones, and . . ."

Jennifer leaned back, turning to face him. "And what?

I should have listened, but my brother is in real trouble. He's been kidnapped. I'm sure of it. I have a video in my purse, and a picture of the house he's in."

She expected support but saw the beginnings of a sneer. He said, "So what now, you want the Taskforce to assault a place in Mexico? Is that it? Because you got a voice message from your brother? Jennifer, we're not the damn A-Team. You just made me kill two men in Mexico to save your ass. *You* did that, whether you like it or not, and it didn't do a damn thing for your brother. All it did was prove a point."

She dropped his hand. "What the hell does that mean? My brother's not worth it? He's probably being beaten to death right now, by men just like the ones you killed!"

He said nothing.

She said, "Pike?"

"It means maybe I can't see the forest for the trees anymore. Maybe I can't separate our relationship from the job. Maybe this was just a bad idea."

What?

She said, "Stop the car. Right now."

"Screw that. We need to get away from the border. Get away from the damage."

"Stop this car right now or I'm jumping out."

He looked at her, trying for bravado, but she saw apprehension at what had slipped out of his mouth. He pulled over, letting the other cars pass.

She said, "Who talked to you?"

"Nobody. I'm just thinking. I mean, I need to keep my head, and I'm not sure I can with our relationship. I'm not sure it's right. Listen, I left a site survey early, got to Atlanta, then caught the first flight to El Paso because of you. I shortchanged a mission because of you. I'm not sure I can do both anymore."

She stared at him for a second, then said, "So you mean because we're together in the Taskforce, we can't be *together*? Are you asking me to choose?"

He looked out the window. "I don't know. I don't *know*. I'm making decisions out of emotion, and I can't do that in this world. With our business."

She smiled, relieved at his answer. "So Knuckles talked to you."

He said, "No, nobody talked to me."

"Liar. He talked to me before I flew. Before the stakeout. He suspected and gave me the same line of bull." She took his hand again and said, "Look, I can't answer how you would react in combat without me in the mix, because I don't know what you guys did before I arrived. I *do* know that all decisions have a basis in emotion. Just because emotion is there doesn't make it wrong. It's only wrong if the emotion leads to a bad one."

"Jennifer, I just *made* a bad decision! I misused Taskforce assets and funding to get here. *And* killed two men. Based on our relationship."

"And that was a *bad* decision? I've seen you 'misuse' Taskforce assets before. All for the good."

He looked out the window again, saying nothing. She said, "Answer me this: Would Knuckles have gone to Mexico for his brother? With the voice mail that I got?"

He said, "Knuckles doesn't have a brother."

She took a breath and exhaled. "Just say he did, would he have gone to Mexico?"

He thought, and said, "Yes."

"Would you have come and helped him, if he'd called, using whatever means were at your disposal?"

He nodded slowly. "Yes. I would have."

"Then what the hell are we talking about?"

Pike closed his eyes for a moment. "You really twist up what I'm thinking."

She squeezed his hand and said, "No I don't. Others are doing that. And you know it."

He let go of her hand and put the car in drive, saying nothing. She said, "You know that, right? I wouldn't stay if I thought what you said was true."

He said, "I know. It's just that we can't be pulling shit like this. The other times you mentioned were for national security. Averting risks to our nation, not something personal like this. It was wrong."

She said, "Listen to the tape. I don't think it's just personal. I think it's a Taskforce problem. Something bad's going on, and I think it affects national interests."

As she pulled out the recorder he said, "Jennifer, drugs might be a national problem, but they're not Taskforce business. There's a whole agency dedicated to that."

She said, "Just listen. Jack might have been working on the cartels, but he found something different. There's an American on here talking about something much bigger than drugs."

"What?"

"Our GPS constellation."

19

Not for the first time, Arthur Booth considered bringing mittens with him to work. The temperature inside his trailer was damn near freezing due to the number of servers, and it wasn't like he was going to be banging away on a keyboard any time soon. Well, unless there was an anomaly in the system, which had happened only a few times since the Air Force officially accepted the latest upgrade to the GPS Architecture Evolution Plan.

Located behind the wire on one of the largest secure areas within the Department of Defense, the trailer was nowhere near as nice as the control room it supported two hundred meters away, but it was supposed to be temporary, and anything beyond the barest of requirements was a waste of money in the eyes of the defense contractor that maintained it.

Boeing had won the bid to create the next-generation Global Positioning System and had been working nonstop for over a decade to implement it. Designed to replace the aging, monolithic mainframes with a distributed network, along with launching more robust and capable satellites into space, it was an enormous undertaking that had to be accomplished seamlessly. Sort of like upgrading a propeller aircraft to a jet-capable one—while the aircraft continued to fly. Given the criticality of the system, it couldn't be treated like cable TV, where the United States could tell the world, "Sorry for the inconvenience, but GPS will be experiencing some unpredictable outages over the next ten years. . . ."

And so Boeing built the system with robust backups, monitoring the architecture on a twenty-four/seven clock. The new AEP operational control segment at Schriever Air Force Base was fully functional now, monitoring the health of the global constellation of satellites, and Boeing, using Booth's station, monitored the health of the control segment, reacting to any anomaly it found.

Booth, however, was watching for a very different reason. He *wanted* an anomaly. Wanted official access to the control segment. Wanted to be able to ostensibly solve a problem while introducing a new one.

Booth was a hacker and always had been, although he would say he was of the breed known as "ethical." With ethics being decidedly in the eye of the beholder. He never compromised systems for financial gain, like eastern European Mafia groups, or for general mayhem, like a high school script kiddie defacing a pop star's website. He only hacked for what he perceived as the greater good, exposing corporations and government evil, as it were.

Hacking, in and of itself, was nothing more than unauthorized penetration of computer systems. It was an action, not an attribute that could be spotted across a room at a party, and thus, like the group he sometimes worked with, he remained anonymous. The same skills he employed as a hacker were in great demand in his work as a computer technician, and thus he commanded a significant salary from Boeing, complete with a secret security clearance.

His initial foray into government employment had been with the CIA, where he'd applied to work in a cell developing some decidedly nefarious computer applications, something at the time he'd thought would be right up his alley, using his skills for the greater good in defense of the nation and gaining a sense of self-worth he couldn't obtain by writing code designed to increase advertising sales. Unfortunately, he couldn't pass the lifestyle polygraph test, which was designed to determine if there was a risk in exposing an applicant to national secrets. Apparently, he had been deemed risky and had been denied employment. Luckily for him, there was no such thing as cross talk among the divisions of the government, and Boeing didn't require anything more than a background check, which had come up pristine.

Booth finished the initial survey for his shift and sat down, exhaling hard in an attempt to see his breath in the cold air but coming up empty. Having nothing else to do, he turned on his personal laptop after inserting a thumb drive with a boot segment that would control the laptop's operating system. He placed his thumb on a small biometric scanner at the base of the keyboard and unlocked the system. Wading through various partitions, he pulled up an executable file called POLARIS.

He absently tapped the interface, checking for any glitches from his programming the night before, proud of his chosen name. Polaris was the North Star, which was the old-school, analog GPS that had guided navigation for centuries. He thought the name very apt, as the program would revert the world back to using it.

The executable file seemed to work fine and, in truth, would have worked fine a week ago. All he was doing now was refining the aesthetics of the interface while he waited to inject it into the GPS constellation, changing it from code only a computer maven could understand into an intuitive screen that anybody could use.

Booth hadn't come into Boeing with any intent to harm. He wasn't a mole who had spent decades wheedling his way into the inner circle. He was just a guy with expertise in computers who needed a day job so that he could execute his night activities and still eat. He worked so that he could *work,* righting the wrongs of the world as he saw them. That notion had changed as he became aware of the extent to which the GPS system controlled government and corporate actions. The satellite constellation was a sterile machine that did nothing but send out streams of ones and zeros. But the people who used the signals did some pretty nasty things.

Booth had worked with the hacktivist group Anonymous on multiple occasions and had even taken leave to protest Wall Street during the heady days of the Occupy movement—wearing the ubiquitous Guy Fawkes mask that was an Anonymous hallmark—but those had always been separate and distinct from his work at Boeing. It wasn't until the United States government began killing its own citizens in Predator drone strikes that he decided to act.

The solution had been elegant in its simplicity, and he'd often wondered why he didn't think of it before. He'd marched on Wall Street using analog methods when the digital destruction of that enterprise was staring him in the face the entire time.

GPS had been created solely as a military application, and as such it had been designed with safeguards in mind. Since the satellites blindly launched signals continuously, the military was worried that the very position, navigation, and timing features that would allow US smart weapons technology to dominate a future battlefield could also be used by an enemy, and they were determined to prevent that from occurring.

In essence, while incredibly complicated in execution, the concept of GPS was fairly simple. A receiver acquired a signal from a satellite, along with how long it took that signal to reach it. Once it had three or more of those signals, complete with the time it took each to reach its location, it simply triangulated its position based on its inherent knowledge of the satellites' location. Easy.

The key was the timing signal, as it had to be nanosecond

precise to get an accurate location, and that was what the military adjusted. All thirty-five of the satellites currently in orbit had an application called selective availability embedded within them. With a flip of a switch, the military could turn on this feature for any satellite they wanted, which, in essence, simply altered the timing broadcast. In other words, the receiver would think it took X nanoseconds to reach it, when it really took Y. Thus, the receiver would triangulate an incorrect location. The military controlled the degree of offset, and the greater the aberration, the greater the error, but civilian use of the system had overcome the military monopoly.

The Department of Defense had begun to lose control of its creation since its inception, like water eroding a riverbank. It was just too good an application not to be capitalized on in the civilian market, even with selective availability. GPS became more and more entrenched in the public world, with the timing feature becoming embedded into the United States' national architecture. Everything from bank transactions to cell phone towers to power grids used it. So much so that President Bill Clinton abolished the use of selective availability in the year 2000, and the new Block III satellites scheduled for launch in the next decade didn't even include the feature.

But it was still there on the legacy systems that were currently in space. All Booth had done was create a program that could access it. With his own personal switch, he could cause every single GPS-enabled device to fail—including the military-only encrypted signal—whether it was a red light in New York City that solely needed accurate timing or a train switchyard that needed accurate positioning of its customers. Or, in his mind, a corrupt banking system that utilized GPS timing for every single transaction and a fleet of Predator UAVs armed with Hellfire missiles looking for something to kill.

Creating the program had been simple. Getting into the satellites was what had proven hard. The 2nd Space Operations Squadron was responsible for all functions of the GPS constellation, and it controlled them from inside a building that had more security than the CIA. His trailer was only a stone's throw away, but he wasn't allowed on the floor of the new operational control segment and could only access the system when asked to because of an anomaly, using the network inside his trailer. And so he was forced to wait.

His freezing little work trailer did provide one benefit, though. Because of its criticality, the entire GPS architecture was air-gapped from the World Wide Web, completely stovepiped to prevent hackers such as him from infiltrating. The only connectivity was with his trailer— which *was* wired into the Internet, but through Boeing work systems that weren't involved in the GPS maintenance. It had been a simple matter to fix that.

Now, in theory, once the script was embedded in the satellites, he could activate it from anywhere. Which was a good thing, because he wanted to be nowhere in the chain of evidence when it went operational. It would look like a simple hacking penetration of Boeing, causing some security analyst to lose his job back in DC but not pointing at Booth.

It was why he'd gone to El Paso in the first place. Two weeks ago he'd been surprised when his dealer had "bumped into" him in a bar in downtown Colorado Springs, the nearest town from his work at Schriever.

Booth had never been into heavy drugs, but he had a marijuana habit that was out of control and had racked up quite a bit of debt. His dealer had always been courteous, but the menace of nonpayment had hung above Booth's head like an anvil waiting to fall. That threat had come crashing down with voters passing Amendment 64. Now that marijuana was legal in Colorado, the dealer saw his profits dwindling and had demanded immediate payment on the debt, something Booth couldn't afford outright. The dealer hadn't punished him—yet—but instead had given him time to collect the money, and he had introduced Booth to a man named Carlos, a supposed hacktivist from Mexico.

Booth had gone along, but he had suspected from the beginning who he was talking with. Carlos knew computers but not much about the hacking fraternity, which had raised Booth's suspicions. Not a great deal, but some. Because of events he'd rather have kept buried, he knew a thing or two about activities in Mexico.

Two years ago, the group Anonymous had threatened Los Zetas because they had allegedly kidnapped one of its members in Mexico, saying they were going to expose every corrupt official involved with Los Zetas unless the man was released. Los Zetas, in routine fashion, threatened to kill ten men for every one exposed. At that, Anonymous had backed down, claiming the man had been freed. No corrupt officials' names had been released. Booth had no idea if the man had even been kidnapped but had worked with Anonymous to locate the officials collaborating with the cartel, compiling a database in an effort he felt was worthwhile.

After the Zetas' threats, and further indications that they were actively recruiting their own hackers to track down Anonymous members, Booth had become somewhat of an expert on the cartels, working to protect his own skin instead of exposing Mexican corruption.

Using those same computer linkages, he'd researched Carlos and had found a few interesting things. Not much, but enough to determine that if he was aligned with a cartel, it was Sinaloa and not Los Zetas, which gave him the confidence to continue. Sinaloa hated Los Zetas, and thus would probably pay him a bonus instead of cutting off his head. In the end, he didn't care how POLARIS was released, as long as it didn't lead back to him. Like the group, he wished to remain anonymous.

He was gazing at his creation, toying with the idea of adding a row of slide switches that looked like an old stereo equalizer bar, when a flashing light caught his eye from the bank of computer monitors. He stared for a full second, in a little bit of shock. It was an alert sent from the operational control segment located in the secure building two hundred meters away. There had been a glitch, and they were requesting that he find it. Nothing crucial, but enough to warrant a bug fix. Enough to warrant his rooting around in the new operational control segment for hours.

20

The digital recorder ended for the third time and I dropped it on the bed, turning away from Jennifer and rubbing my eyes. I was still not seeing the smoking gun that would get the Taskforce chasing after her brother. But I knew she wouldn't want to hear that.

She said, "What's that look? Can't you see they're talking about national security issues? This isn't about drugs."

I dropped my hands, waited a beat, then said, "Jennifer, I don't know what they're talking about. That fat-ass guy just blathers on about freedom of information and a bunch of computer crap."

"He talked about our Global Positioning System. One of the most sacrosanct things the United States controls."

"He *mentioned* GPS. He didn't talk about it. He also mentioned Wall Street and WikiLeaks. This isn't enough to act. What do you want me to do, call Kurt for a fishing expedition? I'm probably in enough trouble for coming down here in the first place."

Colonel Kurt Hale was the commander of the Task-force, and while we'd known each other for close to fifteen years, he *was* in command. Make no mistake, he was a close friend, but he was still my boss. He cut me more slack than most, but this was asking for a poke in the eye.

Jennifer was quiet. I almost saw the smoke coming off of her brain as she tried to come up with something that would persuade me to call Kurt. Finally, she whispered, "But Jack's going to get killed."

I softened my tone, seeing the hell she was going through. "Jennifer, I know he's in real danger. I believe you. It's just that we're not a hostage-rescue force. That's not what we do. We don't even have any authority to operate in Mexico. You want Omega for a hit, and we don't even have a target."

The Taskforce called every stage of an operation a letter from the Greek alphabet, starting with Alpha for the introduction of forces. Omega meant we had authority from the Oversight Council—our own extralegal body of wise men hand-picked by the president—to execute operations on foreign soil. Operations that often had repercussions extending way beyond the action itself, possibly with second- and third-order effects that were worse than the problem we were trying to prevent. Which is why we answered to the council instead of ourselves. Why we couldn't go hot-rodding after her brother.

I moved to the window and cracked the curtain, wishing we'd spent some time searching the Internet instead of pulling over at the first hotel we could find, in this case a La Quinta Inn. Best described as "clean and serviceable," it didn't have a whole lot of ambience.

Out in the parking lot I saw two black-and-white police cars pull up, both older models looking like they'd been borrowed from the set of *CHiPs*. Something about them seemed odd, but I didn't focus like I should have. Instead I turned back to Jennifer.

She was standing in the same place, her eyes slightly unfocused as she went through probabilities in her head. Torturing herself.

I went to her and said, "Look, we can't assault the place, but we aren't helpless. Kurt has the ear of the most powerful people in the world. We can get him to move on this. Get some official help."

She drew some hope from that and nodded, wiping her eyes. I had just started to say something else when I heard footsteps on the concrete balcony outside our room. A lot of footsteps. My instinct went into the red zone, but it was too little, too late.

The door splintered inward from the force of a metal police battering ram. Five uniformed men piled into the room, guns drawn. I pushed Jennifer to the floor and shot my hands in the air, shouting, "Don't fire! Don't fire!"

Two of the men covered down on Jennifer while three moved to me. The man with the battering ram turned around and covered the exit to the room. All were Hispanic, and as with the police cars outside, something seemed odd. By the time they'd closed on me, it clicked what it was: Their uniforms were mismatched. Some had name tags, some didn't. Some had patches on their shoulders, others didn't.

I shouted, "Jennifer, they're fake!" and exploded, trapping the pistol of the first man and rotating his arm in a vicious circle, forcing him to fling himself over the torque or have his wrist shatter. He thumped the floor and I hammered him in the temple, ripping the gun out of his hand. I launched up from the floor and drove my fist under the chin of the next man like a piston, hearing his jaw crack as his head popped backward. I whirled to the third man.

He pointed a pistol at my chest and shouted, "Stop! Stop right now."

One of the men who had gone to Jennifer was on the floor, rubbing his face. The other had her hair in his hand and a knife to her throat.

Keeping his own weapon on me, in accented English, the third man continued. "Drop the gun. You cannot beat us both. You shoot me, she dies. You shoot him, *you* die. Neither has to happen. If we wanted you dead, we could have just started shooting."

I did as he asked, kicking myself for not paying more attention. For letting Jennifer's pain supersede my survival instincts.

He said, "We are going to handcuff you both and leave here one at a time. Act like you are being arrested. She goes first. If she says anything outside the door to anyone who has come to watch, you die. You go second. If you say anything outside the door, she dies. Understood?"

I nodded my head. He turned to Jennifer, and she did the same. My hands were cuffed behind my back and our

Taskforce phones, Jennifer's tablet, and the digital recorder were shoved into Jennifer's bag. I watched her being led out of the room, a man on each side. Shortly, it was my turn. The leader picked up Jennifer's purse and nodded.

We went down the stairs and I hung my head like I'd seen on numerous episodes of *Cops*. Sure enough, there was a small crowd, all pointing and whispering. None moved near us. My heart sank when I saw only one police car. I'd expected them to transport us together, but Jennifer was already gone.

We pulled out of the parking lot without lights, ignoring the crowds. We drove for two blocks, then circled behind a grocery store, the police car stopping adjacent to another sedan, both screened by the loading docks used for large trucks. A gun was placed to my head and I was jerked out, a man on each arm. As if I could do something with my hands cuffed behind me.

They opened the trunk of the sedan, and in the dim glow of the exterior lighting I saw it was already occupied, feeling a small measure of relief. I was unceremoniously crammed into it and knew instantly the body wasn't Jennifer's. It was a man who stank as if he hadn't bathed in a week.

And he was weeping uncontrollably.

21

Eduardo looked out the window across his estate, surveying the lights twinkling in the ghetto of Juárez. He hated it here. Hated having to live in this dump and longed to get back to Mexico City. Back to the land of the rich. But earning *plaza* boss came with a price, and he'd been entrusted with the fight for Juárez by Sinaloa, so here he would stay. At least until he could clean up the mess.

Behind him, Carlos said, "This will work. Things are coming together very well."

"Well? You let a woman escape from your grasp. Here, in the heart of Juárez. It's absolutely shameful. I look incompetent, and we still don't know who took the reporter."

Carlos began to fawn. "You don't look incompetent. She had help. We couldn't predict that. Nobody even knows she was here. Nobody knows of her escape, and I'm working to rectify the situation. I was able to set up a screen on the north side of the border after she fled our net." He gave a shallow smile. "The Americans spend so much time checking vehicles that it worked in our favor. She didn't cross with any speed. We followed them to where they're staying, and it's still close enough to the border to be useful. I hope to hear some news soon, and we will learn who they are. Of greater concern is the traitor in the ranks. My plan will work."

"You really think he is part of my circle? I cannot believe that."

"There's one way to find out. You already have a meeting planned. Let it be known that we're moving forward with Mr. Fawkes. Tell them he's flying down tomorrow or the next day. Give out a flight number. Then we simply check all outgoing calls before anyone is allowed to leave."

"Is he flying down?"

"No. Not yet, but that's not the point. We need to set a trap with false information. You don't want Los Zetas to know anything real."

"What makes you think the traitor will call from here?"

"Tell them they are to remain here overnight. Give them some excuse. He'll call. I guarantee he'll call if he thinks he'll miss getting the information out."

Eduardo turned from the window and said, "Okay. That's easy enough. What of this Mr. Fawkes? Surely you know who he is by now."

Carlos said, "Yes. He checked out. He's Arthur Booth, a midlevel computer technician working for Boeing. I believe he can do what he says. He was almost giddy on the phone today. He's completed the task and wants to pass what he calls the POLARIS protocol. All we need to do is meet him now."

"What is this protocol?"

"I'm not really sure. He said he'd explain it when we met, but what I do know is that it will affect the navigation systems of the surveillance drones on the border."

"So you don't even know what it does? How it works?"

"My meeting with Booth in El Paso was just to establish the connection. We didn't discuss the specifics of the protocol. The point was to get him on our side, and it apparently worked."

Eduardo's lips split into a sinister grin. "Okay, Carlos. I'll let you hold the keys for now. Call the men."

Two hours later, sitting in the conference room with Eduardo and the other men of the inner circle, Carlos felt his phone vibrate. He spoke briefly, then held up a hand. When Eduardo nodded, he said, "Things are looking up."

22

I bumped along in the blackness of the trunk, having given up trying to find out who the man with me was. All he did was beg me not to talk, then began weeping again. Clearly, he was convinced we were going to die. I wasn't so sure he was wrong, so I spent the time trying to prevent that outcome.

I had been to a multitude of defeating-restraints courses during my time in the military, and after all the instruction one thing stood out: Prior planning beats MacGyver shit every day. Almost all handcuffs operate with a universal key in order to allow any officer to free a suspect, be it for health and safety reasons or just for convenience, and I, like many operators I worked with, had taken to carrying one in my wallet.

In over twenty years I had never, ever used it, and Jennifer had made fun of the habit on more than one occasion. Now I was wishing I'd forced her to do the same.

I wormed around, digging my wallet out of my pants pocket and then losing it for an instant in the bouncing. I scooted my ass backward, sweeping my hands until it connected with the leather. Working by feel, I opened it and dug my fingers in until I hit the pocket for business cards. This was where it became critical, and my lack of planning was causing issues.

I'd simply buried the key at the base of the pocket, surrounded by a bunch of business cards I always carried that supported my job as an intrepid archeological explorer. If I dumped all the cards and shook the wallet to get the key, I'd give away that I was up to no good. When they opened the trunk they'd see a confetti playground and know something was awry.

Why didn't you go the distance? Tape the damn thing to the license or a single card? It was like buying a fire extinguisher for your house, then storing it in the attic.

I cradled the wallet and squeezed its sides, then began shaking, using one hand to keep the cards in. If the key was set right, I knew it would fall, because it had done so numerous embarrassing times in the past, usually at the airport with a twentysomething TSA agent grinning lasciviously at Jennifer over the implications. But that would be pure luck, and with mine, it was probably trapped at the base underneath the cards.

The car went over a speed bump hard enough to bounce both of us into the roof of the trunk, causing me to lose the wallet again. I slapped the metal, sweeping aside detritus that had accumulated in the trunk. The car stopped just as I closed my left hand over it. I began shaking it and heard the doors open. When they slammed shut, the key fell into my hand. I rolled over onto my back and shoved the wallet into my pocket just as the lid opened.

I was jerked out, seeing a sign for a sleazy roadside motel called the Traveler's Inn.

Uh-oh. Jack's motel. Not good.

The man was pulled out behind me, and for the first time I saw he was Hispanic and about sixty, wearing cheap rubber sandals and a stained white T-shirt. When he saw the location, he began to wail until he was cuffed in the head.

We were led straight to room number twelve, with one of the men opening the door using a key from his pocket. We got inside and the men pushed me into a corner, sitting me on my haunches with one of the guys standing over me. The door was shut, and the captors began speaking in Spanish. The older man began to wail again as he was shoved to his knees.

The leader of the group began a lengthy soliloquy in Spanish, none of which I understood, but I could tell the man on his knees did. He became catatonic, not even flinching when a large bowie knife was produced, the blade about twelve inches long.

I felt the sweat break out on my neck and began working the key into the lock, an almost impossible task without being able to see the cuffs. Like everyone else, the guard in front of me had his eyes focused on the older man, watching the snot roll down his face as he blubbered.

The bowie knife came down, and as much as I had

seen in the world, it still didn't register as real until both carotid arteries had been slit and the blood began to spray from the damage. I involuntarily flinched, trying to sink into the corner of the room. I heard the gurgles as the knife bit deeper; attempting to sever the head from the body. The knife was stopped momentarily by the spine, and I closed my eyes, focusing on the task of staying alive. I felt the key sink into the hole and gently worked it left and right, trying to seat the pins correctly. Trying to calm the raging adrenaline flowing through me from the fear. I would only get one shot.

I heard the leader shout in Spanish and opened my eyes to see the bowie knife begin cutting the hands off the corpse. One flopped free, held only by a tendon. The man chopped at the floor like he was slicing garlic, and the hand separated. He worked on the other one, sawing through tendon and bone. They placed both hands on the chest of the corpse, then faced me. *My turn*.

In English, the leader said, "This man was an informant and met a traitor's fate. You are involved in his actions, and we wanted you to see what happens to those who oppose us."

Feeling bile in my throat at my helplessness, I simply nodded.

The leader flicked his eyes at the person guarding me, and he placed his hands on my head, pushing it into the wall, exposing my neck. The leader said, "We want to know why you were in Mexico. We want to know what you were doing."

I saw the man holding my head pull out a blade. Much smaller than the bowie but lethal nonetheless. He leaned in, showing me the knife, his eyes locked on mine. I rolled to the left, a prehistoric instinct to get away from the danger, a low grunt escaping as I strained to get out of his grasp. I twisted my wrist, and I felt the lock click free.

A small snick that opened up a world of hurt.

I whipped both hands to my front and lashed out with the wrist still clamped, slashing the guard's face with the teeth of the open handcuff. He screamed and started to roll back, but I trapped him against the wall, grabbed his wrist with the knife, and drove it deep into his eye socket.

The man with the bowie knife shouted and drew his gun. I jerked the dead guard in front of me and used him as primitive body armor, rushing forward, barely registering the weight, the rage of survival adrenaline making me feel superhuman. He fired multiple times in my direction and I felt the rounds impact the corpse. He tried to back up and I threw the body on top of him, then turned to the leader.

He had a look of shock on his face, still with his weapon in its holster. He scrambled to get it free but I was already on him, wrapping one arm around his neck and trapping the weapon with the other. I bent him backward, batted his hand away, and drew his pistol. I jammed it into his chest and pumped two rounds, letting him fall.

I whirled around and raced to the bowie wielder still under the body, now frantically trying to free himself. He raised his pistol and I stomped on his hand, the round going harmlessly into the wall. He screamed something in Spanish and I jabbed the barrel into his forehead.

He shook his head violently from left to right. I held for a second, then softly nodded up and down. And pulled the trigger.

I stood, coming to grips with the carnage, needing to think. I began searching for keys. I found them on the leader and went to the car that had carried me, seeing Jennifer's purse in the front seat. I pulled out my phone and began dialing, leaving the parking lot with the battered tires of the sedan screeching, heading to the border.

Kurt picked up on the third ring, immediately asking why I was in El Paso and why I had left our mission early. I cut him off.

"Sir, it's too hard to explain. Jennifer believes there's a national security threat here on the border, and her brother's wrapped up in it. I thought she was full of shit, but the cartels have just taken a huge gamble to capture us here, in America. She was correct, and I need a team right fucking now. Where is Knuckles? He should be CONUS with the bird."

"What the hell are you talking about? Cartels? Capture you? What are you doing? I can't even get to the Oversight Council until tomorrow. Forget about Knuckles and talk to me."

I was flying down Interstate 10, headed back to the border bridge, and realized I didn't have the facts to convince him. There was no way to get Oversight Council approval for operations in Mexico on a timeline that could save Jennifer. It just wasn't what the Taskforce did. We were slow burn, not crisis management. Unlike in my previous life, we didn't sit on alert.

I pounded the steering wheel and said, "Sir, is Knuckles in the United States? Is he here with a package in the aircraft?"

Kurt's voice grew concerned at my shrill tenor, saying, "Yeah, he's here. In Atlanta. What the hell is going on? You sound like you want a Prairie Fire."

And his words broke free the best that the United States had to offer. *Prairie Fire* was the code phrase for the potential catastrophic loss of a Taskforce team and was used only under the most extreme circumstances on official missions, when everything else in the United States arsenal had failed. The words had been uttered a single time in the entire existence of the unit, but it was the one thing that Kurt could execute on his own, without Oversight Council approval, because Taskforce lives were not held to the same standard as Taskforce missions. I had never given the phrase serious thought, egotistically figuring that if I had communication and could utter the words, I could solve the problem on my own before the Taskforce could ever break anything free quickly enough to help.

Now I held the phone and savored the words. "I need Knuckles to divert to González airport in Ciudad Juárez. I'll meet him there. I'm calling a Prairie Fire. I say again, I'm calling a Prairie Fire."

He said nothing for a moment, and I saw the exit for the bridge. I coasted for a second before he came back on.

"You know what you're doing, right? You got a real Prairie Fire?"

"Sir, listen to me closely. You and I have been through a lot, but nothing like this. I just saw a man get decapitated in front of me. I'm covered in blood from three dead men in a hotel. Jennifer is in the hands of fucking savages, and if I don't get some help immediately, she's going to be slaughtered. Or worse."

I turned onto the bridge and heard, "You got them. Update me as soon as you can."

23

The door at the top of the stairwell opened, spilling light into the room, and Jennifer knew someone was coming down. *Finally.*

She regretted the thought as soon as it came into her head. She knew whoever was on the stairs would offer nothing good, but she'd been shackled in the dark for over three hours, on top of the two-hour ride in the trunk, and the shock of the capture had worn off, leaving her wanting to see why it had occurred. Wanting to learn the fate of Pike and her brother Jack, even if it hastened her own demise.

Initially, when she'd been taken out of the trunk and brought down to the basement, she'd been dismayed to find it empty, expecting to see Jack bound and shackled like she had been. She'd been tossed unceremoniously on the ground, and the lights had been extinguished. She'd waited for Pike to join her. Waited for him to arrive so they could plan their escape. After some time in the dark, she realized he wasn't coming and now wondered if he was still even alive. She thought so—hoped so—simply because of the way she had been treated.

The men hadn't been unduly violent like she'd expected. She wasn't smacked around or made to do anything lewd. There was little respect, but they hadn't been overtly cruel either. They'd treated her more like a piece of livestock, prodding when she moved slowly and showing little concern for her welfare when shoving her in or pulling her out of the trunk.

In truth, after the fear of instant death had worn off, she'd become more concerned about carbon monoxide poisoning during the ride, the leaking exhaust fumes filling the trunk and making her nauseous. Taking solace in small comforts, she initially had just sagged in the dark of the basement and drawn in clean oxygen, trying to clear her lungs of the stench of the exhaust.

Left to her own thoughts, she'd reflected on the enormous risks her kidnappers had taken. Imitating police officers on United States soil and kidnapping two United States citizens was brazen, and she knew her brother had found something much greater than drugs. She couldn't put her finger on what it was, but she knew enough about cartel operations to understand what the impact would have been if the mission had gone wrong. She was valuable for a reason she didn't understand. She might not have known what was at stake, but she knew two things for sure: One, she had been captured by a cartel, and two, she was now in Mexico.

Trying to penetrate the feeble glow from the stairwell, she heard more than one person descending and sat up, using her shoulder against the wall to make up for her hands being shackled behind her back. The overhead light blazed on, and a man was thrown in front of her, hitting the ground hard. At first she thought it was Pike, her stomach clenching in fear when she saw the man's battered face, only relaxing when she spotted a mustache.

Three other men followed him into the room, one in a business suit, two with jeans, rough shirts, and pistols in their hands. The business suit kicked the prostrate man in the stomach hard enough to lift him an inch off the ground. The man grunted, then began coughing. No one paid a bit of attention to her, conducting the actions as if she didn't exist.

One of the guns reached down and pulled the man's head up by the hair, and the suit began to interrogate him. They spoke in Spanish, but, having grown up in Texas, Jennifer could understand the gist of what was said. She visibly reacted when she heard the words *reporter* and *phone,* the suit waving a cell in front of the man's face. He turned away, and the suit nodded at the gunman still holding his hair. The gunman cranked the man's head until he could do nothing but stare at whatever the cell phone showed. The suit yelled again, and the target spit a glob of bloody phlegm onto the phone.

The suit jumped back, holding the cell away from his clothes. He shook it, like a man flinging filth off a shoe, his hands holding the phone between two fingers. Not able to get rid of the goo, he cursed and tossed it to the other gunman, eliciting a laugh from the enforcer holding the man's hair. The suit began questioning again.

Jennifer struggled to keep up with the conversation. Struggled to find an anchor for her brother, searching to translate the Spanish in her mind and failing. She saw the suit bend over the man and whisper in his ear. She unconsciously leaned forward, straining to hear. She heard what she believed were the words *honor, trust,* and *death.* She closed her eyes, focusing all of her concentration on her hearing. She heard an explosion of noise, a concussion that snapped her eyes open, and she knew what it was.

Gunshot.

She saw the suit rise from the body, the head punctured right between the eyes. The suit handed the weapon to the gunman, then walked to her.

She looked up at him, and he said in English, "Sorry for making you wait, but we had a few other matters we needed to attend to."

LOOKING AT THE target house through night vision, Knuckles said, "Well, this is possibly the goofiest plan I have ever heard. Outside of *The Boondock Saints,* that is."

I said, "Really? You're a SEAL. Goofy Hollywood bullshit is what you do."

He put the NODs down and said, "You really think this car will let us penetrate?"

"I know it will. They're waiting on me to show up in the trunk."

After getting the go-ahead for the Prairie Fire, I'd traveled into Mexico using my stolen car. I'd stopped short of the border and camouflaged the blood splatter on my clothes with dirt from the side of the road, making my shirt look like I worked at a mechanic's shed rather than a slaughterhouse. Proud of myself, I'd approached the Mexican checkpoint like a hundred other beat-up sedans, but mine drew instant focus.

It had dawned on me why immediately: I was in a car that they were supposed to let pass with no issue. But now there was a gringo driving it solo. I had sat behind the wheel in a panic but showing nothing outwardly. *Stupid, stupid, stupid*. Then I realized that it was smart. I could use this asset.

I'll pull an Entebbe to get out Jennifer.

When the border official approached and asked a question I didn't understand, I just stared at him, locking eyes until he backed down, giving him the death glare that he wanted.

He waved me forward, and I drove to the international airport coming up with a plan. In 1976, Israel had rescued ninety-eight hostages inside Uganda by landing on the airfield posing as the Ugandan president, Idi Amin. They'd driven a Mercedes specifically designed to look like Amin's off the aircraft, complete with presidential flags and other adornments, and had lulled the opposition. Instead of questioning the aircraft, Idi Amin's soldiers began scurrying about in a panic at the surprise visit. The end result was one of the greatest hostage rescues in the history of warfare. And I was now driving the Mexican version of Idi Amin's Mercedes.

I'd met Knuckles at the Abraham González International Airport's fixed-base operator center for general aviation, having already rented an SUV at the main terminal. Away from the commercial hub of the international concourse, it was a small island still in the land of make-believe. Every FBO I had been in catered to the richest bastards on the planet and thus had no security whatsoever. If you could afford to fly a plane in here, then you were clearly on the up-and-up.

Knuckles had brought the Gulfstream IV that was "leased" to my company, Grolier Recovery Services, and it was still loaded with a package. Meaning it had all manner of death and destruction embedded in the nooks and crannies of its frame that I could use, from suppressed sniper rifles to full-on explosive breaching charges.

He and the team, of course, had been a little confused at the change of direction. We'd talked in the FBO conference room, a perk provided for folks flying in on general aviation in an attempt to lure corporations back to Ciudad Juárez. When I'd closed the door, Decoy had been the first to speak, in a subdued tone I'd never heard from him. "Is that blood on your shirt?"

I said, "Yes. Before anyone says anything, I understand that you have no standing here. No cover for status. No protection. If something goes wrong, we're in a world of hurt."

I paused, judging the reaction and not getting a lot of love. I continued. "You're probably pissed that I left Turkmenistan early, and I understand that, but I need your help. Jennifer is being held by the same group of savages that I'm wearing on my shirt. I need you to focus on that and forget the implications. I don't want any Taskforce bullshit here. We will not get out clean. I can promise that. If you don't want in, then say so now. I can't order you to do anything."

I had waited on the response, wondering what the answer would be. It came from Knuckles, of all people. My friend, and now my Judas. He said, "Jennifer, huh? So this is personal?"

I turned to him, shocked, and saw a grin.

He said, "What the hell are you babbling about? We got a Prairie Fire alert for a teammate. You going to give us a plan or sit there begging?"

I stood for a moment with my mouth open, about to let fly a few choice words until what he said sank into my brain. Relieved, I laid it out. The whole crazy Idi Amin plan.

It had sounded great at the FBO, but now, as I stared at the house with night vision, it wasn't looking so hot. In fact, it looked downright suicidal.

Since I had Jennifer's phone in her bag, along with her tablet and the digital recorder from her brother, there was no way to track her actual location. All I had was the last known location of Jack's phone, which she'd pinpointed on her earlier ludicrous recce attempt. As much as I had berated her before, it was now my only anchor.

The house was set up on a hill with a circular drive leading to it, sitting about two hundred meters past a large iron fence with an electronic gate. Outside, on the front porch, were two watchers, both armed with some type of long-gun variant of the AR-15. Probably sold to them by our Justice Department. On the circular drive was an old sedan like the one we were sitting in, which I was convinced had transported Jennifer.

All we had to do was penetrate the perimeter fence and get up to the front door. No small task, but while waiting on Knuckles to arrive, I'd conducted my own recce and studied the gate, seeing no cameras or speakers or anything else to check on arrivals. While I watched, a car had approached and had simply sat outside for a moment doing nothing, then the gate had opened. I couldn't prove they weren't talking on cell phones, but I was fairly sure they simply let in anyone they expected. And they were expecting me in a trunk.

I said, "You ready to roll?"

"Yeah. No sense waiting. This either works or it doesn't."

I turned around to the backseat, getting confirmation from Retro and Blood. I started the car, and Retro said, "Hope Decoy can hit them. I don't like a Navy guy watching my back."

I pulled into the slot in front of the gate and said, "You'd rather have a Marine?"

Blood, from the back, said, "As a Marine, given the choice, I'd much rather be on the outside shooting right now."

I said, "You'll be shooting soon enough."

We waited, headlights to the front, wondering if we

were going to initiate a firefight just by being here. After a pause, the gate triggered, the giant piece of iron sliding to the right on its track, slowly inching open. When it was enough for the car, I proceeded forward, saying, "Remember, no shots early. We need total surprise."

I continued up the drive at a slow pace, watching the gunmen on the porch. They showed no alarm. I keyed my radio. "Decoy, you got both?"

"Yeah. A little spread, but no issue."

"You got to hit them quick. I can't have a gunfight right out front. The first thing I want them to hear is the breach."

"Roger all. Good luck."

"Luck starts with you."

We reached the end of the drive and paused, our headlights blinding anyone from seeing the death inside the car. The man nearest to us approached, nonchalantly walking toward the driver's door. I opened it and swung my leg out. I saw his jaw drop in surprise when he was finally able to see inside, then his head split open from a suppressed sniper shot. The second man, still not understanding, remained on the porch, fiddling with his long gun. He took one confused step toward us and his head snapped back. He collapsed into the wall, then rolled forward in a heap.

I said, "Game on."

And we launched to the front door.

24

The suit squatted down until he was at eye level with Jennifer. "You may call me Carlos." He pulled a laminated card from his pocket and said, "From your identification, I see you're Jennifer."

"Where is my brother? What have you done with Jack?"

Carlos's eyes widened slightly, and he looked back at the ID. "Jennifer Cahill. Yes. I didn't make the connection before. Jack said he'd just called a friend. So you're family?"

"Yes. We're family, and I want him freed."

He said, "I would think you'd be more concerned about what we're going to do with you."

The words caused Jennifer to inwardly flinch, but her face betrayed no fear. A few years ago, in Guatemala, she'd been in just such a position and had barely survived. Back then, Carlos's threat would have been paralyzing, leaving her catatonic, but she'd learned a thing or two about survival since. The fear did nothing but sharpen her will to live.

She said, "Where's my brother?"

Carlos appraised her for a moment, then nodded. "Okay. I respect your courage, so I'll tell you. I don't know. We had him, but he was taken from us. I thought it was by the US law. I now know it was by a competitor." He pointed at the dead man behind him. "That traitor fed our information to our enemies. They have him now."

Jennifer closed her eyes, fearing Jack was dead. Just like her uncle had been in Guatemala.

Carlos said, "What I want to know is what he told you."

She took a breath, starting the dance she knew was coming. "I never even talked to him. All I got was a voice mail message."

Carlos tapped her ID against his thigh, thinking, then said, "I'm sorry, but that's not good enough. I need to know everything he said."

"You can check my phone. Listen to my voice mail. I'm telling you the truth."

"Unfortunately, your phone hasn't arrived yet. But I will do that, make no mistake. I need to know what he told you off the voice mail. How much did he say about Predator drones? This will go easier if you talk now. By the end, you'll be screaming all you know anyway."

Predator drones?

She shouted, "Nothing! I never talked to him. I'm just an anthropologist. I don't know anything about drones."

Carlos smiled. "An anthropologist, huh? Answer me

this: If you never talked to him, how did you know what motel he was at?"

"He told his editor where he was staying. That's all."

Staring at her, Carlos whispered, "And did the editor give you the address to this house? Is that why you crossed the border and drove right to this location earlier today? Was it the editor who killed my men so that you could escape?"

Jennifer felt her face blanch, searching for an answer that would make sense. When nothing came out, Carlos continued. "Yes, I see you understand. Your story doesn't ring true, does it? I will have my answers. How did you know to search for this house?"

Before she said anything she heard a beep. He pulled a cell from his pocket and listened. When he hung up he said, "Looks like your partner is finally here."

Jennifer felt a brief glimmer of hope, relieved that Pike was alive.

Carlos stood and said, "We'll see what his story is, but I can promise it won't be as gentle as this conversation."

He nodded at the gunman who'd caught the phone and both walked up the stairs, leaving her alone with the final man. She felt the spark of hope snuffed like an ember dropped in water.

The gunman stared at her stoically, holstering his pistol and not saying a word. He was crossing his arms over his chest when a large crack split the air, causing dust to sprinkle from the ceiling. The man gave a slight jump, his hands out from his sides, staring up, confused by the noise. Jennifer understood completely.

Yeah, my partner's here, asshole.

THE DOOR SPLINTERED inward as if it had been cloven by a giant ax, large sections of wood spearing into the walls inside. We entered before the shock wave had even settled, guns and eyeballs flowing in like water out of a split in a bucket.

I focused on my sector and ignored the spitting of a suppressed HK UMP to my right, only registering that a potential threat had been eliminated. I saw a man exit a room ahead, apparently startled awake at the sound of our explosive breach. He raised an AK-47, yelling commands, and I pumped two rounds into his chest. He dropped and I continued on, the lead man in the stack. I heard Retro shout, "Door," and held up, covering down a hallway.

I heard it breached with a shotgun, then the sharp crack of a weapon from inside followed by the low pops of our suppressors. Three seconds of silence and I felt someone tap my shoulder. I leapt to my feet and jogged down the hallway.

JENNIFER ROLLED ONTO her back, tucked her legs, and raked her arms up. The cuffs caught on the soles of her shoes for a second. She wriggled and jerked, ripping the skin on her wrists before they broke free. She leapt to her feet, hearing gunfire erupt from above. She took two hops at the guard as he began to turn. She threw her hands over his head, cinching the chain of the hand-cuffs into his neck. She rotated around until they were back to back, then bent over, raising him off the ground by the chain alone, the metal biting deep into his wind-pipe.

He wheezed and gurgled, flailing his hands in the air. She strained her arms, feeling the cuffs digging into the flesh of her wrists. She rose on her feet and bounced, once, twice, and felt his neck snap. She tucked and dropped him over her shoulder. Untangling her cuffs, she ripped his pistol from his holster and sprinted toward the stairs, one thought in her mind.

Get the man with the phone.

A DOOR TO my right swung open, and I raised my weapon, fingering the safety. A flash of dirty-blond hair filled my HoloSight, and I recognized Jennifer.

I felt a wave of conflicting emotion but shunted it aside immediately, leaping past her to cover the far side of the door. I keyed the radio and said, "Jackpot, jackpot, jackpot."

The team collapsed around her in a protective bubble and I heard, "Pike, Decoy. Got a squirter leaving in your infil vehicle. You want me to engage?"

I locked eyes with Jennifer and smiled. "Negative. We got jackpot now. Move to exfil Bravo. We're too deep into the house and we're going to need your breach of the fence."

"Roger all."

Jennifer, her hands cuffed and holding a Glock, said, "Pike, there's a guy here we need to find."

Unlocking her wrists, my smile fading, I keyed the radio again. "Decoy, continue to exfil, but don't breach the fence until I call." I heard, "Roger," and said to Jennifer, "Your brother? He's here?"

"No. But there's a guy with a phone that's the key to his location."

I tossed her cuffs to the ground and brought my weapon back to high ready. "Forget him. We're out of here."

I started getting the team moving when Jennifer said, "I'm not leaving without that phone!"

Knuckles looked like he was going to lose his mind. He backed up to her, still focusing on his sector of fire, and hissed, "What the fuck is it with your family and drug lords? I've never seen someone get in more trouble than you."

Two men scrambled down a staircase we'd passed on entry, spilling into the hallway and firing pistols. Retro and Blood cut them down, but the narrow confines of the corridor were a funnel of death and a stupid place for a discussion. I said, "Keep going toward the back of the house. We'll clear the route to exfil. If we find him, great. If not, we're leaving as soon as we hit an exit."

Jennifer grimaced but nodded. We started moving at

a fast jog down the hallway, bypassing rooms and looking for an exit. Leaving uncleared sections of the target was like pulling my teeth with a pair of pliers, but I wasn't looking to kill everyone here. All we wanted was to find Jennifer, and we'd done that. My team wasn't big enough to dominate the building, and getting into a gunfight now was just asking for someone to get hit.

We reached the end of the hall and broke into a large den set up like a conference room, a long oak table upended at the far side with gun barrels hovering over it, French doors showing the lawn of the backyard. The barrels began to spit fire and I broke left, shooting on the run and diving behind a couch, while Knuckles went right. The rest of the team met a fusillade of bullets, and I saw Retro go down while Jennifer leapt back into the hallway.

I began to suppress the table with controlled pairs and shouted, "Back out, back out!"

Out of the corner of my eye I saw Knuckles dragging Retro through the door. One man rose an inch too high behind the table, his weapon snapping forward, and I stroked the trigger, popping him upright before he fell backward. The firing went into a lull as they all ducked. I seized the opportunity, retreating back into the hallway, jerking Retro the final way behind the cover of the wall.

Knuckles was on him, stripping the plate hanger off his chest and feeling for blood. He poked something and Retro sat up with a scream. Knuckles said, "In and out of the thigh. He's bleeding, but femoral's okay."

A man appeared down the hallway from the direction

we'd come. I snapped five rounds his way and he ducked back into a room. "We've got to move. Blood, get him up. Knuckles, take point. Find another way out of here. Jennifer, take Retro's UMP."

She said, "Pike, wait. That guy you hit has the phone. I saw him when he went down. He's the key."

I pushed her forward, down the hall. "Move!"

Blood got Retro into a fireman's carry and said, "You want to leave this many men to our rear? You saw the doors at the back of the room, right? They'll be shooting at us on the open lawn."

Knuckles said, "He's right," and began ripping through a bag strapped to his leg, jerking out a simple breaching charge. He prepped the blasting caps, unwound the Nonel tubing to its full length, then attached the initiation device. Saying, "This is the last time I go anywhere without frag grenades," he lobbed the mess deep into the room, the tubing fluttering from the charge to the detonator in his hand like the tail of a kite.

Now committed, I slapped against the doorjamb and said, "Jennifer, on Retro. Cover him from threats in the hallway."

We stacked left and right of the door, ineffectual fire coming through the gap. Knuckles glanced my way, and I nodded. He initiated the biggest flash-bang I'd ever used.

We flowed in, shooting four men staggering about in a daze. Two more were down from the charge, one dressed in much nicer clothes than the others, with only a pistol at his side. *The boss. No wonder they had last stand going.* Knuckles and I played clean-up while Blood went back out for Retro. He returned with Retro over his shoulder, Jennifer right behind. She ran to the first man I'd shot and went through his pockets, pulling out an old-fashioned flip phone.

I said, "You happy now? Can we go?"

She nodded and I got on the radio. "Decoy, blow the breach. We're on the way."

25

Mark Oglethorpe, the secretary of defense said, "Individual interruption? Yeah, that's possible. The GPS signal is pretty weak and it doesn't take much to cause interference, but it's still a lot harder than people think, especially to affect a UAV flying at altitude."

Colonel Kurt Hale saw the rest of the council relax a little in their chairs and was glad at the change in conversation.

In accordance with the charter for Project Prometheus, he'd sent a flash message to all thirteen members of the Oversight Council about the Prairie Fire alert. He had the authority to launch without council approval, but by no means could he do so without informing them. It had taken about forty seconds for his phone to ring, with the president requesting his presence at an Oversight Council meeting the following morning.

Bright and early, Kurt had driven straight to the Old Executive Office Building, adjacent to the West Wing of the White House, and was met by George Wolffe, the deputy commander of the Taskforce.

A career CIA case officer, Wolffe had been sent early to bend the ear of the director of the Central Intelligence Agency for any information coming out of Mexico. Kurt had Pike's situation report on the specifics of the operation but needed the broader scope of the impact.

George smiled, and Kurt knew it was good news. "So far, it's being laid out as a gangland hit between rival cartels. The biggest story is who was killed. Apparently it was the number one guy in Juárez for the Sinaloa cartel."

Taking the stairs at a fast walk, looking at his watch, Kurt said, "No mention of Americans?"

"None. The prime suspect right now is Los Zetas. That's what's on the street and what'll become solidified over the next few hours."

They both exited at the second floor and saw the Secret Service agents already positioned outside the conference room. Which meant the president was inside, and they were late.

In truth, Kurt felt some trepidation about the meeting, now made worse by his late entrance. Project Prometheus itself had almost imploded six months ago based on a crisis engineered from Iran, and Kurt had resigned because of decisions being made that were, in his mind, ridiculous. Now he was back in charge because President Warren had said so, and he was about to brief something that was unpalatable. Something his enemies might want to use to harm him, regardless of the good or bad for national security.

Entering, Kurt nodded at the group while George

took a seat in the back, out of the line of fire. Kurt moved to the head of the table, right next to President Peyton Warren. He raised an eyebrow and Kurt said, "Sorry, sir, I was getting some last-minute updates."

Before the president could respond, he began the briefing, laying out everything he knew, including the fact that the Taskforce's cover was secure—so far. He spent the next thirty minutes getting peppered with questions, but none were what he would have considered irrelevant. It seemed the Taskforce had turned a corner, which was unexpected. The organization, he knew, had prevented more than one catastrophic event since its inception, but always after fighting the council for authority to execute.

Maybe preventing a worldwide pandemic by disobeying council orders has convinced them of the Taskforce's worth. Or maybe the council is just getting used to breaking the law of the land.

In the past, he'd seen these same men spend most of the time asking questions related to how close they were to getting exposed. How close to wearing handcuffs instead of how best to prevent a calamity.

Today, the queries were a relief, but they made him a little wary as well. A tinge of paranoia was a good thing, as it brought healthy debate. Treating Taskforce missions as routine was dangerous, because complacency bred mistakes, and he didn't like the mantle of failure resting on his shoulders alone. Surprised, he realized he *wanted* the skepticism of the past.

After the initial blow-by-blow of the operation, Kurt

began explaining why the mission had been executed, and the briefing finally became contentious because of Jennifer's actions in Mexico. In effect, she'd forced a Prairie Fire alert because of personal reasons, not through an official Taskforce operation. Before it could turn into a feeding frenzy, Kurt had diverted attention by describing what her brother had possibly stumbled upon, which had led to the ongoing conversation about UAVs.

The SECDEF repeated, "Jamming GPS isn't rocket science. Basically, all you need to do is pump out a stronger signal, but that's very localized and really only works within a small footprint. In other words, airplanes, tanks, and other things might lose signal, but only for as long as they were in the jamming zone. Seconds in most cases. It's not catastrophic. Spoofing the signal itself and tricking the UAV to fly somewhere else is much more sophisticated, and not something we've seen yet, at least on DOD drones."

President Warren said, "Just because we haven't seen it doesn't mean it isn't a threat. If the Mexican cartels have managed to find a way to affect GPS—even locally—it could have repercussions worldwide. Especially if it gets in the hands of a peer competitor during wartime, or in the hands of some group looking to harm us in peacetime."

The SECDEF nodded. "Yes, sir. That's true, but only if they've actually got something. I just don't see it. Iran has been trying to develop a capability like that for years, and they haven't gotten anywhere."

Secretary of State Jonathan Billings said, "But they *did* get one of our drones."

"No, they didn't. We lost that RQ-1 through a glitch. As soon as it lost link with the satellite, it landed like it was supposed to do. As I said, they've been trying almost as hard to develop cyber capability as they have to develop a nuke, and they still can't do anything like that, no matter what their propaganda machine puts out. How could a bunch of drug runners create such a device without any scientific capability whatsoever?"

Kurt said, "The expertise is on our side. They'd do it just like they have in all of the Mexican law enforcement organizations. They'd extort it from the inside. We're not sure if it's just UAVs they're interested in. The man on the tape was talking about the entire GPS constellation."

The SECDEF bristled. "Well, they'd have an easier time building this magic device from the ground up in Mexico. The constellation is run by the Air Force's Second Space Operations Squadron, and all of them have ironclad security clearances. It's not like we let a janitor into the control floor and have him keep an eye on things for a smoke break."

Kurt held up his hands. "Hey, sir, I'm just saying it's a method. We had Hansen in the FBI and Ames in the CIA, both with ironclad security clearances. These cartels can bring a hell of a lot more money to bear than the USSR ever could."

The president said, "It's worth a look. Check everyone in the squadron. See if anyone has taken leave in the last week, and if so, find out if they were in El Paso." The SECDEF nodded, and he continued. "I'm more concerned with cyber. Could they get through from the outside?"

"No, sir. The GPS constellation isn't connected to the Internet. They'd have to be on Schriever itself. Affecting a single UAV is one thing, but the backbone architecture of the entire constellation is a different story altogether. I don't see that as a realistic threat."

President Warren ran down the rabbit hole, saying, "If it did happen, what's the impact?"

The SECDEF paused. "Really, that's hard to assess. If they hit the civilian signals alone, we'd have little impact. Theoretically, if they somehow could take out the military signals, we'd lose all precision weapons. We'd be back to dropping dumb bombs. It would also play hell with all of our mounted and dismounted movement, mainly in our logistics. Truthfully, it's sort of like asking the impact of losing our radios. We take GPS for granted now, like talking on a radio. We could still fight, but it would be much more inefficient."

Kurt saw Billings's brow scrunch. He said, "Military signals? You mean they're different?"

The SECDEF said, "Yes. The military has its own architecture, and it's encrypted and hardened against jamming. Losing the civilian bands wouldn't affect our ability to react to contingencies."

Bill Crosswell, a former four-term congressman with a penchant for political survival, spoke up. Having spent most of his adult life in the trucking business before turning to politics, he'd been tapped by the administration for secretary of transportation. "Mr. President, that's not exactly accurate. The military is tied to the civilian signal much, much more than they know. It's true they can drop the bombs, but they might not get the bombs because the civilian industrial base that makes and delivers them is tied into the GPS. Transportation has a hand in the constellation, and I see it every day."

The president slapped the table with an open hand. "So what's the damn impact? Can someone give me a straight answer?"

All the men at the table jerked upright at the action, not uttering a word. Eventually, Alexander Palmer, the national security adviser, said, "Sir, bluntly, we honestly don't know. Because the signal is not licensed or anything like that— because using it only means buying a receiver—we just don't know how far into our national grid it has gone. For the government, I can tell you that the telecommunications, power, and transportation infrastructure rely on it a great deal. The loss of the precision timing alone would cause significant damage if it went out. As for the private sector—banking and all that—we just don't know. Big-ticket things like the New York Stock Exchange claim to have atomic-clock backups for the timing signal, but there are a multitude of smaller elements tied into the exchange that don't."

President Warren began to scowl and Palmer backpedaled. "Hey, it's not something we've studied. It's become so ubiquitous it's like asking how far the Internet has penetrated. We think of the Internet as watching You-

Tube, but it has become a backbone for everything from remotely starting your car to turning out the lights in your house. GPS is the same way. We can guess, but we really just don't know. GPS is just too good to not use, especially since it's free." He pointed at the secretary of defense. "In the end, Mark's right. It *is* a bunch of drug runners, something I don't feel is a realistic threat."

"Unless the assholes actually *do* have something and sell whatever it is to someone else." President Warren saw the D/CIA snap up his eyes at the comment and said, "What?"

The D/CIA spoke up. "Sir . . . we've got movement of a Hezbollah cell from the tri-border region of South America to Mexico City. Coming in two days. It's probably nothing, and I'm not trying to be an alarmist. We've been eyeing them for a while because of the cartel's penetration of our border, and NSA picked up the intercept last night. I thought it was strictly CIA business, but maybe it's connected."

President Warren turned back to Kurt. "What's the next step? Do you have one?"

"We've got the phone trace of the informant in the Sinaloa cartel. That could lead us to Jack, Jennifer's brother. I have no idea what he knows, but apparently everyone down there thinks it's critical. We could at least get some intelligence to flesh out the threat. If there is one."

"Really? That's it?"

Kurt paused for a moment, the statement aggravating him. "Yes, sir. That's it. I have the ability to rescue an

American being held by the drug cartels because they think he has knowledge of a threat against American interests. That's *all* I have."

Kurt saw George Wolffe roll his eyes at the back of the room, then rub his forehead. Kurt kept his face neutral but didn't back down from the president's glare.

President Warren pressed his lips together, then nodded. "I suppose I had that coming. Pike wants to hit a rival cartel now? Make it a clean sweep down there?"

Kurt smiled and said, "We can only follow the bread crumbs as they fall, but I can't predict where it leads."

President Warren said, "Where? We don't even know *what* it's leading to."

Kurt said, "That's true, but Jack Cahill might."

26

Jack's days and nights had blurred, dreading the stairwell light and the next visit. After his initial conversation about the Sinaloa cartel he had been ignored, and he wondered if he'd been forgotten. He'd seen enough butchering that he certainly wasn't going to ask about his status. Being ignored was better than the alternative.

He had grown accustomed to the entrance and exit of what he called the "enforcers" and had learned how to keep them happy. The bald *sicario* was another matter. This morning, he'd been pulled out of the basement by the strange, slight man with the scar on his forehead, and he'd felt mind-numbing fear. The *sicario*'s actions instilled it. He seemed to float about the room like a frail hummingbird, but his eyes were hypnotic, exposing the lie of frailty. Jack knew he was crazy, but in a different way. A stronger way.

If he'd been in a coffee shop in Dallas, going about his life, Jack would have seen the *sicario* and laughed, saying, "He's not all there," before sipping his four-dollar grande latte. Now, living in this man's world, he knew that was incorrect. He was *beyond* all there, like an elemental thing, sensing the very pulse in Jack's neck. And yet, Jack knew he wasn't all there.

Put into a car, he'd been told the person he'd seen on the video was coming to Mexico City, and he was to point him out. They'd driven close to an hour, then parked outside the Benito Juárez International Airport. Going into the waiting area of terminal one, the *sicario* had said nothing at all, treating the entire trip as if they were meeting family. No threats, nothing about what would happen if he tried to escape. He'd simply parked and locked the car, resting his dark eyes on Jack for a second, then had turned his back and entered the airport.

Jack had scurried to keep up, the eyes searing his brain with unquestioned obedience, any thoughts about escaping sinking like a coin tossed in the water, flashing more faintly the farther he walked.

They'd entered the throng of people all waiting outside the exit to customs, the *sicario* pushing aside illegal taxi vendors and family members waiting on loved ones returning home, all turning in initial anger, then melting back at his stare. They reached the front, separated from the exit by a metal railing, and he spoke for the first time.

"The contact's plane has landed. He will be coming out soon. Point him out to me."

Jack nodded and began scanning the flow of people exiting, praying he would recognize the man, bringing forth the memory from the digital recorder. The tension in his body increased with each passing minute, the people exiting in little bursts. They stood for over an hour, Jack beginning to see the contact in everyone who appeared, imagining what he would look like with a haircut and clean-shaven or in a suit. Maybe wearing a sombrero. Perhaps camouflaged in a dress with a wig. Anything to please his crazy captor.

Eventually, the *sicario* tapped him on the shoulder, causing Jack to jump. He flicked his weird eyes toward the exit and turned without a word. For a brief moment, Jack considered running. Racing through the crowds and shouting his predicament, causing a commotion that would set him free. As if his thoughts were floating on the air between them, the *sicario* turned back and Jack felt his eyes penetrate. He rushed to catch up.

They'd returned to the mansion and Jack had been led to the same study as before, the mustached leader who had originally questioned Jack waiting behind his desk. The *sicario* set a directional microphone and digital recorder on the table. When the leader went to pick it up, he said, "El Comandante, I didn't get a chance to use it. He didn't show up."

The leader scowled like a child and said, "Didn't show, or didn't get pointed out?"

Jack felt his survival time shrinking to seconds. He said, "I swear, he wasn't at the airport. Maybe he came earlier or he's coming later, but he didn't leave while we were there."

Indifferent, the *sicario* said, "I think he's telling the truth. Your information was 'within the next couple of days,' correct? It's the same flight number each day. He might show tomorrow."

The leader said, "I might need you back in Juárez. It's on fire right now and we may have an opportunity."

"What has happened?"

"I'm not sure. There's another player on the board, and he's hitting Sinaloa. I have to think about it. Get more information. I'll talk to you later with a decision."

Thrown back into the basement, the first thing Jack noticed was that he had a new neighbor. A boy of about eighteen was sitting in the corner in stylish jeans and an expensive shirt. Looking at Jack with the catatonic stare of someone not yet understanding what had happened to him.

Or maybe understanding completely.

27

"Koko, roger. That's our target."

Jennifer rolled her eyes at her call sign, wishing like hell she could change it to something more dignified. She turned to Pike and said, "Well, that pretty much eliminates the capture/interrogation plan."

"Yeah. I agree. It wouldn't be too smart to kidnap a Mexican law enforcement guy in the Federal District."

After exfiltrating Retro across the border, linking up with some doctors read on to Taskforce activities, they'd received the go-ahead to explore from the Oversight Council. Flying from Juárez to Mexico City, otherwise known as the Distrito Federal, or DF, they'd begun to track the phone of the person who had received the call from the Sinaloa traitor.

The primary trace had shown up centered on a tidy row of town houses located in the northeast of the city center, just outside the historic district in a middle-class neighborhood. Since the phone location itself wasn't down to the meter, but instead had a circle of probable error upward of the size of a football field, they'd spent most of yesterday locating the specific bed-down site, collating the multiple pings of the phone into layers that allowed them to neck down exactly which house contained it. The research done, they'd begun static surveillance this morning to refine a course of action.

Jennifer had noticed a man in some type of police uniform exit the garage of the town house, followed by a woman carrying a baby, whom he kissed before walking to a car farther up the street. Since the garage serviced all three houses, at best it meant their target lived next to a policeman. At worst it meant the target *was* a policeman. She'd had Knuckles and Decoy tail the man until he was far enough away to get another ping that wouldn't be contaminated by their previous traces. And had confirmed the worst.

She said, "You think that phone intel was bogus? They killed a guy for no reason?"

"Maybe, but more than likely it means the cop is bogus. Playing both sides of the fence. Either way, we can't take him down."

Jennifer felt the only lead to her brother withering away. "What about a B and E, just to see what he's got in the house? Might give us something."

"Yeah, but I just saw his burglar alarm go back in. We can't do a surreptitious entry with a baby and mother inside."

As he was speaking the garage door opened again, and the mother exited pushing a stroller.

Jennifer said, "There goes the alarm. Want to try it?"

Pike thought a moment, then said, "A daylight B and E on an unknown floor plan? We don't even know the lock-set."

"I'll use a window. I can pop that with a credit card."

"Jennifer, the windows are all barred."

She pointed above the garage. "Not on the second floor."

Jennifer saw him wavering and drove home the slipping time. "Pike, it's an empty house but won't be for long. We're wasting an opportunity to neck down the threat."

He sighed. "You mean neck down your brother's location."

"Yeah, that too, I guess. I hadn't thought about it."

He smiled at her joke and keyed the radio. "Knuckles, what's your location?"

"Coming back down the south side, about two blocks away."

"Hold what you got. There's a woman in a stroller headed your way. Get eyes on her and give us early warning when she starts heading back to my location."

"Roger all. What's up?"

"Koko's going to do something stupid."

Jennifer smiled and opened the glove box, pulling out the little tool kit that came with the rental. She selected a small flat-head screwdriver and Pike said, "You see any chance of compromise, get out. Don't push it, understand?"

She nodded and slipped into the alley between the garage and the building next door. Barely three feet wide, it stank of garbage and had a stagnant stream of some ominous liquid running down the middle. She saw that the little corridor ended in a brick wall, connecting the town houses to the next building. She reached the wall, glanced back down the alley to the street, and began to climb like it was a chimney, placing one foot on the facing wall and one behind her, then doing the same with her hands. She inched up until she could get her hands on the parapet of the roof, then pulled herself over.

She keyed her radio. "I'm up. Moving to breach."

Keeping low so as to remain out of view of the street, she reached the first town house, scuttling under the windows to the second one. She said, "We're positive on the location, right?"

Pike said, "I'll be absolutely positive until you tell me I'm wrong. Second one in."

Great. That's a lot of confidence. She inserted the screwdriver into the jamb of the window, then gently rocked it back and forth, springing free the latch. She placed her hand on the pane and pushed, but the window remained closed. She studied it for a moment, then saw the problem.

Painted shut.

She ran the edge of the screwdriver around the pane, digging out as much latex paint as she could, then wedged the flat end back into the jamb. She lifted the handle, hearing the window groan from the leverage. She gave the handle another pull and the window popped free, sounding as loud as gunfire. Jennifer froze, straining to hear someone coming to investigate. After thirty seconds, she opened the window fully, then slipped inside.

She debated leaving the window open but decided to close it to prevent anyone from becoming curious on the street. She saw she had entered a nursery, with the cloying, sweet smell of diapers and powder.

Her radio came to life. "Pike, woman is headed back."

"How far out?"

"Look on your map. See the park to the south? All she did was circle it with the kid. Now she's coming home. You probably got six or seven minutes, unless she stops again."

"Roger all—break. Koko, exfil."

She left the nursery at a trot, saying, "Pike, I just got inside. I haven't found anything yet."

She entered the master bedroom and quickly surveyed, hearing, "I can't help that. Get out."

She swept the closet in the bedroom and found nothing. Moving down the hall, she entered a third room, a tiny cubicle. She saw a filing cabinet and a desk. She ran to the desk and began shuffling papers, all in Spanish.

No good. I can't tell if any of this is important.

She heard, "Koko, you copy? I have the woman in sight now. She's about three minutes out headed right toward me."

And the first thing she's going to do is put that child in the nursery. Pike's right, you need to leave.

But she couldn't leave with nothing. Couldn't abandon her brother. Jennifer opened the filing cabinet and pulled out a folder, seeing official documents. Each was a printout of some kind with a picture of a person in the upper left corner. Most had a red X drawn across the face, but one was untarnished. None were her brother.

"Koko, this is Pike. She's entered the garage. Status?"

Out of time.

She took a picture of the one unmarked document with her smartphone and heard the door close downstairs. She gently closed the drawer with the files, then began to ease out of the room but heard the woman cooing to the baby on the stairs. She froze, knowing she couldn't get down the hall without the mother seeing her.

She heard, "Damn it, Koko, what's the story?"

She clicked her transmitter twice and heard, "Well, that's just great. Another damn teammate ignoring my exfil call. I'm coming in. I'll get her attention and you get out."

She clicked rapidly four times.

"Roger all. Story of my life. I'm standing by."

She heard the woman pass by the office and waited. The mother began singing in Spanish, then began making shushing noises. Eventually, Jennifer heard her footsteps on the stairs. When she was sure she was clear, she slipped out of the office and glided as lightly as she could to the nursery.

She saw the baby in a crib, sound asleep. She opened the window and it gave a slight screech. The baby woke up and began to cry.

Jennifer flung herself out onto the roof, thinking, *Sorry about that, Mom.*

No sooner did she have the window closed than she

saw a shadow in the room. She flattened against the wall, then slithered back to the alley. She dropped into the goo at the bottom, splashing the foul liquid on her shoes.

Reaching the car, she saw Pike's scowl. She closed the door and he said, "Tell me you have the exact grid to your brother, because this favoritism stuff is getting old."

She shook her head, feeling the tears well up and hating them in front of Pike. "I don't think I found anything at all."

28

Carlos waited outside the customs gate of terminal one at Benito Juárez International, feeling like someone had poured sandpaper into his eyes. He hadn't slept in close to twenty-four hours and wondered how many Sinaloa hit men were now hunting him. The very fact that he was alive would be enough to brand him with suspicion. It wouldn't matter that he'd escaped the assault on the Juárez house by the skin of his teeth. To Sinaloa, it would look planned. Or he'd simply be made an example of so they could pretend they knew what was going on.

As for him, he had no idea. He'd received a call that the second American, Jennifer Cahill's partner, was being brought through the gate, then all hell had broken loose. Instead of fighting, he had chosen to run, and had spent the last twenty-four hours driving from Juárez to Mexico City, weaving through towns and avoiding the major thoroughfares to keep him out of Sinaloa clutches.

He'd made two phone calls on the way. One to Mr. Guy Fawkes—aka Arthur Booth—in Colorado, telling him the time was almost right to come to Mexico and having him start to dig into Grolier Recovery Services. Use his skills to penetrate and find out what they really did, because something wasn't right about that company.

After hanging up, he had laughed at the thought. *Something isn't right. That's putting it mildly.*

The supposed anthropologist woman had had the balls to drive across the border by herself into cartel territory and had found the house with nothing more than a voice mail, then had managed to escape a ring of Sinaloa men, killing several in the process. If that weren't strange enough, the man with her had somehow managed to escape *his* captors, drive across the border, find the *same* house, then slaughter everyone inside with a team of killers.

Yeah, something wasn't right, and he asked Mr. Fawkes to find out what that was. In truth, he wasn't so sure that Arthur Booth wasn't behind it to begin with. The entire cycle of events had begun when he'd captured the reporter at their initial meeting. Carlos would treat Booth as an enemy until he could prove otherwise.

His second call had been to South America. If the PO-LARIS protocol actually worked and wasn't just some trap to cause the implosion of Sinaloa's grasp on the Juárez *plaza*, then it would be worth money to others, and that was all Carlos had left.

They'd been approached on numerous occasions by Lebanese Hezbollah, and had actually helped them once or twice when it would pay off without risk, but for the most part, Sinaloa had stayed away from anything smacking of Islamic terrorism. The cartel's fight with the government of Mexico was something they could handle, and they didn't want to give the United States any reason to interfere, which is what would happen if they started assisting Hezbollah on a grand scale, but now Carlos's fight was over. He would be dead if he ever went back to Sinaloa, and he couldn't have cared less what the Americans did after he had his money. And so he'd called a Hezbollah contact, saying, "I have something that will help in your fight against the drones. You fear them in Pakistan and Yemen, but I can make that fear go away."

Not having any insight at all into the phenomena of global jihadist movements, Carlos didn't understand the difference between al-Qaeda and Hezbollah, and, like most of the world, assumed they were painted with the same brush. They'd agreed to meet, and now Carlos waited on their arrival outside the international terminal, hoping he didn't see a group of foreigners wearing something that looked like a bedsheet, highlighting who they were and putting cross hairs on him.

He needn't have worried. Three men exited, looked around, then focused on the sign in his hand. All appeared more Latino than like an Arab terrorist, wearing jeans and T-shirts with cheap rucksacks on their backs. They sported thick mustaches but no beards.

The tallest one approached and said in English, "You are looking for an investment in South America?"

Carlos replied, "Yes, I'm always looking for good investments."

The man smiled at the correct answer and held out his hand. Carlos shook it, saying, "You have no bags?"

"Just our backpacks. We can buy what we need if we stay longer than anticipated."

Carlos nodded and led them to the car rental counter, saying, "Who did I talk with on the phone?"

The tall one said, "None of us. We understand you have something that will help our brothers' fight in Waziristan."

Carlos had no idea what he was talking about, beginning to feel lost. "I have an ability to confuse the Predator drones. Is that what you mean?"

The man smiled and said, "Yes. That's what I mean. So you know, we are but a conduit. Another man is coming, from *Waziristan*." He said it in a condescending manner, as if Carlos was a child.

Carlos held his gaze for a moment, then said, "I don't give a shit where he's coming from. As long as he has money. A lot of money."

29

Jennifer, her eyes behind a set of small binoculars, said, "Holy crap, Pike—that's the cop!"

I jerked the binos out of her hands and focused. Sure enough, the target of the house we had left two hours ago was now leaving the residence of the kid on the document Jennifer had brought with her from the B & E.

What the hell? This whole thing was turning into a real-life version of *The Usual Suspects*. All I was missing was hearing someone say Keyser Söze was behind it. I wanted to turn the operation off but couldn't because of Jennifer. She was hell-bent on finding her brother, and since she could play me like a violin, here we sat with her pathetic lead from the B & E. Only now, the damn thing had actually gone somewhere.

The one clue she'd taken from the house had been a photo of a document in Spanish with a picture on it. We'd sent it to the Taskforce and had found out the kid in the picture was the son of a textile tycoon and had been kidnapped yesterday. Just one more statistic in the multimillion-dollar ransom industry in Mexico.

The family lived in a wealthy area west of the city center called Polanco, where all of the houses were set behind high walls and gates. Why the cop had the kid's picture we didn't know, but Jennifer was convinced it was because he was in on it. Convinced it was a lead to her brother.

I, on the other hand, was convinced the whole thing was asking for a compromise of Taskforce activities but had reluctantly let it go since the Oversight Council had sanctioned further operations. I was a little surprised we'd been given clearance to explore the lead at all, and my heart just wasn't behind it. For once, I wasn't demanding to be allowed to do something because I thought the risks far outweighed the rewards.

It was a cold calculation, but Jennifer's brother wasn't worth Taskforce exposure, and I wasn't as sure as everybody else that there was some overarching threat. Even though the Oversight Council flinched at the mere mention of my name, I understood when to push things and when to back off, and this was a case of needing to back off. Except Jennifer had looked at me with her damn puppy eyes. And the council had sanctioned it.

Jennifer said, "What do we do now? He's getting away."

"Do? What do you want to do? Run him into a ditch and demand answers?"

Her face grew dark. "Yeah, that would be fine."

"Well, that ain't happening. How about we ask the family what they know?"

"You mean go knock on the door? With what? They won't even let us in."

I tinkered with the idea a little longer, probing it like a tongue working a piece of meat stuck between the teeth. Yeah, that's a gross analogy, but it explains exactly how I was feeling. Wanting to free the irritation in my mouth, but knowing the slop left over would be disgusting.

I said, "Let's go. You lead the way. You're much less threatening. Get them to let us in. I'll take over from there."

We called Knuckles, letting him know what was going on, then parked outside the gate of the mansion, punching the buzzer of the keypad outside. A man came on speaking Spanish, and Jennifer said, "We're here to talk about Felix. We'd like to come in."

There was nothing for a moment, then a woman's voice in heavily accented English said, "Who are you? What do you want?"

Jennifer stared into the camera and said, "I'm here to help. Please. Let us in."

She said, "Go away or I'm calling the police."

I thought for a split second about pushing the issue as if we were the kidnappers, just to get me in the door. Knowing that would be cruel. Before I could lean over, taking control, Jennifer said, "My brother is kidnapped by the same savages who have your son. I know they're together. Please, please let me come up."

Her voice was dripping with emotion that couldn't be faked. Instead of leaning forward, I leaned back lest they see me in the car and suspect a trick. The gates parted.

We drove up a circular path and parked out front, the mansion much larger than what could be seen from the gate. Two men exited the top of the stairs, not overtly threatening, but not friendly either. We walked up, and one motioned to me, telling me to spread my arms. I did so, and was thoroughly searched. Not in a sloppy way either. He literally cupped my balls, which told me he was doing it for real, as that is the last place a man will put his hands and the first place a killer will put his weapon because of it. He wasn't an amateur, which meant his employer wasn't either.

He had me face to the left, putting Jennifer in my sight, and continued. For her part, I saw a man cup her breasts and knead. I suppose I should have been aggravated, but the guy did it like he was working a lump of dough and clearly had no ulterior motives. I began to wonder how the child of someone who hired professionals like this could have been kidnapped.

They both stood up and waved to someone inside. For the first time, I noticed the sliding door behind us was four inches thick. A ballistic door. Bulletproof. They'd searched outside in case we were carrying a suicide vest.

What the hell? Who is this guy? The only thing that came into my head was Keyser Söze.

We were led into a room and met by not a man, but a woman of about fifty with a stern visage that exuded control. Someone who was clearly used to being in charge, but her trembling hands belied the act. In English, she said, "Who are you?"

I said, "We're here to help you. I promise."

She flicked her eyes at the man who'd searched me, and without a beat he punched my kidney, bringing me to my knees. He drew back to punch again, and I trapped his hand, gasping for breath.

I rotated against the joint, then rolled over, bringing him with me to the ground. All I was thinking was escape. I saw the other man moving in and released the joint lock, collapsing my hands around my target's head, screaming, "Stop, or I kill this motherfucker!"

Everything paused like it was in slow motion. I said again, "Back off or he's dead. Jennifer, go to the door."

She said, "No." Then turned to the woman. "I want my brother, and you know where he is. You might not realize you know. But you do."

I heard the words and screamed, "Jennifer, get your ass outside the door, right now!" I saw the other man glide my way and torqued my target's head. "Back off!"

Jennifer shouted at the woman, "Your son is with my brother. Please, we need your help!"

I heard someone shout, *"Alto!"*

The guy in my arms relaxed as if on cue.

30

A man entered the room and said again, in a lower voice, *"Alto."*

He waved a finger, and the guard advancing on me faded back like a robot. The woman began to weep, sagging against the wall and putting her face in her hands.

He looked at everyone in the room, guaranteeing compliance, then said, "I am Arturo Gomez, the father of Felix. Let him go and no harm will come to you."

I did so and the bodyguard stood up, then joined his partner, another robot under the control of the man who had entered. Both eyed us, ready to spring forth, but did nothing more. I rose from the ground and said, "I'm Pike Logan and this is Jennifer Cahill. Her brother has been taken and we believe it's by the same people who hold your son. Any information you could give us would be appreciated."

"Are you American law enforcement?"

Jennifer said, "No. Just family."

"Why should I trust you?"

I said, "You should trust me more than the law around here. Who is that cop who just left?"

"Why do you say that? He works with the kidnapping task force. He's the lead investigator on my son's case."

Of course. That's why he had all the pictures. It made perfect logical sense now. Except the phone trace led to him, which meant he was helping the kidnappers by providing them all the information on the investigation. Possibly even setting up the snatches.

I said, "I'm just paranoid, I guess. Can we sit down and talk?"

He nodded and led us to an anteroom. After settling onto a couch, he began recounting the loss of his son, talking in a monotone as if he'd repeated the story a hundred times. The boy was a student at a university south of the city and had been taken from the campus. The last known location was about four miles away from the university, in a residential area where the suspects were seen driving. Not a whole lot of help.

I said, "You have pretty good security here. Didn't you have anything on your son?"

"Yes. He had a bodyguard, who was killed trying to protect him. We found the corpse and my son's car."

"But someone was left alive, right? Someone saw the suspect's vehicle."

"No. Only the bodyguard was with him."

"Then how did you get the report that they'd been seen miles from the campus?"

Arturo looked at his wife like he'd let something slip he shouldn't have. She spoke in Spanish, and he nodded, then said, "My son has a tracking device implanted in his arm. We haven't told anyone until today. The company that's supposed to locate him told us to keep it a secret to protect him, but they have failed."

Great. They got suckered. There was a plethora of anti-kidnapping companies selling RFID chips the size of a grain of rice and claiming they had GPS capability, but in reality, all that thing could do was identify the body after it was dead because the chip could be read from only about three feet away. It was basically the same thing people used to identify runaway animals in the United States. The companies here made a fortune on services for the "tracking," but the truth was it did little good because the actual locating device was the size of a cell phone, and once it was taken farther than three feet from the subject, it did no good.

Two things about the statement caused me to think, though. One, this man was smart enough to do the research and would know it wouldn't work, and two, there was a second location. If it wasn't an eyewitness, then it was something else.

I said, "Nothing small enough to embed under the skin could transmit a location. I'm sure you know this."

"Yes. I do. The actual transmitter is built into the belt he was wearing. It has a battery life of forty-eight hours once activated and is supposed to send a location every fifteen minutes. It only sent one."

"But it did send one? The residential location?"

"Yes."

So it had worked at least once. "How does it send the location? What's the method?"

He said something to one of the bodyguards and the man left the room. He came back carrying a brochure. He handed it to me, and I saw the specifications of what was being billed as an "antikidnapping alert" device. I said, "So it works on the cell network, sending an SMS text to a server, which then plots on Google Maps?"

"It's supposed to. But it hasn't since that one time."

Which meant the belt was without cell service. Unable to reach a tower. So to find it, we would need to bring the tower to it. Or it meant that the damn belt had been tossed. *Think good things. The belt is still active until proven otherwise.*

I said, "Can you get me the number of the belt? What it's using to transmit to the company?"

He nodded and rattled off some more Spanish. One of the bodyguards got on a phone, and something else Arturo said finally penetrated.

"You said you've not told anyone until today. Do you mean until you told us?"

"No. I told the investigator just before you arrived. The company is doing no good, and I thought he could use the information."

Holy shit. Use it is right.

I leapt to my feet, saying, "Jennifer, give him your contact information. Call her with the number as soon as you have it."

I dialed Knuckles and began giving instructions, walking at a fast pace to the front door.

31

The *sicario* listened to El Comandante rail and realized he was now finding threats in every shadow, paranoid. It was a cycle the *sicario* had seen many times before. When you assume the mantle of leadership through treachery and murder, you cannot retain control without starting to find the same everywhere, whether real or imagined.

Hearing a break in the stream of vitriol, he said, "El Comandante, with all due respect, do you really think someone attacked Sinaloa so Los Zetas would remove you? There are many cartels vying for the Juárez *plaza*. Maybe it was Beltrán Leyva, or someone in the Gulf cartel. Sinaloa has many, many enemies."

"I'm being blamed for it! I have to travel to Matamoros to explain to the capo why I attacked them, and I had nothing to do with it. Sinaloa is going on war footing, and Los Zetas are not pleased. Someone is trying to get me out. That's the only explanation. Someone who knows Juárez."

Someone like me, thought the *sicario*.

"Do you wish me to go to Juárez? Attempt to find out what happened and punish those responsible?"

El Comandante rubbed his face. "No. Take the journalist to the airport again today. I'd like to report some good news when I leave. Find the man coming from America and find out what he has that Sinaloa wants."

The *sicario* could read between the lines clearly enough. El Comandante no longer trusted him and wanted him close. He believed the *sicario* was involved in this ludicrous attack and feared what he would do once in Juárez.

He said, "If the man doesn't show today, what do you want me to do?"

"Kill the journalist. Dump him in the desert, then return back here. You will be coming to Matamoros with me."

As an offering to the capo. The *sicario* betrayed nothing on his face, simply saying, "It will be done."

He entered the basement, seeing their new captive cowering in the corner, afraid to even meet his eyes. A young man, most likely from a rich family. The *sicario* was probably the foremost expert on the mechanics of kidnapping that Los Zetas had, but he'd never done it for money, like Los Zetas were known for in Mexico City. In Juárez, he did it for one thing, and no amount of money would alter his captive's fate.

He waved the journalist to his feet, feeling the irony of his work in Juárez. He had been tempted multiple times with huge amounts of cash but had always remained loyal to Los Zetas. Always executing exactly what the *jefe* wished, condemning his soul to hell in the process. Walking back up the stairs with the journalist in tow, he wondered if that loyalty would now be his death.

THEY HAD BEEN on the road for close to thirty minutes, the *sicario* aggravated at the antics of the cars around him. Yesterday, the drive had been novel, not the least because he was operating a brand-new BMW 5 Series instead of the usual clunker that blended in around Juárez and allowed him to work his deadly skills. In Juárez a car like this would have been as bad as driving a fire truck with the lights spinning, but here it had been a diversion from the traffic. Now, the satellite radio, heads-up display, and other electrical wizardry no longer held his interest, and the idiots in the vehicles around him began to grate.

With thoughts of his meeting with El Comandante swirling in his head, he uttered his first words to the journalist that weren't a command.

"Tell me, what is it like in the United States. Is it like here?"

He heard nothing and glanced at the journalist in the passenger seat. The man sputtered for a moment, then said, "I . . . I don't know what you mean."

The *sicario* said, "Do you live in fear? Do people in your cities fear men like me?"

At first the journalist said, "Yes," followed by a pause, then, "Well, no, that's not true. There is no one like you in America. At least not in my world. The only people that run into men like you are criminals. If you do nothing wrong, you don't have anything to fear. Unlike here."

The *sicario* pondered the statement, wondering how the journalist could believe such a thing. Surely his world and the journalist's were not so removed from each other.

He said, "Life is nothing but a series of interconnected events. There is no right and wrong, only moving forward, making the best of each circumstance. Good and bad is a myth to explain away things, nothing more."

When the journalist didn't reply, he said, "Do you agree?"

He could tell the man was working up his courage. He smiled and said, "There is no right or wrong answer either."

Finally, the journalist said, "No. I don't agree. We create our own destiny by the path we choose. Right and wrong *do* matter."

"So you've done something wrong on your path of life, and it led you to me. You deserve this?"

The journalist's eyes widened. "No! I've done nothing bad. I don't deserve to be here."

The *sicario* stared at him for a moment, causing the journalist to turn away. He said, "And yet here you sit, next to me. A killer working for men who you would say have done only bad. How did right and wrong matter on your path, then?"

The journalist said nothing, and the *sicario* was disappointed. He had hoped to glean some truth he had missed in his life. Hoped to learn a secret from another world he had yet to experience.

They rode in silence for a few minutes. Then the journalist surprised him by asking, "Do you have a family?"

"I did, but they're dead now."

The journalist paused, then said, "May I ask how they died?"

"In a war. They were killed in a raid."

"And you don't think that's wrong? When it happened, did you feel it was justice?"

The images of the *campesinos* fleeing from his machete flashed in his mind, and he shunted them aside. The day before that attack, he had been told of the death of his mother and sister at the hands of the rebels, and his rage had flowed through the peasant village in retaliation. The *campesinos* were long dead, but their ghosts punished him still.

He said, "When I was a child we had a coop of chickens. It was our livelihood, with my mother bartering the eggs for other things. One day, I went to feed them and found all of them slaughtered. A fox had come in the night and had killed every single one. He didn't eat them. Just killed them. He had taken our livelihood. Was the fox evil?"

The journalist said, "You can't compare a chicken coop to human beings. The fox is an animal. He doesn't know the difference between right and wrong."

The *sicario* pulled into the parking area for terminal

one and said, "Or there is no right and wrong. Only interconnected events." He turned off the car and said, "Do you see? Or do you have a different explanation for your fate?"

The journalist seemed to withdraw into himself, disappointing the *sicario* yet again. He wanted a new truth. A new reason for what had happened in his life. Instead, it looked like he was instilling a new reality into the journalist. The one true reality.

They entered the terminal, and, like before, the *sicario* muscled his way to the front, his slight frame not nearly as powerful in exacting compliance as his gaze. He positioned the journalist and began to wait, sure he would end up killing the man in another couple of hours, and was a little sad at the prospect. He would have liked to talk again. Explore the differences in their lives a little more.

Forty-five minutes in, growing more positive the journalist would be sacrificed, he was beginning to construct a plan for disposal of the body when he saw the man visibly start. Thinking he had spotted the courier, he followed the journalist's gaze, then did a double take before his eyes reached the doors exiting customs, having a flash of recognition of a man on his side of the ropes.

Carlos.

He studied the face to be sure, then backed away. It *was* Carlos. A respected member of the Sinaloa cartel's operations in Juárez, he had been marked for capture by Los Zetas numerous times but had always escaped either through luck or through a change in focus of El Comandante. The *sicario* had studied his life intently, learning his patterns and methods, and had nicknamed him El Traje because of his habit of always wearing a business suit, like he did today.

Why is he here? El Comandante had said the leadership had been killed. Decimated in a military-type attack.

He saw three men approach, and a discussion ensued. He wished he could hear what was being said, but the directional microphone was in the BMW, too large to use unobtrusively here.

He sidled up to the journalist and said, "Did you see the man? Is he here?"

His face white, he said, "No. No, he hasn't come through."

Sure he would tell the truth if the man appeared, if only to save his life, the *sicario* said, "Who did you see?"

The journalist ducked his head and said, "No one. I thought I saw him, but it wasn't the right guy. He'll come, though, right? He'll come."

Carlos and the men began walking to the rental car counters, and the *sicario* had a choice: continue waiting here or follow them. *Maybe Los Zetas' information was only partially correct.* Maybe someone *was* coming, but it wasn't the man the journalist knew.

He made his decision, pulling the journalist with him to the car and circling around to the exit for the rental lot. When the three men appeared in a yellow Toyota, he waited. Soon enough, he saw Carlos drive up in a dented, beat-up American sedan like he was accustomed to using in Juárez. He let them get a few cars away before beginning to follow, knowing the traffic would keep them from eluding him.

After winding through Zona Rosa they pulled over at Chapultepec park and exited, walking toward the lake that fronted Paseo de la Reforma Avenue. The *sicario* parked as well, pulling out the directional microphone and saying, "Do as I say and you may yet live through the day."

When the journalist didn't respond, he said, "Do the *right* thing. Follow me."

The park itself was very large, with paths intertwining throughout and food vendors hawking their products, giving the *sicario* plenty of options to approach without being seen. He passed the lake without finding his quarry and looped around a strip of food vendors, searching the tables. He came up empty. He was preparing to go deeper into the park, away from the lake, when the journalist said, "There. At the paddleboats, on the bench. Are those the guys you were following?"

The *sicario* looked at him curiously and the journalist said, "Please remember that when we talk to the leader again."

They settled onto a bench screened by a row of shrubs and the *sicario* placed the headphones on his ears as if he were listening to music. The microphone looked like a black tube with a pistol grip on the bottom, connected to a small box with two dials. He laid it alongside his leg and angled it toward his target.

He fiddled with the gain on the box for a second, then adjusted the volume. Satisfied, he began to listen, turning on the digital recorder.

Within seconds, he knew he had made the right choice.

32

I was driving as fast as I could in the traffic, weaving in and out, trying to get a handle on our target. And a handle on our authority.

Jennifer was on the phone, talking to our pilots, getting them to feed the number the father had sent into the embedded collection capability hidden in the aircraft, and Knuckles was working the trace of the cell phone for the cop.

I jerked the wheel to swerve around a jackass who had decided to stop in the middle of the street, causing Jennifer to slap her hand against the door and me to start cursing. The only good thing about the dumb-ass drivers in the Federal District was the fact that I couldn't do anything bad enough to get pulled over, because everyone here treated all traffic rules as advice only. Lanes, red lights, whatever, it was only a guide and not something to be followed if you didn't feel like it.

I heard Jennifer talking to the pilots and wanted to snatch the phone away from her. "Yes, that's the number. We need you to suck that thing in. . . . No, it's not a blanket. We aren't trying to prevent it from talking. We need to draw in an SMS text. . . . *No*, we're not conducting unauthorized surveillance. It's sending a code. We need the code. What do you mean you don't have the capability? I know you have it. . . ."

I finally had heard enough. I snatched the phone. "Hello? Who the hell is this?"

"Jim Beam."

Dumb-ass pilot call sign. "Jim, did you hear what was just said? Do you have an issue with it? Because I'm on a road that leads to the airport and I could be there just as quickly as I could execute this mission."

"Hey, I heard everything she said, but I can't start affecting the cell network in a foreign country just because you guys called. I need authorization. We diverted to Mexico for transport only."

"This is *my* mission, and I'm Pike Logan. I say again, Pike Logan. I'm authorizing the operation. Do you understand?"

"Uhh . . . no . . ."

What the hell? Another new guy?

I saw Jennifer roll her eyes and wave her hand for the phone back, but that insult was too much to let go. I took a breath and said, "Okay. Well, clearly, you haven't heard about me. But we *did* meet, right? You remember what I look like?"

I heard him talking to someone next to him, then, "Uhh . . . yeah. Brown crew cut, scar on your face? You had the hot chick with you, right?"

Now I really wanted to throw the phone. "Yes. That's me. I was running Taskforce collection operations before you got your pilot's license. Now put that number into the collection device and turn it on with the largest gain you can. We're trying to get an SMS text that is out of range of the nearest tower."

I heard nothing for a moment, then, "The package in the plane isn't authorized for Grolier Recovery Services. All you are authorized for is transport. I need someone from headquarters to release."

Jesus Christ. The Taskforce actually separated the individual capabilities of the aircraft? I should have known, because I'd seen it a hundred different times in other scenarios where I was authorized but others weren't. This was a first for me, though. As a civilian, I wasn't supposed to be read on to what was in the aircraft, but I was, and now I needed it and I had no time to work through the bureaucracy.

A car appeared out of nowhere, playing NASCAR and causing me to slap my hands on the steering wheel, swerving around him. I put the phone on speaker so I could use both hands to drive and tossed it onto the seat. Jennifer locked eyes with me and put a finger to her lips. She said, "Just got authorization from Kurt Hale. Code four-seven-four-Alpha-Zulu. Authenticate."

The pilot said, "Code what? What the hell are you talking about?"

She said, "I just gave you the authorization! Come on. Authenticate or find another job."

"I can't authenticate . . . I . . . I have no idea *how* to authenticate."

"When did you leave CONUS? Did you get the new procedures?"

"We haven't been home since we left for Turkmenistan. What procedures?"

"Well, welcome to the new world. Get in the air, or start calling Southwest Airlines for employment."

The pilot muttered something unintelligible, then spoke to someone beside him. Seconds later, he came back on and finally agreed. Jennifer said, "Fly south. The target is in the south. Suck up every signal you can get, and lock that number."

She hung up and I said, "What the hell was that?"

"You were getting nowhere with the macho crap. You guys change operational procedures every five seconds, so I figured I'd give him what he wanted. Authorization."

Weaving through the traffic, I shook my head at how easily she had manipulated the system and said, "Get Knuckles on the phone. Leave it on speaker." When he came on I said, "You got 'im?"

"Yeah. He's continuing east, toward Zona Rosa. When he gets there, he's going to be near a ton of embassies and government buildings."

"We need to stop him before then."

I heard nothing for a moment, then, "Pike, you sure about this? He's a Mexican federal agent. We take him down and we're wrong, this will be a world of hurt. We have no cover for action here whatsoever."

Jennifer rolled her hand into the grip above the SUV window and looked at me, knowing what he said was true, but also knowing that her brother's fate hung in the balance. I had the Oversight Council's authority to continue, but that was predicated on my judgment. And I wasn't sure that my judgment here was correct.

Every bit of evidence said this guy was doing exactly what he was supposed to do: finding the textile tycoon's son as a kidnapping investigator. He was a uniformed member of the Mexican Federal Police and had a reason for having the son's name and face in his house. If I captured him and was wrong, there would be no way to control the repercussions. *Everything* pointed to his being what he said.

Except for a single phone call from a member of the Sinaloa cartel. And if he was crooked, he was now informing them of our only edge. Informing them of the technological link that would lead to Jennifer's brother.

I glanced at Jennifer for support, wanting something more than my instinct to make the call, and got nothing. She knew the same things I did, and I could tell she didn't want the decision. She wanted her brother.

I said, "Yeah. Get me a grid. Box him in. We're taking him down."

3 3

Booth's hand hovered over the "complete transaction" button, reluctant to push it and confirm his reservation. Wondering if taking POLARIS to Mexico City was such a hot idea after all, especially after his last conversation with Carlos.

The man had thrown away all pretenses of being a Mexican version of Anonymous, going so far as to pay for the trip down, as if he didn't care what Booth thought about him. He appeared to only want the protocol. Or maybe Booth himself.

It had been over two years since he'd dug up the corrupt officials working with Los Zetas on behalf of Anonymous, but he knew their memories were long, and their taste for vengeance was legendary. It was nearly impossible to determine the playing field at any given time in Mexico, and Booth now wondered if he was putting too much faith in the hatred Sinaloa had for Los Zetas. Maybe they were allied now. Or maybe, like the hacktivist groups Booth worked with, they were so fragmented that

Carlos was working both sides of the fence, taking PO-LARIS for Sinaloa and selling Booth to Los Zetas.

The investigative work he'd done on behalf of Carlos hadn't helped his attitude any. Grolier Recovery Services had smoke all around it. On the one hand, it had found a temple in Guatemala that had actually made some press, meaning the discovery had been real. On the other, it had done little since. A trip to Syria on behalf of a university that went nowhere because the country was in a state of turmoil, a trip to Egypt that looked more like a tourist agenda than anything a professional archeological company would conduct, and most recently, a trip to Turkmenistan where the employees did little, if anything.

Digging in deeper, exploring the linkages any company has in the digital age, he'd found a hefty amount of obfuscation and security. The company ISPs redirected off mirrors, making it hard to determine exactly where the host was, and they employed encryption protocols that were something he would expect out of Apple protecting the next-generation iPhone, not a firm doing routine business. Especially a firm of this size. Some of the ISPs crossed paths with other, interesting ones coming out of Washington, DC.

On top of all of that, the company supposedly had over ten employees, but he could find tax records for only two: a Nephilim Logan and Jennifer Cahill. The rest were ghosts, on the books officially but with little else to show for the trouble. A token payment here, an issued credit card there, but nowhere near what should have existed.

The final kicker was a Gulfstream IV aircraft leased to the company. He worked for Boeing, the world's largest aerospace company, and outside of a handful in the upper echelons, nobody flew around on private jets. How on earth did this company manage to pay for the thing? And why would they?

On the whole, the company stank, and Carlos had brought them into the equation. He didn't care if it was some DEA front out to destroy whatever Carlos was into, but he wondered greatly if he would be pulled into the net. Wondered how much of Carlos's blood would splatter on him if an action occurred while he was down in Mexico. No way did he want to end up like Bradley Manning, chained to a bunk at Quantico on suicide watch, or Edward Snowden, running from country to country. And what he was doing would be considered exponentially worse than giving diplomatic cables to WikiLeaks or a top secret slide show to the press.

But at least Manning and Snowden had done something. Created some good in the world at the risk of their well-being. Created transparency in a government that was cloaked in darkness, the worst being the so-called drone program working to keep the fat cats on Wall Street in business. There was no telling how many people were being targeted right this minute, all enriching the oil barons. If he could, he would crack open that vault of information and let it fly free, much like Manning and Snowden had done, and cause the light of day to expose the rot hidden in the darkness. But he couldn't. Unlike them, he had no access to official databases. No means to expose the destruction being wrought at the hands of his own government. All he had was the ability to stop it, and that was worth the risk.

He punched the transaction button, getting an immediate e-mail back with his flight itinerary. He checked to make sure it was correct, seeing the American Airlines flight would leave in two days, with one stop in Dallas before going on to Mexico City. Two days to figure out what Grolier Recovery Services is really all about. Not enough time to figure it out alone.

He logged on to a message board and began recruiting.

34

Waiting on a miracle from our aircraft, I had Jennifer vector me in on the unmarked police car. Luckily for us, the cop hadn't taken a high-speed avenue of approach from the Gomez residence, but had traveled east up a street called Presidente Masaryk, which appeared to be rich man's land, with high-end car dealers and jewelry stores lacing the boulevard. It was a four-lane road separated in the middle by a little island of foliage and trees, which meant you weren't going to assault coming from the wrong way. Not unless you were driving a bulldozer.

Blood, in my only singleton vehicle, was to the north, staged and waiting on instructions. Knuckles and Decoy had circled around and were driving west, coming the wrong way, unfortunately, but that was okay. I didn't think an assault on this road was terribly smart anyway, given the high-end stores and outward security. I'd already seen two separate black Suburban convoys, traveling security for some rich guy or gal, so my preference would have been for our target to leave this section of the city.

Two things worked against that, though. One, if he kept going east, he would run into the area around Zona Rosa, which I knew contained multiple embassies—along with the Mexican version of the FBI—making the security impossible for an assault, and two, the longer I let him drive around, the longer he had to give his GPS locator information to the cartel.

I didn't know if he'd phone it in or if he'd just wait, figuring if it hadn't worked yet it was no threat, but I didn't like his having the information and running free.

Jennifer said, "He's one block up. Right in front of the traffic circle."

I relayed to Knuckles, having him hold up short with eyes on the circle to see which way he went. My traffic began to flow, and I asked for lock-on.

"Same location. He hasn't moved."

"Okay, break-break. Blood, come down south. Hit the traffic circle and head west. Give me a visual."

"Roger all."

We pulled over and waited, giving me one vehicle short and one long on the road, with the target in between. I was always a stickler for human eyes versus technology because I'd been burned in the past when relying solely on some magic device. In this case, I didn't know if the target was truly stationary or if he'd dropped his phone in the trash.

Two minutes later, Blood said, "Okay, I have eyes on. He's out of the vehicle and at some sort of cantina next to a pizza shop. He's inside, and he's talking to a bartender. The bartender doesn't look happy."

"What are the atmospherics?"

"It's mostly just outdoor tables. Inside it has a few more seats and a long piece of lumber in the back for the people wanting some booze. Your kind of place. He's at the bar with a guy polishing glasses on the other side. Nobody outside, and from what I can see, nobody inside. I don't think they're open for business yet."

My mind was running through the potential opportunity when Blood came back on, his voice slightly elevated. "Cop just pulled his gun. The bartender's got his hands in the air."

What the hell? More Keyser Söze shit. "Is he arresting the bartender?"

"Not from what I can see. The bartender is now at the cash register."

And it became clear. *He's shaking the guy down for cash. Extorting money out of him.* Which confirmed he was crooked. I put the car in drive and Jennifer said, "What are we doing? What's the plan?"

I ran through the options and keyed my radio. "Blood, hold what you got and stand by. Knuckles, close through the circle and get eyes on. Wait until you see my car. I'm going to block his in. We'll then enter together. Get him on the ground, and we'll get out."

"You want to take him in the cantina? Really?"

"Yes, really. Go in hard shouting '*policía*,' and get him

in our car. It'll be out front. He's shaking that guy down for cash, and it'll look like we rescued him. Blood, you copy?"

"Ahh . . . Roger."

"You're our blocker. Anything comes in behind, they're yours. Decoy, you take the front as lead element on exfil. We're headed south. Any questions?"

Knuckles said, "Yeah, do you have the number for an attorney in Mexico?"

I said, "I'm sure Mr. Gomez will provide one if we get his kid back."

I pulled in behind the cop's unmarked car in front of the cantina, seeing him through an open door at the bar. His weapon now holstered, he was stuffing something into his pants. To Jennifer, I said, "You got the wheel. Get this thing ready to run. Coordinate with Decoy for a route out toward Paseo de la Reforma."

She looked at me, surprised at how quickly this had erupted, but she nodded. I exited and saw Knuckles to my left, coming down the sidewalk from the pizzeria, a Glock held low by his leg. We paused out of sight of the front door. He nodded, telling me he was ready, and I peeked around the corner. I saw the cop holding his pistol in a two-handed grip, aiming it across the bar.

Shit. Not what I wanted. Now it's hostage rescue.

I said, "Gun out, gun out," and entered quickly. I went left, covering the cop, leaving the bartender for Knuckles behind me. I put my front sight post on the cop's chest, shouting, *"Policía, policía!"*

And triggered a shit storm.

The cop gave a small jump when I entered the room, his eyes springing open at my words. He snapped his head at me, then back on a target to his front, seeing something in his mind's eye that wasn't there. He began jerking the trigger, getting off two shots before his chest erupted in a spray of blood. I heard the blast from my rear, then a snapping of rounds from a Glock. I whirled in the direction of the shot, seeing the bartender leaning against the wall, two holes in his chest, a double-barreled shotgun hanging limply in his hands. And Knuckles's smoking barrel.

Holy shit.

He glanced my way, still covering the room, saying everything without speaking. In two steps I was on the bartender, leaving the cop for Knuckles. I grabbed his shirt, rapidly becoming soaked with blood, and yanked him across the bar, slamming him to the floor. I searched, finding no other weapons, then began to triage him, but it was too late.

He was dead.

Knuckles finished with the cop's destroyed body and found his phone. He looked at the log and said, "One call made."

In a calm voice, I said, "We need to go before a crowd shows up."

We left the bodies where they lay, with me wondering how it would have worked out for the bartender if I hadn't entered. *Why did he go for the shotgun?* The only good thing was we knew for sure the cop was an evil cuss.

Getting to the sidewalk, I saw we were clear. If anyone had heard the shots, they weren't coming to investigate. *Yet.* We jumped into the back of Jennifer's car and I called Blood and Decoy for exfil. She hit the gas without saying a word.

With Jennifer weaving through traffic, Knuckles said, "I took the shot. I'm not sure whose bullets hit him."

I said, "You did the right thing. It was a gunfight. You couldn't let him continue with a loaded shotgun."

He said, "It was a double barrel, and I think he fired both. I killed him after he was no threat."

I saw where this was going and immediately went to damage control. Not for the mission, but for Knuckles. "Bullshit. It was my call to enter. I did it when I saw the cop's gun. I should've looked into the bar to see what he was aiming at. I should've pulled back. Screw all that innocents-killed crap. He had a shotgun and was shooting. I only heard one barrel. You probably saved my life."

Knuckles nodded, but I could see the cost. I said again, "You made a right call. And you aren't that good of a shot. The cop probably hit him."

He laughed for the first time, a stilted thing, but a laugh nonetheless. I said, "Check your gun. Let's get back into the mission."

He glanced at me, then dropped the magazine and racked the slide of his Glock, clearing the chamber and checking its function before slapping in a new magazine.

Making sure it was ready for another fight. Something I knew he would understand.

Jennifer heard the conversation and waited until we were through the traffic circle before talking, concentrating on driving instead of the chaos behind us. When we were back into the regular flow she asked, "What the hell happened? What was the shooting?"

Knuckles said, "You wouldn't believe me if I told you. The cop's dead, and we didn't shoot him."

She said, "Then what was that conversation about?"

I said, "It was about a situation I shouldn't have put us in. The cop's dead, and we're clear."

She looked at me, getting my eyes in the rearview mirror. She saw not to ask. She cut to the chase, which surprised me. "So what do we have? Since he's dead, they didn't get the information about the GPS device?"

Knuckles said, "He made a call."

I saw her face fall, and the look aggravated me a little, given what we'd just gone through to save her brother. Given what I knew Knuckles was now going to question for the rest of his life. But we still had a mission. A way to make the bartender's death mean something.

I said, "Knuckles, get a trace of the number he called. Jennifer, keep going south, toward the grid Mr. Gomez gave us for the last sighting."

I got on the phone, calling the pilots. "What have you got?"

"Nothing. We didn't get anything. The city's too big. Saying 'fly south' didn't help any."

"Stand by."

Knuckles talked into his phone for about a minute, then nodded at me.

I said, "You got a grid on your phone now? From the Taskforce?"

The pilot fiddled around a little bit, then said, "Yeah, I got it."

"Vector on that, right now."

"Pike, I can't do loops in the sky. Air-traffic control is already bugging me about loitering."

"Come back to the airport on that grid. Tell them you have a maintenance issue and are returning. Fly low and slow. We *need* that ping."

"How am I going to explain that after I land? When I don't have an issue?"

"Figure something out."

"I'm not sure I should jeopardize the cover for this. We don't do this sort of thing, ripping around by the seat of our pants. I'll fly out to El Paso first, like my flight plan says."

After what we'd just been through, and the stakes, I was sick of his posturing behind some bullshit security classification, in no mood to hear some damn pilot at twenty grand second-guess what I was ordering when I was dealing with the blood.

"Screw the cover. You're jeopardizing someone's *life* right now." I took a breath before continuing. When I did, it was cold rage coming through. "You turn that fucking plane around or I can promise you you're jeopardizing your own life. Do you understand that, or do you need to call the Taskforce for confirmation?"

I heard nothing for a moment, then, "Roger. Turning back now."

About damn time that guy realized who I am.

35

Felix Gomez had grown somewhat used to his situation. The violence of his abduction, the loss of control, and the feeling of impending doom all competed for his attention, but he'd managed to adjust. The first night had been the worst, when he'd been literally catatonic in fear, but that had steadily eroded as he realized that they meant to keep him for his worth and had no inclination to torture him for amusement. The night before, he'd even managed to fall asleep. He'd had nightmares, but all in all he was holding up better than the others who were with him.

A man of about fifty and a boy not much older than him, both seemed on the verge of a nervous breakdown, their faces reflecting a hollow shell devoid of hope.

Perhaps it was because of their respective timelines. The old man had told him he'd been here for over a week, and the younger one was running up against a week and a half. Felix knew the average time for successful negotiation and repatriation was five to seven days. After that, the kidnappers either felt they were being jerked around, or that the families simply couldn't come up with the money, with the victim usually found dead alongside a dusty road, bound and blindfolded with packing tape. Another *encin-tado* to add to the statistics. Both of the men with him were running out of time and knew it.

Or perhaps it was the fact that he hadn't been abused like the two other captives. The older one's face was swollen, with a bloodshot, purple black eye, and he was missing his index finger on one hand, the stump covered in dirty cloth. A "proof of life" sent to someone to communicate that Los Zetas meant business. The younger one had a bandage on his upper arm that was mottled red, fresh blood seeping from the wound over the crust of the old. Felix had no idea what that represented, but nothing of the sort had happened to him. Maybe if he'd been treated to constant abuse, he'd be as mentally crushed as they were.

It might also have been his faith in his father. He knew Arturo Gomez would move heaven and earth to free him, and had the power and money to do so. He was sure they were tracking him right now, because he had an ace up his sleeve. Well, underneath his sleeve, that is. He unconsciously rubbed his left triceps, where his ace was buried.

Initially he was petrified the men would undress him when he was placed in the basement, but all they'd done was take anything that could have been of value for escape, such as his shoes and cell phone, leaving everything else as he wore it. Leaving his belt, which was much, much more valuable for escape than his cell phone. Had he been able to call, he had no idea what he would have said to get them to his location, but his belt was sending that out constantly.

He wondered if his father was even now planning his rescue.

The lights flashed on and his two roommates scurried to their designated eyebolts, the older one silently weeping.

Felix did the same, as the enforcer Felix had taken to calling El Barbudo, or the bearded one, came down the stairs. In one hand he held a fillet knife. In the other was a machete. He ignored the other two blubbering captives and came straight to Felix, throwing a pair of handcuffs at his feet. Felix manacled himself to the eyebolt.

His arms drawn out before him, his hands locked, El Barbudo gave him a choice. Tell which arm held the antikidnapping chip or have them both cut off with the machete. Felix felt his world collapse, the reason for the other boy's upper-arm wound becoming crystal clear.

How did they know? How did they know?

He feigned innocence, and El Barbudo raised the machete, lightly touching the upper bicep of his right arm. Manacled to the eyebolt, his arm in perfect position for getting hacked off at the shoulder, Felix whispered the answer. Ten seconds later, he was screaming. A minute passed, and the man was holding the little device in his hand, covered in a coating of bodily fluid. He dropped it on the floor and stomped. The glass shattered with a small pop, the sound a tiny punctuation of Felix's dwindling chances for survival.

El Barbudo unlocked his arms and tossed a bandage on the floor. He left, dropping the room into darkness yet again. Felix sat in the gloom, weeping, his face now reflecting the same hollow shell of the other two captives'.

Devoid of hope.

36

The pilot put me on hold, and I was sure it was just to aggravate me. Jennifer saw my face and pulled one hand off the wheel, slapping my shoulder. I glanced her way and she said, "Give him a break. He's working the problem."

From the back, looking at a tablet, Knuckles said, "Keep going straight. Right up ahead at the school. That's the location. The last place his GPS pinged. The phone trace is about four miles away."

I motioned for Jennifer to stop the car. There was no sense in driving around in circles, and if the target ended up being near the trace, I didn't want to burn it by rolling aimlessly. We were far south of the city center, on the edges of Mexico City proper, located in a cul-de-sac with a primary school at the end. Why it pinged here at a dead end was beyond me, but there were a ton of parked cars, so maybe it was a transfer point to a different vehicle.

I stared at the phone, willing it to speak, and was startled when it did.

"Pike, this is Jim. We flew right over the plot and got nothing. We're headed back to the airport."

Damn it.

"Listen, that plot was general. All we know is it's tied in some way. If I remember, you collect in a cone off the left side of the aircraft. Is that correct?"

"I'm not at liberty to discuss the capability."

I rolled my eyes. "Okay, fine. I want you to do a slow left turn with that grid at the center. One loop, with like a two-mile radius."

I heard nothing for a moment, then, "All right, all right. We're looping now."

We waited, knowing it would take only a minute or two, me putting the phone on speaker and setting it in the seat. It looked like Jennifer was actually holding her breath. Knuckles said, "What do you want to do if this fails? Hit the phone trace?"

Jennifer scowled as if he was putting out bad vibes. I said, "I don't know. This will probably be it, unless the Taskforce can give us a lead to the threat from the other end. We can't hit a phone just because the cop called it. We have no idea what it's tied to."

Jennifer snapped daggers at me with her eyes, and I knew we were going to part ways on how this shook out. She wanted her brother, but we were operating on the mission profile that the brother would lead to the threat. If we couldn't find him, then he wasn't worth Taskforce time that could be better spent working the problem from another direction. It was a hard truth, but it was reality.

I said, "Jennifer, if this doesn't pan out, we need to

turn what we know about your brother over to the proper authorities. It's been forty-eight hours. Let them work his abduction while we do what we do: find the threat."

"What good will the authorities do? The US won't conduct any investigation down here, and you just watched a Mexican federal agent get killed because he was working for the cartels. You really want me to go to them?"

I started to say something and was cut off by the pilot. "Loop complete. Dry hole."

Jennifer closed her eyes, her lips set into a grim line. *End of the road.*

I said, "Roger, Jim. Thanks anyway. Get back and work your cover. File a flight plan for the US tomorrow. We'll contact the Taskforce and give you further guidance."

Jennifer said, "Bullshit! This is bullshit. I'm not giving up. You can fly back, but I'm staying."

She pounded her fist into the dash, frustrated. I reached forward, grabbing her wrists. "Jennifer! Stop it."

She glared at me as if I was at fault, and the pilot spoke again, the line still open. "Pike, Pike, we're getting something."

We all stared at the phone. I said, "What?"

"A string of SMS on the line. Apparently the backlog that hadn't gotten out yet."

No way.

"You're getting SMS texts? Right now?"

"We *were* getting a steady stream, but it just stopped midtext. It's dead."

Jennifer was pinging off the seat, wanting to talk. I held up my finger and whispered, "Call the Taskforce. Let them know it's coming." She started dialing furiously, and I said to the pilot, "Get that data to the Taskforce. Tell them it's from me. They'll know what to do with it."

Five minutes later we had the plot. Fifteen separate pings that were all on the same house. The last one time-stamped five hours before, which was ominous. Clearly, the SMS stream had been interrupted by something before it could complete the backlog of updates. Hopefully it was a dead battery.

The good news was the target was about four miles away as the crow flies, and within two hundred meters of the phone trace. Inside the circle of probable error.

The Taskforce had already pulled satellite photos, complete with an imagery analyst's description of what they thought we were up against, which was a fairly large estate in a neighborhood full of large estates, called Bosques de las Lomas. I gave the tablet with the down-loads to Knuckles, telling him to come up with a plan for in extremis assault, then called the rest of the team to my location.

While they were coming, Knuckles said, "You want to hit it now? Or wait until we can get some detailed intel from a recce? We don't even have our shooting package here. Body armor, breaching charges, long guns, all that shit."

I looked at Jennifer, who was frothing at the mouth, and said, "I'm leaning toward hitting it. What do you think?" Giving him the out.

He stared out the window for a moment, then exhaled. "Yeah, we need to go. It'll be a two-hour round-trip for the kit, and we don't have that kind of time. That data stream shutting down could be because of the cop's phone call. Which means they could all be getting packaged for transport right now. We know the stream was active as of five minutes ago."

I saw the tension leave Jennifer's body and said, "So how do we hit it?"

"Well, an explosive breach is out of the question. I say low-vis and slow. Get in through the pool area. It looks like a damn jungle. Get over the wall and start from there. Taskforce hasn't identified any guards on the outside, so we can make it to breach unobserved. My bet is they're hiding in plain sight, using the exclusive neighborhood as security. Hell, the cops probably know it's a *narco* house."

"What's your take on the manpower? I'm thinking no more than five. Just guards for the kidnapped folks. Enough to run errands and provide twenty-four/seven coverage."

"Yeah, but this isn't like Jennifer's show in Ciudad Juárez. We know at least two are in there—Jack and Felix—but there may be more, and they may not be able to move on their own. We'll need to secure the entire objective before exfil."

I said, "You think we have the manpower for that? Four guys?"

"Five. Jennifer comes in with us. We'll do the clearing, but she can help with security, hostage screening, and other shit, freeing us up to take every room with four on assault. Overwhelming them."

I said, "Whoa. She's not an assaulter. She can pull security outside for anyone coming up the drive. Give us early warning and other things, but she's not coming in. Anyway, someone needs to stage for exfil."

Jennifer cleared her throat from the front seat. I'd forgotten she was there. She said, "I'll do it. I can do whatever you want."

I said, "Jennifer, I get you want to save your brother, but let us handle this."

I saw the other team vehicles pull up, and Knuckles said, "Remember what I told you in Turkmenistan? Is that happening here? Because we need her inside the target. She doesn't enter, and I can't recommend assault."

Am I trying to protect her? Jennifer wasn't trained as an assaulter. She could shoot, no doubt about it, but she would only slow us down, and speed was the one edge we had. The one thing that would allow us to defeat everyone in the house, by moving faster than they could react individually. I saw Decoy and Blood get out of the cars and a thought sprang unbidden into my mind.

She'll get hurt.

It was like a subconscious truth springing forth, clouding my deliberation, making me question my decisions. I trusted Knuckles's judgment more than anyone on earth's. Right now, more than my own. I asked, "You think she can handle it?"

He looked at her and said, "Yes, I do."

In a weird bit of role reversal, Jennifer had finally made it to the inside, convincing Knuckles of her worth, and I was the one keeping her out of the action. Keeping her safe from harm. Protecting her because of what she meant to me.

Decoy opened the back door, looking at me expectantly.

I turned to Knuckles and said, "It's your plan. Brief it."

37

Jennifer came over the barrier last, being the only one who could scale the fifteen-foot brick wall without any help. When she landed, she was sweating profusely from helping to push all four of us up. I don't know why, but I found that funny.

I'd gone up first and waited on the top, the wall being about a foot wide at the apex, but luckily not embedded with broken bottles or strapped with razor wire. Blood, the designated point man, came next. I pulled him up, then hoisted up Knuckles. Once he was set on top, Blood and I both went over, giving us two guns on the ground if we ran into trouble instead of one man on his own.

The foliage was extremely thick, reminding me of working in the jungles of Panama. Blood had moved only a few feet, but I had to look hard to see him. The pool area was still out of view, but I knew it was only about fifty meters away.

After we had everyone together, spread in a tight wedge, I signaled Blood, and we began moving like a patrol at Ranger school, only with suppressed Glocks instead of any type of long gun.

We went about twenty meters before I saw Knuckles take a knee and hold his fist in the air, a relay from Blood. I followed suit and took a knee, looking at Knuckles. He shrugged, telling me he didn't know why Blood had stopped. I saw him lean into Decoy, who whispered something. He then leaned my way and hissed a word I didn't understand. When he saw I wasn't getting it, he held his left hand like he was mimicking a pistol, index finger out but with the thumb inverted and pointing at the ground. The hand signal for *enemy*.

I tensed, getting ready for a fight, aggravated that I'd trusted the Taskforce analysts on the guard force outside the compound. He pointed again and hissed a word.

What the hell is he saying? "Fighter"?

I got sick of the dance and slid over to his position, keeping my voice low. "What is it? A guard?"

He whispered back, "No. A tiger."

"A what?"

"A fucking tiger. Blood says there's a tiger up there."

I shook my head, trying to figure out what that meant. Blood was a former Recon Marine but had spent most of his time with the CIA in the Special Activities Division. I wracked my brain for some code word that we didn't use in the Army but that he might have used as a Marine or paramilitary officer in the CIA.

And came up dry.

I slid through the foliage toward him, moving as

slowly as I could. I reached his position and leaned into his ear. "What's up?"

From a knee, he pointed forward, and sure as shit there was a Bengal tiger staring at us about ten feet away, its tail twitching and its mouth open and huffing.

My first thought was *How many others are in this little zoo?* but I didn't get to dwell on it long, because the cat darted right at us. We both leapt up, our Glocks spitting rounds, and it kept coming.

Heedless of the noise, the entire team crashed backward, everyone now firing at the wraith coming through the jungle. I could see the bullets hitting its side, the forty-five slugs pummeling the body. The cat leapt in the air right at Decoy, hitting him in the chest and knocking him to the ground. Decoy jammed his barrel into its mouth and pumped two rounds, ending the fight. He kicked the beast off and stood, breathing hard.

He whispered, "Never get outta the boat."

On a knee, we all began chuckling silently, except for Jennifer, who didn't get the immortal line from *Apocalypse Now*. I whispered back, "That explains the lack of a guard force here."

We waited in silence for an additional five minutes, checking to see if there would be a reaction from the house. I knew they couldn't hear the suppressed weapons from this distance but wasn't sure about the noise we'd made thrashing through the brush. When nothing appeared, I signaled Blood to continue.

We made it to the edge of the pool area without incident, keeping inside the vegetation, and Knuckles and I left the team, moving forward on our bellies for a view.

A giant wall of glass fronted the pool, and inside an ornate den I could see a man with a beard watching a wide-screen TV. I scanned the room and saw a door to the left, cracked open, which, being the only intel we were going to get, would be the first room we cleared after breach. To the right the glass wall continued on to a small gazebo, complete with a gigantic barbecue grill set into another expanse of brick and an outdoor fireplace.

How do they use all this stuff with a damn tiger roaming around? I figured there was a cage for it somewhere in the jungle and let it go.

I scanned to the left of the glass and saw a large wooden door. *Breach point.* I looked at Knuckles and he nodded. I pulled back into the foliage, getting the team in close.

"There's a breach to the left of the glass. Knuckles, you got it. Blood, you're his backup. Remember, quiet as a mouse on the lock. Inside the house I can see one room with an open door. It's on the left, and our first interior breach. I'll take lead toward it."

I turned to Jennifer. "There's a man in the den sitting on a couch. That's your target. You enter first and go right. You'll see him. We're coming in right behind and going left toward the door."

She said, "I'm first in?"

"Yeah. He needs to be dealt with immediately, but I need all the rest of my guys to enter the room. I have no idea how big it is or what's inside. Once he's down, fall back to us. Pull security on the door we enter."

She didn't speak and I said, "You good with this?"

"Yeah. Yeah, I'm good with it. Just didn't think I'd be first."

Knuckles winked at her, and I saw a little smile slip out before she began checking her weapon. I said, "Any questions?"

Nobody uttered a word. I tapped Knuckles on the shoulder, and the plan was in motion.

38

Knuckles slithered around the pool on his belly, staying in the foliage, Blood following close behind. I saw Blood take a low knee, his pistol on the door, then Knuckles duck-walked forward the last few meters. He tried the knob, then turned and waved his hand in front of his face in a deliberate motion, like a director signaling "cut."

Unlocked. Perfect.

He stayed put, keeping the movement down, and we all collapsed in on Blood's position. I got a thumbs-up from the people around me, then pointed at Jennifer. I could tell the adrenaline was flowing, but her hands were steady. She inhaled and exhaled, then nodded.

I pointed at Knuckles, and we rose, running to the door in a crouch. Two feet from it, he pulled the latch down and swung it open, letting us flow into the target like hornets looking for a victim.

Jennifer entered and jerked right, out of my sight. I spent no time on the target in the den, trusting her to eliminate the threat, running straight to my breach, knowing I had four other men doing the same. I heard the spitting of her Glock and kicked the door inward, leading with my weapon. I saw a man behind a huge desk working a computer, the fat cigar in his mouth spilling to the floor at my entrance. He lurched forward toward a pistol, and I drilled him in the forehead.

The room wasn't that large and was secure in a half second, before Jennifer even made it to us. We bounded back into the den and began clearing, racing silently through the large expanse, checking nooks and crannies. We reached the end of the den, which choked into a hallway that stretched away, deeper into the house. To my front I could see a stairwell leading up, with a door immediately on my left.

I let the stack catch up, waited for the tap on my shoulder, then swung open the door. I almost bounded into it before I realized it was another stairwell, this one going down. And it stank.

The holding cell.

I said, "Jennifer, stay up here. Cover our back."

She nodded, and we began bounding down the stairwell, one man covering while the other moved. Two-thirds of the way and the stairwell took a right-angle turn. Blood held up, putting his barrel around the turn for cover, and Decoy rounded the corner. We each took turns covering as the next man went, a dangerous game of tag.

By the time I had reached the bottom, someone had found a light switch, and I saw three men staring at me with a mixture of fear and hope, unsure where to place their trust. They were looking a little worse for wear, to put it mildly.

But no Jack Cahill.

All three were Latino. None were Caucasian. I held a finger to my lips, then heard Jennifer's Glock snap, followed by a fusillade of rounds from an unsuppressed weapon.

Oops. They know we're here.

We raced to the stairs, turning the corner and seeing Jennifer at the top firing controlled pairs and ducking back. Knuckles looked at me with a smug grin and I said, "Yeah, yeah. Good idea to bring Jennifer."

If we hadn't left her at the top, we would have been as badly trapped as the captives themselves, with no way to get up the stairs. A grandpa with a .22 could have prevented movement out.

We reached the top, staying in the protection of the stairwell, and Jennifer said, "Three guys came down the stairs. Two are still in the stairwell, one is dead."

I leaned out and saw a body on the floor, about twenty meters away. I said, "Jennifer, suppress the stairwell. Blood, Decoy, get to the other side of the hall, back into the den."

They nodded and I leaned over Jennifer's shoulder, putting rounds into the banister of the stairwell. Jennifer followed my lead. Decoy and Blood made it across without issue and began to move down the hallway under the protection of our guns.

Before they reached the stairwell, Knuckles and I slid out, moving on the opposite side of the hall. We got within view of the stairwell and pied off the corner, preventing escape. Blood and Decoy turned into the opening and began firing. I heard one unsuppressed shot, then Decoy appeared, giving an all-clear. I turned and found Jennifer right behind us. I said, "Go down the stairwell. The hostages are there."

Her eyes lit up, and I remembered.

"Jennifer, your brother wasn't down there."

She took that in, nodding vacantly. I said, "Check them for injuries and get them ready to move. Find out what they know."

She nodded more forcefully and took off at a trot. We continued clearing, finding nobody else. The remainder of the house was empty. We rallied at the head of the basement stairs.

I said, "How are they?"

"They can move," Jennifer said. "They're a little beat up but ambulatory."

"Okay, Blood, Decoy, figure out the gates to this place and bring in two vehicles. Knuckles, Jennifer, get them ready to load. I want to be out of here in less than a minute. No telling if any of these guys called reinforcements."

Jennifer said, "Jack was here, Pike. They said that. He was here and taken out this morning."

I said, "What? Here in this house?"

She nodded, her eyes boring into me, looking for the magic answer that I didn't have. Truthfully, the words were like a hammer. Like being a Son Tay raider in Vietnam.

If we'd only gotten the intel earlier.

"Decoy and Blood, go. Get the vehicles up here." After they left I said, "You sure?"

She said, "Yes. He was *here*."

I ran through the risk and decided. "All right, listen. We have no more than five minutes to SSE this place, and that's pushing it. Go find phones, laptops, CDs, thumb drives, whatever. Knuckles, take the last two rooms we cleared. The ones with desks. Jennifer, take the first room we entered. The dead guy in there looked important. I'll take the den and kitchen. Ignore the second floor. It's nothing but bedrooms."

Jennifer gave me a grateful smile and we split up. I found nothing of interest in the den. The kitchen was the same, so I continued into the garage. I saw two Mercedes and a BMW, with a fourth spot empty. On the wall was an impeccably kept little key assortment, like you see at a valet stand. Three of the slots held two sets of keys or key fobs. The last slot held only one fob. A keyless-looking thing for a BMW.

And Jack had been taken from here in some type of vehicle.

I snatched it off the rack and returned, finding Decoy leading the captors to the front door. Knuckles had a couple of phones and a thumb drive. Jennifer had a hard drive she'd ripped from a computer.

In forty minutes we were out of the area and driving back to the city center. We segregated Felix from the other two and released them at the Zócalo in the historic district, giving them each a wad of pesos. I suppose we should have taken them to their respective houses, but the fewer people who saw us, the better. They'd have to make do with finding a taxi or using a pay phone. Felix, on the other hand, was a little more personal to us.

When we pulled over, the two were weeping uncontrollably, profusely praising and thanking us over and over. We admonished them not to say a word about the team, and, if asked, to say they had escaped on their own. I didn't worry about them going to the authorities, because they were free and that was all that mattered in their minds. They knew going to the authorities wouldn't get them any justice, so they wouldn't bother. Very few kidnappings were reported in Mexico, and they probably didn't trust the police not to take them back. The story might get out, but they had nothing to really go on, other than saying we were gringos.

We drove to the Gomez residence in Polanco and let Felix buzz us in. We went straight up the circular path, parking behind a late-model BMW. The bodyguards came flying out the door, guns drawn, and Felix waved at them. They looked flabbergasted. One shouted inside, and Mrs. Gomez came out. She saw Felix and went berserk.

He flew up the steps and was whisked inside. Arturo came out, wiping his eyes.

He said, "How did you do it? How did you find him?"

I said, "You found him. It was your GPS device."

He pointed at Jennifer. "Did you find her brother as well?"

"No. He was there this morning but was taken out before we arrived."

He grew solemn and said, "I'm so sorry. I can never repay you for what you've done. However I can help, I will."

I stared at the BMW in the driveway. I pulled out the key fob I'd found and said, "You ever seen one of these?"

Confused, he said, "Yes, of course. I have the same thing. Why?"

"Is this the key to the car? How's it work?"

"It's keyless entry. Come here."

He led me to the car, showed me his own key fob, then stuck his hand in the handle. The doors unlocked by proximity alone, and the seat began moving back. He said, "It controls the car."

I leaned in and saw what I was hoping for: a little cover near the rearview mirror that opened up, exposing a red button like an old bomber switch. "What does this thing do?"

"You press it if you have car trouble, and someone from BMW gets you help. It works through satellite." He pulled out a smartphone and tapped an app, saying, "Look, with it I can find my car using my phone. It shows where it is on a map."

I bounced the fob in my hand, getting the sniggle of an idea. "You serious about helping me?"

"Of course, whatever I can do."

"You know a BMW dealer around here?"

39

Sitting in his hotel room on Tower Road, just outside Denver International Airport, Booth placed two Garmin GPSs in the windowsill and waited for them to lock on to a signal. His flash drive already inserted, he stuck his thumb on the biometric scanner, disabled his software booby traps, and pulled up POLARIS, toying with his new interface.

It looked marvelous, exactly like the dials and switches on a 1990s-era stereo. The "volume" control set the desired length of time, the "radio tuner" set the degree of disruption of the timing signal, and the "equalizer" switches were each associated with a section of the world. He'd even designed a delay system allowing the settings to be uploaded for execution at a later date.

A person pretending to be Tom Cruise in *Risky Business,* jamming the volume and equalizer settings to the max while "tuned" to the highest FM "frequency," would fatally disrupt the satellite-timing signal worldwide and subsequently render useless anything that leveraged the GPS constellation.

At least in theory, that is. While Booth was pleased with the aesthetics, sure that a child could use his program, he realized that he had no idea if it actually worked. It wasn't like he could test the code as he wrote it. He'd had to create it whole, without any measure of success, then inject it based on faith.

Not wanting to fly out of Colorado Springs for security reasons, he'd made the drive to Denver International, coming up a day early and getting a hotel. Throughout the trip, a nagging thought had spread like oil on water: *What if the system doesn't function?*

Why fly all the way to Mexico City, put himself at the potential mercy of a suspected cartel boss, and then pass something that was little more than a broken string of ones and zeros? The protocol would do nothing, and his risk would be worthless. Unlike Manning and Snowden, he wasn't exposing information, he was *using* it. He was the first to actually exploit the network for good instead of merely talking about it.

He consciously focused on the goal of stopping the United States' injustice the world over, but he couldn't keep another nagging thought from intruding: If it failed, he'd get no money at all. No way to pay off his drug debts. No way to escape.

Then he thought about the man receiving the protocol. Carlos. If POLARIS didn't work, money would be the least of his problems. Maybe Booth should stay here. Just call it a day. Why go to Mexico and risk the wrath of someone like Carlos?

But that outcome was predicated on POLARIS's failure. Something he could test right now. If POLARIS executed like he'd programmed, it would be worth a great deal of money. And he was the only one who could make it function. Carlos could threaten, but he needed Booth's help. *If* the thing worked.

After checking in, he'd sat on the bed and contemplated a test.

It was a risk, because the disruption would definitely be felt, causing the 2nd SOPS and Boeing to go crazy trying to figure out what had happened, but that, in itself, was worth the test. He'd buried the protocol deep, cloaking it with the GPS constellation's own code, making it impossible to find without shredding the software that gave the satellite life. This would force them to clean the satellites one by one to prevent interruption of the overall constellation, a massive, time-consuming process. In the end, a doppelgänger of Booth would root around, trying to locate what had caused the issue, but he would have little luck finding the protocol if he didn't know where to look.

Theoretically.

His GPS gave a little beep, and he saw an icon of a Volkswagen Beetle centered directly over his hotel, blinking silently. On, off. On, off. Beckoning. Booth made up his mind.

He plugged the other GPS into the computer and waited for it to mate to the protocol. The GPS satellites were continuously circling the earth, and he needed to know which ones were overhead in order to only affect North America. It was a bit of a technological marvel that the average person took for granted when cursing their GPS, but the satellites broadcast an almanac of locational data that the little receiver then synchronized before searching the sky for the strongest signal.

He saw a string of numbers, labeled SVN 54, SVN 67, SVN 32, and continuing until all operational satellites were listed. He now knew the location of every one, and POLARIS synchronized the data. He turned to the laptop, engaging the "equalizer" button for North America but leaving the others alone.

He touched the "volume" dial until it showed six seconds, the timing packet used by the 2nd SOPS when working the constellation. His mouse icon hovering over the tuning dial, he debated on the degree of timing offset. He had no idea how effective his protocol was and wanted to be able to register a disruption with his crude little handheld GPS, so he went ahead and dialed it all the way to the right.

He connected to the Wi-Fi in his room, logging on to the Internet, then pulled up Tor, a browser package that utilized a volunteer network of computers that would randomize his ISP, preventing a searcher from knowing who he was or what he had sent over the Internet. He smiled at the irony of using something developed for the military to cloak his attack against that same body.

Once his computer had accessed the Boeing desktop in his little frigid trailer, he stroked the keys, turning off the Boeing firewall. Everything set, his mouse icon hovered over the power button to the virtual stereo deck. He glanced once more at the second GPS sitting in the window, seeing the car still blinking in the correct spot. He clicked "on."

The little GPS blinked, then flashed the message, "Acquiring Satellites." Two seconds later, it showed his location as somewhere in northern Canada. Two seconds after that, it went through the same process again, the icon ending up back at his hotel.

A QUARTER OF a mile away, at the 7-Eleven on Tower Road, a man attempting to buy gas for his rental car received the message "Unable to complete transaction" from the fuel pump. He ran into the store to pay, dismayed at the line. He waited at the end, glancing at his watch every five seconds, growing more and more frustrated. The line didn't move as the cashier tried to get her machines to function. He felt the time slip by and wondered if he would make his flight. He needn't have worried.

ON I-70, A mother desperately trying to reach the airport before her plane left heard her GPS say, "Recalculating." Shoving a pacifier into her crying baby's mouth, she unwittingly drove past her exit while it bounced back and forth. Seven seconds later, when it finished calculating, it ordered a U-turn, causing her to scream in frustration.

She prayed her aircraft was delayed. Her prayer would be answered.

IN THE CONTROL tower of Denver International Airport, the largest airport in the United States by area and the fifth busiest by volume, the air-traffic controllers were hard at work synchronizing a dizzying array of fuel-laden flying bombs.

One of the first airports to be upgraded to the Federal Aviation Administration's NextGen architecture for enhanced efficiency, it depended on GPS for accurate approach and takeoff instructions. Because NextGen was fairly new, the tower maintained the legacy radio guidance, should any receiver fail.

In the span of three seconds, every single receiver began sending false positioning codes. An unforeseen catastrophic event, the massive data conflict caused the mainframe computer to lock up, crashing every heads-up display and scope showing inbound and outbound traffic. The radio guidance continued to work flawlessly but was tied to a computer system that was no longer functioning.

The room filled with screaming voices as the air-traffic controllers tried to maintain separation of aircraft by eyesight alone, one man rebooting the system while another pulled an ancient set of binoculars from a closet.

At six thousand feet, United flight 762 continued to descend as instructed. On approach for landing, the captain correctly assumed that continuing with his last instructions was a better course of action than retaking to the sky with no one at the wheel in the tower.

On the ground before him a Cessna 182 took off, the new pilot inside trying to decipher all the shouting in his radio. Climbing higher and higher, the pilot of the Cessna never saw the wing of the Boeing 757 that crushed his cockpit like he was a gnat hitting a windshield. Never saw the 187 souls screaming on their way to earth. Never heard the captain grunting in the radio as he tried to get the plane to respond. Never felt the fireball that erupted when the aircraft sliced into the earth, spewing flaming jet fuel, luggage, and body parts.

STARING AT HIS blinking little Volkswagen Beetle icon, Booth was very, very pleased. His code, created out of whole cloth and built in the dark of a basement, without any testing, had worked flawlessly. He giggled to himself at the number of inconveniences he had caused, wondering how many people across the United States had just heard that annoying little GPS voice. Or how many had had their ATM withdrawals spoiled, forcing them to start over after the six-second test.

He heard a siren and glanced out the window, noticing for the first time a giant black cloud growing from the airport.

40

A small trickle of blood still flowed from the gaping wound in El Comandante's head, tracking down his outstretched arm before dripping silently to the hardwood floor below the desk. The flow told the *sicario* that the attack was fairly recent.

He scanned the office, seeing a computer ripped open, wires sprawling out like electronic intestines. The desk had been rifled, with papers scattered about, but two separate bundles of US one-hundred-dollar bills lay in the drawer, untouched.

It didn't add up to a *narco* hit. The bodies lay as they had fallen. No messages sent through mutilation, no sign of methodical execution, and nothing of value had been taken. Yet someone had ripped through a Zetas safe house, killing everyone inside. Just like the Sinaloa safe house in Juárez. Someone with intelligence and the skill to use it.

Who would that be? Who would have the capability to penetrate both Sinaloa and Los Zetas, then attack with a scalpel, hitting two distinct houses, getting nothing in re-

turn? No law enforcement proclamations about stymieing
the drug trade, no riches from the houses themselves?

He turned and found the journalist staring at the
corpse, his face pale. Scared by a dead man. The *sicario*
found it humorous.

He said, "Sit on the floor in this room. If you move,
you will look like El Comandante."

He searched the rest of the house, finding more bodies, but from what he could tell, all were lying exactly
where they had been hit. There were no *narco* banners
left at the scene, no propaganda or bragging, no graffiti
designed to intimidate. It was as if whoever had come had
killed for no other reason than because they could, like
the fox in the henhouse of his youth.

And like that same animal, they had taken the livelihood of the *sicario*.

Going down the steps to the basement, he realized that
he would now be targeted. El Comandante had planned on
taking him to Matamoros, which meant he'd probably already poisoned the leadership, offering the *sicario* to deflect
blame from the Sinaloa attack in Juárez. This assault would
do nothing but confirm it, leaving him on the outside.

He reached the basement, and, as expected, it was
empty, although it wouldn't have surprised him to find
the kidnap victims killed outright as well, like the chickens by the fox.

He went back up the stairs, contemplating what he
should do. He couldn't remain in Mexico City, as all of
his contacts here were Los Zetas. He couldn't trust them

for help, and the city itself was foreign. Ciudad Juárez was more his style, a place where he understood the rhythm and flow, but after the Sinaloa hit, he was sure anyone associated with Los Zetas was being targeted, and he had no illusions about his picture hanging on someone's wall, just like Carlos's photo had been on his. It was pure luck that he hadn't been here when the assault went down in the first place. An interconnected event like all the other ones he'd experienced in his life. All that remained was how he would use it.

I need safety. Someplace to hide. But there is no place in this country.

He had one other alternative. A thing he'd always kept but never felt he would use. Maybe it was time to invoke his escape clause with his US passport. Disappear into America for good. What had been a scary, last-ditch solution before his trip to El Paso he now saw as his only option. Before, he'd been afraid of using it, but now he understood that he could cross the border and survive on the other side. Even thrive, provided he had money. A stake to get him started, which he was fairly sure he could obtain by selling the BMW and any other jewelry or watches he could find in this house.

He opened the office door to find the journalist sitting on the floor with his head in his hands, apparently in emotional shock. A lone rooster left prancing in the yard, pecking at the dead around him and waiting on the fox. *Baggage at this point.* He realized it would be easiest to do it right here and leave the body with the others.

He withdrew his Sig P226 and racked the slide. The journalist snapped his head up, seeing the end of the barrel.

He threw his hands in the air, shouting, "Don't! Please don't! Remember I can still identify the contact. Carlos told those other men he was coming tomorrow. Without me you won't find him."

The *sicario* had maintained surveillance on the meeting in the park, more than likely at the exact same moment a team of killers was ripping apart this house, and had learned that the mysterious contact from the United States was flying into Mexico City tomorrow morning. Not that any of that mattered now. He couldn't have cared less about the American or what he was doing with Sinaloa.

He said, "El Comandante wanted the contact. I do not."

"Carlos said he was selling the device. It's worth a great deal of money. Don't you care about that?"

The words gave the *sicario* pause. Carlos *had* said that. Had admonished the men that they would need to bring a great deal of money to get the device—whatever it was—and they, in return, stated a third man was coming who would have the money. After the meeting had ended, and Carlos had left, he'd hoped to learn more about the third man, but the men began speaking in a language he didn't understand, disappointing him.

He sighted down the barrel, considering. Truthfully, if the journalist ran out of the house right now, he could do little to harm the *sicario*'s chances of getting to America. He had no idea of the name on the passport or of the *sicario*'s intentions. What was he going to do, run to the nearest policeman and start ranting? The most he could accomplish would be providing a detailed description, but without something more than a story of abduction, the police in Mexico would toss that in the trash.

It's worth the risk.

He holstered his pistol, seeing the journalist sag against the wall. Not giving him any time to recover, he said, "Get that money in the drawer. Search El Comandante's body. Take his wallet, watch, rings, and anything else of value."

He left and did the same to the bodies in the hall, stripping them of anything that he could sell, then methodically went room by room looking for anything of value he could scavenge. He saw evidence of a search in the other rooms as well, but once again, articles an ordinary thief would never have passed up—and certainly not a hit man from the Sinaloa cartel—were left behind, confusing him as to who had perpetrated the attack.

Nine minutes later they were driving away, the BMW's backseat holding two garbage bags of valuables the *sicario* intended to sell in the thieves' market of Tepito tomorrow afternoon. It would take a few phone calls, but Tepito was a free-for-all of black-market goods where one could purchase anything from weapons to the latest bootleg copy of a Hollywood movie.

The hardest would be the BMW, given its previous owner, but Tepito was overrun with Korean Mafia—a strange set of circumstances, but real nonetheless. The right man wouldn't care who owned it, only what he could glean from its parts.

The car brought up another dilemma: He couldn't lie low in a hotel that would ask no questions about a gringo chained to the toilet, as the BMW would be talked about, and probably stripped by morning. He would need to stay at a higher-end hotel, with parking and security, and that meant leaving a trail.

He said, "Have you stayed in Mexico City before?"

The journalist slid his eyes like it was a trick question but answered. "Yes. I reported from here a few times."

"Where?"

"The Sheraton next to the United States embassy, on Reforma Avenue."

The *sicario* took that in and nodded. It was a huge risk, but nobody from the cartels would dare do anything due to the security.

"We're going back there. Remember what I said about circumstances and making the best of them?"

"Yes."

"This is one of those times, but not like you think. I should kill you right now, but I have not. I will not hesitate to do so if you try anything inside the hotel while I'm checking in." He floated his eyes on the journalist, and the man shrank back. "I understand the frailty of life much more than you, and I do not hold my own existence to the same level as you. I am the fox that kills for no other reason than he can, and like the fox, I will be exterminated eventually. You did well today. Continue, and you might return to your life where right and wrong keep the predators at bay."

The journalist nodded, saying nothing.

The *sicario* said, "Remember, you exist solely to identify the gringo coming from America. I hope for your sake you can."

41

On the wide-screen TV a past administrator of the FAA bloviated on and on about what he perceived had gone wrong in Denver. Having served when air travel was a novelty and the technology was based on lessons learned from World War II, he was the perfect man to discuss the intricacies of modern-day air travel. Or at least the only man the network could get to fill in some dead air. He pointed at a chart detailing the exponential increase in aircraft juxtaposed over the static manning hours of the air-traffic controller, extrapolating human error based on the government's refusal to address grievances he had championed years ago. Kurt turned away in disgust.

In his heart, he understood he shouldn't fault the network. They were only doing what they existed to do: entice someone to watch their channel so advertisers would buy time. Like many times in the past, though, he knew what they did not. He knew the secret, and in this case the secret was bad indeed.

George Wolffe stuck his head in the door. "Principals' meeting in forty-five."

Kurt leaned back and rubbed his eyes. In the end, it was only a matter of time before he was called. The National Security team would deal with the mess created by the GPS blackout, but his organization was the only one with a thread that could lead to the prevention of a second catastrophic event. Not that he thought it was very strong. Or even something he'd really call a thread. More like a tendril of smoke.

He said, "Any more information on the probes of our systems?"

George grimaced and said, "Yeah. I was going to wait until after the meeting. You don't need to hear this now."

"What?"

"There's a YouTube video posted. The usual idiot in the Guy Fawkes mask. He says Anonymous is going to expose a secret government spy ring in four days."

"You think it's us? Or coincidence?"

"I think there's no way it's a coincidence. We've had probes on all our systems linked to Grolier Recovery Services, and they've been very, very good. Hacking cell can't track them back. All they know is they're happening."

"What could they find? How bad could they expose anything?"

"No gun, but plenty of smoke."

"That's just great." He stood up and stretched. "Let's go see what the Beltway's knee-jerk reaction is to the blackout. Deal with this later."

They exited the building into a parking garage in Arlington, getting into a nondescript Toyota sedan. George said, "You going to brief them on the penetration?"

"Yeah. I suppose I have to, but I'll wait until after they finish hyperventilating about the GPS constellation. It'll probably cause three or four heart attacks."

FORTY MINUTES LATER he entered the conference room in the Old Executive Office Building, feeling like he'd just left it. Ordinarily, Kurt and George briefed on a quarterly basis, getting approval for operations that were drawn out and boring but by their very nature had significant risk of United States exposure. At least that had been the framework. Now it seemed they spent more time briefing because of some crisis than they did controlling the long-term efforts that were the core of what the Taskforce did.

He saw five men in the room, unofficially called the "principals" of the Oversight Council. It was a moniker that had grown out of the power and experience the men brought to the table. While all thirteen appointed members of the council were needed to approve any Taskforce operation, these five men routinely met to discuss the operations' implications, and 90 percent of the time, the rest of the council fell in line with whatever they wished.

Alexander Palmer, the president's national security adviser, said, "Thanks for coming."

Kurt said, "It's becoming routine. What's the damage?"

"For actual loss of life, pretty much what you see on

the television. A 757 crashed, killing everyone on board. It's being blamed on a computer malfunction in the tower, but the cause of that malfunction is still unknown. To the public, anyway."

"And nonlethal damage?"

"We're still trying to assess, but it'll be in the billions of dollars. The secondary repercussions to our national air transportation alone were significant. Every major airport in America was affected, and while it was very brief, it caused a lot of panic, but luckily no other catastrophic events. Everywhere else worked fine with the legacy systems. Beyond that, we had an enormous amount of lost bank transfers and credit purchases, power outages, downed cell phone signals, and a ton of other things we haven't even begun to assess. It's a mess. Nobody knew how far the GPS signal had extended into our national framework."

Kurt nodded toward the secretary of defense. "I thought there was no way anyone could affect the constellation. Jam individual signals, but not affect *every* signal."

The SECDEF said, "It wasn't every signal. As far as we can tell, the glitch affected only the satellites orbiting over North America."

George Wolffe said, "Glitch? Is that what we're saying? This was an accident?"

The director of the CIA said, "We don't know. For six seconds, the satellites spit out a bad timing signal. It didn't impact any of our operations overseas. All UAVs continued normally, but here, in the United States, it caused a lost link with every drone in the air. If it was done on purpose, it was most likely a test."

Kurt said, "Well, it looks like it was successful. Can't you guys figure out the difference? I mean, isn't there some egghead who runs this shit who can tell? Find out what happened?"

The SECDEF said, "We're working that now through Second SOPS and Boeing, but so far we've come up with nothing. There isn't anything in the software architecture that shouldn't be there. It's like the satellites had a Tourette's moment, then went back to normal."

"So what's next?"

"We've scrubbed everyone in the squadron and they're clean. Nobody is on leave anywhere near El Paso or anything else that sends a spike, which is what I expected. Those guys live and breathe space operations and take it very seriously. No way would they be involved in an event like this. It's something else, and we don't have a thread. All we've got is what you have."

"You mean Jennifer's theory about her brother? Seriously? That's the best we can do?" Kurt looked at the D/CIA. "You guys don't have anything? What about the Hezbollah team?"

"They're in Mexico City, but that's all we know. No linkages to this at all other than the timing. The council's already given execute authority to explore further. We're wondering what your next steps are."

Earlier, Kurt had sent them the situation report from the second hit, so he knew they were fully aware of the dry hole as far as Jack Cahill was concerned. What surprised him was that they were willing to continue in the face of so little evidence that it wouldn't do any good whatsoever. Running amok in a foreign country conducting lethal operations was not something they should have been doing. Maybe once, when there was a distinct threat and a payoff, but twice with nothing in return was pushing the limit.

He said, "Honestly, I was going to tell Pike to stand down. We've conducted two overtly hostile actions in an allied country. On top of that we have no cover for action whatsoever down there. If Mexico investigates any of it we're in hot water. There is no backstopping."

Kurt saw Alexander Palmer look around the room, getting a nod from each man present. He said, "We don't want you to stand down. We want you to continue full bore on the problem."

What the hell? Because we're the right tool or just the easiest tool?

Kurt replied, "Uhh . . . yeah, well you realize we're coming dangerously close to compromising the project, right? Maybe we should discuss this with the full council. Put other agencies in play. Get the State Department to lean on Mexico to produce Jack or get the DEA to start working it."

"We don't have time for that, and engaging them would mean pulling you off. We can't do both, and you already have a lead. Something we can work with. It's slim, but you haven't been compromised yet doing operations that were worse than these. Remember what Pike did in Europe a couple of years ago?"

Kurt said, "Yes, sir, I do, but the situation's a little different now. Someone is probing all of Project Prometheus's computer networks, possibly making connections that they shouldn't."

Kurt laid out what he knew about Anonymous, the YouTube threat, and the potential for the entire effort to be exposed.

Taken aback, nobody said anything for a moment. Finally, Palmer broke the silence. "I thought your cover backstopping would prevent this. Isn't that the whole reason we created such a gigantic beast?"

"It will, to a point, but the actual protection was hiding below scrutiny. If anyone really wanted to dig into one of our companies, like Grolier Recovery Services, they'd find something that was a little off-kilter. I mean, seriously, the only way to look exactly like a real business is to *be* a real business. You can't do what we do without looking a little strange."

The SECDEF said, "That's not what you briefed when we started this. We were told it would be untraceable."

Kurt looked at the D/CIA for support, the one man in the room who should have understood. When he received no help he said, "Nothing is untraceable, especially nowadays. Shit, the CIA had their rendition flights cracked by a bunch of amateur tail watchers at airports. They did everything right and someone made a connection between a flight taking off in Pakistan and one landing in Egypt. Next thing you know, the entire history of the aircraft is out, mainly because of the interconnections on social media."

All looked toward the D/CIA for confirmation. He sighed and said, "He's right. There's only so much you can do. There will always be a digital trail that someone can piece together. The best defense is not giving them a reason to start piecing. Which begs the question: Why is someone probing Grolier?"

Kurt said, "We have no idea, and we're looking hard. Whoever it is is pretty damn good. We've got the best hackers in the world and they can't track them back. The bottom line is someone is probing our networks. If that YouTube video comes out and CNN smells a story, they're going to be all over Grolier Recovery Services. It'll stand up to basic scrutiny, but it won't survive if Pike's still in Mexico chasing after drug cartels. It'll be the crack that breaks the dam, leading back here, to this room."

Alexander Palmer said, "The video isn't being released for four days? Is that what you said?"

"Yeah, most likely because they don't have any smoking gun yet. They're still digging."

"So you've got four days to figure out this GPS thing, then get back here and smile for the CNN investigation. Sounds like a normal Taskforce day for Pike Logan."

"Don't put that on him. We don't pay Pike to make decisions on the fate of the organization. He'll do what we say, but only because we say it. Don't put him in the crosshairs like that unless you're willing to back him up when it goes to hell."

Everyone remained silent, understanding the insult Kurt had just thrown out. Palmer said, "I'll pretend I didn't hear that. You created this organization for a reason, and that reason is here. Continue with the search."

"Sir, in good conscience I need to formally state that I'm not sure I can handle the repercussions. Suppose CNN takes a cursory look at the CEO of Grolier Recovery Services' flight history? They'll find that both Pike and Jennifer flew to Turkmenistan on a leased G-Four belonging to the company, but flew home separately on commercial birds, only they didn't go home, they went to El Paso, then traveled by car to Mexico, where the G-Four linked up with them. It'll stink to high heaven."

Alexander Palmer raised his voice for the first time. "Then I guess you'd better stop that YouTube video from getting out. In the meantime, find out who's fucking with our GPS constellation. Is that clear?"

Kurt glared at him, wanting to say what he knew he should not. Understanding he was on fragile ground after he'd bucked this very council six months before, he settled for "Yes, sir."

Palmer softened his voice. "Kurt, we get the threat to the organization, but it's nowhere near the damage of someone having a remote control to our GPS constellation. I can't believe you're fighting us on this."

"Sir, I understand, and I'm not fighting the fact that

it's dangerous. I just don't think I can do anything about it. The thread you're talking about is nothing. A rumor that Jennifer believes."

"Then I guess we're fucked, because Jennifer's brother is all we have."

42

Booth walked through customs, shocked at the lack of English-speaking people. It was a boiling mass of humanity, but everyone he attempted to engage simply smiled and shrugged. It was disconcerting, to say the least. He'd been to Europe and the Far East, and in both those locations, while he definitely felt like an outsider, most everyone spoke at least some English. Here, nobody did.

And they live just across our damn border.

He exited with a throng of people, then stood, looking around in a daze. A man came up and said, "Taxi?"

He said, "You speak English?"

The man repeated, "Taxi?"

Booth said, "Yes, yes. I need a taxi." And began following him out the door. He walked five feet before a policeman intervened, shouting at the man. Bewildered, Booth simply stood, watching the exchange. The unlicensed cabby took off at a fast walk, and the policeman handed Booth an envelope.

He opened it, seeing instructions from Carlos to take

the metro to a stop called Insurgentes. Taken aback, he said, "Where's Carlos? Why did he pass me this?"

The policeman simply stared at him. Seeing he was getting nowhere, Booth said, "I don't know where the metro is."

The policeman scowled and walked away. Booth saw a line at the end of the hall, ending at a glass window with a woman behind it. Most of the people were Hispanic, but a few were foreign. He joined them, and when he reached the front, he found to his relief the woman behind the glass spoke English. She asked where he was going, and he said he wanted the metro.

She said, "This is the taxi line. The metro is at the other end of the hall." She gave him instructions, then turned to the next person in line before he could assimilate them. Brushed aside, he left the counter.

He fumbled about, following the directions to the best of his ability while dragging his little carry-on suitcase, and eventually found the stairs leading to the Terminal Aérea metro stop.

Reaching the bottom, he was once again confused as to what to do. The place was a dirty, swirling mass of humanity. He watched people go to a counter behind glass, not noticing that several men were now studying him as well. A plump, lost gringo wading into a school of piranhas.

As instructed, he bought a ticket to the Insurgentes metro stop, then moved to the train platform. When it arrived, he was swept on board with everyone else, all

Mexican and all rattling in Spanish. He took a seat at the end of the car, crammed in by the people continuing to board. Three men were hovering over him, two looking out and one staring at Booth.

The Mexican above him said, "Gringo. Where you go?"

Booth stared at the floor. The man poked him with a shoe. "Gringo. I talking to you."

Booth said, "I'm meeting a friend. Please, leave me alone."

The man pulled out a knife and said, "Pay tax. Gringo tax."

At the sight of the knife, Booth recoiled, blubbering. The man leaned in, his stench flushing what little fresh air there was on the train. He said again, "Pay tax."

Booth stabbed his hand into his pants, pulling out his wallet. He looked about, waiting on someone to stop the mugging, but nobody seemed to notice. He withdrew all of his cash and handed it over, his hands shaking.

The Mexican said, "Computer."

Booth hugged his laptop to his chest and shook his head. The man lowered the knife until it was level with his eyes and repeated, "Computer."

Booth looked left and right, hoping someone would help but seeing that nobody was paying them the least bit of attention. In fact, all were studiously looking away. The train pulled into the next station, and the mass began to ebb and flow. The two men closed off their corner, preventing anyone from interfering with the mugging.

People packed into the car, the brief emptiness filled

with soiled shirts and dirty feet as the riders crammed together. The man traced Booth's ear with the knife, and that was enough.

Booth flung the laptop at him, shouting, "Take it, and leave me alone!"

The man grinned, showing a jack-o'-lantern mouth with the front teeth missing. He turned, saying something in Spanish to his compadres, then grunted. Magically, a knife had grown out of his stomach, the area around the hilt growing black with liquid. He sat down heavily, and Booth saw the laptop jerked from his hands. He followed the arm and recognized Carlos standing above the downed mugger.

Carlos hissed at the mugger's two friends and they disappeared through the open door. He grabbed Booth's arm, jerked him to his feet, and followed suit, exiting just before the train left for the next stop.

Carlos said, "You're two hours late and you took the wrong train. Idiot."

As he walked up the stairs, gasping for air, it was almost too much for Booth to absorb. He said, "I'm late because of a plane crash at the Denver airport. Didn't you see the news? Every damn flight is late coming out of Denver because of it. Why did you change the instructions? Why aren't I meeting you at the hotel?"

"No. I didn't see the news." Getting to street level, Carlos grinned. "I thought maybe you were working for the US Federales, but I think it's safe to say your stupidity proves otherwise. Either way, we aren't going to the hotel I sent you. You're just lucky my people kept an eye out for you."

"Federales? What are you talking about?"

"Nothing. You have the protocol?"

"Yes, I have it. Of course."

They walked down an alley toward a dented sedan with the trunk held in place by a rope. Carlos motioned for him to get in.

Driving west, Carlos said, "I'm going to want you to show me how it functions."

"I don't think that's smart. I've already tested it with my own GPS and it works. Every time you do that, you give them a chance to plug the holes. Trust me, it worked. Better than I expected. I think I caused the plane crash in Denver. You pay me for it, and then you can launch it after I leave. After I'm back in the US."

Carlos slammed the brakes and threw the car into park on the side of the road. He turned to Booth, baring his teeth. "You need to understand something. You belong to me now. You will do what I say, or I'll turn you loose right here. You'll last about an hour after I make some calls."

Booth recoiled, nodding his head over and over again, the fear of this newfound world making him wish he'd never boarded the plane. Making him wonder if Bradley Manning or Edward Snowden had ever put himself in danger like this. The thought brought a small tendril of pride at his audacity. Small, but large enough to give him the courage to continue. He might not make any money on POLARIS, but he'd at least get it released. Others could talk the talk, but he was walking the walk. Snowden and Manning had garnered a legion of people preaching their hero status. What Booth was doing would be exponentially better.

Carlos started driving again, saying, "I really don't care what happens to you after I get POLARIS, but you'll care a great deal if the thing you brought doesn't work. You'll care for hours, I promise."

The words sucked the courage out of Booth like a dental vacuum rooting around a mouth.

They drove in silence for another twenty minutes. Then Carlos pulled against the curb next to a run-down building of crumbling brick surrounding two roll-up doors.

He said, "Follow me," and walked up a narrow stairway on the side. At the top, he held the door open, letting Booth enter. Inside was a one-room flat with a sofa bed and a corner kitchenette, the toilet in the back competing with the rest of the space with its odor alone.

Carlos said, "Put the computer on the table and turn it on. Show me how it works."

Booth did as he was told, then said, "Do you have Wi-Fi? Internet here?"

Carlos looked bewildered for a moment, then said, "No."

"It won't work without a connection to the Internet." When he saw Carlos's face grow dark, he whined, "I'm telling the truth! Think about it, I have to connect to the satellites somehow. I can show you how it works, but I can't prove it does without Internet."

Carlos stared at him, and Booth was sure he was considering putting a bullet in his head. Eventually, he sat down in front of the laptop and said, "Show me."

Booth pulled up his stereo interface and began to explain, detailing how to control the protocol. He was discussing the equalizer tabs and how they corresponded to sections of the earth when someone knocked on the door.

Carlos jerked his head at the noise and drew his pistol. He held a finger to his lips and crept to the door. He leaned in, putting his eye against the peephole.

Booth heard a cough, no louder than a hand clap, then saw Carlos's head snap back. He felt a spray of liquid like someone had popped a wet towel near his face, then watched Carlos crumple straight down.

In shock, Booth touched his face, and his hand came away with a viscous fluid tinged in red. His mouth opened and closed like that of a fish gasping on a dock, and the door exploded inward. What entered was something out of the Brothers Grimm. A man of normal height, wearing normal clothes. Normal ended at the neck. The man had no hair on his head, and his forehead was smudged, as if someone had sculpted a bust and then scraped the forehead in anger before it was set.

In his hand was a large pistol, pointed directly at Booth's head. The barrel didn't register at all because of the death above the sights. A hypnotic stare coming from beyond the world Booth lived within.

The golem said, "Close the computer."

Booth did so without hesitation, waiting on a further command, the sweat spreading on his body like a rash. The man said, "Make any indication you do not want to comply and you will be dead. Do you understand?"

Booth nodded furiously.

"Follow me."

Booth stood, and for the first time noticed another man on the landing, crouching down and holding his arms over his head.

The man looked up, and he saw it was a gringo.

43

I did a double take in my rearview, noticing that the statue behind the cross was a skeleton. "What the hell is that?"

Jennifer set her smartphone down and glanced backward. "It's a church for Santa Muerte, the patron saint of death. It's a bastardization of Catholicism, and pretty popular with those on the illegal side of things."

Leave it to her to actually know the answer.

"You mean it's some kind of cult?"

Jennifer said, "Yes and no. It's not a cult like you mean, with only a few people belonging to it. La Santa Muerte's huge down here, but it's also definitely frowned upon by the Church. The Mexican government thinks it's nothing but a way for the drug cartels to sanctify what they're doing, and it's officially illegal, but I guess around here being illegal doesn't mean a whole lot."

We were just south of Eje 1 Norte, only a half mile or so from the tourist area of the historic district and the president's palace, but had crossed some border that separated the good guys from the bad. The Tepito barrio was just across the road, and according to all the research

I could find, it was about as bad an area as I could possibly imagine. Known as the thieves' market since colonial times, the barrio was home to every sort of illegal activity, from prostitution to gun running, and the people who lived there were known throughout Mexico as fighters. Tough guys who took pride in their rough-and-tumble existence.

Merchandise was sold throughout in all manner of tiny little shops or right out in the streets, each alley clogged with stolen, smuggled, or counterfeit items. The people here knew which alley to go to for drugs, weapons, CDs, or phones, but we didn't have a clue. All we knew was that the little blue marble on our smartphone, representing the BMW from the *narco*'s kidnapping house, was located in the heart of the barrio.

After we'd dropped off Felix yesterday, his father had taken Jennifer and me to a BMW dealer to see what we could do with the key fob. The dealer was closed because of the late hour, but Arturo had pulled some strings. I'd heard him shouting into a phone and figured his son's rescue was paying off.

I'd wanted to go just by myself, because it was a long shot and I didn't want to get Jennifer's hopes up. I wasn't sure what the thinking would be back home and needed to contact Kurt Hale before I did anything else. The last thing I wanted was for Jennifer to think we were still on the hunt for her brother, only to have the Oversight Council pull us home. I'd probably end up tying her to the airframe to prevent her from doing something stupid.

After a little baksheesh exchanged hands, courtesy of Arturo, the BMW dealer read the fob. It turned out that not only did it work the doors, ignition, and windows, but it had the maintenance records for the car stored on its embedded chip, including the VIN and other identifying characteristics. In other words, a partial lead. It would take some hefty convincing to make the lead pan out, as I'd have to get the Taskforce to penetrate BMW of North America and create a BMW Assist account tied to the VIN for us to track the vehicle.

It was almost a 100 percent guarantee that the *narco* didn't have that sort of thing operational in his car—what crook would want Big Brother to have the ability to track him?—but it was about only a 50 percent chance that he'd taken the extra step of removing all the electronic infrastructure that allowed the feature to work, especially since that infrastructure was probably threaded throughout other operational capabilities like arteries in a body.

We'd taken the information back to our hotel in the Zona Rosa and I'd given the team what little we had, telling them to return to their rooms for some shut-eye. We all needed some decompression time after the activities of the past couple of days, and I wasn't sure when we'd get another chance. It was the way of such operations. You might get sleep for the next four months because the command decided to pull the plug, or you might be up for the next four days.

Used to the stop-and-go, they left, but Jennifer had

stayed behind. I let her, given her brother's life was at stake.

I had contacted Kurt on our company VPN, an encrypted network that bounced around forever through various ISPs to cloak who I was calling. He took the information, but, as expected, he was decidedly lukewarm on doing anything with it.

Jennifer, behind me and off camera from the VPN, had pleaded with him, trying the same hand she had with me about a threat to the GPS constellation, but he wasn't buying it, and I understood why. Hell, I wasn't even buying it. The evidence was simply too weak, and we were literally flying by the seat of our pants down here, conducting operations without a shred of backup should someone get rolled up.

In the end, Kurt said he'd prep the intelligence picture—a nice way of saying he'd have the hacker cell penetrate BMW—but we were to stand down until further notice. We agreed to talk again the following morning, and I signed off.

After the call had ended, I'd sat for a minute reflecting. Jennifer had cleared her throat, reminding me she was in the room, and I told her to go get some rest. She didn't move.

I joked, "What? You want to sleep in my room tonight?"

She slowly shook her head and said, "No. Not with your attitude about my brother."

Trying to lighten the mood, I said, "Usually the

woman waits a little longer in the relationship to start withholding favors to get what she wants."

Jennifer's face was flint. Not a bit of humor at all. She said, "Usually the man I sleep with isn't such a callous ass."

I realized the joke was a mistake. I'd just brought our relationship into the equation of what should have been a team member–team leader discussion. I needed to get that back.

"Jennifer, listen to me closely. I care about your brother, and I'll do whatever I can within the limits of what's possible, but right now, you need to get your head on straight. This is a Taskforce operation, period."

She said, "You never seemed to care about that in the past. You always did what you thought was right, regardless of Taskforce rules. Remember in Prague? You rescued all those sex slaves when you could have simply used a beacon. Now, when it's someone I care about, you've turned into a by-the-book soldier."

It was true, I'd taken a significant risk assaulting a house full of Albanian Mafia who were trafficking in young girls, but she was failing to remember that the only reason I'd done it was because she had demanded the assault. I thought it prudent to let that remain unspoken.

"Jennifer, one of those girls could have positively ID'd the terrorist. That's why we went. Just like we did today, in case you have forgotten. We just hit a house we thought was holding your brother, but he wasn't there. I'm sure there were a few girls out the night we hit the house, and we didn't go running around the countryside chasing them."

"Because the girl with the knowledge *was* there. If she hadn't been, you might have chased her down."

I said, "Jennifer, please . . . don't make this hard. You know I'm correct here. Don't make me play team leader."

She took my hand and said, "I don't want my team leader. He's kind of an asshole. I want my Pike back."

Damn it. Unfair.

"Jennifer, listen, if we're stood down tomorrow, that's the end of it. They'll take the aircraft and head home and there's nothing I can do about it. I can't call a Prairie Fire for your brother."

She held my eyes. "I'm not asking them. I'm asking you. If they fly home, we stay and find my brother. Just the *real* Grolier Recovery Services. That's all I want."

She stared into my soul, waiting for an answer I knew damn well I couldn't give, but my resistance was eroding just from her presence. I was beginning to wonder if I'd lost the ability to control my own fate. If somehow she'd planted a chip in my head and had a remote control in her purse.

She was the exact opposite of me, always following the rules and chastising me for bending them—or breaking them outright. Now she was begging to do exactly that. I should have found it a relief, like I was rubbing off on her, but I didn't. All I felt was a loss of control. Well, my conscious brain did anyway. My subconscious was another matter entirely, and it apparently held more sway.

"Okay. Damn it, okay. We'll find your brother."

She smiled. "That wasn't so hard, now, was it?" She kissed me, then moved to the bed.

I said, "What, *now* you want to stay?"

She propped a pillow under her head and lay down. "I always want to stay when Pike's in the room. That asshole team leader is a different story."

Christ. She drives me batshit.

She leaned to face me and smiled. "You going to sleep on the floor tonight?"

The comment meant more than the words alone. It was something she'd said a long time ago, in Bosnia, when we were both being hunted and she didn't trust me as far as she could throw me. Whatever remote control she had was obviously tied to her mouth.

I thought about saying the exact same thing I had in Bosnia, then curling up with a pillow next to the bathroom. Well, for a nanosecond anyway. I'm not *that* stupid.

We'd gotten a hell of a lot less sleep than we should have and then had to wake up extra early to allow her to execute her little walk of shame back to her room before the team showed up. I felt like I was in high school, but she insisted. I guess it would have been a little awkward with her being the "first" to arrive while wearing the same clothes she'd had on yesterday, her hair looking like she'd just awakened.

As it was, Knuckles was the first in, knocking on my door a mere two minutes after Jennifer had left. He took one look at me and shook his head.

What, is it painted on my face?

I said, "You're getting here a little early, aren't you? I was going to sleep in, glad I didn't."

He rolled his eyes, pushed past me, and said, "Shut up. I saw her get in the elevator."

I said, "Who?"

Before he could answer, another Johnny Eager Beaver knocked on my door. I let in Decoy, and the conversation was dead. Thirty minutes later, everyone had arrived but Jennifer. When she entered, Knuckles caught her eye and gave a theatrical scowl. She winked at him, just to rub his face in it, I suppose.

Oh, man. His scowl turned real. I glared at her, then got the room's attention. I brought them up to speed, telling them about the VPN last night and the potential for future operations, which, given the current state of affairs, wasn't that great.

They broke for breakfast and I waited with dread for the morning VPN with Kurt. Honestly, I didn't see how I was going to access the BMW data if Kurt told the team to stand down. I might be able to do it from DC, but Mexico was a different kettle of fish. The hacking cell activities were taken about as seriously as an actual hit, and getting them to work unauthorized would take some creative skill. Skill that might get me kicked out of the Taskforce for good.

The VPN initiated, and I found out how quickly things could change overnight, along with a reminder that I should watch the news while on operations. A horrific airline crash due to some GPS blip had caused the Oversight Council to switch into full-alert mode, and we were given carte blanche to find Jennifer's brother. Kurt and I both agreed that it wasn't going to do anything against whatever threat was out there, but it sure made me happy. I could have my cake and eat it too.

Six hours later, I was sitting with Jennifer outside the Santa Muerte cult of death church, and the blue marble marking the BMW was blinking steadily inside Tepito. The *narco* hadn't gutted the system from his car, and the Taskforce penetration had worked. BMW Assist was giving us great assistance.

We'd downloaded the BMW app to our phones, plugged in the user name and password, and voilà—we were tracking the car. It was all I could do not to access the system, get the car on the line, and shock the hell out of whoever was in it by saying, "BMW, how can I assist you in selling cocaine?" *That* would have been good theater.

Instead, I'd sent in Knuckles and Blood for some dismounted reconnaissance, with Decoy on a leash as backup in a sedan. I picked the recce team with a purpose, given what we had to work with. Jennifer was usually perfect for this kind of thing, because nobody expected a woman, but in this case, with the homogeneous nature of the barrio, she'd stand out.

Knuckles had black hair that he always wore long, like a hippie. Blood was African-American, and while he wouldn't exactly fade into the landscape, he had a better shot than Jennifer or me. With a two-day growth of beard and some ratty clothes, both looked like they belonged in Tepito. Which was fine for a recce, wandering around like they were looking to offload a shipment of bootleg CDs.

What we would do once we found the target was another story entirely.

44

Blood came on the radio. "This market is very tight. Not a good place for an assault. It's packed with people."

I looked at the map on my phone, getting a fix on both their positions in relation to the BMW's blue marble. "Don't start thinking assault just yet. Develop the situation. You still have a couple of blocks to go. Maybe it'll thin out."

Jennifer gave me a look, chomping at the bit. Off the radio, I said, "Calm down. You don't want your brother killed in a cross fire by a bunch of Mexican banditos who are reacting to our actions. Let's get eyes on. Might be better to wait for the BMW to move. Get it in a more favorable location."

"But my brother may no longer be with it."

"Have some patience. We don't know anything yet."

The radio came to life, with Blood giving me his opinion of my recce plan. "Who the hell thought I'd blend in here? I don't think these people have ever seen a black man. Everybody I bump into looks like they want to kick my ass. And it's really crowded, so I'm bumping into a lot."

"That's just the neighborhood. Don't aggravate anyone. Maybe buy some fake Nike basketball shoes. Make 'em all happy."

"I'm five-seven. I don't play basketball, you stereotyping asshole."

"Then buy a sombrero. Just don't get anyone mad. Break-break. Knuckles, what's your status?"

"About the same as Blood. Everyone eye-fucking me like they want to fight."

"From what I'm seeing, you're closest. Looks like the marble is about a hundred meters south, down an alley to the east."

"Roger."

"Decoy, what's your location?"

"I'm staged on a north-south thoroughfare near the Tepito metro stop, but, Pike, I can't do shit with the vehicle. There's no way to get it through the market with any time to react."

"Roger all. Just hold tight. They'll be coming to you if things go bad."

As soon as I said it, things began to go bad.

"Pike, this is Knuckles. I tried to make the turn into the alley and I've been stopped. Three guys jabbering in Spanish at me. I can see the nose of the BMW inside a roll-up door about seventy meters away."

"Okay, back off. Let it go. Blood's going to try from the other end."

I heard shouting in the background, then, "Crowd's

gathering. I'm about to be sacrificed to Santa Muerte. I don't think they like me shopping here."

"Can you get to Decoy at the metro?"

"No. It's through them."

"Overtly hostile?"

"Naw. Not yet. Just apparently want to pick on a gringo."

"Roger all. Forget the car. Exfil the way you came in. Decoy, you copy? Circle around to the north of the market and go dismounted. Help him break contact. Throw money around if you have to."

Blood came on. "Pike, I'm at the corner on the other side. I can see a group of men inside the roll-up door with the car. Believe it or not, most look Asian, but there's one guy who looks like Satan with a bald head, and two are definitely Caucasians."

Jennifer exclaimed, "Jack! That's Jack. Come on!"

Before I could stop her, she was out of the car and sprinting across Eje 1 Norte, disappearing into the Tepito marketplace.

I shouted out the open window for her to stop, but it did no good. I leapt out of the car myself, running through the traffic and into the barrio, giving orders on the radio. "Blood, lock down that exit. Don't let them get out the east end. Knuckles, Jennifer's headed right to you. Hold your ground as best you can without getting into a fight. Decoy, close on Knuckles."

I entered the market and was immediately stymied by

the mass of people. An alley about five feet wide lined on both sides with multicolored plastic tarps, it was jammed with a moving anthill of people, all buying, selling, or just hanging out, with the air swirling with a myriad of spices from outdoor taco vendors.

I was slowed to a fast walk, bumping through the crowd like a pinball and getting glares from men who looked like they'd shown up directly from the central casting of a spaghetti western. At least by their faces, because I don't remember any spaghetti western with characters sporting Adidas T-shirts and tattoos, but make no mistake, they all looked like hard men. I saw no sign of Jennifer. Either everyone was getting out of her way because she was a woman, or she'd already been dragged down an alley somewhere.

I keyed my mike again. "Koko, this is Pike. Status."

Jennifer said, "Closing in on Knuckles's position."

Damn. She is flying through this place.

"Do not, I say again, *do not* engage until we can develop a plan. Link up with Knuckles and wait on me. Acknowledge."

I heard nothing but couldn't be sure it wasn't because I was barreling over a guy selling some sort of food on a cart. He cursed me and I said again, "Koko, acknowledge."

"Pike, I see Knuckles. I'm on Knuckles now. Break-break. Knuckles, where's the car?"

Knuckles said, "Koko, stand by. Pike, I got eyes on her, but we got another problem."

I squeezed between two vendors, shaking my head when one began waving scarves in my face. "What?"

"There's a group of Asians coming out of the alley that has the BMW. I think they saw the crowd of banditos forming up and didn't like it. The good news is the banditos quit messing with me. The bad news is the Asian guys are now focused on them, and it looks like they're working into a fight."

Jennifer said, "I see them. They're Korean. Korean Mafia. They own a ton of warehouses around here. The car is probably in a Korean property, and they're protecting their turf."

How the hell does she always know this stuff?

"Jennifer, hold what you got. Decoy, what's your distance?"

"I'm there. I can see Knuckles. Coming in at his six."

"Okay, listen up—"

"Gun. Bandito pulled a gun."

Here we go.

"Everyone down. Get out of the fight. Blood, what's your status?"

"East end is fine. I'm eating a taco. Guess they don't have an issue with a black man after all."

"Can you still see the gringos?"

"No, but they never exited the roll-up. They're still inside."

A gunshot split the air no more than thirty meters from me. People started screaming, running in all directions.

Then the shooting started in earnest. I jammed against a wall and said, "Knuckles, what the fuck is going on?"

"Gunfight at the O.K. Corral. Or the Kimchi Corral. You pick."

"Get down the alley. Get to the car."

"I can't from this side. I'll have to penetrate the cross fire."

Jennifer said, "This is Koko. I got it. I'm on the near side. I'm going in."

"No! You stay put, I'm on the way."

Knuckles said, "She's the only one who can get there."

I reentered the flow of people fleeing the market, not wanting to say it, but I did. "Koko, move."

Working upstream, I reached the intersection in time to see Jennifer turn the corner to the alley, running in the middle of a group of women escaping the gunfire. I caught a glimpse of a Glock in her hand, and I knew she was about to commit to a shooting war to save her brother. And all I could do was back her up.

"Blood, get down the alley. Enter the building."

"Roger. By myself?"

"Koko's on the way and I'm right behind her."

I heard him say, "Good to go," just as I rounded the corner. The roll-up door with the BMW was much, much closer to my side of the alley than his. Even so, we reached it at the same time. He might not have played basketball, but Blood could run like a damn cheetah.

We entered with pistols drawn, seeing nothing. I heard a door slam at the top of a flight of stairs and we both began running up them. We entered a small apartment with only a couch and a table. At the back was an open sliding door to a makeshift balcony, the curtains flowing in from the wind and the roof to the next building just below it. Jennifer was nowhere to be seen. I was running to the balcony when a Korean appeared out of a side room carrying an AK-47. He raised his weapon and Blood drilled him twice in the chest, throwing him to the ground.

I saw a flash of someone jumping a roof fifty feet away and recognized Jennifer's hair blowing in the wind. I wanted to chase after her dumb ass but knew I couldn't leave the area uncleared. Blood was outside the door to the only other room and I ran to him, squeezing his shoulder.

We entered to find the space empty, losing precious seconds.

45

We sprinted to the balcony, me screaming into the radio, "Koko, Koko, stop what you're doing. Do not go any deeper into the barrio."

"Pike, I've got my brother in sight! He's being pushed forward by a bald guy who looks like the devil."

Christ. I knew it would do no good trying to get her to stop. Which left me running after her. I tossed the key fob for the BMW to Blood and said, "Get that car out and shadow us north."

"What are you going to do?"

"Chase her crazy ass."

I gave a SITREP on the radio, getting everyone moving north, the dismounts going to Decoy's vehicle and Blood inside the BMW, paralleling my line of march, then took off out the balcony, jumping roof to roof.

One building over I saw Jennifer behind some concrete bricks, trading shots with someone on the other side. I jumped the gap and slid in behind her while she was in the process of reloading. She freaked out at my sudden appearance, trying to take my head off. I blocked the strike and slammed her against the brick.

I said, "What part of 'stop what you're doing' do you *not* understand?"

"Pike, my brother is on the next roof. I saw him. He's with the guy shooting back."

I peeked over the wall and saw three men running.

Shit.

I said, "Cover me. Do not move until I'm covering you. Do you understand?"

She nodded and I leapt up, giving chase. I reached the next building and jumped over the small gap, landing in another makeshift terrace with an old couple looking like they were enjoying the excitement and ignoring the fact that bullets were flying. I vaulted over a low wall, crashed through a clothesline, and heard a shot snap past my head.

I flattened behind the cinder blocks and heard Jennifer return fire, hoping she was taking the time to aim. I pulled up, getting my pistol over the brick and centering my sight post, seeing one man with a gun flanked by two men crouching with their hands over their heads. I radioed, "Jennifer, move."

The distance was way outside the envelope for a surgical shot from a handgun, but all I wanted to do was get him to quit shooting back. He cracked a bullet our way and I held high to compensate for the drop of the .45-caliber slug. The round impacted the brick right next to his head, smacking him with spall. He recoiled from the spray of brick, then kicked the other two men. They jumped to the next building.

Jennifer went by me without slowing down, leaping from cinder block to tin roof, closing the gap. I jumped up as well, falling in behind her. She cleared the next building, falling onto the same roof as the men, the drop causing her to roll on the tar-covered concrete. As the gunman raised his pistol, I took a knee and fired a double tap that went wide. He squeezed the trigger at the same time and the man to his left slammed into his arms, throwing the shot into space.

The gunman screamed and turned the pistol onto Jennifer's savior. The man backed up with his hands out, shouting something I couldn't understand. He reached the edge of the building and fell backward just as the pistol went off.

Jennifer screamed, racing to the edge while firing at the gunman with an off-hand hold. He ducked, kicking the final man in the ass as Jennifer's rounds pinged the cinder block around him, and they jumped to the next roof. Jennifer looked down to the street, holstered her pistol, and flung herself over the parapet. The last thing I saw was her hands on the ledge; then they disappeared.

I leapt across, saw the gunman fleeing with the final man, and let him go. I raced to the edge and leaned over. Seven feet below me was a balcony, with Jennifer holding Jack in her arms, putting pressure on a shoulder wound that had already coated his shirt with blood.

I dropped to the balcony, seeing a horrified family inside, all cowering on the couch. I showed my pistol and shook my head at them, then went to Jennifer.

She said, "He's hit bad. He's hit bad. He's bleeding out."

I moved her hand and smiled for the first time. Yeah, he was hit, but it wasn't bad. Well, not bad as far as gunshots go. He'd have more danger from infection at the hospital than the wound itself.

I said, "Keep up pressure," then keyed my radio, vectoring in everyone to my position. "Jackpot. I say again, jackpot. Need exfil and I don't know my exact position. Somewhere north of the market right next to Trabajo Avenue. Need medical ASAP. Precious cargo is wounded."

Decoy came on. "I got your position on the phone. I'm north, headed your way."

"Who do you have with you?"

"Me and Knuckles."

"Need more room. Blood, status?"

"Coming in hot right now. BMW seems to get everyone out of the way. Be there in thirty seconds."

Five minutes later we were on the street with a crowd of people starting to circle. I shouted at Blood, "How much money you got?"

He said, "Not enough to get these guys to quit, but we have a couple of garbage bags in the back we need to dump for space anyway. They're full of watches and shit."

I pulled them out, surveying the crowd. One man was

in front of the others, holding a rusty crowbar and looking like a badass. I walked up to him and said, "Let it go."

Of course, he didn't speak a lick of English. He raised the crowbar and I dumped the bag in front of him. When the watches, rings, and other bling spilled around his feet, he lowered his weapon, looking confused.

I swept my hand above the loot and said, "All yours."

Once I tossed the other bag on the ground, they started jostling with one another, and we were on the way to a hospital with Jack bleeding all over the red leather seats and Jennifer hyperventilating over his wounds.

His eyes fluttered open for a moment, and he gained consciousness and tried to sit up. Jennifer stopped him, cooing. When he recognized her voice, he slurred, "Jennifer? Are you dead too?"

She laughed for the first time and said, "No. And neither are you."

He leaned back and said, "What are you doing here? Did Mom send you?"

She smiled. "Yes. Mom sent me. Along with some friends."

He chuckled, then grimaced from the pain it caused. "Friends, huh? Who on earth did you convince to come down here to this hellhole?"

"Some people who don't mind a little trouble." She caught my eye and smiled. "Someone who does what's right."

He closed his eyes and said, "Does what's right . . . I knew that would make a difference."

She said, "What's that mean?"

He didn't answer and she let it go.

She held his hand and leaned forward, saying, "Thank you, guys. Thank you for doing this. I owe you big-time."

Blood said, "You don't owe me shit. I get a paycheck."

Now that we were relatively safe, I let my anger spill out over her activities in the last hour. I said, "Blood may not care, but you sure as hell owe *me*. Jesus, you ignore every single order I give, running into a Korean Mafia house and slinging lead with no backup whatsoever. What the hell were you thinking?"

Blood said, "Hey, cut her some slack. She was rescuing the PC. You'd do the same in her shoes."

"I would *not*. No way would I do something that stupid."

His face split into the same smile he always used when he knew he was right, a disarming bit of trickery he'd learned at the agency. "You do that all the damn time. The only difference is the person you're ignoring is a continent away."

I harrumphed, then saw Jennifer returning Blood's smile with one of her own. So damn proud she'd ignored me. I tried to maintain my anger, but it was a lost cause. Her actions had saved her brother, after all. He'd have been gone for good if she hadn't raced off on her own, and being mad about her actions was a little selfish. I certainly couldn't argue with success, and whenever I'd done something like she had, I didn't smile because I was proud of ignoring the command. I smiled because I'd succeeded in the mission, which was something I was always throwing in Kurt Hale's face.

Now it was being thrown into mine.

I poked one more time, because I didn't like being treated like the damn command I always flouted. "Well, I'm glad we got your brother, but let's hope he can do something against the threat. You were sure he was the Holy Grail, and apparently so was the Oversight Council."

Jennifer got a little truculent at that. "I *am* sure he can, but this mission isn't a failure if he can't. Is it? Do you think that?"

She was staring daggers at me, and I heard the unspoken end of her words: *Do* you *think that, or does the asshole team leader?* I saw Blood catch the look in the rearview, a question on his face, wondering. Someone else reading the tea leaves like Knuckles. Seeing things beyond a simple team member–team leader relationship. I honestly hated how smart these bastards were. Nothing got past them for long.

I backtracked and said, "No, of course not. I just meant I hope he's got some useful information. That's all."

Blood said, "Check in your foot well. I gave the car a cursory once-over for bad shit, found the goody bags in back and something else."

"What?" I started rooting underneath my seat. "What did you find?"

"A digital video recorder and a directional microphone. No idea what's on it."

I pulled it out, put the headphones on my ears, and started listening. Jennifer saw my eyes squint and said, "What is it?"

I held a finger in the air and said, "Shhh." I listened a little bit more, then turned around, seeing Jack unconscious in the back, Jennifer keeping pressure on his wound. She waited. I continued listening until she couldn't take it. She said, "Damn it, what are you hearing?"

I pulled the headset off and said, "I take back everything I just said about your jackass maneuver."

"What?"

"Your brother just bought us a ticket to the dance."

46

The *sicario* finished taping Booth's ankles to the metal rod he'd broken from the towel rack, pinning them to the bar. He pulled the feet until they hung over the bathtub, then taped the bar to the ceramic edge. Now stretched out like a calf for slaughter, his hands chained to a cast-iron pipe that jutted out from under the sink, Booth began to writhe up and down, but he'd waited too long. His eyes wild, he grunted through the gag in his mouth, only growing still when the *sicario* turned to face him, a demonic vision that caused instant compliance.

"You understand the reason I have you like this, correct?"

Booth shook his head violently side to side.

"I want to know who those men were who chased us. What they represent. I don't expect you to tell me the truth right away, but you will. Everyone does when I start peeling the soles of the feet. It's very, very painful."

The *sicario* pointed to a bottle of bleach on the

counter. "I prefer the bathtub because it's much easier to clean. The bleach flushes all traces of blood down the drain, but I'm told it burns like fire on open wounds."

A low moan escaped Booth's throat, barely penetrating the rag stuffed in his mouth. The *sicario* jerked it out and said, "Well?"

"I have no idea! Please, dear God, I don't know. Why would I? I'm from America! Maybe they're friends of Carlos! You killed him. Not me."

"If that's true, then there was no reason to bring you here. I should have left you dead like the other man on the roof."

After shooting their way clear of the team following them, the *sicario* had dragged Booth down a rickety flight of metal stairs to a balcony and pushed him through into a shabby apartment. The family inside never even saw the pistol in his hand. They took one look at his visage and disappeared into another room.

They reached the street unmolested. The *sicario* jabbed Booth in the kidney with the barrel of his weapon, pushing him back into the crowded market. Burrowing through the mass of people, they left the street vendors behind and entered a warehouse district. The *sicario* saw two men carrying a pallet toward a dingy, beat-up van and waited until they'd finished loading. When one moved to the driver's door, he approached and did nothing more than show his pistol. The men fled, running down the street toward the market. He'd thrown Booth in the back, spending a minute tying his hands with loose cord. Satisfied Booth couldn't interfere, he'd driven to a run-down hotel five miles away.

While he weaved through the traffic, the gunfight had spun relentlessly in his head, rattling around like a loose marble in a can. Initially, when the shooting started, he'd thought it was a setup by the Koreans, but they'd allowed him to leave without incident, instead sending men to the gunfire in the market. They'd also seemed genuinely pleased at the car he'd brought, along with the loot.

That meant it was someone from Sinaloa or Los Zetas, but the man and woman on the roof were gringos, and the woman could *shoot*. The people chasing him had skill. They had reminded him of his Special Forces unit in Guatemala, one calmly firing while another moved under protection. He'd never seen such a thing with the brutish killers employed by Sinaloa and instinctively knew there was no way it was a cartel. It was something else.

Which left the fat gringo taped to the bathtub.

The *sicario* said, "You gave me the answer I expected. All that remains is to see how much I peel before you tell me the truth."

He pulled a folding straight razor from his pocket and opened it, watching for a reaction. His captive saw the blade and began trembling as if he were having a seizure, causing the chain on his hands to rattle against the pipe. He fixated on the blade; then his eyes rolled back in his head and his body grew still.

The *sicario* sat back and tapped the razor against his palm, considering. While he had no compunction about mutilating the man, such work was tiring and messy, and should be done only with a purpose in mind. He knew the power torture held and had used it many times to elicit confessions. In this case, he needed real information, and the time and trouble of the work had to be measured against what he would gain. The gringo clearly had never been in any bit of danger in his entire soft life. The sight of the blade alone caused him to pass out, like a woman seeing blood.

But that may mean nothing.

He stuffed the rag back into Booth's mouth, then filled a glass with water and splashed it into his face. When Booth awoke, he rolled left and right as if he was confused, then saw the *sicario* standing over him. He began to shriek through the gag. The *sicario* raised his finger to his lips, and Booth went silent. The *sicario* removed the rag.

"You ready to tell me what I want to know?"

Booth began crying, weeping so hard his lungs starting hitching, the tears mixing with his sweat and the phlegm rolling from his nose. He choked out, "All I came here to do was to give up the POLARIS protocol. I don't know anything about what's going on between your cartels. I don't know who those people shooting at us were. I met Carlos in Colorado. He was supposed to pay me money if I gave him the protocol, but you killed him. You can have it. You take it. Just let me go."

The *sicario* gazed down at the blubbering mass of humanity and decided he was telling the truth. He'd heard what Carlos had discussed with the three men from the airport. He knew Carlos was trying to sell what this man was bringing. Whatever it was, it had nothing to do with drugs, which raised doubt in his mind that the man and woman who chased them were working with Booth.

Why would the US government set up some elaborate sting in Mexico for something that had none of the trappings of the drug trade? No guns, no precursor chemicals, no transfer of aircraft or boats, and certainly no actual drugs. Just some weird protocol that was worth money to foreigners. It was too complex a trap even for the Americans, and this man was clearly way out of his league. He didn't even pretend to know a script to recite.

It didn't answer the question about the team who had chased them, but ultimately that didn't matter. Time was all that counted now. The quicker he began his run to America, the better. He had captured Booth for the cash he represented, but in so doing he had somehow drawn the focus of another group. Leaving behind all of this as soon as he could gave him his surest chance of survival, even without any money. It was too bad for Booth, but at least the *sicario* would now make it painless. If anything, Booth should have felt thankful that he didn't experience the flaying of his feet before he died.

The *sicario* peeled the tape from the bathtub, leaving Booth's ankles trapped on the towel rod, then unlocked his hands from the sink pipe, cinching the handcuffs behind Booth's back once he was done. Booth did nothing to resist, simply staring at the *sicario* with wide eyes. He rotated the body around and hoisted him into the tub, grunting with the exertion of getting Booth's pudgy carcass over the edge.

He dropped Booth on his back in the tub, his head against the far side and his legs bent at the knees, his feet hanging over the edge and touching the tile of the bathroom floor. The *sicario* moved his head until it was resting near the drain, then raised the straight razor. Booth began grunting through the gag, twisting his head side to side.

The *sicario* hesitated, then pulled the rag from his mouth, a string of drool trailing from the cloth to his lip.

"You have something you wish to tell me?"

"Yes! Yes! Please don't do this. I came because Carlos asked. I understand he was your enemy, but that doesn't make me the same. Please. You kill me and you lose the POLARIS protocol. My laptop is encrypted. I am the only one who can work it."

The *sicario* gazed at his beast for slaughter, considering, then grabbed the hair of the head and twisted until the neck was exposed. Booth began shrieking, "You wanted money from the BMW, but you didn't get it. Sell the protocol! Sell it! You kill me and you're killing more money than you would *ever* have!"

The *sicario* paused again. The sacrificial lamb was only trying to save his miserable life, but what he said was true. He'd lost all money for the journey north with the interrupted transfer of the BMW and other trinkets he'd taken from the Zetas house. The only things he had were the two bundles of bills from the office, and that would last about a month, provided he lived frugally. He'd heard Carlos talking about a great deal of cash for the purchase of the protocol. Maybe a day or two to investigate would be worth it, even with the mysterious team on the loose.

"Where is this transfer? How was Carlos going to sell it?"

Booth's eyes grew wet, and his head lolled to the side in defeat. "I don't know. Please, I don't know. All I did was bring the protocol. Carlos was supposed to pay me outright, but you killed him. He was going to sell it to someone else, but he knew all that, and he's dead. Please, please, don't kill me. I don't *know*. . . ."

Waste of time. But the *sicario* hesitated still. He had hunted men who had taken great care to survive, and he had always proven the precautions they took were worthless. He had been given hard targets with nothing more to go on than a photograph and had brought the head home dripping from the neck. All of those men had been Mexican. People who understood the terrain and how to hide. People who knew they *needed* to hide. Not like the three foreigners. He had a great deal of information from the meeting with Carlos, and he knew he could find them again.

The *sicario* put away his razor. "You will show me how to work this protocol. You will give me the keys to unlock it. Understand?"

Booth nodded over and over again. "Yes, of course. It's all yours. I'll show you everything about it . . . then you'll let me go?"

"Perhaps. But, to maintain our relationship of honesty, I'll most likely kill you tomorrow."

47

Kurt said, "We're going to need the entire council for a decision. I've got a thread to work, but it's unorthodox, to say the least."

Alexander Palmer said, "Look, give us what you have and I'll determine if it's worth bringing the president and everyone else back into a room."

Kurt had already sent a report on the safe rescue of Jack, along with a preliminary analysis of what he knew. Since then, Pike had done a thorough debrief and the Taskforce had translated what was on the digital recorder that Jack's kidnapper had taken.

Kurt said, "Here's what I know right now: Jack went with the kidnapper—we're calling him Baldy—on two separate occasions to the Mexico City international airport. His purpose was to identify a Caucasian man who was bringing some software package down to Mexico to sell to the Sinaloa cartel. Both times he was unable to complete the identification. On the second visit, Jack's original kidnapper—a man named Carlos—showed up at the airport and met three men. When the Caucasian smuggler didn't show for reasons unknown, Baldy decided to follow Carlos and recorded a meeting in a park with the three unknown subjects. They discussed something called the POLARIS protocol, which is apparently an undetermined method to defeat our GPS constellation. Some time later Baldy took Jack back to the airport, where he was able to identify the Caucasian smuggler. Baldy followed him to a meeting with Carlos, where he was apparently going to transfer the protocol. Baldy interrupted the meeting, killed Carlos, and took the Caucasian with the protocol. Pike managed to track their location and rescue Jack, but lost Baldy and the man with the protocol. These are the facts that we know right now."

The director of the CIA said, "So it's a real thing? Someone has the ability to interdict our GPS constellation?"

"Yes, apparently. Unfortunately, he's still loose in Mexico, in the hands of the Zetas drug cartel, either willingly or as a captive."

"Who were the three men Carlos met in the park? Who's trying to get it? Another drug cartel?"

Kurt shook his head. "No. It's much worse than that."

The secretary of defense leaned back and rubbed his face, saying, "I don't think I want to hear this."

Kurt said, "I guarantee you don't. Baldy took a recording of the meeting with Carlos using a directional microphone, and it came in crystal clear. Most of the conversation is in English, discussing monetary terms for transfer. Sometime during the meeting, Carlos left and the three men began discussing the purchase of the protocol. In Arabic."

The D/CIA said, "Are you telling me it's the Hezbollah crew? They're tied into this?"

"I can't confirm one way or the other, but the Arabic translation indicates that, yes, they're working for Hezbollah. They discuss bringing another man in. A money guy, and they talk about him as if he's from a different organization. They say he's coming from Waziristan, Pakistan, which indicates al-Qaeda. Because they mention the organization being different from theirs, it means they *aren't* al-Qaeda. Which, understandably, could mean a hundred other Arabic terrorist organizations, but given the Hezbollah team movement the CIA tracked, I'm betting it's them."

The SECDEF exclaimed, "Are you saying we have a Hezbollah crew that's working *with* al-Qaeda? And they're both going to get this protocol?"

"Whoa," said Palmer, "Hezbollah is Shiite. AQ is Sunni. Why would they cooperate? They're on the opposite sides of the fight in Syria, so why would they be on the same side here?"

Kurt said, "Well, they *have* cooperated in the past, but in this case, it looks like the usual animosity is still in play. Apparently, the guy coming is a moneyman for AQ, and he thinks he's getting the protocol for use against our drones in Pakistan. Hezbollah wants his bankroll, but on the tape they talk about using him to buy the protocol, then killing him because they want to keep the protocol for themselves. They know we'll figure out how to defeat it given enough time, and they don't want some back-woods Taliban bullshit triggering it too early. They want it for their Iranian masters in case we strike them. To give them an edge in the fight."

The principals committee sat in stunned silence for a moment, then began talking among themselves, ignoring Kurt, the chatter rising as the implications settled in. The secretary of defense, arguing with the secretary of state, finally exclaimed, "You don't get it! It gives them more than an edge. It'll even up the fight at any time. They don't have the reliance on GPS that we do. Our systems depend on it, and losing it means much more to us than them. It'll put our force back to Vietnam. Maybe worse, because we've ditched all the Vietnam-era equipment."

The secretary of state said, "But surely we can find it. Get rid of it like a computer virus at home. Right? I mean, we know it's there now."

"I hope we can. But hope is not a method. It's just that: hope. We don't know how it works, so we're having trouble finding it. Boeing and Second SOPS have been going around the clock since this started and found noth-ing. The software upgrades are all clean. Nothing's stand-ing out, and we might have to wait until it's triggered to find out how it works. Because of that, we'll have to take the damn thing into account for any military operation. Prepare for not being able to access GPS in every OPLAN we have."

The D/CIA said, "Operation Gimlet. What do we do

about that? We only get one shot, and if the GPS is disrupted, it won't work."

Kurt said, "What's Gimlet?"

Palmer held up his hand. "Nothing. Not Taskforce business."

"Screw it," said the SECDEF, "read him on. He deserves to know what's at stake."

Palmer looked at the D/CIA, who nodded. He said, "We have an asset deep in the Syrian army. He's tasked with placing a beacon on the chemical-weapons stockpiles hidden around the country. Gimlet is the operation to take them out. We need to have precise locational data because some of the munitions are hidden in urban areas. Others are in hardened underground bunkers, requiring a precision strike with massive ordnance."

Jesus. So that's why they were pushing so hard. Why they're willing to risk the cover. Hezbollah gets POLARIS, and Gimlet ends up in disaster. Kurt said, "What's the timeline?"

"Most of the beacons are in place. The asset is conducting a tour of the facilities and has two left. The problem is the beacons only have a battery life of five days, and the asset will not get the ability to execute a second time. We don't even know if the munitions will be in the same place a week from now. We're set to execute in forty-eight hours, right before the beacons begin shutting down, but without GPS we're not going to be able to. We can't afford to end up slaughtering a bunch of civilians, or worse, only incinerating half of a target and releasing the other half of the nerve gas on the population."

What a mess. But it makes this sell a little easier.

Palmer said, "So, now you know. We've got a critical operation in play, and it's time sensitive. What's your next step? Do you have anything on Baldy or the Hezbollah guys?"

Kurt said, "No. Nothing. No phone numbers, locations, or anything else, and Mexico City is one of the biggest cities on earth. We could spend ten years there and get nowhere without a lead."

"So you're saying we're screwed? All this time spent on building the capability, all this effort developing a super-secret surgical strike force, and we're now helpless?"

"No. That's not what I'm saying. Pike has an idea, but it's pretty extreme. Like I said, we're going to need the full council for this decision."

"Well, spit it out. I'll determine if the president calls a council meeting."

"Okay," Kurt said. "The potential killing of the AQ courier is an edge for us. We know the name he's using from the recording, which means we can locate him when he flies and take him out."

"What good will that do? He doesn't have the protocol. The Hezbollah guys will still get it."

"You remember the Ghost? The terrorist we captured in Dubai?"

"The guy who tried to kill our Middle East envoy?"

"Yeah. Pike thinks we can use him. Get him involved to help us."

"What? How the hell can he help? Isn't he in the Cloud?"

"Yeah, he is. Pike wants to take out the AQ courier and inject the Ghost. Have him go to the meeting with Baldy and the Hezbollah guys. They've never met, so they won't know the difference, and the Ghost can talk terrorism like a master. He can lead us to the meeting; then we take them all out."

Kurt saw nothing but shock at the idea. Palmer said, "Are you saying you want to use a terrorist we captured to penetrate another terrorist cell?"

Kurt smiled. "Does this meet the criteria for a council meeting? Like I said, it's out of the box, but in my mind, it's the best chance we have. Unorthodox, I know. But that's it."

"How on earth are you going to get him to agree?"

"That'll be up to Pike."

48

The town was small, as American towns go. A square patch outlined by parallel streets and no buildings with more than two stories. Main Street was a throwback to quieter times, with bunting in the windows and every store a stand-alone family affair, sporting names like Cowboy Collectibles and the Blue Pine Motel.

Surrounded on all sides by great swaths of national forest, Panguitch, Utah, was like an island of Americana that someone forgot to tell to grow with the times. A town where everyone still waved when they drove by, whether they knew you or not, and the chosen vehicle was a pickup, preferably a four-by-four dually.

My kind of place, although the damn hybrid rental I was driving wasn't helping my reputation any.

I was a little shocked that the Oversight Council had given me the go-ahead for my plan. Okay, a lot shocked. They were usually a bunch of handwringers, and I would have thought a request to recruit a terrorist I'd previously captured would be dead on arrival, but they'd said yes.

I'd flown into the closest airport, located in Cedar

City, and driven about an hour, looping around the national forests on Interstate 15 and other back roads. Pulling into town, I'd checked into a roadside hotel and then set out to meet the county sheriff.

I'd never been to any of our Cloud locations before and was a little interested in how they worked. When we developed the Taskforce, we had one overarching problem: what to do with the guys we captured. Contrary to popular belief or what the news blabs, we don't set out to kill everyone. Capture is a much, much better option because it allows us to extract more information that leads to further dismantling of the terrorist threat. Allows us to start painting a picture of the network.

Too often, the intelligence community hears a name or a reference to something and doesn't know why it's important. But the terrorists do, so if you can get a thorough debriefing, you can start building the connections, then wait for some bit of chatter to spike interest. You hear the name Abu Bagodonuts, and while you'd otherwise have thrown it away or stored it for future reference, now you *have* the reference, and you know that ol' Bagodonuts is a passport forger or whatever, and you can start piecing together the puzzle of what they're trying to do.

The problem was that we operated outside official channels, so we couldn't very well march into a New York City courthouse and throw the terrorist on the floor, trussed up and whining, then fly out with a big S on our chests. So we'd come up with our own solution: the Cloud.

Camp X-Ray at Guantánamo Bay would seem to have

been the logical choice. I mean, according to the world press and jihadist propaganda, we capture and torture the shit out of terrorists there on a daily basis, without any oversight whatsoever, right? In reality, Gitmo is the most overwatched prison on earth, with a permanent international Red Cross office that has instant access to any and all detainees. Once you go there, you're pretty much treated like a king—at least as far as prisoners go—with soccer fields, prayer rugs, cable TV, and the ability to bitch about the food and get on a worldwide stage. Make no mistake, once someone's interned at Gitmo, there's little information coming out. The only talking the terrorists do at the prison is screaming about imaginary abuses to CNN.

In the early days we could have used a CIA black site in a foreign country, but that went by the wayside with press revelations about "secret prisons" and the enormous backlash from the countries who had agreed to work with us because we promised we could keep a secret. Which we couldn't.

We kicked around starting our own version, black site lite, as it were, but eventually decided that involving foreign governments was probably not the way to go, considering the Taskforce was illegal under our own laws. They'd want to know how we got the bad guys, which could expose the existence of the Taskforce and create a potential leak that we couldn't control. So, no new black sites.

Someone finally came up with the idea of using the terrorists' own techniques against them. While they were all separate entities and sometimes fought among themselves, Islamic radical groups were also interconnected and used those connections to further their goals. Know a guy you went to school with who now works in a bank? Get him to transfer some funds off the books. Have a buddy you met at a training camp from a country you want to enter? Get him to coordinate travel. It worked out very well for them, and it turned out we could do the same thing.

There are a plethora of special operations folks who have served and are now in the private sector, working in a host of legitimate roles, from schoolteacher to insurance salesman. Having risen to the cream of the crop, they all still held a deep patriotic bent and would help if asked, and so we did.

We reached out to a very select few who were now working in law enforcement. The idea was to hide the captured terrorists in plain sight, at a jail in the United States that was run by someone who held a security clearance and had worked in special operations. Someone who could stash the guy, allow interrogations, and ensure his health and welfare was taken care of while keeping it all under the good-ol'-boy hat.

And the Cloud was born.

The name was a play on cloud computing, whereby we'd remove the terrorist and his "data" from the real world and "store" them in a special place that nobody on the outside could see or touch, locked away from other prying eyes, accessible only by authorized members of the Taskforce. One of those locations was here.

The Garfield County sheriff's office was a few miles out of town, on a road that ran along the Panguitch creek. On the same property was the county jail, used pretty much exclusively for household domestic violence calls, drunk drivers, or, more dangerously, marijuana growers, who were staking their claim more and more to the surrounding national forest lands, playing cat and mouse with the Forest Service response teams.

The sheriff's name was Bob Marley, something I'm sure he hated now that the marijuana growers had started to move in. He had some history with special operations and had agreed to use his jail as a Cloud location, one of many sprinkled throughout the small towns of America. He was responsible for the man I wanted to see, but first I had to prove who I was.

I pulled my hamster-powered hybrid in front of a corner coffee shop that looked straight out of a Norman Rockwell painting, parking between a Jeep and a Ford F-250 pickup. I shut the door, getting some stares from two old guys sitting on a park bench out front. One said, "How well does that thing work when it snows?"

I passed by them and said, "Not so good, but the hamsters under the hood are trained to dig."

I entered the café without waiting on a response and glanced around. There was another pair of old guys sitting at the counter drinking coffee, a man and woman in a booth to my right, and in the back, a solo man with a laptop in front of him, facing the door. He was dressed in a plaid shirt, jeans, and a cowboy hat. I was expecting someone in uniform, making identification easy, but there was nobody here like that.

I walked up to the guy in back and he stood. I said, "Sheriff Marley?"

"Yep." He shook my hand and motioned to the opposite seat in the booth. After the waitress had come and gone, he said, "How can I help you?"

Feeling like I was in a *Mission: Impossible* movie, I slid across a thumb drive. He plugged it into the laptop, did some fiddling around on the keyboard, and waited, giving me a smile.

49

I couldn't see his screen but knew the thumb drive was conducting a sync with the laptop, each interrogating the other to make sure the ciphers matched. After a second, he leaned in and said, "Alpha Echo Seven Seven Seven."

I pulled out my phone and tethered it via Bluetooth to his computer, the access codes automatically locking on because of the thumb drive. The screen showed AE777 on one line and ZG502 on another. I said, "Zulu Golf Five Zero Two."

He smiled again and closed the laptop. "You don't look like an intel weenie."

I said, "Neither do you."

He laughed and said, "I'm just a small-town sheriff. You Army?"

"Yeah. Well, I was. Doing something different now. Like you."

"Something different, but nothing like me, I suspect. I was One Seven-Five, back in the day when I was a barrel-chested freedom fighter."

And I knew I was in like a tick on a hound dog, to use a phrase that seemed to fit in around here. One Seven-Five was First Battalion, Seventy-Fifth Infantry. A Ranger, like me.

I said, "No shit. I spent some time in Third Batt. Not as nice as Savannah, but I guess you didn't see much of that city while you were there anyway."

As expected, he immediately felt a bond, and I saw him relax. We of course spent the next few minutes playing the "You know Sergeant Humpty-Hump?" game, figuring out where we'd crossed paths. He didn't ask outright for everywhere I'd served, but he was smart. He peppered the name list with men who'd moved on to a different, more select unit. A special-mission unit I was also once in. It didn't take him long to confirm I wasn't an intelligence analyst.

Eventually we ran out of war stories, and he said, "What's an Operator doing here? I've had this guy for over a year, and the only people who've shown up might as well have been driving a hybrid car and wearing a lab coat."

I skipped telling him about my rental. "I'm not here to get information out of him. I might be moving him to another location, depending on what he says."

He nodded, not asking any more questions, knowing it wasn't his place to do so. He'd only been read on to his specific activities with the Cloud and had no knowledge at all of the Taskforce, but he was smart enough to be able to guess.

I said, "How many other guys in the Cloud do you have here? Will they know he's gone?"

"None. He's my first, and from what I know, they never put two in the same place."

Good thinking. It was weird getting a glimpse into part of the Taskforce that had been kept secret from me. Especially since I'd helped create the organization and was one of the Operators who fed the detainees into this system.

I said, "Can you give me some background on him before I go in? What's he like? How's he act?"

"He's not bad at all. Actually, he's pretty polite. Never gives us any trouble. His only request has been books. He reads constantly. Nothing like the drunks we usually deal with."

That gave me a little alarm. The terrorist was a Palestinian assassin from a refugee camp in Lebanon. He went by the name the Ghost, and he was very cunning. He'd come close to killing some of my team in Dubai using an ingenious heat-detonated improvised explosive device he'd created in about ten minutes using parts from a hardware store. He was a killer who had never registered on our radar, which meant he'd been very, very good. We weren't even sure if we had his actual name, since we'd found five attached to him. If he'd been here a year, he'd probably come up with some idea of how to escape.

"You realize his danger, though, right? This guy tried to kill the sheik of Dubai and the American envoy to the Middle East with an explosive device that cut the cables to an elevator. He is *smart.* I don't care how polite he is, treat him like Hannibal Lecter."

Bob held up his hands. "Yeah, yeah. Don't get me wrong. I'm glad he's not flinging shit through the bars or going on a hunger strike like I read about at Gitmo, but I treat him with the respect he deserves. Don't worry, when I was read on to the Cloud I was given my left and right limits. I'm out of the Army, but I still have some discipline." He took a sip of coffee and said, "Although when you see him, you might second-guess whether we have the right man. He's a scrawny little guy with Coke-bottle glasses that make him look like the kid who got bullied at school. Doesn't look like a master terrorist. But then again, neither did the ones I took out in Iraq. Don't worry, I get it."

I didn't want to let on that I was the one who'd captured him, because as far as the sheriff knew, he might have been taken off a flight by the TSA. It didn't sound like the Ghost had changed much, though. Although I guess he wasn't getting any time to hit the gym.

"Has he talked about Islam or thrown any propaganda at you when you dealt with him? Killing infidels or anything like that?"

Whether I continued would hinge on his answer. The Ghost was a killer, but he wasn't what I would call a radical jihadi. At the end of the day, he was a Palestinian nationalist who happened to be Muslim. He had no interest in a global caliphate or taking the war to the capitalist kafirs. His interest was the injustice he perceived had been committed against the Palestinian people. At least that was my take, and after reading the file of his extensive interviews, I knew it was also the take of the intelligence analysts. He, naturally, hated Israel and all it stood for, along with the United States for supporting that country, but he'd been screwed by Hezbollah as well, and I hoped to use that.

I wanted a second opinion, though. The Ghost might have fed the analysts whatever he thought would help him out, then dropped his guard around the prison personnel, letting something slip out about his true mental state.

Bob said, "No. Not really. Honestly, I haven't even seen him pray like the devout ones do. When he looks at you, you can tell he'd probably like to put a knife to your throat, but I don't think it's because of Islam. I'd be giving him the same looks if I were locked up in a secret prison. Like I said, he's pretty polite otherwise."

"Have you talked to him extensively? Engaged him in conversation while he's been here?"

"No. Not allowed to, beyond the normal day-to-day activities. The only ones allowed to engage him are guys like you who come in with a thumb drive."

Should have expected that.

"Look," Bob said, "I've only got a two-hour window when I can get you in and out without anyone else seeing. I don't think I'm going to be able to give you anything more than those analysts."

I nodded and stood, throwing enough money on the table to cover both of our coffee orders. "Let's go."

50

Alone in his cell, the prisoner wrote a verse in Arabic. He knew the men would come and take it, scrutinizing the words for some secret meaning, but they would never find his name threaded in the text. *Abdul Rahman*. Through repeated interviews they had gained much information from him, but they had yet to learn his true name. He kept it secret, a token of his resistance, and enjoyed hiding the name in innocuous text that they would study for hours. It was a small thing, but it allowed him the mental fortitude to continue.

They called him the Ghost, and had managed to connect him to several *kunyas* and aliases he had used in the past, but were frustrated by his true name. A frustration he enjoyed giving them.

The interviews had grown more and more infrequent, with the last one happening over a month ago. In truth, he missed them. Much to his surprise, he had never endured what he would consider torture; instead, the interrogations had become a match of wits. Initially, when he'd first arrived, the Americans had come in hard, threatening him with all manner of things and making his life miserable with various physically coercive techniques, but it got them nowhere, as there were very few men on earth with the willpower he possessed. He'd endured much worse in the past—true torture—and he'd survived intact.

About a month into his detention they'd shifted tactics, and he found himself slipping. He had followed his own strategy, sure of his intellect. Giving up information that he knew would be worthless or dribbling out a web of deceit that sounded accurate, he had been surprised when the interrogators had come back with a different picture, asking more questions. A picture that was accurate.

The men and women would talk to him for hours, tripping him up with his own lies and using insidious psychological techniques to reveal what he wished to keep secret. Realizing they were much, much smarter than they let on, he had begun to parse his words so he said nothing that they could use, yet they always managed to get something. The interviews had grown to be a challenge he looked forward to, but they came less and less frequently now.

As they had learned from him, he had gained a greater understanding of them. While he no longer underestimated their intelligence, their actual knowledge of his world caused him to laugh. It was like watching a child paint a picture of an animal he or she had never seen, based only on a description. The painting bore a resemblance but its errors were glaring.

In some cases, he helped them refine the picture, as

with Hezbollah. That group had used him for its own ends and had eventually tried to kill him. Ultimately, he wasn't sure if the reason he'd been captured wasn't because the group had betrayed him. He detested their arrogance and had no compunction about feeding the Americans what he knew. Hezbollah might have professed to be the resistance against Israel, but he'd seen up close that all they really wanted was their own political dominance in Lebanon, and they used the threat of Israel to maintain their massive armament. Israel's disappearing tomorrow was their worst fear, as they would lose their reason to exist.

In other cases he tried to dilute the picture even more, giving false information that would only confuse or conflict with intelligence they already knew, not wanting to enhance the Zionist dogs' ability to harm the Palestinian cause. Hamas, the Palestinian Islamic Jihad, Fatah, or any other group looking to push Israel into the sea was off-limits in his mind. He would protect them at all costs.

The one area that the interrogators actively pursued was al-Qaeda, wanting more information about them than anything else. Unfortunately for them, he'd honestly had little contact with that group and couldn't have provided much information even if he'd wanted to.

He wondered if that was the reason the interrogators had quit coming around. They'd realized he couldn't help them in their quest against al-Qaeda and thus left him to his lonely cell. Left him with nothing more than books and a chance to exercise once a week.

He missed the game. It was the only one he had, and he needed the stimulation. He understood that he would never be allowed to leave, would never have his freedom again, and that is what hurt him the most. He had considered suicide but had rejected it outright. It just wasn't his way. Instead, he'd turned to thoughts of escape, studying the prison routines and plotting.

The task was daunting to say the least. Getting out of the prison would be nearly impossible, but that was the easiest challenge he faced. He knew he was in the United States but had no idea exactly where and had no passport, money, or connections to facilitate escape. Fading into the background, like he would have done in his home country of Lebanon, would be impossible here. Even so, he enjoyed the mental challenge and had come up with a multitude of options, if the opportunity presented itself.

The light in his cell flicked off, then back on, signaling that someone was coming to visit. It startled him, since it had been so long since his last interrogation, and he was embarrassed at the excitement he felt. He put his back to the door and placed his hands through the slot, waiting to be cuffed, mentally preparing for the duel.

He felt the steel on his wrists and stepped forward, facing the mirror at the back of his cell. He saw it open, and was shocked at who came through it.

The man said not a word, waiting on the door to close again. As the echo of footfalls faded, he spoke. "Hello, Ash'abah."

The Ghost smiled at the Arabic butchering of his nickname but said nothing, staring at the man in the mirror to confirm. He didn't really remember the height or the color of his hair, but the blue eyes and the scar on his cheek were branded like acid on his brain. It was the man who had captured him.

"You can call me Mr. Pink. Have a seat."

The Ghost did so, turning around and sitting at his small table, remaining silent.

"You remember me, don't you?"

He spoke for the first time. "Yes. You're the man who stopped my attack. The man who brought me here."

Pink grinned. "How about that airplane ride? You couldn't pay money for high adventure like that."

The Ghost barely remembered his drugged trip on the Skyhook extraction system. A violent jerk off the ground, spinning in the hurricane-force wind, then being hoisted in the back of an aircraft. From there, it was one sedated journey after another, until he'd ended up here.

The Ghost said, "What do you want? I don't think it's answers you seek. That's not your skill."

Pink smiled. "Perceptive, aren't we. No. I want you to listen to something. And then I have a favor to ask."

The Ghost was off balance, his routine shaken by this strange turn of events. He felt the redline of danger but nodded.

The Ghost watched as a digital recorder was placed on the table. Pink held up the headphones and said, "May I?"

The Ghost nodded again, and Pink placed them over his ears. He hit "play," and the Ghost focused on a conversation in English, then in Arabic. When it was complete, he returned his eyes to Mr. Pink.

"What you heard was a Mexican drug cartel member talking to Hezbollah about selling nuclear secrets from the United States. There is an American who is bringing them down. Did you understand the Arabic?"

The Ghost said, "Yes. Someone is bringing money to pay, and the men speaking intend to kill him."

"Yes. That's correct. That someone is coming from Pakistan, and he's due to arrive tomorrow. The American with the secrets arrived yesterday."

"What does this have to do with me?"

"We cannot let Hezbollah get nuclear secrets. They'll turn them over to Iran, helping them with their quest to build an atomic bomb."

"So?"

"We want you to pretend you're the man coming from Pakistan and lead us to the meeting."

51

At first the Ghost thought he'd misunderstood. The statement was so ludicrous it defied logic. He thought his English had failed him.

Pink said, "You'll be in no danger, and we won't ask you to do anything overt. Just lead us to the meeting. We'll do the rest."

The Ghost couldn't help but smile. The idea was preposterous. It was a trick of some kind. "So, you're going to take me out of here, fly me to Mexico, and allow me to meet with members of Hezbollah?"

"Yes, that's about the sum of it."

"But I can't do that under your watchful eye, with you handcuffed to me. If that were possible, you wouldn't need me. You're going to have to let me go on my own."

"I know."

The Ghost shook his head. "I don't know what your little interrogators told you, but clearly you think I'm an idiot."

"No, I don't. Remember, I'm the one who caught you. I do not underestimate anything about you."

The Ghost said nothing for a moment, contemplating. The idea was fantastic, and clearly a lie. There was something else at play here. Why else would this man—his sworn enemy—come begging? They were trying to set him up for something.

He said, "Pretending what you said is true, why would I help? You consider me a terrorist as well. What makes you even fantasize that I would help?"

Pink said, "Let me ask you a question: Do you hate the United States?"

"Yes."

"Do you hate Hezbollah?"

"No."

"Really?" Pink smiled. "Hmmm . . . seems to me that you have every reason. They sold your ass down the river in Lebanon and don't care one little bit about Palestinians. They're currently fighting *against* Sunni insurgents in Syria. Fighting with a Shiite dictator who hates you for daring to defy him. They're trying to prevent the creation of a government that would help your cause."

When the Ghost didn't respond, Pink said, "I've read your file. I've seen the assessments of your intelligence. You should be proud to hear that they're off the charts compared to any other detainee. What's funny is that with all those smarts you get tripped up whenever talking about Hezbollah. We have very little for Hamas and other Palestinian groups, but quite a lot on Lebanese Hezbollah. Why is that, do you think?"

Pink leaned back in his chair, tipping onto the back

legs and locking eyes with the Ghost. He rocked back and forth while the Ghost remained silent. Finally, he said, "The man coming to the meeting works for al-Qaeda, but he's Palestinian. Is your hatred for America so great that you'll let him die so Hezbollah can help out Iran?" Pink leaned forward on the table. "It's really just a question of who you hate more. The enemy of my enemy and all that Arabic bullshit."

They sat for thirty seconds without speaking, Pink content to let the silence blanket the room like a fog. Finally the Ghost said, "Let's say I do lead you to this meeting. What's in it for me?"

Pink said, "You'll get to prevent the death of a countryman, and have my undying gratitude."

The Ghost scoffed and Pink continued. "You know I can't promise you release, but I *will* talk on your behalf. We've got everything we're going to get out of you. Any information you have now is old and stale. Not worth our time. I'll do what I can, maybe get you moved to some sort of house arrest where you get to see more than these four prison walls. That's the best I can do. No way will they release you, because you'll go right back to killing people. You and I both know the truth of that."

Despite himself, the Ghost began considering the offer. He had no doubt that Pink was lying about something in the mission, but he hadn't lied about what he could offer. He could have but didn't. Reluctantly, the Ghost felt a grain of respect for the man across the table. He wouldn't admit it, but Pink had spoken the truth about Hezbollah and Iran and had pushed the correct buttons much more adroitly than any of the interrogators before him. Pink wasn't like the people who had questioned him this past year. He was someone more like himself than the Ghost cared to admit. Which meant he was someone to guard against.

All of that, however, was superseded by one thought: escape. His biggest issues were first getting out of prison, and second getting out of America. And this man was offering to do both for him.

As he was spinning these thoughts in his head Pink spoke again.

"I'm sure you've already considered the greatest benefit. You help me and you might get the chance to escape. There's no way you can get out of this prison, and even if you could, you'll last about thirty minutes on the street in America. I'm going to take you to a foreign country and give you a passport to get there."

The Ghost felt his face flush and saw Pink smile. Before he could recover, Pink said, "Of course, it'll be my job to prevent that, but hey, a man can hope."

Despite himself, the Ghost smiled back. *He's inside your head right now.* Nobody had done that in his entire existence. His slight build and unremarkable features had allowed him to earn the nickname the Ghost. Had caused him to be underestimated by every one of his enemies. His intelligence had allowed him to kill all of them. All but one.

The man across the table.

Yes, he's someone to watch against.

But the challenge intrigued him. Worst case, he could thwart the murdering thugs of Hezbollah, something he would relish. Best case, he escaped. Then he thought of the man he was to replace.

"What of the person coming from Pakistan? If I'm to pretend I'm him, where will he be?"

Pink said, "I won't lie to you. He's going to be kept from the meeting. That has nothing to do with you. You come or don't, he's gone either way."

The Ghost appreciated the honesty once again. "How will I pretend I'm him? They'll know I'm not."

"They have no idea who he is. They've never met him. You've played this game enough to pull it off. Last time we met, you were acting like a citizen of Saudi Arabia. Surely you can act like a Palestinian with a different name."

"I know nothing of al-Qaeda."

"Neither do they. You know enough about underground organizations to fake it. Look, I'm not saying it's risk free. The only thing risk free is staying here in your cell. You want to do that for the rest of your life?"

The Ghost said, "If I agree, what's the next step?"

Pike pulled two devices out of a bag, each a small black box the size of garage-door opener affixed to a metal band.

"These are GPS trackers. They'll get fastened to your ankles underneath your pants. You'll notice there are two of them, and that's for a reason. The trackers will have a geographic boundary that I'll program once we're in the country. Each one also has a small explosive charge. If you exceed the boundary I've set, it'll sever both of your feet at the ankles."

The Ghost simply stared and Pike continued. "I told you it would be my job to prevent escape."

52

Walking down the promenade of Motolinía Street, the *sicario* kept his pace the same as that of the shoppers around him, occasionally stopping to gaze into a window or buy a trinket. Wearing a hat and wig, he no longer looked like an apparition from hell, but instead blended in nicely with the multitude of tourists and locals out to enjoy the sunshine. His purpose was different, however. Having suspected a car following behind him less than thirty minutes ago, he was trying to determine if he was under surveillance. If he was being targeted by Los Zetas. Or perhaps the phantom gringo hit team from Tepito.

Originally, he'd planned on driving straight to the meeting place, leaving Booth taped and gagged in the trunk, but had opted to stop short and take the walk to the final destination. Having captured many men, he knew the tactics well and understood he was safer on foot, moving in a crowd.

It wasn't the best of circumstances, as it left Booth to his own devices in the trunk while he was gone, but he was fairly confident he'd instilled enough fear into the man that he wouldn't attempt to do anything rash. He'd told Booth what would happen should he attempt to escape. He'd kill him, plain and simple. Maybe slow, maybe fast. That all depended on the circumstances at the time. Either way, he'd take the life out of the man for disobeying, no matter where on earth he chose to run.

It wouldn't be for vengeance or because of any emotion. It was just what he did. The only thing he did. He had no other skills, but the one he possessed was valuable, he knew. He watched soccer on TV and thought to himself that in his own way, he was just as good as the best players on the field. They kicked a ball, which was seemingly easy, but only one in a thousand could do what the men on the field could do.

It was the same with him. The *sicario* had seen the masterpieces hanging in the museums, painted by men who had a talent that defied description, and thought to himself that he was like them, only in a different type of art.

And he wasn't wrong.

Walking up the promenade, he knew this skill meant little here. He was entering a world of strategy and negotiation where violence was of no use. The big question was whether the men Carlos had contacted really had money and the desire to purchase Booth's protocol. Something he would find out in the next few minutes.

It had turned out to be relatively easy to locate the men. Leaving Booth chained in the bathroom, the *sicario* had returned to the airport and cornered a man who worked at the rental car counter he had seen the foreigners use. Knowing they had to have shown a passport and international driver's license, he'd bullied the rental clerk into divulging that information. From there, he'd contacted an informant for Los Zetas who worked in the immigration department at the airport. Someone who'd provided information in the past for cash.

The contact was a risk, because the man could just as easily tell others in Los Zetas that he'd shown his face, along with the information he'd sought, but he didn't see any other way around it, and the danger was slim. The immigration agent had no idea of the ongoing status of Los Zetas, so his appearance would get back to them only as a coincidence.

For a single American fifty-dollar bill, the agent had given him the inn the three men had provided on their immigration cards. A midlevel hotel in the Zona Rosa.

He talked to reception at the hotel, and a couple of twenty-dollar bills later, he had the room number of one of the men. He'd slipped an envelope under the door with his cell phone number and had waited.

The man had eventually called, as the *sicario* knew he would, and they'd arranged for an initial meeting. The *sicario* had picked a famous restaurant and bar called La Opera, near the tourist section of the Zócalo. Unlike previous occasions, when he was a valued member of Los Zetas, he didn't want to meet anywhere near their territory. He'd chosen the Zócalo because of its proximity to the presidential palace and other government buildings—

meaning tight security. For once, he feared his own associates more than the officials who hunted them.

He reached the corner of 5 de Mayo and took a left, leaving the walking promenade behind, fairly certain that nobody was still following him, if anyone had been at all. He passed by the entrance to La Opera and continued to the next block. He stopped, standing next to a vendor selling tacos and studying his back trail. Nothing suspicious appeared. He looped around and entered the restaurant, his eyes taking a moment to become accustomed to the gloom.

Like the streets outside, the bar was starting to pick up, the late-afternoon crowd hitting happy hour as in bars all over the world. He'd picked this time specifically because the streets would soon be packed with vendors selling everything from "handmade" sombreros to watches and packs of gum. A sea of people that he could escape within, should it become necessary.

A man in traditional Mexican attire, complete with a sash, approached and asked how he could assist. The *sicario* said he was meeting someone, and before the host could respond, a swarthy gentleman came forward, speaking in English. "Do you wish to have a margarita?"

The *sicario* responded, "No. A glass of water would be fine."

The restaurant host looked confused, but the swarthy man smiled and stuck out his hand. The *sicario* shook it, pleased that the foreigners had the ability to follow instructions.

Each now sure the other was whom they were supposed to meet, they moved to the table already obtained by the foreigner. After sitting, the man said, "You may call me Farooq. It means 'one who distinguishes truth from falsehood.'"

The *sicario* smiled and said, "As in 'one who will not pay for something that doesn't work'?"

"Yes. That's about the sum of it."

"You may call me Pelón."

"And what does that mean?"

"A man with no hair."

Farooq looked confused, as if there was a hidden meaning, and the *sicario* said, "It's just a nickname. If you'd prefer something with substance, something that's closer to my nature, you may call me Muerte."

"Which is?"

The *sicario* rested his eyes on him, and Farooq instinctively recoiled from their weird glow, as they all did, no matter the nationality. "Death. I am death."

Farooq said, "As in you'll kill me if I don't pay for services rendered? Really? Trust me when I say your threats mean nothing to me, and it's not how I like doing business."

The *sicario* said, "I mean no threat. You asked. It's simply who I am."

Farooq said nothing for a moment, and the *sicario* let the silence stretch, not concerned. Eventually, it was Farooq who broke it. "So now you have this protocol? What happened with Carlos?"

"I killed him."

Farooq searched the *sicario*'s visage for the bluff but was left wanting. He made a move to stand, saying, "I'm not sure I can continue, under the circumstances."

The *sicario* caught his wrist and said, "Don't leave. I have what you want. Carlos was but an impediment. You shouldn't care who profits, only that you get it."

Farooq sat back down and said, "We were called here by Carlos, a man my organization has worked with in the past. I don't know you at all. No offense, Mr. Death."

The *sicario* realized he was losing the sale, losing his chance at a stake for a new life, but he'd never conducted such negotiations. All he'd ever been tasked with was punishment. He had no tact or skill in this world, unlike Carlos.

He said, "Farooq, I speak plainly, but it is only because of my nature. I have what you want. All I ask in return is what you were going to pay Carlos. That's it."

"We only pay for results. Can you prove it does what Carlos said?"

"I'm not sure what Carlos told you it does, but I can bring the man who will explain it all. He can show you it works, on the Wi-Fi network of this restaurant."

"Can you do this now?"

"Yes. I'll have to leave and fetch him, but it won't take but about fifteen minutes."

"Do so."

"Before that, I'd like to know what Carlos knew. How much is this worth to you?"

He saw Farooq's eyes flick to the left and knew he was about to get cheated. He had no idea what had been discussed for the monetary transfer, and he wished he could take back the ignorance of his question.

Farooq said, "Carlos wanted a wire transfer of one million dollars. We could not afford that. We discussed a cash transaction of one hundred thousand. He agreed."

The *sicario* knew about the other man coming and had not played that card. He did so now.

"You said Farooq means one who separates falsehood. Please don't play me for a fool. I want the wire transfer from the other man. As you agreed with Carlos. Where is he?"

Farooq slid his eyes to the bar, saying nothing. When he faced the *sicario* again, he said, "He is coming, but the protocol had better work."

"It will. I'll prove it shortly. When does he arrive?"

"He's on an airplane as we speak. Coming here."

53

The hat was a little big, and the jacket made me feel like a bus driver, but both were needed to get me through security. Jennifer looked a hell of a lot better, in my mind. Like the stewardess everyone fantasizes about having instead of the ninety-year-old tart who gave you a sour look when you asked for another beer.

Reaching the TSA checkpoint, Jennifer said, "Let me lead. If anyone says anything, let me answer. Whatever you do, don't try to fake being a pilot."

A little miffed, I said, "What's that mean?"

"I know you. You think you're smarter than everyone else, but you'll get us in trouble trying to talk flying. Just stick with the hotel or the airport. Please."

"I can talk flying. It's just a bunch of buttons and dials. These TSA agents know less than I do."

She gave me an exasperated look and said, "Pike, please. Let me do the talking."

I smiled, letting her know I was just teasing. She didn't know a damn thing about flying a plane either, but she knew plenty about airports. Her deadbeat father was an airline pilot, and after he'd left the family, he'd spent his limited time with her dragging her around the world while he worked. Leaving her in hotel rooms as he went out to find some cougar to bed. The memories weren't nice, but it did give her a healthy appreciation of how airports worked. I was more than comfortable letting her take the lead.

My Bluetooth chirped, and Knuckles came on. "I'm set outside customs."

I said, "According to the flight status, his aircraft is on the ground thirty minutes early. Shouldn't be long. You got the ABS ready?"

"Yeah, but I hate using this stuff. I'm going to get it on myself."

"You do, and it'll be a very long flight to Mexico."

ABS was our not-so-subtle nickname for the medication we were going to apply to the moneyman coming from Pakistan. A topical solution that was fashioned into a tube of ChapStick, ABS stood for Atomic Blow-Shits. A small amount applied anywhere to the exposed skin would cause incredible diarrhea within a matter of minutes. Knuckles, having purchased a ticket on American flight 833 to Mexico City, like our target, would use it on him when given the chance.

Unlike other countries' international airports, those in the United States had no separated transient area for folks just passing through. If you landed in America, even if only transferring to another flight out, you had to go through US customs. Thus, Knuckles could pick up our target as he exited, at a choke point he would have to use.

It had caused a little consternation in the Oversight Council, because the man from Pakistan was flying under the name Gamal Hussein, which, unbeknownst to him, was on our no-fly list. He'd managed to get a US visa— admittedly for transit only—but that alone caused a spasm in Homeland Security and further investigation, because he shouldn't have gotten a visa to use a bathroom in the United States. It did work in our favor, though, because we couldn't have affected his application in time if it had been denied. We could, however, remove him from the no-fly list, which caused some on the council to question what the hell we were doing.

I'd have questioned it too, given the plan I'd come up with. Kidnapping a foreign national inside a working United States airport, without informing TSA or anyone else that we were operational, was a bit much. Throw in the fact that we were going to inject a known terrorist in his place, letting him fly to Mexico out of our control, and I could see why some were jumping up and down. The no-fly list was the least of our worries.

We reached the door to the Known Crewmember access in terminal C, and Jennifer presented her badge. The TSA agent checked it, then a second form of identification. He tapped on the computer and let her through. I watched her dragging her roll-aboard and followed suit. It was surprisingly easy; the agent only wanted to make sure I was in the database. Had he checked last night, I wouldn't have been.

Started in 2011 in response to pilot demands after

9/11, the Known Crewmember program allowed pre-screened participants to bypass security at select airports, one being Dallas. Given that we were bringing in some dangerous kit in our carry-ons, we definitely needed to bypass security.

We'd brainstormed a bunch of different ways to penetrate the airport and had decided on a combination. Posing as TSA agents had been the first choice, but having flown through a myriad of airports, both Jennifer and I had rejected it. TSA agents knew each other and habitually worked the same stations. Any time I had traversed a security point during a shift change, I saw them saying hello or good-bye, or just kidding around. That, coupled with the TSA's natural suspicion, meant we'd be asking for trouble by trying to impersonate them.

We definitely needed to get equipment into the sterile area of the airport, though, and putting it through an X-ray machine was a nonstarter. Who could do that but wouldn't be known to the TSA agents themselves? Who was transient but trusted at the airport? Why, an airline pilot and his loyal flight attendant, that's who.

We'd had Knuckles buy a ticket and go through traditional security. His role was to babysit the Ghost on the flight. Outside of giving Hussein the shits, he would have nothing to do with the assault.

Decoy was in the transfer van outside of terminal A, acting like a baggage handler for American Airlines. Blood, dressed as an airport janitor, would be outside the freight elevator of terminal A, ready to push a large refuse cart with some decidedly different trash inside. With any luck, we'd be getting him inside the sterile area using some equipment in Jennifer's carry-on bag.

I smiled at the TSA agent and pulled my little bag through, seeing Jennifer just inside the entrance to the secure area. We were in the middle of the mission, but I couldn't help but feel distracted by the sight of her in a flight attendant outfit. I swear I didn't want to, but the scarf, hat, and little wings were something out of a soft-core porno movie.

I'd said as much when she'd met me in the lobby of our hotel, and she'd promptly kicked my leg. And not in a teasing way either. She'd done it hard enough to bruise the hell out of my shin.

No way was I going there again, although I *really* wanted to jerk her chain about it one more time. She was a little too sensitive about such things, and an easy target.

We had a little walk to get from terminal C to terminal A, and I was growing concerned about the timeline. Hussein coming in early threw things off a bit, but not by much. We took the Skylink train, then hoofed it to gate A6, the end of the line. Terminal A was next to corporate aviation, which had allowed access to the airfield using our Gulfstream as a prop.

This far down the terminal there were no restaurants or newsstands, so there weren't a whole lot of people hanging around. The closest was a bar at A10, and only one flight was preparing to leave at gate A8, so we could work in relative safety. All we had to worry about were the cameras, which, luckily, didn't focus on our door.

We found the access door leading to the freight elevator in a little cubby and Jennifer opened her bag, with me shielding what she was doing. She handed me a key card attached to a USB device that looked like a big-brain scientific calculator, then took her bag into the restroom.

My Bluetooth chirped, and Knuckles came on. "I have him. He doesn't look much like his passport photo on the visa application, but it's him. He's in line to exit customs with his bag."

"How long?"

"Line's about ten minutes. From there, he's got to walk to Delta six. Maybe twenty or twenty-five minutes tops."

I said, "Roger, we're at Alpha six. Jennifer's changing and I'm about to bring in Blood."

I turned on the calculator thing, then dialed the computer geeks at the Taskforce. "I'm set. What's the sequence?"

The key card was a blank designed to duplicate the RFID code used by the door reader. The code was randomized daily and synchronized with the official cards through an encrypted handshake. Mine was a bit more manual, so I had to input today's code courtesy of the hacking cell.

The man on the other end tapped his keys for a second, then read off a sequence to me, which I tapped on the calculator pad. It was too bad we couldn't do more operations inside the United States. Being a member of a US counterterrorism team really gave us an edge cracking security at official US facilities, but the Taskforce charter restricted us from operating on US soil. Since this target wasn't a citizen, we'd been given special permission.

I held the card up to the pad and hit "send." Voilà, the door magically opened. On the other side was Blood, wearing a janitor's uniform for the Dallas airport and standing behind a large Rubbermaid trash receptacle.

We only had a fifteen-second gap before the open door started to bleat an alarm, so I didn't waste time with small talk. I held it open and waved him through. Once he was inside, I said, "Any issues?"

"None. Van is downstairs and it's only a thirty-second ride to the corporate side and our aircraft."

I cracked the lid on the Rubbermaid and found the Ghost staring back at me, scrunched down at the bottom and looking lost. I winked and closed it back up just as Jennifer returned, now wearing her own janitor's outfit, which didn't look near as sexy.

Probably why you don't see movies with janitors getting it on.

She'd applied some disguise makeup, which gave her a broken, downtrodden appearance. It was more than likely the first time she'd ever made herself look intentionally unattractive, but it allowed her to blend in better as an airport janitor.

I said, "You've got about twenty minutes and a long way to go, so you need to get moving."

Blood said, "Maybe we should take the train."

"No. These Rubbermaid bins stay in the terminal with the people assigned to that terminal. Nobody takes them to another terminal on the train, and I can't have some TSA agent start asking any questions."

I, of course, as an intrepid pilot, wouldn't be walking from terminal A to terminal D.

I confirmed, "What's the gate?"

Jennifer said, "Delta six. Far end."

"Roger that. See you there."

54

Ten minutes later I exited the Skylink at gate D12 and began to walk toward the end, to gate D6, where Hussein's flight to Mexico City was berthed. I called Knuckles. "Status?"

"He's next up. Coming out now."

"Koko, Blood, you copy that?"

"This is Blood. Roger. We've entered the far side of terminal D, but we've got to walk the entire way to the gate."

The D terminal joined the access walkway to the other terminals at gate D40, which was hell and gone from D6. "Roger all. Pick it up a bit."

I stopped at D7 and took a seat, just another weary pilot hanging around. I got eyes on the bathroom at D6 to orient myself and hoped the timing worked out to use it. I really didn't want to flex to another bathroom, but that wasn't my call. It was Knuckles's, and the digestive system of Hussein.

Knuckles came on. "He's out of customs and walking back upstairs to the terminal. Ten minutes."

I said, "Roger," and felt the anticipation start to build.

Blood came on. "We're ahead of him. We'll be good. Want us to let him pass?"

"No. Keep coming, but you can slow it down."

A minute later, and Knuckles was cursing. "ABS in place, I say again, ABS in place, but I got some of it on me. I *knew* that was going to happen."

Oh boy, that's not going to be fun.

"What did you do?"

"I went to swipe his arm, and right as I did, he turned my way to look at a monitor. He knocked the ChapStick into my hand. I'm moving out, away from him."

"What gate?"

"Gate eighteen, I say again, gate eighteen."

"Pike, this is Koko, we're at sixteen. I can see Knuckles. Target's got to be close. We'll pick him up. We have the eye."

"Roger all. Track him and execute as planned. Trigger when the ABS takes effect."

Knuckles said, "I'll bet I can do that for you."

"You'd better hope not."

I waited a bit, looking calm but fired up with a fight-or-flight response. I saw Knuckles first. He passed by me, no acknowledgment at all, and took a seat at D6, milling around with the people waiting to go to Mexico. A minute later, I saw the garbage bin come into view. I scanned the crowd and found Hussein. I tracked him with my eyes, watching him take a seat. He didn't appear to be in any distress.

Hope that damn ABS stuff functions as advertised.

No more than thirty seconds later, Knuckles shot up and scurried to the bathroom. *Well, I guess it works.* Right behind him was Hussein.

Jennifer and Blood let them both get inside, then pulled the bin in front of the door, placing out little cones that said "Closed for Cleaning." Blood went inside, then returned to the door, waiting.

A third party inside going to the bathroom.

Eventually, a Hispanic man and small boy exited, returning to gate D6. Blood disappeared again, then called. "Execute, execute. Come on, make it quick. This place smells like something died in here."

I stood up and walked to the bathroom, dragging the two carry-ons. Blood pushed in the Rubbermaid and Jennifer stayed outside, holding a cleaning bucket and a mop, pulling security.

The stench hit me immediately, a green fog of unbearable odor. Then I heard the bowels being forcibly evacuated. It was so bad I didn't think I could continue. Blood was on the other side of one of the stalls, his face scrunched up and pointing toward a door. I opened my carry-on and pulled out a Taser, locking zip ties, a screwdriver, and a syringe.

I handed Blood the screwdriver, and he placed it into the slot to unlock the bathroom stall. He nodded and I kicked it in, seeing Hussein doubled over on the toilet, farting and shitting his guts out.

I didn't even need the Taser. He was so destroyed by the ABS he couldn't have resisted if he wanted to, which made me wonder if Knuckles could still get on the plane.

He looked up in agony, and I said, "Wipe what you have."

He doubled over and began another round. *Damn it.*

We couldn't sit here for an hour while he shit his brains out. We needed to go. *Note to self: Take into account the time for ABS to subside.*

Blood said, "What are we going to do? We pull him now and he's going to spray all over the place like a damn baby."

I said, "Go through his bags. Get the boarding passes and get the Ghost ready to go. Knuckles, you alive?"

I heard a weak, "Yeah."

"You going to make the flight?"

"I'll make it. Just give me a minute."

"Koko, how are we looking?"

"Okay from this end. Nobody's approached."

Blood had the Ghost out of the bin, and he looked green from the smell. I couldn't imagine what he must have been thinking about this clown fest. Probably wondering how on earth we had managed to capture him.

I heard Knuckles flush, and he came out, sweating profusely and walking unsteadily. I said, "You okay?"

"No. Hell no."

I couldn't help it. A grin slipped out. He scowled and said, "You think this is fucking funny?"

I scrunched my lips together in a terse line, then said, "Well, yeah. Might be worthy of a new call sign. Perhaps 'Ass Wipe.'"

He looked like he wanted to hit me and I held up my hands, saying, "Jennifer's got the antidote. Get it from her bag before you go."

He nodded and moved to the Ghost. He checked his ankles, seeing a green light on both GPS trackers. He said, "I'm your babysitter. You can call me Mr. Black. Don't do anything stupid because I'm really not in the mood."

The Ghost nodded. Blood said, "Found the boarding passes."

He handed them to the Ghost, who checked to make sure the name was the same on his newly forged passport.

I said, "You guys go. We'll give you a data dump when you land. Go to a restaurant inside the airport, before you leave the secure area, and call. We'll feed you the next steps."

The flight time was about two and a half hours, which was cutting it really close, but we had an entire Taskforce team in a safe house nearby who would complete the initial interrogation and exploitation of everything Hussein had with him. We would know before they landed what Hussein was supposed to do.

I turned back to Hussein, who was now sweating like Knuckles but ambulatory, realizing we weren't there to help him. He made a half-assed attempt at escaping, trying to pull up his pants at the same time. I punched him in the head, knocking him to the floor of the stall, his pants falling back down to his ankles. I hit him with the syringe in his thigh and he went limp. We flex-tied his arms and legs, then dumped him into the Rubbermaid container, the stench wafting out as if it contained a dead animal.

55

The trunk of the car jerked open, and Booth squinted his eyes at the glare coming from the sun. When he could focus, he saw the crazy bald man standing above him, wearing a wig and holding a knife. He began to panic and the man said, "Stop. I'm cutting your bonds. It's time to show the people that your protocol works."

He relaxed, letting the man cut through the tape around his ankles and wrists. After it was complete, he was jerked out of the trunk. The man put his weird eyes on him and said, "Do exactly as I say, and you will live another day. Try to run, and I will make your death infinitely slow. There is nowhere I won't find you. Understand?"

Booth nodded, afraid to speak.

"Bring your computer and whatever else you need. You are going to show a man how your system works."

He gathered his things, including the two GPS devices, and followed behind his captor. He knew his last test would have caused a massive reaction at Schriever Air Force Base and was worried about doing another such test. He'd end up causing another blackout in the Northern Hemisphere, and that might potentially create an all-out push to find his protocol. It would still take some time, but he didn't like the odds of discovery, especially since he was sure he would have to do it a third time, if only to instruct whoever was purchasing the protocol.

By the time they had left the walking promenade of Motolinía, he had the beginnings of an idea. His GPS would lock on to four different satellites to obtain a location, showing the man it functioned. All he needed to do at that point was demonstrate a discrepancy. What if he affected only the specific satellites the GPS was using? Then he wouldn't harm the entire constellation. It would cause some disruption, as undoubtedly some-one else was also using those four satellites, but there were thirty-five in the air, and other devices could switch seamlessly to another satellite. It wouldn't cause a wholesale blackout. In fact, if he attacked only two of the four, he'd still get a shift in signal. The 2nd SOPS would see it, but it would be looked at as a signal anom-aly instead of a catastrophe.

He spent the rest of the walk working out the specifics in his mind, figuring out how to attack only two satellites. He hadn't designed the protocol that way, but he could use the data from the GPS to isolate them.

Still running the mechanics through his head, he didn't notice his captor had stopped and bumped into his back. The man scowled, then opened the door to a restaurant called La Opera, waving him through. The room was covered in burnished wood that had the look of age, the ceiling ornately sculpted and the bar to the right fairly crowded with businesspeople. He was led to a table in the middle and presented to another man who could have been Mexican. Booth heard the name Farooq, and when the man spoke, Booth realized he was not from Mexico. Realized his POLARIS protocol was about to be turned over to America's enemies.

The thought did not alter his calculations one bit, as his sole concern was survival. It was like passing a billboard right before slamming on the brakes to avoid an accident, something that registered and then was immediately forgotten.

He gave up the deception of using "Guy Fawkes" and stated his real name.

"A pleasure, Mr. Booth. Pelón here says that you can cause American drones to stop flying. I'd like to see that."

Booth looked from his captor to Farooq, slightly confused. He said, "Yes, the POLARIS protocol will do that, but it's not designed to affect drones. It affects the GPS constellation, which is what the drones use to operate. You know about GPS?"

Farooq said he did, and Booth gave a quick class on POLARIS, describing how it functioned. Farooq said, "So this works with all GPS devices? Bombs, ships, cruise missiles?"

"Yes. If it uses a GPS, it will become ineffective."

Booth saw the gleam in Farooq's eyes and knew he was doing something very, very wrong. But it was too late to worry about the repercussions. Way too late to wonder about making any money. Not if he wanted to continue living with the soles of his feet attached.

Farooq said, "Show me."

"We need to be near a window. Can we change tables?"

They called a waiter and moved deeper into the restaurant, getting a high-backed wooden booth next to a window. The waiter pointed at the ceiling above them, where a hole was circled in paint. He said, "That's Pancho Villa's bullet hole. He ate here and shot the ceiling."

Booth found the comment surreal. Twenty minutes ago he had been taped up in the trunk of a car, put there by a man he was convinced was insane. Now he was about to show another man who was undoubtedly a terrorist how to thwart one of the United States' greatest technological advantages. And he was getting tourist tidbits from the waitstaff. The situation caused a nervous giggle to escape. The snigger died instantly when Pelón looked at him.

He set up his two GPSs in the windowsill, then showed Farooq the interface he had designed while they locked on.

Farooq said, "You must have Wi-Fi for this to work?"

"Yes. Well, you need to have Wi-Fi to load the settings." He pointed toward a dial on a screen. "You can use this to delay the action. In other words, if I turned this dial, when I hit 'send,' the operation wouldn't happen until the time I had set."

Farooq nodded, and Booth said, "One thing about the time I forgot to mention. Not the time delay I was talking about, but the actual time of disruption. You need to be sure you set it to exactly what you want, because once it begins, you can't turn it off. POLARIS is synced with the constellation itself, and the disruption also affects the program."

Farooq said, "You will give me this computer? Is that what will happen?"

Booth said, "No, no. You need to bring another computer. This one is mine and has biometric safety features that only I can operate. It's also got about four hundred different security tripwires. You try to mess with the program on this system, and you'll end up formatting the hard drive, wiping out all traces of the protocol. I'll have to transfer a clean copy of POLARIS to your own system."

Booth heard the GPS chirp and quit talking. He tapped a few keys, received the almanac information, then the specific information of the satellites the GPS was tracking. He locked two of them into the interface, dialed up the timing offset, and said, "Watch the GPS on the right. The one with the car. See where the car is located?"

"Yes. Where we are now."

"Watch what happens when I hit 'send.' "

CAPTAIN LISA DONNOVAN was the first to see the anomaly. As the Payload System Operator on duty in the control segment at Schriever, she was responsible for monitoring every signal in the entire GPS constellation. And she could not believe her bad luck.

Here we go again.

She had had the misfortune to be on duty for what was now being called the "blackout" the day before, and to say it had caused some consternation was an understatement. The echo went all the way to the chairman of the Joint Chiefs of Staff, with her trying to identify the problem while simultaneously answering questions thrown at her by a multitude of people.

She immediately notified the Mission Commander, who ordered a status from the other system operators on the floor. Like last time, the network and mechanical functioning of the satellites were fine. It was just the signal. Unlike last time, it was only two satellites.

She waited for the other satellites to start going crazy and relaxed when they didn't. Her squadron commander appeared above her shoulder, firing questions. He didn't remain long, and she knew why: He now had to report to higher, and she was glad it wasn't her job.

The Mission Commander had the Satellite Vehicle Operator pull the two offending satellites and ordered them to try to replicate the event.

Everyone began working the issue, but like last time, they got nowhere. She felt like Chevy Chase in *Christmas Vacation* trying to get the lights on his house to work but unable to find the magic switch.

The damn things just decided to put out a bad signal.

56

The light above the conference-room door began flashing, a red and white signal meaning someone uncleared needed to enter. Kurt Hale blacked his PowerPoint screen and quit talking.

An aide who looked to be about twelve came in, apologized, and ran over to the secretary of state, Jonathan Billings. After muttering a few words, he left again.

Billings said, "Sorry about that. Unfortunately, I have more going on than just this issue. Continue."

Kurt turned on the Proxima projector. "As I was saying, the transfer was a success, and the Ghost is en route to Mexico City with Knuckles. Pike and the rest of the team are following in the Gulfstream. We've completed the initial interrogation of Hussein and have the instructions the Ghost is to follow once he gets there."

"And you're sure he's not going to disappear?"

"Not if he wants to keep his feet."

The secretary of defense said, "Billings, quit worrying about it. He's only going to be on the ground for a couple of hours. Once he's met them, we take them out." He looked at Kurt. "Right?"

"Well, close," Kurt said. "That was the original plan, but the instructions tell him to meet the Hezbollah guys first, then they'll have a follow-on meeting with the American who has the hack. They want to ensure he's who he says he is and that he's got the money. They gave him some double-oh-seven instructions, full of tradecraft."

The D/CIA said, "How long will that take?"

Kurt understood exactly where the question was directed. "We'll still be within the window for Operation Gimlet. Shouldn't be more than a day."

Billings said, "Why would they do that? You'd think they would want to get the hack as fast as possible."

"Because Hezbollah's paranoid. I don't know, maybe they're worried that we'll try to trick them with a plant."

After the chuckling died down, Alexander Palmer said, "Okay, so we're still tracking for Gimlet. What about exposure of the Taskforce? What's the story on the YouTube video? Anything more?"

"We're still getting probed, but we can't pin it down. The real concern is that we're getting probes on other cover organizations, including the Taskforce headquarters under Blaisdell Consulting. They're making linkages somehow. Might just be guesswork, but with enough of that we could be in trouble. All they have to do is throw everything against the wall and see what sticks."

The D/CIA said, "Great. This will be the Church

Committee all over again. The press is going to explode with joy. And you know who's going to get the brunt of this? Me. That's who. It's always the CIA that gets hauled in front of Congress."

Kurt said, "We might have one lead. My guys have gone back and we did find an anomaly from right before all this started. We had some exploration into Grolier Recovery Services from an ISP in Colorado Springs. We don't know the specific location, but it's definitely Colorado Springs."

The SECDEF said, "Not really. The flavor of the day is the NSA. My people."

The D/CIA said, "And you think this is connected to the group Anonymous?"

"Better than that: I think it's connected to this GPS issue. It's way too much coincidence. I think we find the guy with the hack, and we find the YouTube people."

"I don't know about that. Seems like a stretch."

Kurt said, "Schriever Air Force Base is in Colorado Springs. These probes began right before the first disruption. I don't think it's a stretch."

"Say you're right. How will you find them even if you capture the guy? I mean, they don't call themselves 'Anonymous' for nothing. Your hackers can't locate them through the digital trail, but you think this guy will be able to? He probably doesn't even know their real names."

"They had to talk somehow. We can't find them through a digital trail going back from Grolier, but if we move forward from him, I bet it's a different story."

"Then what?"

"Then we take them down."

Palmer said, "Huh? Here? In America?"

Kurt said, "Hell yes, here in America. Those little fucks are about to expose our most closely guarded secrets. They want to play with fire, I say let 'em get burned."

The principals said nothing, looking back and forth to see if anyone agreed with the extreme measures before stepping into the water themselves. Finally, Billings said, "You know, Anonymous threatened Los Zetas a while back, and Los Zetas made an attempt to find them. When they said they were going to kill ten men for every person Anonymous exposed, the hackers backed off."

Kurt said, "Yeah, what's your point?"

"You're basically saying you want to act like a drug cartel."

"What the hell? You guys were the ones that didn't seem concerned with any of that before. All you cared about was Operation Gimlet. What was it you said? 'Better stop that YouTube video from getting out'? How did you think that was going to happen?"

Palmer held up his hands. "Hey, we aren't going to solve that question with the principals. That's definitely one for the entire Oversight Council. The president needs to be involved."

"Well, you'd better involve him soon because we're running out of time. We catch that guy with the GPS hack and you can execute Operation Gimlet as planned, but we're going to need to squeeze him immediately to protect Project Prometheus. I can't wait until after we capture him to begin debate. We're—"

The light flashed above the door again, and Kurt cursed, exasperated. A man entered, looked around the room, then ran to the secretary of defense.

After he left, the SECDEF said, "That was from the Air Force chief of staff. There's been another outage. Another test, but this time only two satellites were affected, which means he can pick and choose what he attacks. I hope it wasn't a proof of concept for Hezbollah and they now have the hack."

The comment brought a low murmur, with Kurt hearing the term *Gimlet* three different times. He attempted to calm them down.

"They can't. They're waiting on the money guy. They're waiting on the Ghost."

The D/CIA said, "I cannot believe the fate of our national grid and defense architecture rests in the hands of a Palestinian terrorist who's sworn to kill us. I cannot believe I agreed to this."

Kurt smiled. "Look at the bright side: This goes bad and the press finds out, nobody's going to care what Anonymous does."

57

Using the original reservation from the captured man and his new passport, the Ghost checked into his small boutique hotel without issue. In line two people behind him stood Mr. Black. Outside of the initial instructions in the bathroom, he'd said not a word to the Ghost the entire flight, never even acknowledging that they had met. That fact gave him some confidence that the Americans wouldn't do something stupid and inadvertently get him burned. He had enough to worry about trying to pass himself off as member of al-Qaeda without the Americans causing trouble. On top of that, he had to start working on a means of escape.

As instructed, he went to his room, opened up a pre-arranged Yahoo e-mail account, and sent an instant message. He waited for five minutes, then received his response from Mr. Black. An e-mail would be coming shortly.

He puttered around the room, unpacking his things and cataloging what he would need to do to evade the clever little net they had created for him. First, of course, he'd have to find a way to remove the two ankle charges he was wearing. It wouldn't be easy, because they were banded to his legs with metal that utilized a laser-cut key. Not impossible, though. He'd more than likely lose a little skin in the process, but he was sure they could be cut. The problem was the time needed to do so. The Americans would know everywhere he went, along with any instructions he had been given, so somehow he would need to introduce a delay. A meeting of some sort where only he would be present. Well, him and someone with a hacksaw who wouldn't ask questions when provided enough cash. He just had to make sure the meeting was somewhere near the one in his instructions. He had no idea what boundary that devil Mr. Pink had set and didn't want to find out the hard way. All Pink had said was if he felt a vibration, he had three minutes to get back on the inside.

He'd toyed with the idea of telling the men from Hezbollah what was happening and securing their help—becoming a double agent, as it were—but ultimately discarded the idea. They were planning on killing the original man who came, and he was fairly sure they'd do the same to him the minute he showed them he was being tracked.

The second problem was securing a passport. Even if he managed to get out of his electronic bonds, the name on the passport he was using was poison. He wouldn't get very far having it as an identity. On this point, he was fairly sure he could leverage Hezbollah.

The final problem was money, and he had already fixed

that to a certain extent. He had the captured man's credit cards, which still worked, as proven at check-in. The e-mail coming would have the bank account information for purchasing the nuclear secrets, and he had no intention of giving all of that to Hezbollah or whoever else was involved. Some of it would be his nest egg for a future life.

He heard the laptop ping with an e-mail and felt a rush, just like he had in the past before going operational. He read the enclosed instructions, seeing he had a little walk in front of him, along with some link-up instructions. Hezbollah didn't have his flight itinerary and apparently wanted to make sure they met the right guy.

He sent an instant message confirming receipt and left the hotel room, feeling strange conducting a meeting on behalf of the Americans he despised. Strange for being used to turn on members of Hezbollah, whom he also hated, in order to prevent the transfer of nuclear secrets paid for by al-Qaeda, with whom he had no quarrel.

Strange indeed.

As INSTRUCTED, HE had the taxi drop him off in front of a Sanborns department store next to the independence monument on Paseo de la Reforma Avenue. Before continuing to his destination, he accessed an ATM located outside. He withdrew the maximum daily amount his credit card allowed, then began walking north, looking for the second intersection from the Sanborns. He passed the first—an alley more than an intersection—and glanced down the street, seeing a sign that caused him to stop in his tracks: VISA APPLICATIONS DONE WHILE YOU WAIT.

He debated, ultimately deciding he couldn't pass up this gift thrown in his path. He rushed down the little street and entered the small kiosk, knowing it was a risk. Knowing Mr. Black would more than likely question what he had done, but he could feign being lost. After all, his destination was one more street up, and he'd never been in this city.

Five minutes later, he returned to the main thoroughfare, now armed with two passport photos of himself. He reached the second intersection and took a right on a street called Rio Lerma. After a hundred meters, he began looking for the restaurant, fairly sure it would be easy to spot. There couldn't be that many Lebanese food vendors mixed in with all the taco stands.

He smelled it before he saw the sign, a refreshing blend of spices reminding him of home. He reached the entrance and read a cheesy sign in English proclaiming something about Aladdin's carpet. Here he knew he had to be very careful not to let slip in any way that he was from Tripoli, no matter how much he would have liked to reminisce about home.

He parted the beads hanging from the door and went to the order counter, saying hello in Arabic. The man behind it beamed, asking where he was from. He stated Pakistan, then, before the man could engage him in conversation, he gave the phrase from the instructions.

The man's smile vanished, and he told the Ghost to

wait. He disappeared in the back, and when he returned, he carried a cell phone.

"Hit redial."

The Ghost said, "Who am I calling?"

"The people you are to meet. I don't know anything else. I just run a restaurant. Please. Leave before you call. Please."

The Ghost did as he asked, dialing the phone from the sidewalk. A man answered and he repeated the phrase from the instructions.

The man wasted no time with pleasantries or questions. "Go to the Sanborns you passed on your way to the restaurant. Enter, move to the café in the back, and get a table. Place a newspaper on the table open to the front page and take a seat facing the door. Ensure the table is away from anyone else. When approached, give the security phrase."

Before the Ghost could respond, the man hung up. The arrogance aggravated him. *Pretentious kafirs.* It reminded him of why he hated them. Convinced they were superior to any other group, they always acted like everyone else should bow before their almighty presence.

He was tempted to ignore the instructions just to set the tone but knew that would be asking for compromise. *He* was the one hiding something, not them, and making them suspicious or angry wasn't the way to escape the grasp of Mr. Pink.

Fifteen minutes later, he was sitting as asked, wondering if buying a cup of coffee would set them off. The restaurant, set in the back of the department store down a small flight of stairs, was practically empty due to the time of day, with a few patrons drinking coffee or eating dessert, but not many. He'd scanned all of them upon entering, a casual once-over to determine if they were surveillance or security, but was convinced they were not.

He heard the front door chime and saw two men coming into the restaurant. They were dressed in western clothes but were not Hispanic. At least not to the eyes of a man who'd spent most of his life in Lebanon.

He didn't stand, waiting on them to commit to his table. When they did, he uttered the phrase from the instructions in Arabic. The first nodded and sat down on his right. The other moved to his left.

"I am Farooq. This is Hashim. Thank you for traveling here to us. What shall we call you?"

For a split second he almost spit out Ash'abah—the Ghost—wanting to shove a little of their condescension back down their throats, as the nickname had been given because of his skill in Lebanon and even the mighty Hezbollah feared what he could do. But that would have been suicide, so he said, "Gamal Hussein," just like his passport called for.

Farooq nodded, satisfied, and said, "Did you have any trouble coming through the United States?"

The Ghost thought, *Well, yes. Gamal had an extreme case of travel sickness that caused him to be shoved into a giant garbage bin.* He said, "Yes, as a matter of fact, I did. There was a tick on their no-fly list. I had to go through extra questioning before being let on the plane. Someone with my name from somewhere else is on their list. I do not want to use this passport to get home. Can you help with that?"

Taken aback, Farooq said, "Can't your people do it? We aren't here to facilitate your travel."

"My people aren't here, in Mexico. You are, and you require my money. All I'm asking is that you help me return." The Ghost slid across the two passport photos he'd taken earlier. "I don't wish to sound demanding, but the price for me to help is a new passport. I don't trust the one I was given anymore."

Farooq stared at the photos for a moment, then passed them to the other man, Hashim. "Okay. But it will be a Lebanese passport. Is that an issue?"

The Ghost couldn't believe his luck. "No. That will be perfectly fine, as long as it has a visa for the United States. I can't get through their airports without one."

At this, Farooq scowled. The Ghost said, "Given how much money I have brought, I don't think that's too much to ask. Especially since you and your leaders will benefit most from what I'm buying."

Farooq said, "Yes, the device is very expensive, but it will help *you* out with your drone attacks more than it will us, which is why we asked for you to pay in the first place."

Drone attacks? How will nuclear secrets help al-Qaeda stop drone attacks? And what's this about a device?

He'd known all along that Mr. Pink was hiding something but never imagined it could be the very reason for the mission. He decided to proceed cautiously, not knowing what the real Gamal had been told.

"We're happy to pay, depending on what it is."

"It's just like I sent in the e-mail. A way to stop the drones from operating."

The Ghost relaxed. Whatever e-mail had been sent, it most assuredly hadn't been directly to Gamal. There would be go-betweens, especially with how hierarchical Hezbollah was. They'd never let a nobody like this talk directly with anyone in Pakistani al-Qaeda.

He said, "I never got the e-mail. I was just told to bring a sum of money here and evaluate whatever it is that you found. Please, forgive me, but you will have to repeat yourself."

Farooq smiled, pleased to explain what he was responsible for locating. "There is a man who has a way to turn off the GPS that the Americans use. Make it so it doesn't work, which means the attack drones won't work. He's willing to sell it to us but wants a large amount of money. A million US dollars."

The Ghost ignored the money, focusing on what Farooq had said earlier. "What do you mean, turn off the GPS?"

"Just like I said. He has some computer program that is tied into the satellites. He can turn individual satellites off, just the ones that affect certain sections of the world, or the entire GPS architecture. Not only that, but he can do it at any time that is set. It'll turn the Great Satan's drones and all of their GPS-guided bombs into junk. Isn't that worth a million dollars to you?"

The Ghost heard the words and didn't think a single instant about drones or bombs. He was thinking about the GPS ankle cuffs on his feet. About escape.

"Yes. Yes, that is definitely worth a million dollars to me."

58

Booth heard the door to the shoddy hotel open and felt the fear return. The crazy man was back. He jerked his hands out of reflex, feeling a sharp stab of pain from the metal of the handcuffs digging into his raw skin.

The door to the bathroom swung open, and his captor was there, holding a box in his hands. The sight caused Booth's imagination to go into overdrive. What did it contain? What horrific device was he going to use?

How on earth did I end up here?

Booth said, "Please, please. I've done everything you want."

"No. Not everything."

He opened the box, and Booth shut his eyes, feeling dizzy.

"Look at me."

Booth did, and saw the man was holding a new laptop computer.

"I need help with this. I don't have the skill you do."

Booth sagged on the floor. "Yes. Of course. Whatever you want."

The killer bent down and unlocked his wrists. He turned and left the bathroom without a word. Booth stood up, hesitated a moment, then followed, finding the man plugging in the laptop on the nicked table in front of the television.

"I have opened a bank account that can be accessed by the Internet. I need you to configure it for the transfer of my money."

"I . . . I can't do anything here, without Wi-Fi."

The killer placed a small device next to the computer, saying, "I bought this. It's supposed to give Internet over the cell network."

Booth recognized the device as a MiFi hotspot. He stood, unsure if he was allowed to move.

The killer said, "Can you not do it?"

"No, no. That's easy. I can do it."

When he remained still, the killer fixed his hypnotic glare on Booth and said, "Then do it. Now."

Booth scuttled to the chair in front of the table and went to work. His captor said not a word, watching. Within fifteen minutes, the computer was configured and online.

Booth said, "I need the bank information."

He was passed a sheet of paper, and he went back to work. A few minutes later, he had the bank account online but now had to ask for specific information from the killer. Information he did not want to know. Things that would make him worthy of extermination. He sat with his hands trembling on the keyboard.

"What are you waiting for?"

"Sir, I need your account information. Your password and account number. And the name you used to open the account."

The killer said nothing for a moment, then passed Booth another sheet of paper and a United States passport. Booth was stunned.

American. This lunatic is from America.

Booth felt the eyes on his neck as he typed, his hands trembling so hard he was continually having to backspace and correct. He reached a screen for synchronization of a token and was confused.

He said, "This account has two-factor authentication. Did they give you anything? Any other device?"

"Yes. They gave me this." He handed across a digital gadget that looked like a small pager, with a screen in the center. "They were going to explain it to me, but I said you would do it."

Booth recognized it as an RSA SecurID key fob. He took it and opened up a new window. He authenticated the fob on the RSA website, then said, "I need a PIN. Four digits."

"Why? What is that thing?"

"It's just a second authenticator. You type in the password you gave me to get to your account, which will allow you to see any activity that's been done and other mundane things, but if you want to transfer money, you need a second authentication. This key fob provides it. You type in your PIN and it spits out a number. You type that number into the computer, and it allows the money to be transferred."

He gave Booth a number and said, "What happens if I don't have that device?"

Booth, working the new PIN, said, "All you can do is check your account. Get a balance, see what's happened with credit cards, that sort of thing. If you want to materially affect the account, you need the key fob."

Booth finished and tentatively turned around. "It's set. Remember, you still need me to transfer the protocol at the meeting."

The killer smiled, his yellow teeth conveying little warmth. "Don't worry, I have no plans to kill you today. Our meeting is tomorrow morning. Perhaps after that."

59

"So the Ghost actually made contact with Hezbollah and returned to you? I have to say, I had my doubts. So did the Oversight Council."

The streaming video feed from my laptop was breaking up some, our hotel Wi-Fi becoming overloaded with the encryption required for my company VPN. Kurt looked a little bit like the old Max Headroom guy, his face in one location before jerking to another. Luckily, the audio, while distorted, was coming through fine.

"Yeah, he came back, but make no mistake, he doesn't buy the 'nuclear secrets' thing. He knows what this is about now, which I figured would happen."

We'd set up a secure meeting site for the Ghost in Zona Rosa, wanting a clandestine encounter, but after I'd quizzed him via Yahoo! Messenger, I'd learned that the Hezbollah crew hadn't asked where he was staying. I'd decided the James Bond stuff was more risky than simply going to his hotel room two floors above mine—both because of Hezbollah and because of him. I had no doubt he would attempt to escape, and the longer I let him wander around, the more ideas he would come up with. Better for him to sit in his hotel room.

Kurt, thinking just like me, said, "If he knows it's a GPS threat now, aren't you worried he'll want to get the hack himself instead of helping us out? The only leash you have on him is those GPS cuffs."

"No. I was actually counting on that to help us. The hack doesn't turn off the signal. It sends a false one. He'll be afraid that if the thing is initiated, his cuffs will think they're now in South America and explode. He knows he only has three minutes to rectify that or start spending his life walking on pegs. He'll want it shut down as soon as possible. No way will he allow some Hezbollah assholes to run around with it."

"The council is not nearly as convinced as you. They're regretting the decision to let him loose."

"Tell them the meeting is tomorrow. Both Hezbollah and the man with the hack will be there. If they hadn't let the Ghost travel, we would be sitting here with our thumbs up our asses, wondering if we were going to lose our precision weapons in some future war."

I saw Kurt grimace and said, "What?"

"That meeting is critical. We don't have the time to chase these guys. We're no longer talking about a *potential* strike."

He filled me in on Operation Gimlet, and I felt the pressure increase. I wasn't sure tomorrow's meeting would be the final one because I had no idea what Hezbollah and the man with the hack were thinking. It could simply be an introduction to get everyone comfortable, with a follow-on meeting for exchanging the goods. We still didn't know how the hack was initiated, and the meeting location they had chosen wasn't exactly conducive to major computer operations. It looked like all of that was moot, though. I wasn't going to get the chance to develop the situation. Tomorrow's meeting would be the last, no matter what they intended. And it would be up to me to engineer that.

He finished, and I said, "Okay, sir. I got it. Now you can go tell the council that the Ghost decision wasn't the best one. It was the only one. No way would I have been able to interdict in such a short time span without it. One thing, though: Given what you've said and my force structure down here, I'm going to need lethal authority. With only one shot tomorrow, I can't capture everyone *and* get the hack. I'm not sure what this meeting is about. If they show with the hack, that's my focus. Anyone who gets in my way, I'm killing."

Kurt said, "It gets worse, I'm afraid."

He told me about Anonymous and the exposure of Grolier Recovery Services, which would lead to the exposure of the Taskforce itself. A YouTube video was set to lay open our organization in two days, and apparently this same American traitor had information that would allow us to stop the release, making my operation infinitely harder.

What an asshole.

Not only was the traitor selling the capability to cripple the United States, but he was also about to expose its most classified organization. I couldn't wait to get my hands on him.

It was too bad I couldn't use them to kill him outright.

60

The Ghost decided to walk to the meeting in order to get a better feel for the terrain. He might need to escape on foot, and he wanted to know how many routes were available. He'd thought Mr. Pink would tell him no, but it turned out he preferred the Ghost on foot as opposed to in a cab. Easier to catch, especially with the tracking devices.

Paralleling the main thoroughfare of Paseo de la Reforma, he entered a long park, with various monuments and paths threading next to the highway. He considered taking one, just to see where it would go, but decided against it. He knew the meeting location was adjacent to the highway, so there was no way to get lost if he kept it in sight. The path, while it might give him some ideas, could also get him confused and cause him to miss his contact window, something he couldn't afford to let happen.

He passed by a monument on his right and did a double take. It was a statue of Heydar Aliyev, the leader of Azerbaijan, a prominently Shiite country in the Caucasus.

The plaque, in both English and Spanish, heralded his triumphs.

The Ghost continued on, shaking his head. Why on earth was there a monument to a president from a country that had absolutely nothing in common with Mexico? He put the thought out of his mind and returned to the mission. Or more precisely, *his* mission.

He had demanded that he meet Farooq before the actual sale so he could deliver the Ghost's new passport. In no way was any money exchanging hands if he didn't have that. Farooq had agreed. In demanding to get it before the meeting, he hoped to ensure the passport was actually created, as he knew what Hezbollah intended once the sale was complete.

Once he had that, he would ask the American for a test of the system to ensure it functioned. If it did, he would give half of the money in his account for purchase. Al-Qaeda had provided Gamal two million dollars, and from what Farooq had said, the sale was for one million, which would leave him a nice tidy sum to escape with.

Insh'Allah, he would leave with the device, following Hezbollah—ostensibly believing he was going to share in the treasure. A lamb being led to the butcher. Like Mr. Pink, Hezbollah was under a false assumption. They thought they were going to kill him. Mr. Pink thought he was going to wait on a signal from the Ghost to trigger an interdiction. None realized what was really going to happen.

As soon as they stopped at whatever kill zone Hezbollah had picked, he would initiate the device, knocking out the GPS in the ankle cuffs. Then he would slaughter the Hezbollah members. Afterward, he would flee with his new passport and money, finding someone to cut off the cuffs and leaving the cursed Mr. Pink and Mr. Black to pick up the pieces.

He would never be found again. He had *earned* the nickname the Ghost, and he would put that to good use.

He passed a throng of street vendors selling food and T-shirts in a parking lot and saw his destination: the National Anthropology Museum.

He walked up the stairs, past a fountain, and looked for Farooq. He was nowhere to be seen. He checked his watch and saw the meeting time was less than five minutes away. He grew concerned about a trap, snaking his hand into his pants and rubbing the initiation device Pink had given him. Basically a small pager tied into the cell network and slaved to Pink's phone, it had two buttons: one benign for signaling the meeting was over and he had the device, and one for initiating the assault. Mr. Pink had said the second one was also a panic button. If anything went wrong, all he had to do was press it and forces would intervene.

The irony wasn't lost on the Ghost that he was relying on Pink to rescue him if something went bad, but he had no intention of reciprocating if everything went as planned.

He saw a man sprinting up the stairs and recognized Farooq, a laptop bag swinging behind his back.

He reached the top out of breath and said, "I'm sorry. We got caught in a massive traffic jam. We're late. We need to get inside."

Should have walked, you idiot.

The Ghost said, "No. First my passport. I won't transfer the money without it."

Farooq fished in his pocket and pulled out a key. "It's in a locker downstairs. I was supposed to get it before you came, but I ran out of time."

The Ghost felt the trap. *They didn't make the passport because they intend to kill me.*

"Without the passport there is no deal. I can't get home on the one I have."

Farooq turned and pointed down a set of stairs leading to an underground parking area. "It's in a locker down there. Please. I didn't place it there. I only had it made and delivered. It is done, I promise. You can retrieve it afterward."

He was sweating and looking like he was on the verge of panic. Looking truthful. The Ghost considered. *They would know I would go straight to the lockers, and they couldn't kill me here, in broad daylight in front of tourists. If it's not there, I'll simply have to find another way out. After I kill them.*

He took the key and they entered the museum. They purchased tickets and moved through the line of people. The Ghost noticed a strong police presence, but nobody searched either of their bags. They entered into a large open area with a giant fountain raining water from the ceiling, kids splashing about. Farooq consulted a map and said, "Come on. He's out back, in the Mayan temple section."

They moved through an exhibition hall, ignoring the displays and exiting on the south side of the building, into an outdoor area lined with paths and displaced temples. Farooq, seemingly knowing the terrain, went behind the stonework, almost running on the granite path. They turned a corner and the Ghost saw two men sitting at a picnic table, looking expectantly at them. He casually slid his hand into his pants and pressed the first button, letting Mr. Pink know the meeting was on.

Farooq took the lead, introducing a Caucasian as Arthur Booth and a Latino as Pelón. Booth said nothing, sitting meekly on his bench, a laptop in front of him. Pelón nodded, locking eyes with the Ghost. In that stare the Ghost saw his essence reflected back at him.

The man was a killer, just as he was.

61

Farooq couldn't see it, but the talent that had allowed the Ghost to survive in the cauldron of Lebanon was predicated on a sixth sense that others lacked. He had an inexplicable gift for feeling danger, and he was staring it in the face. Unlike the pretenders from Hezbollah, this man was death.

The Ghost saw Pelón's eyes narrow and knew the man recognized the same skill in himself. The two remained in a trance for a moment, neither speaking, ignoring the other men at the table. Farooq broke it, saying, "Shall we conduct business?"

Keeping his eyes on the Ghost, Pelón said, "Certainly. Have a seat."

Farooq gestured to the Ghost and said, "Gamal here has your money, but he insists on a test before transferring."

Pelón, still staring at the Ghost, said, "You people saw it yesterday. Transfer the money first. I'm not a traveling amusement park."

Booth said, "I have to give you a class on it anyway.

Let's kill two birds with one stone. Pay him, I'll teach you, then I'll place it on your computer."

The Ghost said, "I didn't bring cash. I thought we were doing a wire transfer."

Pelón broke his gaze and gestured to Booth, who brought out the portable MiFi device. Pelón said, "Let him have your computer and he'll get you to the Internet."

The Ghost did so, and while it was being worked, Pelón said, "What do you do, Gamal?"

Farooq looked confused, as there was to be no mention of their past, but the Ghost understood. "I do the same as you. Only in a different place."

Pelón smiled, as if he'd learned something profound. "I have often wondered if there were others like me. Besides in Mexico, I mean. Others who do what I do. I've asked an American, and he told me no, that such men are evil and exist only in evil places. I wondered if he was wrong, or if Americans simply had no evil in their world."

The Ghost answered as if the other men did not exist. "Americans have a quaint notion of evil. They don't know the meaning of the term, unlike those where I am from."

Now Farooq looked completely baffled, but he remained silent.

Pelón nodded, saying, "Tell me, do others fear you where you are from? Do they know your name?"

"Yes. I am known as the Ghost."

Farooq's eyes squinted, as if he were searching for something lost in his memory. The Ghost realized he'd said too much. Given away his shield. His secret. Should Farooq make the connection and realize his skill, he would have a much harder time killing them, as they would be on their guard. Even so, he was glad he'd told the truth to Pelón. A man who would understand.

Before Pelón could respond, Booth interrupted, saying, "Okay, we're ready to make the transfer. I just need Gamal to input his account and password, and I need you to use your token."

Annoyed, Pelón glared at him, and Booth shrank back. Pelón said to the Ghost, "I'd like to talk to you again. After we have completed our business. I have so many questions."

The Ghost nodded, keeping his face neutral, wondering if the others understood Pelón wasn't all there. Wondering if the man was completely insane. It didn't matter, as they would soon be done, but unlike Farooq, he sensed the danger within Pelón. A killing instinct that was barely contained, like a vat of acid held in place by masking tape, the liquid dripping down.

He tapped in his account information, then watched as Pelón pulled out a digital device, read a number, and tapped that into the computer. When it was done, Booth said, "How much?"

Looking at the Ghost, Pelón said, "How much does he have?"

"Close to two million dollars."

"Then that's what it will cost."

The Ghost said, "Wait, I was told one million."

"The price has changed. Unless you don't want it. I'm sure it's worth much, much more than that to others."

Farooq tugged his sleeve. "It *is* worth much more. Pay it now and I will talk to my people about reimbursement."

You mean after I'm dead? The Ghost decided he would enjoy killing this ingrate liar but knew his escape hinged on turning off the GPS. Money was something he could always get. He still had the real Gamal's credit cards for a head start.

"Okay. So be it."

Booth completed the transaction and opened his own laptop, going through a biometric authentication, turning off his security traps, and establishing a connection with his two GPSs and the cellular Wi-Fi. When it was complete, he began showing the Ghost the various dials and switches on the screen, describing each one. He turned the final dial, detailing how it affected the timing signal, making it the heart of what would generate the false locational data. His words took a moment but finally sank into the Ghost's brain.

"Wait, wait. I thought this device turned off the GPS signal. Isn't that what I'm paying for?"

Booth said, "No, it renders GPS devices here on the earth inoperable by sending a false timing signal. In effect, it causes them to think they're somewhere else."

"You mean it tricks the receivers here? Instead of shutting ting them off?"

"Yes."

The Ghost felt sweat pop onto his neck as his heart rate skyrocketed. *The ankle cuffs are going to think they're outside the boundary.*

He said, "We don't need to test it. If that's it, let's transfer the system to our computers. We're taking too much time here."

Farooq said, "No, no, it'll only be for a few seconds more. Show him the car on your GPS."

Out of options, the Ghost snaked his hand into his pants, found the panic button, and triggered it, pressing it over and over. He said, "Wait, before you do, explain to me again how it works."

Booth started to say something, and Farooq cut him off. "Who cares about the science? It works. Watch."

And he hit the enter key.

The Ghost saw the car disappear, then reappear in Canada. And felt both cuffs begin to vibrate. He felt a colossal urge to run, but he knew it would do no good. He had three minutes before both feet were amputated. Farooq said something that came out as white noise.

Farooq spoke again, then touched the Ghost's sleeve. "Gamal, are you okay? Look, now the car is back where it is supposed to be. See? You can control how far it moves as well as how long."

The Ghost felt the vibrations cease in both cuffs.

He took a deep breath and said, "So all the GPS receivers are working again?"

Booth said, "Yes."

He jammed his hand back into his pants and hit the

first button, the nonpanic one, in an attempt to stop the assault he knew was coming.

Farooq continued. "Show him how you can do it without Wi-Fi. Show him the delay."

Booth said, "If I want, I can set up multiple strings of outages for as long as I'd like." Using the laptop track pad, he turned another dial, saying, "For instance, I could shut off just the GPS receivers in Mexico for five minutes, then set the entire constellation to go out permanently in twelve hours. Now, if I were to hit enter, we'd get two outages of varying degrees and varying lengths of time."

Farooq said, "That way, you can set it when you have Wi-Fi, but it won't release until you're away from Wi-Fi."

The Ghost was pressing the nonpanic pager button again when Mr. Pink and a woman he didn't recognize rounded the far side of the stone temple. He heard noise behind him and saw Mr. Black and an African-American closing from the opposite direction.

Pelón took one look at the woman and leapt to his feet, pulling a gun from inside his jacket. Farooq slammed the lid on Booth's laptop with his hand still on the keyboard, drawing a howl. The GPS screen went blank.

And the Ghost felt the ankle cuffs vibrate again.

62

Sitting at a corner table inside the small museum cafeteria, Jennifer said, "I find it ridiculous that I'm out here while Knuckles and Blood get to roam around the museum. They don't care one bit about what's in this place."

I said, "We'll come back when this is over."

She said, "I have a degree in *anthropology*. This is one of the largest anthropology museums in the world!"

I started to say something when my phone buzzed for the second time, meaning the meeting was over.

That was quick.

I looked at my screen and felt a jolt fire down my spine. Next to me, Jennifer said, "Pike, he just alerted."

I said, "Let's go," just as my radio came alive, Knuckles and Blood confirming the worst. Something had gone horribly wrong, and my beautiful plan was turning to absolute shit.

With the five-man team I had—well, four men and a woman—I was hard-pressed to accomplish both primary tasks of capturing the American hacker and taking down the device he'd created. Whoever had picked the place of the meeting had done a pretty good job. The anthropology museum was wide-open, with multiple halls and levels in addition to a plethora of outside exhibits. On top of that, it had a large security presence to prevent theft and damage. Enough to preclude any shenanigans from either side during the sale of the device.

I'd decided to wait until after the sale, allowing the men to split up and leave the museum, with the Ghost alerting us when the meeting was over, triggering surveillance. I'd left Decoy outside in an SUV, giving us some flexing options should we need to mount up, and tasked Knuckles and Blood with tracking the American. Jennifer and I would take the device and the Hezbollah crew, along with the Ghost.

I wasn't comfortable allowing anyone else on him, feeling he was my sole responsibility, and was glad the assignments had already been decided by our previous actions. Whomever we had chased on the rooftops of Tepito would recognize Jennifer and me, but they hadn't seen Knuckles or Blood, meaning they could conduct a proper follow. The downside was they couldn't identify the targets like we could, as we had no photographs or anything else. I wasn't too worried, though, because the guy who had the American was definitively strange looking and would be easy to spot. All they had to find was a devil dragging a Caucasian.

Allowing them to split up and leave was a risk, but I

didn't like the odds of successfully conducting an assault inside the museum, then escaping with an American in tow. Especially if we were going to leave some dead bodies behind. Too great a chance of compromise inside a treasure that Mexico valued highly.

And now I was being forced into it.

Speed-walking through the open courtyard, Jennifer took the first left she could find into the exhibit area, weaving through the displays but not moving fast enough to draw stares. I went through our options and began coordinating the assault, shifting mission focus from what I'd given previously.

"All elements, all elements, priority is the device. I say again, priority is the device."

Knuckles said, "Coming in from the west. Copy you want to forget second target?"

Jennifer reached a large glass door and we were through, into the garden area full of old relics and temples. I said, "Roger. Good copy. If we can, we'll take him, but the device has priority."

We rounded a temple and I saw the Ghost sitting with three other men. The one on the end reacted first, and I recognized the devil from Tepito. He raised a weapon and began firing. Jennifer split right, behind a stone head, and I went left, diving into the protection of a brick wall. I rose and saw the American running full out toward the museum, screaming, with his arms over his head, the devil firing at his back. I snapped two rounds, hitting the devil in the upper body and causing him to drop the gun. But it didn't put him down. He whirled and sprinted into the temple behind him.

I focused back on the table, seeing Knuckles and Blood closing on the Ghost and one other man running through the trees toward the fence that fronted Paseo de la Reforma Avenue. Blood broke left, into the temple, and I leapt up, reaching the Ghost at the same time as Knuckles.

Out of the corner of my eye I saw Jennifer take a knee, pulling security toward the museum. Knuckles closed down the other half of our circle, facing the direction the other target had run and getting a status from Blood on the radio. I turned toward the Ghost, who was lying on the ground.

I jerked him to his feet, pointed at the two laptops on the table, and said, "Is this it? Which one is the device?"

He screamed, "No! Farooq has it. The man running toward the road."

I dropped him, turned to Knuckles, and said, "Go."

He took off and I began coordinating, "Decoy, bring the vehicle down Paseo de la Reforma. Precious cargo is on foot, headed to the fence. Interdict him. Blood, Blood, status?"

I had barely gotten the words out of my mouth when he rounded the corner of the temple. "Both guys are in the crowd. I never saw the American, but the other guy is headed to the entrance. You want me to move to the front?"

"Negative. We're getting the device."

The Ghost grabbed my arm. "It's running. He's initiated it."

Shit.

I said, "Let's go. Jennifer, get on the Ghost. Get him out of here."

We began crashing through the foliage and I heard the Ghost shout something at my back. I ignored him and continued on, huffing into my radio. "Knuckles, what do you have?"

His answer came back the same way, as if he were panting it out. "He's at the fence. He's climbing. I'm not going to reach him before he's over."

"Decoy, Decoy, status?"

"I'm coming. I'm coming. I got him when he clears the fence. Pike, the GPS in our car has gone haywire."

Blood had left me behind, running through the woods like a deer. He closed on Knuckles and I heard, "He's over. Decoy, Decoy, he's over."

"Roger. I see him. I see him. He's coming to the road about a hundred meters up."

I said, "Stop his ass. Run him over if you have to."

I saw Knuckles ahead, halfway up the fence, Blood leaping up right behind him. I sprinted as fast as I could, hearing the worst.

"Pike, Pike, he's got help. A car just hopped the curb and he's in it. They're mounted now."

Interdict the car? Have Decoy slam into them?

"Can you stop them?"

"Not right here. I've got cars in between us. Knuckles, I got you. I'm ten seconds out."

I leapt onto the fence and said, "Pull over. Pick us up."

I flipped to the far side, hung for a split second, then dropped to the sidewalk, seeing Knuckles and Blood diving into the vehicle. I sprinted to the open door and heard a pop to my rear, at the museum, as loud as a gunshot fired right next to me. I crammed into the back of the SUV, Decoy hit the gas, and Knuckles said, "What the hell was that?"

I said, "I don't know. Get moving." Then it dawned on me.

Oh man. The ankle cuffs. The GPS thinks he's out of the boundary.

For a moment I couldn't concentrate because of what I'd done to the Ghost. I'd promised him safety, and I'd maimed him for life instead. Quite possibly killed him. *That's what he was shouting when you ran away.*

He was a terrorist, but he was also human. He was my charge, my responsibility, and I hadn't thought through what would happen if they initiated the device for any length of time greater than a simple five-second test.

The SUV jerked to the left, slamming my body against the door and bringing me back to the mission. Decoy said, "See that yellow sedan? That's him."

"Get on him. Knock him off the road. Everybody, the device is running. Don't waste time trying to subdue anyone. Interdict the car and kill all inside. Find the device and shut it down."

I called Jennifer, "Koko, Koko, what's your status?"

I got no response. "Koko, Koko, status?"

I felt a sour, nauseous sense of dread. She was on the Ghost when his cuffs had gone off. *Please don't let her have been hurt by my stupidity.*

63

Jennifer watched Pike and Knuckles race into the woods, then turned to the Ghost, putting her front sight post on his head.

"Get up. Now. We need to clear the area."

He screamed, "The device is on! It's on!"

"I know that," she snarled. "Get your ass up, now!"

"My cuffs are going to blow. The POLARIS protocol has tricked them into thinking I'm somewhere else!"

Jennifer heard the words and took a step back, wondering if he was lying. She knew from personal experience the man was deadly and wicked smart.

The Ghost looked at her and pleaded, "Please . . . take them off. I'm running out of time."

Pike had ensured that every member of the team held a key that would unlock the cuffs in case emergency action was necessary, just as every prison guard had the ability to unlock their charges. But doing so would release the Ghost into the world without any controls. Something akin to opening the cage of a wolf inside a nursery.

She knelt down, keeping the barrel of her Glock on his head, the suppressor wobbling from the adrenaline. She touched the ankle cuff on his right leg and felt it vibrating. She leapt back.

"How long? How much time since they started?"

"I don't know. Please, don't let this happen. I won't hurt you. I'll follow you wherever you want. Do whatever you say. Just don't let this thing maim me."

She instinctively wanted to help but now had a second dilemma: If she tried to remove the cuffs, she could have her hands blown off because the time ran out.

She looked into his eyes, enlarged through the thick glasses he wore, and saw despair. Along with resignation. *He thinks he's doomed. He believes nobody like me will help him. Believes I want him to suffer.*

She laid the Glock on the ground and ripped through her pockets for the key. He sat up, an incredulous expression on his face. She knelt down, frantically working the circular laser key into the right cuff. She got it off and flung it far into the woods. Hands shaking, she went to work on the left cuff, wasting precious seconds getting the key inserted. She twisted, and the lock refused to move. Her brain screamed for her to run, screamed that the fuse was reaching the end.

She jerked the key left and right without result, then took a deep breath, willing herself to relax. She pulled the key from the lock, blew on its grooves to remove any blockage, then reinserted it, the clock in her head now banging in a crescendo.

The lock turned, releasing the cuff. She snatched it away and threw it backhand over her body. It went seven feet from her hand and exploded, the shock wave slapping into her head. She felt a stinging pain in her shoulder and rolled on the ground.

She heard nothing in her ears but ringing. She sat up and found the Ghost standing above her, holding her weapon.

The last thing she saw was the barrel of the heavy suppressor coming at her temple.

64

Decoy jerked the wheel to the left, swerving around the last car that separated us from our target. I stopped trying to get Jennifer on the radio, focusing on the immediate mission.

Paseo de la Reforma was a four-lane boulevard in this area, with the inbound lanes separated from the outbound by a median ten meters wide and lined with trees. He could only go straight, the thoroughfare a channelized kill zone.

Decoy said, "Got stopped traffic ahead. Pedestrian crossing."

I saw the right-side window of the sedan come down, and a man hung out with a pistol, firing our way. Decoy shouted and I flattened onto the seat, fighting with Knuckles and Blood to get as low as possible. I heard the windshield pop, the safety glass spiderwebbing from multiple rounds. The salvo done, Decoy snapped upright.

I got an up that nobody was hit, then strained to locate the sedan but was unable to see anything because of the spiderweb of cracks in the windshield. Decoy was driving with his head held just above the steering wheel, looking through a spot of clean glass.

"He's hopped the curb, using the crosswalk."

I hung my head out the window and saw the sedan plow into two people, flipping them over the hood before they spilled back onto the brick walkway. The sedan reached the far side and whipped around in front of the traffic stopped on the eastbound side, pedestrians screaming and diving out of the way.

"Follow him!"

We hit the curb at speed, the jolt bouncing everyone inside. Decoy kept the pedal buried, looking like a little old lady crouched behind the wheel, threading the path the sedan had created. We hit the east side before the light changed and found ourselves behind the target, nothing between us but road. Decoy swung into the lane and began to gain with each passing second, our horsepower greater than the sedan's.

I said, "We gotta end this. Cops will be here soon."

The sedan was rocketing forward way too fast, reaching seventy miles an hour before it hit the next pack of traffic. It slowed and began weaving, still going much faster than was safe. We followed, causing brake lights to flash as the two vehicles swam through the traffic like sharks in a school of goldfish.

We caught up with the sedan at the first traffic circle of the central district. The man popped out of the window again, aiming his pistol, and Decoy hammered the sedan's right rear quarter panel. I saw the gun skip across the roof as the car was flung sideways into the traffic circle.

The driver broadsided a vehicle, regained control, and exited the circle, back on Paseo de la Reforma, now separated from us by a small cluster of cars. All Decoy could do was pound his horn in frustration.

We circled back onto Reforma and once again began to work our way forward, everyone straining to catch sight of the yellow sedan.

Blood, his head hanging out the left window, said, "Got him. Five cars ahead. Florencia traffic circle coming up."

Continuing to weave, gaining ground, Decoy was slowed behind two cars driving the same pace. Frustrated, he jammed the accelerator, splitting the gap between them. He clipped the rearview of the car to our right, spraying the road with glitter before cutting back left, now two cars behind the sedan.

They saw us coming and accelerated, attempting the same maneuver. The sedan ground into the car on the left, then jerked to the right, hammering that vehicle before springing back to the left like a pinball. The two wrecked vehicles on either side slowed, and the sedan jumped forward into the Florencia traffic circle, moving with too much velocity, causing it to skid sideways.

I heard the squeal of tortured rubber and saw a panel truck, tires smoking, slam straight into the driver's-side door of the sedan.

Decoy jammed the brakes and I shouted, "Go, go, go!"

The three of us exited at a run, Blood leaving Knuckles and me behind as he raced to the vehicle. I saw a man jump from the passenger side and sprint to the sidewalk, hitting Florencia and going south. Blood reached the vehicle, batting his way through the crowd. Knuckles and I diverted to the sidewalk, going after the man.

Blood came on the radio. "Vehicle is a dry hole."

Which meant the man in front of us had it.

He was a block ahead but not running as fast as we were, probably because his idea of physical training was smoking a hookah pipe. We closed to a half of a block. I saw him glance over his shoulder, his eyes bugging out of his head with the realization that we were going to catch him. He reached a cross street called Londres and ran straight into a market. I couldn't believe my good luck.

"Blood, Blood, this is Pike. Get your ass down here. He just entered Mercado Insurgentes. Take up your planned position."

Knuckles said, "Same for me?"

"Yeah. I'll go in and flush him."

Mercado Insurgentes was a shopping area a block long, full of stalls no more than five feet across and walkways smaller than three feet in width. It was a maze. It was also the place I had preplanned to meet the Ghost, had I needed an off-site instead of his hotel room, which meant we knew the area much better than the target did because we'd already conducted a recce. Unlike him, we knew it only had two exits: one on Londres, which Blood would take, and one on Liverpool Street, where Knuckles would position.

Knuckles continued running flat out down the block, heading toward the southern Liverpool exit. I sprinted into the market, having little trouble finding my quarry due to the racket he was making trying to escape in the confined space.

The vendors were starting to swarm the congested pathways through the maze, wondering who the jackass was that was knocking over all the souvenir Santa Muerte statues and handcrafted jewelry. I slowed, not needing to rush now. Not wanting to highlight myself like he was doing.

I followed the noise, moving deeper into the market, taking turns by sound alone. Eventually, my target got smart and quit running blindly through the stalls. I started conducting a grid search, saying into my radio, "Are we set?"

"North set."

"South set."

"Roger all. Time to do some quail hunting. Stand by."

I weaved through the stalls, peeking across and between the various tourist junk for sale, systematically going in one direction, then cutting back to another. Slicing the market into smaller and smaller sections of pie.

I caught a flash of movement two rows over and peeked between a shelf of jade necklaces, the owner knowing better than to ask if I was shopping. I saw my target, standing still and facing the other way, a laptop in his hand. I held my finger to my lips and looked at the shopkeeper. She nodded, not saying a word.

I exited, went to the nearest little alley of a walkway, and snuck behind him. He was now one row of shops over, and I could see the laptop through the back of another stall, behind a selection of Mayan calendars. He was up against a wall and could go no deeper into the market. I knew he was close to the southern exit, even if he didn't. I decided to get him to the street instead of wrestling him to the ground here.

I moved right to the edge of the stall, squatted beneath the calendars, and said, "Stop! Stop right there!"

As expected, he jumped like I'd poked him with a cattle prod and took off running, paralleling the wall. I circled around and gave chase, letting him gain distance. "Knuckles, he's five seconds out."

"Roger all."

I saw daylight, then heard the scuffle. I reached a small alcove that led to the street in time to see Knuckles bounce back as the man swung a small pocketknife at him. I heard the cough of a suppressed pistol, then the man collapsed, the laptop bouncing on the concrete.

Exasperated, I said, "What the fuck? You took him down because of that little toothpick?"

"Asshole was trying to kill me."

I couldn't argue with that. I said, "Get Decoy here with the vehicle and lock that door leading in. You get to clean up your mess."

He grunted something and I grinned at him, snatching up the laptop, knowing we'd just accomplished the mission. Well, the half that mattered the most, anyway.

I opened it and saw something that looked like an old-fashioned stereo face. I ran my finger over the track pad and a pop-up appeared, saying the computer was locked for "CareBear" and to enter a password or use a biometric thumb pad at the base of the keyboard.

I waited until it disappeared, then studied the screen. All the switches and dials were in the off position, with an upper box labeled "Satellite Acquisition." The number in the box was zero.

So we're good.

I looked at the bottom of the screen, seeing another box labeled, "Next Disruption." Beside it was a clock showing eleven hours and twenty-two minutes.

And it was counting down.

65

The Ghost watched the fractured response from the security personnel at the museum entrance and knew checking the locker wouldn't be an issue. The explosions and gunfire had caused some reaction, but for the most part the tourists wandering around the exhibits simply looked at each other in confusion. Which is exactly what the security personnel did. Eventually, they started moving inside, but apart from the initial fight at the temple, there was no chaos. No screaming or running amok.

He assumed Pelón and the American were long gone, and he would have been as well except he needed the passport. He left the museum trailing another group of tourists, the woman's pistol hidden in his laptop case.

He knew he should have killed her, should have used her suppressed weapon to punch a hole in her head, but he couldn't bring himself to do it. Her actions had been incredibly brave, and in truth, were something he never would have expected to see from an American. From an enemy.

She had risked her life to ensure his safety. Had shown

compassion he would have never given if their positions had been reversed, along with the courage to use it in the face of great bodily harm. It was an act that had confounded him.

Despite what she'd done, he knew he should have taken her life. She was still the enemy, and the cold, reptilian part of his nature was chastising him for his weakness. But he had been here before.

A year ago, he had seen a close friend begin to crumble from the pressures of a mission and had understood he should eliminate the weak link if he wanted to succeed. But he could not, and because of it, he'd ended up in the hands of Mr. Pink.

He'd often wondered what had happened to his friend, wondered if he was living a life of isolation in a strange American prison like he had been, but he had never regretted the decision. It was his choice to make, as with the woman, and his life was worth less than his honor. Flesh and blood were frail and fleeting. Honor was forever.

He could kill without remorse, but he did so for a purpose. In his world, betrayal was a way of life, just like the mission he'd been given by Mr. Pink. The actions of the woman, on the other hand, were a surprise.

She would return to hunt him, he knew, and regardless of her actions, he would still owe her a debt. And he understood he would never repay it. If she stood in his way in the future, if she attempted to capture him again, he would kill her just as quickly as anyone else. The dichotomy caused no conflict in his mind. It was what it was.

War.

The tourist group he was following continued on to the street, and he veered to the left, traveling downstairs to the parking area. He saw a pack of schoolkids waiting for a bus, all excitedly talking to each other and bouncing around, exasperating their chaperone. On the wall adjacent to the stop was a bank of small lockers, designed to hold umbrellas, purses, and wallets.

His key said seventy-two. He ran his eyes down the row, found the number, and unlocked the door. He pulled it open and smiled. Inside was a Lebanese passport, just as promised.

He took it and began retracing his steps to the park, this time staying away from the four-lane road and moving down the paths that meandered throughout, thinking about his next steps.

The killer with the scarred face had taken his money, but he still had the credit cards. He could withdraw as much cash as they allowed as a cushion, then buy a plane ticket home with them. He thought for a minute and realized the trap he was setting for himself.

The Americans knew the name on the card, knew the account, and they'd be watching. He would need to buy many different plane tickets to confuse them. If he bought enough, spread throughout several days, he'd increase his odds of escaping. Perhaps he'd head to Europe first, while they staged for a flight to Lebanon.

The thought reminded him that he'd have to ditch the credit cards the minute he left Mexico. Buying the tickets here would be a risk, but using the al-Qaeda credit card at any final destination would be suicide. And he had no access to cash because that devil had decided to empty his al-Qaeda bank account. All he would have was the measly amount he could draw on the cards.

The truth rankled him. Why should that man get all of his money? Why didn't he agree to the purchase price?

He reached the first intersection and saw a *sitio* taxi stand, for government-regulated cabs that wouldn't attempt to rob him after he got inside. Not that that would matter. He was on the run now, and anyone who stood in his way, be it for petty cash or his capture, would die.

He gave the cabby the name of a hotel he'd seen on his walking tours earlier, far away from where he'd stayed before with Mr. Pink and Mr. Black, in a decidedly less touristy part of town. He secretly hoped the cabby would try something. Give him some reason to vent his frustration.

The man looked at his thick glasses and started to grin, intent on fleecing him for more money than a simple drive to a hotel was worth. Then he saw the eyes behind the glasses. He turned around without a word.

In the back, the Ghost opened the computer he'd taken off of the table. On the screen was Pelón's bank account, still open with the password in place. He stared at the Web page, considering his options. This man held the key to his future. The chance at a new life, with money that was rightfully his. He didn't care if Pelón kept half, but it wasn't fair for him to have it all.

He tapped some keys, ensuring the password was saved in the computer registry and would automatically be filled in when he reached this page again. He knew he couldn't transfer any money without the digital token Pelón had, but that was okay. He would see any transactions the man made and could track him down. Could find him.

When he did, he'd have a discussion about sharing the money. About giving the Ghost what was rightfully his. Get him to use the bank's digital token to transfer cash into a new account. One that would give the Ghost a new life.

Pelón wouldn't do so out of goodwill, the Ghost knew. After their brief encounter, he understood the man was like a rabid dog, looking for something to bite. And he had the skill to bite deep. The thought brought no fear. The Ghost knew his own capabilities well. If he didn't want to transfer the money, it would be okay. All the Ghost needed was the digital token.

If he had to pry it from the killer's dead hand, he would.

66

The *sicario* watched the people exit the cab, none looking remotely like Arthur Booth. He checked his watch, seeing that he'd been waiting for close to two hours.

It looked like his guess had been wrong, just as he'd been wrong about Booth's having nothing to do with the team that had been chasing them. A miscalculation he regretted. Booth was the only connection, the only common denominator, and somehow they'd managed to find him twice. First in Tepito, then at the museum.

Booth wasn't working with the team; of that the *sicario* was sure. For one, during the attack in Tepito, after initially showing tenacious resolve, the man and woman on the team had abruptly quit the chase, letting them escape. Two, Booth had run away screaming at the museum. If he'd thought they were there to rescue him, he would have stayed, happy for them to appear. Instead, the assault had surprised him as much as anyone else.

Even so, he was sure they *were* tracking him, and Arthur Booth knew the reason why. Had known they *might* be coming again and had said nothing. The *sicario* regretted not flaying the man for answers. Booth had lied to him, which was reason enough to kill him, but he also now had information that could never get out. He knew the *sicario*'s real name.

The *sicario* watched one more cab arrive without result and decided to leave. Clearly, Booth wasn't coming to the United States embassy for help. The *sicario* mentally kicked himself for allowing the man to keep his passport.

Identification was necessary to enter the museum, and so the *sicario* had given Booth his passport just prior to entering. He'd kept the man's wallet but had failed to retrieve the passport after they'd entered. Booth had no money or the ability to get any, but now he had the means to flee the country.

Knowing Booth's fear and lack of ability to do anything in the city—especially without any money—the *sicario* had figured he would show up here, spinning some story about being mugged or kidnapped and asking to return to America, but it looked like that idea had been misplaced hope. There had been a steady stream of people moving inside to the first security checkpoint, but none were Booth.

Perhaps the team is working with the embassy. Maybe this is why he hasn't shown. He is as afraid of them as he is of me.

The man had to be somewhere, though, and the *sicario* understood his intelligence. While he might have been a blubbering mass of cowardice, he was smart. He wasn't wandering the street looking for a handout. He was working hard to find another way to get home.

How? How would he do that?

The *sicario* stood and walked away from the embassy, flagging down an unregistered cab. He climbed in back, seeing two men in the front, both disheveled and dirty. He gave them the name of a store and settled back, thinking of the ramifications.

If Booth were captured by the team or anyone else, the *sicario* had no illusions that he wouldn't give up his real name as soon as he opened his mouth. Doing anything to keep himself out of jail for his theft of computer secrets. That would close down the *sicario*'s only escape route. His island of protection from Los Zetas. He now had plenty of money to live on for the rest of his life, but he couldn't use it if the American authorities were hunting him. He wouldn't be able to get a driver's license, open a new bank account, or do any of the mundane things required to live in the United States.

Beyond that, Booth had lied to him and had fled. The *sicario* could not let that stand. He had one thing he did well, one thing that made him what he was, and Booth had spit on that skill. For that, he would die.

The *sicario* was brought out of his thoughts when he felt the cab stop. He glanced out and saw they were nowhere near his destination. The cab had parked in an alley between two warehouses. The *sicario* understood why.

The man in the passenger seat said, "What happened to your arm?"

The *sicario* noticed his makeshift bandage had begun to leak crimson, the wound he'd received at the museum slowly seeping through.

"I was hurt at work. Why did you stop here?"

The man flashed a kitchen knife with a six-inch blade. "Hand over your money. Maybe I won't carve your other arm."

The *sicario* closed his eyes. The violence followed him everywhere. He wasn't the fox. He was the hen. An animal that attracted death. Why did they come for him? Was it God's plan or another unconnected event on his path in life? A sign of what was to come or just an echo, like thunder in a storm?

He dearly wanted to know.

When he opened his eyes again, the man in front wavered, shrinking from the glare. The driver said, "Give us your wallet. Do it now!"

The *sicario* reached behind his back, and the man with the knife relaxed. Instead of a wallet, the *sicario* withdrew his pistol, placed it on the forehead of the knife wielder, and pulled the trigger, spraying the windshield with blood and brain matter.

The explosion was huge inside the closed vehicle, the smoke and smell of burned powder filling it. The driver held up his hands, saying, "No, no. Please don't."

The *sicario* said, "Move over. Get in the passenger seat."

The driver sat still in fear. "Don't, please. Don't kill me."

"Move over. Now."

"Why? Why why why?"

The *sicario* pressed the barrel into his head and said, "Because I'm taking this car and I don't want to drive sitting in blood. Move."

The driver began to cry, but he opened the door and pushed the body to the pavement. He turned around and said, "We weren't going to hurt you. Please, I have a wife. A daughter."

The *sicario* paused, intrigued. He placed his black eyes on the man and asked, "What does that have to do with anything? Would having a wife and daughter prevent a fox from killing your chickens?"

The driver was confused by the statement. He opened his mouth to speak, his lips sliding over his teeth, but no words came out. He looked at the *sicario* in fear, willing to say anything to prevent what was coming but having no idea what words would succeed. The *sicario* was disappointed. Another man who had no answers. He pulled the trigger, shattering teeth and severing the spinal cord. The *sicario* pushed him out of the seat, letting the body flop on top of the other man's. He closed the door and backed out of the alley, the front tire rolling over an outstretched arm.

He was unsure of his exact location, not having paid attention during the drive, and gave up trying to find the store he'd given them. Instead, he began circling the neighborhood, looking for the familiar black and yellow sign.

He made several left turns and was growing frustrated when he saw what he wanted: a small grocery store with a placard advertising Western Union.

He parked on the side, the passenger door pinned in by a wall to prevent some curious passerby from seeing the mess in the front seat. The store was empty, making his job infinitely easier. He turned and locked the front door, then went to the counter.

The woman behind it had seen his actions, and when she saw his destroyed visage, she shrank back, praying under her breath.

He said, "I'm not here to harm you. I want to withdraw a transfer from Western Union."

She nodded rapidly in relief and said, "I need the MTCN and your first and last name."

He said, "Arthur Booth, but I have no MTCN. What is that?"

"The money transfer control number. It's the number the person sending it should have given you so you could receive it."

He leaned into the counter and said, "I just want to know if a man named Arthur Booth received money. Can you check for me?"

Trembling, she said, "I'm not allowed to do that. Please."

He stared at her for a moment, then said, "Is that what you really want to tell me?"

A man outside rattled the handle of the door, then

knocked. The *sicario* said, "Don't turn this into violence. Check for me, please."

She began typing, and he went to the door. He opened it, said, "We're closed for inventory," then shut it in the man's face before he could say a word.

He returned to the counter and she said, "Yes. An Arthur Booth received four thousand dollars from a Western Union in the United States. The transaction has already been completed."

"Can you tell me where? What store did the transfer?"

Her lip quivering, she said, "No. It doesn't show that. It just shows it was completed."

"Who sent it?"

"I don't know. Usually you don't have to give any information like that. The only person who has to show identification would be the receiver. To prove he was who he said he was."

She seemed to collapse in on herself, fearing what the *sicario* would do. He said, "He wouldn't have to show identification even for that amount of money?"

Seeing a lifeline, her eyes lit up, and she said, "Yes, yes. Maybe. That would be considered a suspicious transfer in the United States."

She began typing again, and he saw her exhale. "It's here. The amount was flagged, and the sender had to provide his name and address."

She wrote down the information and handed it to him. He read it, seeing he would be going deeper into

America than he had intended. The address was for someone named Peter Scarborough in Colorado Springs, Colorado, USA.

He knew Booth was gone. Probably in the air, flying to America right this moment. The *sicario* had no idea where he would go or what he would do to hide.

But this Peter Scarborough did.

67

"What was the heat state when you left?" said Pike. "What's our compromise status?"

Jennifer tried to turn her head, but Decoy held it in place, saying, "Stop moving. Look right at me and keep holding your hair back. I want you to follow this light with your eyes."

She did so, then said, "We're good at the museum. They have no idea what happened. They heard some noises, but when the policeman brought me around, I claimed I'd been mugged. He asked about explosions and I said I had no idea what he was talking about. He took a statement from me, so he's got my name, but I used our cover of Grolier Recovery Services. Made absolute sense to be there. And I had the pocket litter and identification to back it up."

Decoy said, "I don't think she's got a concussion, but we should get her checked out by someone who isn't a witch doctor."

Pike said, "You're the best we've got right now. Put that med-lab training to good use. Patch her up."

Decoy squatted down at her level and gingerly touched her scalp with an antiseptic. She gritted her teeth at the sting but said nothing, waiting on him to "accidentally" poke the wound in retaliation for her mistake.

After dealing with the police, she'd been allowed to go. Well, more precisely, they didn't seem to have any overarching plan, and she'd wandered off. Knowing bad news never got better with age, she'd called Pike. And told him what had happened.

I had the Ghost and was escorting him out. Then I let him escape free and clear. By the way, he has my weapon as well.

She didn't use those exact words, but it had been the toughest phone call she'd ever had to make. She knew full well what the impact would be. While they had been on a high-speed chase complete with a firefight, she'd let a captured terrorist shackled with a GPS locator escape. Not only that, she had facilitated it. She knew her reputation was done. Now she was simply waiting on the fallout.

Strangely enough, it hadn't happened yet. The minute she'd walked in the room, everyone had taken one look at her and wanted to know if she was okay. At first she was convinced it was because she was female and they were showing a protective streak. But she knew the hotwash was coming. She'd seen them before as a bystander, brutal after-action reviews where they analyzed all mistakes to prevent future occurrences. Nobody was spared regardless of their position on the team, and that was where she would be fired.

Pike said, "I think we're good at the market as well.

Decoy managed to get our SUV out of the area before the police showed up, and we weren't stopped getting back to the hotel with the computer."

Decoy placed two butterfly bandages on her cut and said, "Amazing what a wad of cash will do for you in Mexico. Most expensive SUV I've ever purchased, but it was worth it. They even took out the registration history of the rental."

He rose and said, "She's good to go. She's going to look like an abused wife for a couple of weeks, but she doesn't need stitches. The shoulder wound is worse than the head one, but that's just a puncture from shrapnel. It'll heal on its own."

Eyes downcast, she said, "Thanks."

He nudged her. When she looked up he winked and said, "I see what you're thinking. Don't. That was a gutsy move."

He went back to the anteroom of the suite with the rest of the team, leaving her alone with Pike.

Here it comes.

Pike said, "You got any ideas at all where the Ghost was headed? Did he say anything?"

"No. Nothing. He just begged for me to get the cuffs off. If I had done it sooner, I'd still have him. If I hadn't waffled . . ."

He sat down facing her. "Cut that shit out. Look, this was *my* mistake, not yours. I never thought they'd initiate a long-term outage before making the sale. Never figured those cuffs would be something to worry about."

"Pike, you don't need to protect me. I know I screwed up. I know how much the Oversight Council thought this was a bad idea, and I proved them right."

He glanced at the door, making sure it was closed, then leaned in and kissed her forehead, right next to her wound.

"You always think I'm protecting you because you don't understand your own worth. You never have. What you did today earned the respect of every man on this team. They're out there right now wondering what they would have done, and not all are sure they would have risked their lives to save the Ghost. They know it was the right call, but they're wondering if they would have made it."

Staring vacantly at the ground, she said, "Pike, he was screaming in the dirt. I felt the cuffs vibrating. I had to do it. I thought the things were going to go off while I was working the lock. . . . I don't know what I could have . . . "

He lightly punched her in the shoulder, knocking her back into the present. "Hey, you did good. Don't dwell on it. Whatever you do, don't let this action cloud something in the future. Keep your compass. It's served you well in the past and will do so in the future. We'll get him again. I told you, it was my mistake."

She didn't believe him. About whose mistake it was, anyway. She did believe that he thought she'd done the right thing, and that meant a great deal to her. Like it always did. She wasn't so sure of the team. Although Decoy had winked at her, giving her encouragement.

But that guy is always trying to get in my pants. Would he have said it if he knew about Pike and me?

Blood opened the door and said, "VPN's up. Kurt's on the line. Time for a disaster report."

Pike grinned at him and said, "I don't think I've ever had a SITREP quite this bad where someone wasn't KIA. This'll be a record."

68

I exited the bedroom with Jennifer in tow, wondering how I was going to spin this disaster. Well, that's not true. There was no spin in our world. The facts spoke for themselves, and, unlike on the Sunday talk shows, the repercussions were for keeps. Whatever the reason, we had lost both the American and the Ghost. We'd captured the device, but it was apparently ticking down to a catastrophic GPS outage, and we couldn't get into the computer to stop it.

A disaster all around, and spinning words like a politician wouldn't make the facts any different. Our job was to stop the catastrophe. Their job was to cloak how it was done, using their words to protect us. We each had our missions, and while theirs disgusted me, I understood the necessity of both.

After some pleasantries, I told Kurt the entire team was in the room, just to let him know who was listening. They were mostly off camera, and I didn't want him to say something that was only meant for me.

He said, "I'm assuming since you're all sitting here the meeting for the device is over. So, give me some good news. I have a council update in an hour."

I told him what we had with the computer, then how we couldn't affect the countdown.

He said, "And it's going off in twelve hours?"

"Was. It *was* going off in twelve hours. It's down to about seven now."

"Seven. Great. Just perfect. That's about the same time as Operation Gimlet."

"Have them strike early. What's the big deal with that?"

"We can't penetrate the Syrian air defenses with a strike from a carrier group. It's not like Afghanistan. We don't own air superiority. Syria is one tough nut to crack, especially for a surgical attack. The strike package is a flight of B-2 bombers from Whiteman Air Force Base in Missouri. We need the stealth capability, but the trade-off is reaction time. The B-2s are the only ones that can accomplish the mission, and they're already in the air. It's a fifteen-hour flight, and they're halfway to the target."

Shit.

He continued. "Where's the American? It's his computer. Make him crack the code."

"Sir, he escaped."

I told him about the Ghost hitting the panic button, triggering early, and the meeting devolving into a nest of rabbits scattering at the sight of a hawk.

He heard the story, then asked the next obvious question. "And the Ghost? Where is he?"

I took a deep breath, then told that story as well. I saw him put his head into his hands on the screen. I said, "Sir, it had to be done. He was—"

He looked up and interrupted. "Was what? About to escape? What the hell is going on down there? Where's Jennifer? How could she let him get away?"

From the side, away from the team and all by herself, Jennifer said, "I'm here, Kurt. I did what I thought was right. I made a bad call."

She looked like she wanted to crawl into a hole. Completely ashamed to be in the room. It aggravated the hell out of me, but I knew if I said something, it would have no weight. Kurt understood we were close, even if he didn't understand *how* close.

It turned out I didn't have to say a word.

Kurt said, "Jennifer, I understand you're a civilian and haven't been in the military, but the repercussions of this are going to—"

That's as far as he got. Blood stood up and moved into view of the camera, saying, "Whoa, whoa, whoa. Sir, with all due respect, she made the right call. I'd have done the same thing."

Kurt said, "But you don't understand what the council is going to say. You don't understand how this is going to affect our operations. We'll be pulled—"

He was cut off by Decoy, who rose and crowded the camera as well. "Bullshit. You don't get to pick what's right based on what some council will think. It either is or it isn't. And Jennifer's call was *right*."

Kurt leaned back in his chair, rocking and thinking. An operator now working solely in the shark tank of politics, trying to remember what he used to know. What it was like on the ground. He turned back to the camera and said, "Yeah, yeah. Okay, I got it. Maybe I've been in DC too long. The call was right. I'm with you, but that doesn't solve my problem. Pike, you there?"

I pushed through. "Yes, sir."

"You know I'm going to have to pull her. I don't want to, but I need a head. With the report I'm about to give, I need something to show we're not all fuckups. She's going to get flushed. Before you say anything, we've got too much at stake. I have to get Oversight Council approval to continue, and I can't get that without their thinking we're tracking and correcting. They'll need something tangible with this disaster of a report. Jennifer's it."

I could see he didn't believe in the decision. He'd been one of her biggest cheerleaders, against a he-man, woman-hating world within the Taskforce. He had wanted her to succeed. But, like me, he also understood the political dimensions of the fight. Jennifer was going to be sacrificed to allow Kurt to continue. To allow *me* to continue.

The irony was debilitating. My team, who had initially *hated* the thought of a woman in their world, now believed in her as much as they did any man in the Taskforce, and the commander who had fought to allow my experiment to continue, who had believed in her from the beginning, was going to fire her.

Knuckles stood up, squeezing into the group, now making us look like we were in some sort of carnival picture booth, with everyone trying to get in the frame. The one guy who was always calm, his face now radiated real anger.

He said, "Tell that pack of pussies if they want to question our decisions they need to kit up and come downrange. I'm with the team. Jennifer's call was good. Not only that, but it was pretty fucking heroic. Any other organization would be giving her a medal, and those jerks want to cut her free?"

I glanced at Jennifer and saw her sitting against the wall slack jawed. Amazed at the support.

Kurt snarled, "I got it, Knuckles. I don't like it either. That's the world we live in. You want to find the assholes who are about to destroy our ability to wage war, not to mention our economy, or do you want to get called home? The Oversight Council doesn't understand the world you live in. Some do, but most don't. What they do understand is penalty, and I'm giving them Jennifer. It's the price for playing, damn it. You know that better than most. End of story. Let's move on to solving the damn problem. Pike?"

Nobody said anything. The team looked at me, waiting for me to tell Kurt to shove it up his ass. I really, really wanted to, but he was right. I'd dealt with the Oversight

Council and had glimpsed into their world. Not lived within it, but had seen enough to realize what he said was true. I knew how they acted and what buttons Kurt could push to allow us to operate. To succeed. In truth, I respected him for putting up with the BS he did to get the job done.

In the end, I could fight Jennifer's battle later. Right now, we had a much more serious concern. "Sir, this computer's locked, so our first course of action is to get it open to shut off the GPS device."

"Get it up here. Let's get the hacking cell on it. See if we can crack that thing before it's triggered."

"I'm not sure you can do that in time. We've got seven hours, and this guy was a computer geek. The laptop's probably got more booby traps than Indiana Jones. We need to find the American. He can open it. Haven't you guys been able to do anything to neck it down? Who is he?"

"We've got nothing. The guy's got to be someone on the inside, or he wouldn't be able to access the GPS constellation, but we've looked at everyone in the Air Force, starting with the Second SOPS and moving all the way out to the Fiftieth Space Wing headquarters. Shit, we even looked at the guys manning the gates. Schriever is clean."

I said, "We're missing something. That guy is *there*. We're overlooking the footprints. Maybe he isn't in a uniform. Maybe he's a contract janitor or something like that."

"None of those guys would have clearance. They'd

have no access. There's only one civilian contractor allowed on the floor, and he checked out."

"They don't have more than one contractor on Schriever with a clearance? That's bullshit. The place is probably overrun with guys like that. It's full of rocket scientists, and they aren't in the military. Snowden was a contractor with a clearance, for God's sake. Did you check them all? Sir, all we need is a thread. We can find him. Shut this thing down. But we need a thread, and it's there. You guys are missing it."

Kurt said, "We're out of time to fish. The last check took thirty hours to complete. Get the computer up here. We'll take a swing at it with our guys."

Resigned, feeling failure all the way around, I said, "Roger all. We're ready to fly right now. All I need is some help with customs. We'll come right into Dulles."

From the back of the room, Jennifer interrupted. "You guys are sure this traitor is on the inside?" She was holding the computer, with the clock ticking on the screen.

Kurt said, "Yeah. No way would he be able to access the GPS constellation otherwise. He's on the inside. Why?"

She moved forward, bumping the team out of the way. "If he's on the inside, he has a security clearance, right? He couldn't do the work without one."

Kurt leaned forward. "Yes? Why's that matter?"

"Well, when I got my clearance they did a background check. I had to give them fingerprints."

I said, "So what? We don't have his."

She held the computer forward and pointed at the biometric reader next to the keyboard. "Yes we do. We have his thumbprint right here."

The team stood in silence for a moment; then Knuckles turned to the screen and said, "You still want to fire her?"

69

Arthur Booth banged on the aluminum screen door, causing a racket that startled him. He swiveled his head left and right in a panic, looking for a phantom government team to spring from the ground and handcuff him. He heard, "Calm down. I'm coming."

When the inner door opened, a balding man with pale skin said, "Jesus Christ, Booth. You look like shit. What the hell is going on? Why on earth were you in Mexico? You said you were going to Canada to visit relatives."

Booth pushed through the door, saying, "Pete, it's too complicated to get into. You're a lifesaver, though. I'll pay you back the money as soon as I can get into my bank account. I lost my entire wallet."

Booth walked past him, dragging a suitcase and a laptop. Pete said, "Why aren't you staying at your place? I don't get it. Why do you need to stay here?"

Booth sat at the kitchen table and booted up his laptop, the sweat on his neck mixing with his greasy hair. He said, "You wouldn't believe me if I told you. I think there are people from Mexico who are hunting for me. I got mixed up in some bullshit down there. I was sweating bullets just getting clothes and my spare computer from my house."

He saw Pete's expression and hastily added, "Wait, wait. It's not what you think. I didn't do anything. I was just at the wrong place at the wrong time. I said I was going to Canada because Boeing has a flag on travel to Mexico for anyone with a security clearance. Believe me, now I understand why. It'll blow over, but I need some space. I can't let Boeing know about this. I can't lose my job."

Pete said, "Well, you left at the absolute worst time. The AEP upgrade of the constellation is a mess. It keeps throwing out false timing signals, and everyone is going ballistic. We've been digging for days and can't find out why. Of course, the damn Air Force is blaming Boeing. And Boeing is blaming us."

Booth thought about his lost computer. About the clock ticking. He couldn't remember exactly how long he'd delayed the disruption, but he knew full well he'd set it for a catastrophic failure. In the next few hours, America was going to go through a seizure. He no longer cared about punishing Wall Street or stopping drone attacks. All he was focused on now was saving his own pathetic skin.

When his aircraft had broken ten thousand feet, his first order of business was to slam a margarita, amazed that he was flying back to the United States alive. After that, he'd begun to think about what had occurred. Besides the weird kidnapper who'd taken him—a man who still gave him chills even inside the aircraft—he'd been tracked by a team of Americans. He'd wondered if they weren't following the killer but knew that was too much to hope for, especially given that the kidnapper had almost tortured him to death trying figure out who they were. The man had been right, though. It had something to do with the POLARIS protocol, which meant they might know his identity.

He needed to redirect them. Get them worried about something else. Maybe the GPS failure would be enough, but he didn't think so. The initial reports from his Anonymous contact had been that something was fishy with Grolier Recovery Services, and he wanted to know what had been found. He needed any ammunition he could get.

He said, "What's your Wi-Fi password?"

"Chrystalbean pound pound. Capital *C*." He leaned over and saw the website Booth pulled up. "Whoa. Stop right there. Don't you start mucking around with those message boards. I've told you before that messing with those people will get your security clearance pulled, and I want no part of it."

Exasperated, Booth said, "Boeing isn't looking at your router data. Come on. I'm just trying to get some information that could help me."

Pete folded his arms across his chest. "You can sleep here, but you will not pull me into whatever you have going on. The MAC address of your computer is tied to the MAC address of my router. Someone can see every

ISP you hit, and those message boards are tracked by just about every government agency in existence. Not here."

Booth slammed the laptop shut, the pressure he was under breaking the surface. "I'm just trying to chat with a buddy who's doing some research for me. What sort of friend are you?"

Pete refused to back down. "The sort who's willing to send you four thousand dollars on a fucking phone call. Go get some free Wi-Fi downtown."

Booth was about to tell him to stick it up his ass and storm out, but the one rational part of his brain that still worked in his cesspool of panic realized it would only leave him exposed. And he could use a beer. Or twelve. Most of the bars in downtown Colorado Springs had free Wi-Fi.

He said, "Okay, okay. I'll head to Tejon Street. You want to go? I'm buying."

Pete laughed and said, "You mean with my money? Thanks, but I've still got some work to do. I'm trying to puzzle out how that timing signal is being twisted. You've still got a day of leave left. Better use it, because when you get back, it's balls to the wall. If we can't figure this GPS problem out, we'll be looking for another job."

70

The thermal showed the apartment was still empty. Which, given that we'd had eyes on the front gate leading into the parking lot for the past fifteen minutes, stood to reason. We were waiting on the sun to drop below the horizon, and I needed to ensure nobody entered the apartment in the meantime. There *was* one heat source in the target, and after analysis by someone smarter than me, it looked like it was a hamster. I think the wheel-spinning gave it away.

I looked at my watch, now synchronized to the ticking clock on the doomsday computer, and saw we had less than two hours before the GPS constellation went crazy. Less time than that to call off Operation Gimlet, because they wouldn't want the aircraft to penetrate Syrian airspace if they weren't going to drop the bombs. Which, from what I was reading about our chances, was what was about to happen.

We'd flown straight to Colorado Springs and met a cell of Taskforce computer experts, who'd set up an operations center in the Hampton Inn by the airport. With the thumbprint it had taken less time than our flight from Mexico City to find our target: a contractor working for Boeing named Arthur Booth.

He'd taken some vacation time a few days before, ostensibly visiting relatives in Canada. The Taskforce had gone to work, tracking his credit cards and cell phone usage. They'd found cellular data and credit purchases that tied Booth to El Paso earlier in the month, but the recent history was blank. He hadn't used his cell phone or credit cards in days. The last purchase they could find had been for one round-trip ticket to Mexico City from Denver, returning yesterday. He had not used the second leg, which made perfect sense, given I'd seen him at the museum earlier that day running like a girl.

With Arthur Booth's personal digital trail a dead end, the Taskforce dug deeper, scanning official domestic databases, probing with a wide net to find some link that would lead them to the target, and had gotten lucky. Arthur Booth had gone through immigration at Dallas earlier today, with onward travel to Colorado Springs.

Originally ordered to bring the computer to the might of the Taskforce fifty-pound heads in Washington, DC, we'd been redirected midflight to Colorado Springs with a dual purpose. The hacking cell would go to work on the computer here, in a makeshift operations center, and we would go after Booth.

We'd gotten a dry hole at his apartment, but I hoped something inside there would give us a clue as to where he had gone. Ordinarily, we'd just have sat there waiting, for days if necessary, instead of attempting a break-and-enter, but we didn't have that luxury this time.

Which is exactly why we hadn't simply alerted domestic authorities, claiming Booth was a serial killer or something else that would get him on every beat cop's radar screen. We couldn't break him free from the police without raising an enormous flag as to who we were and why we wanted him. The decision had been made to do a domestic Taskforce operation, against a US citizen, which was a big decision indeed.

Operating domestically was forbidden by the Taskforce charter, precisely because we had the ability to break quite a few constitutional protections afforded the average United States citizen. We didn't have congressional oversight like the intelligence community and the Department of Defense. Without this scrutiny, the Taskforce had the capacity to grow into something cancerous, becoming the very threat we were created to fight, and thus the decision had been made to keep it off US soil. Keep the beast at bay in the hinterlands, as it were, doing evil so good may come.

We had operated domestically in the past, but against foreign targets, as we had in the Dallas airport. We'd conducted only one operation domestically against a US citizen, but the threat had been overwhelming—a domestic terrorist attack to destroy our power grid—and it was judged that the Taskforce was the lone tool that could solve the problem. I remembered well the enormous debate surrounding that mission, because I'd been at the heart of it. We had succeeded, and apparently, that had made this debate a little easier.

I was happy with the verdict, but I'd be lying if I said it didn't give me a little unease. With only the Oversight Council as a decision maker, there was the threat of hasty judgments based on emotion or an imperfect intelligence picture, something I'd seen happen only six months ago on another operation, causing Kurt Hale to offer his resignation.

A problem to worry about later. Right now, I had an asshole on the loose that I needed to capture to stop a catastrophe, and little time to worry about any constitutional niceties.

Although there was still a glow of twilight, I judged it dark enough to execute. I turned to Jennifer. "You ready?"

"Yeah. I see my route. I'll use the balconies."

The building was a four-story brick structure with a single access point on the ground floor, secured with a keypad. From our reconnaissance earlier, we'd learned that the entrance could be unlocked from the apartments themselves, as we'd seen a pizza delivery guy speak into a box, then pull the door open. That was now Jennifer's mission.

Dressed like Catwoman, in a black Lycra Under Armour shirt and leggings that fit like a second skin, she was going to scale to the fourth-floor apartment, break in through the sliding glass door, then hit the entrance button.

I said, "Get moving. We're wasting time."

She exited the vehicle; scurried through the foliage, avoiding the pool of light from a streetlamp; and reached the corner of the building.

A voice in the backseat said, "Who is that chick? I didn't think we had any female operators."

His name was Bartholomew Creedwater, and he was supposedly the best computer guy the Taskforce had. He'd probably never once left his little hole inside Taskforce headquarters in DC, and he was treating this whole operation as the time of his life.

Beside him, Decoy said, "I didn't think so either, until I saw her do some shooting in Mexico."

I said, "She's a monkey. She can climb just about anything, which comes in handy during situations like this."

Standing on the railing of the bottom balcony, Jennifer leapt up and grasped the concrete of the balcony above. From there, she began to move like a lizard, seeming to flow upward against gravity.

Creedwater said, "That is positively amazing. Where'd she come from?"

I said, "Cirque du Soleil. She's a gymnast."

We continued to watch her climb, Creedwater acting like he was in a spy movie, his mouth hanging open.

He said, "I wonder if she likes computer geeks."

What? I looked at him, and I swear I thought he was constructing some fantasy in his head. "Hey, keep focused on the mission. I didn't drag you out here so you could watch a show."

We were bringing him and his skills into the apartment

to survey whatever electronic stuff was available, hoping to find a lead. His mission ended at a keyboard. He snapped his mouth closed, embarrassed.

Decoy said, "Yeah, Creed. Trust me, you don't want to go after Jennifer. It'll make some people mad."

I snapped my head toward him, wondering. *Is that because I almost bit his head off for what he's said about Jennifer in the past? Or does he know? Did Knuckles talk?*

Decoy had a little grin on his face, giving nothing away.

Through my earpiece I heard, "On the balcony."

I said, "Roger," signaled Creed in the backseat, and opened the door to the car.

We walked with purpose to the front door of the complex, leaving Decoy behind as early warning in case Booth came back while we were inside.

We reached the entrance just as Jennifer said, "I'm in."

71

We waited less than thirty seconds before hearing the door buzz. A minute later, we were inside the apartment. It was your typical furnished rental, with a cheap sofa, chipped end tables, and absolutely no personal effects. No pictures on the walls, books, or anything else. Sitting next to a wide-screen TV, I saw an Alienware desktop computer that looked like it belonged to NASA. I pointed to it and said, "First things first, get all electronic devices next to that computer. Creed, get to work."

He laid a backpack on the ground and began pulling out all sorts of black-magic devices. Jennifer went into the bedroom.

I watched Creed attack the computer, fascinated that anyone could do what he was doing. I was pretty tech savvy, but this guy was on a whole different level. He had the monitor running script that looked like the Matrix but seemed to understand what he was reading.

I said, "Why can't you guys do this with the laptop we brought?"

Still working, he said, "We scanned it, and there are indicators of little booby traps threaded throughout. The guy who created that program is pretty damn good with code. Trust me, I could get into the computer, but I'm afraid that I'll cause the software program to self-destruct. We lose that thing, and we'll have no way to turn off the threat. Given enough time, I could do it, but not in two hours."

Story of my life.

Thirty minutes later he was done. In addition to the desktop, he'd gone through two tablets and an iPod. He'd collated a list of potential leads from various threads in each system. Known contacts, repeated bills from restaurants, multiple ISP hits, and anything else that stood out. I contacted the Taskforce and had them start their analysis. Given the time crunch, I needed some focus on where to begin. They'd be making an educated guess, but it was better than starting at the first name on the list and moving down.

Working the screen, Creed said, "This guy has been a very bad boy. He's accessed just about every hacking message board in the world."

"How do you know?"

"Because I used to do the same thing. Before I saw the light with the Taskforce."

"Can you work it back? Find out specifically who he talked to?"

"Yeah. Given some time, I could figure it out. Maybe not a name, but I could get the ISP location." He leaned into the screen and said, "I've also got one MAC address unaccounted for."

"What's that mean?"

"I have all of his router information, and included in that are MAC addresses that accessed his Wi-Fi. I can account for the target laptop you captured, these tablets, and the iPod, but there's one more MAC address that's not tied to anything we know of. Could just have been someone visiting, but maybe it's a lead."

"What are you talking about? How's that a lead?"

He started stroking the keys to the desktop, saying, "The MAC is the identification the computer uses to talk to Wi-Fi. It's specific to that computer, and we might be able to locate it."

"How?"

"There's a company called Skyhook. They've mapped close to a billion Wi-Fi hotspots, basically by driving down roads and sucking in signals. If that MAC is talking to a Wi-Fi hotspot in their database, it'll give us a location."

"So those guys can identify *any* MAC? Anywhere? Isn't that a little like an illegal wiretap?"

He smiled, still pounding keys. "No. You have to have their software program installed in your device. In effect, you have to agree to the location service."

"And you think this guy did that?"

He said, "No, he probably didn't do that, but Skyhook doesn't employ people like me. They won't locate you without the software, but it doesn't mean they can't. Well, it doesn't mean *I* can't. All I have to do is get in their system."

He continued typing and Jennifer came back into the room. She said, "Didn't find anything else of value. What's he doing?"

"Beats the hell out of me. Some type of black magic with a computer."

He typed a little more, then said, "Yes! It's here, in Colorado Springs."

On the screen was a Google map, with a glowing icon. Creed went to street view on the computer, and I was looking at the front of a bar called Blondie's.

Amazing. Scary, but amazing.

I called the Taskforce, seeing what they'd done with the data I'd given them. To my surprise, Kurt took the call instead of an analyst.

He said, "Pike, we've got him. The list you sent included a guy named Peter Scarborough. He works with Boeing as well. Both Peter and Booth are directly responsible for the monitoring of the GPS constellation. This morning Scarborough sent four thousand dollars via Western Union to Mexico City. I don't know if they're working together on this, but he's a definite link. Address will be in your phone. Get moving. You have less than an hour."

I said, "Sir, we have another location." I told him about the MAC address, saying, "Getting Peter won't be enough. We can always pick him up later, but we need Booth."

"But you don't know that's Booth's MAC address. It could be from someone who simply used his Wi-Fi, right?"

"Yeah, but this guy doesn't appear to have a lot of friends over. If I go to Peter's address and Booth's not there, I won't have time to redirect."

"You have the same problem in reverse. You get to the MAC address and Booth isn't on the keyboard, we're screwed. Pike, we get one shot. The strike package will be starting their attack run soon."

"You want to call it off? I don't have the manpower for split operations. It's either one target or the other."

"You tell me. The president's inclined to do so, but they're all waiting on word from your operation. That includes the guys entering Syrian airspace."

72

At forty-seven thousand feet, Captain Eddie "Brick-top" Brickmeyer checked the SATCOM radio, making sure the link was still established. Flying straight up the Mediterranean, he and his wingman were closing into range of Syrian air defenses, and he couldn't afford to miss an abort, should it come. The last thing he wanted to do was attempt penetration of a hostile country flying into the teeth of an arsenal designed to destroy any combat aircraft that dared approach, only to find out his mission had been scrubbed after the fact.

He knew the importance of the operation, though, and took pride in the fact that his squadron had been selected. There had been a lot of discussion over the last few years about how the B-2 was a luxury the United States no longer needed. With the end of the Cold War and the beginnings of the War on Terror, everyone had started kissing all the special operations forces' asses while looking askance at his missions, questioning his worth.

Why did we need such an expensive airframe? What terrorist group requires a Stealth bomber to eliminate it?

When would we ever require such technology fighting a substate threat? That's what the almighty SEALs and Special Forces were for. Better just to throw money at them.

Then this mission had appeared. No SEAL on earth could do what he was about to do. And no other aircraft could accomplish this mission. Could fly unseen through a barrage of radar and air defenses, penetrate and destroy a hardened, deeply buried target inside a hostile country.

When the president had asked for options to eliminate the threat of Syria's chemical weapons stockpile, plenty of ideas had been thrown around, but there was only one left standing in the end: a B-2 carrying MOPs, or massive ordnance penetrators, one in each weapons bay.

The MOP was a GPS-guided bomb that contained more than five thousand pounds of explosives. The largest conventional munition in the world, it was designed to burrow deep into a hardened bunker before exploding, rendering that protection moot.

The pilots called it the MOAB: the Mother of All Bombs. It had never been used in active hostility before, and Bricktop was honored to be chosen as the flight lead for the historic mission.

He checked his instruments, talked to his wingman, and began his attack run. In twenty minutes, they'd be inside Syrian airspace. Thirty minutes after that, they'd be a ghost heading back to the Med, but the world would know they had been there by the smoking holes they left in the ground. Whether those craters would reflect the destruction of Syria's WMD or the slaughter of innocents was not something that ever entered Bricktop's mind.

Other than the release point, he had no responsibility for targeting. There really was no need. He knew how precise GPS was. Knew that the encrypted military signal would put the MOAB within three yards of where it was intended. As long as he released it correctly, it couldn't miss, short of a catastrophic failure of the US GPS constellation.

And no way would that ever happen.

ABDUL HAKIM ROLLED over on his pallet and stared at the stars above his head. With the brutal heat of the Syrian desert, he, like most in his village, slept on the roof in the summertime. Dawn was still over an hour away, but he'd found it safer to make the water run before then. Before the soldiers awakened, skittish and willing to shoot at the slightest provocation.

He woke up his younger brother and they gathered the water containers—old milk jugs, gallon jars, and a battered plastic bucket—then descended the stairs to the street below.

Since the beginning of the uprising in Syria the brothers' lives had become hard. Living in Palmyra, in the center of the country, the environment was a challenge, but now with the fighting, it had become downright hostile.

Four months ago insurgents had set off a car bomb in front of the minister of intelligence's headquarters building. They'd managed to kill seven of the dreaded security forces, but the explosion within the close confines of the cramped town had shattered the livelihoods of many more. Abdul hated the violence and dreaded the thought of real firepower coming to bear.

The village had once been known as a major tourist pathway. Built on an oasis in the middle of the Syrian desert, it had been a Roman center for trade. Called Tadmor by the locals, the sheltered town had erupted in 2011 with protests against President Assad. Unfortunately for the inhabitants, Palmyra had something else besides relics that the government desired to protect. Something worth much more to them than a few musty stone arches.

Protests here were treated differently than the initial outbursts elsewhere. Here they were crushed with ruthless efficiency. The soldiers patrolling the streets knew nobody was watching this desolate desert town, but their hostility was driven by more than the simple absence of press. After the first protest and the forceful regime response, the people realized that the soldiers feared more than just losing the town. They feared losing what they'd been charged with protecting.

Abdul knew none of this, of course. All he understood was that they no longer had running water, and if he wished his family to drink today, he needed to collect enough before the sun rose. Before the soldiers woke and began scanning for targets.

He had no idea that their paltry little weapons were nothing compared to what was on its final approach to his location. No idea that his entire world was held hostage by a radio signal weak enough to be broken by a clap of thunder.

73

The *sicario* debated whether to clean up the mess or just leave it as is. He decided to leave it. Peter Scarborough hadn't changed his story at all, and the *sicario* had wasted precious time making sure. He wiped his knife on Peter's jacket, staring into the man's lifeless eyes, the neck wound gaping open, like a second mouth under the one with the tongue lolling out.

He hadn't died easy. After the *sicario*'s mistake in letting Booth escape with his lie, he had wanted to make sure with Peter. Leave no stone unturned. Peter had given him an answer at the mere threat of violence, but that hadn't been good enough. The *sicario* had left the soles of his feet at the far end of the bathtub, strips of flesh looking remarkably like thick-cut bacon from the grocery store. Fatty lengths of meat that were now curled in a pile. It hadn't been pleasant—for Peter anyway—but at least the *sicario* was sure.

According to him, Arthur Booth had called from a bar named Blondie's about an hour ago, and he was probably still there. The longer the *sicario* waited, the greater the chance Booth would leave. He closed his knife and stood, studying a map of Colorado Springs.

Peter lived in a small brick rental house just off Platte Avenue on the east side of town, in an area that was probably the place to be in 1950 but now had seen time erode its façade. Most of the houses were small, and none had been built after 1970. Blondie's was a mile or two to the west, in the small downtown area of Colorado Springs. A two-story bar in the renovated part of town only a couple of blocks from his hotel.

The *sicario* rubbed a smudge of blood from Peter's finger off the map, left when he'd pointed out the location. He tossed a towel on the body and walked out of the bathroom.

Opening the front door, he stood for a moment, glancing up and down the street and seeing nothing but leaves blowing in the shade. It was so different from his life in Ciudad Juárez. Trees and sidewalks. Children playing. No graffiti. No trash. The American journalist had been right. Nobody in this world had any comprehension of men like him. No comprehension of how protected and insulated they were.

They still assumed that there was a cause and effect in life, never understanding the meaning of the fox in the henhouse. They truly thought that doing good would beget good, just because of the action—and in turn that doing evil would beget evil. It was completely alien to him, and he wondered yet again if he'd missed out on some greater truth.

He'd slit Peter's throat from ear to ear, and even while

he'd bled out the *sicario* had seen Peter didn't believe it would happen. Didn't understand how it *could* happen. This after his feet had been peeled like a grape.

The *sicario* had done the work, halfway studying his response, and was amazed. He'd killed many, many men in Mexico, and when the time came, they were always resigned, understanding that death was knocking on their door and accepting it. Peter had begged until the last moment, even after the torture applied against him. After he'd screamed out the answer for the hundredth time. Believing he could alter the outcome.

Strange.

The *sicario* walked out the front door to his rental car and drove away, not bothering to check around him like he would have in Juárez. There was no reason to look for the hunter here, because there *were* no hunters here. He was unique, like a predator that had been inadvertently packed in a crate and shipped across the ocean, arriving in a new land looking for food.

His confidence was a mistake. Had he spent half of a second looking, he would have seen another predator. One who was his equal.

I PULLED INTO an alley behind Blondie's, calling Knuckles on the radio. I'd left Creed at the apartment to find out what else he could about the hackers Booth had been in contact with, then had alerted the rest of my team, telling them to move to the bar and prepare for assault.

A block off of Tejon Street, the ribbon of pavement I was on led through a large pay-for-parking area behind the strip of bars running down the middle of downtown Colorado Springs. Full of college kids and business professionals out for a good time, the area posed a significant risk to surgical operations.

Knuckles came back. "We're out front. No parking available except for a handicapped spot. I'm assuming the Taskforce will cover the ticket."

I said, "Don't worry about that. You got the computer?"

"Yeah. Hacking cell couldn't do anything with it. Clock's still ticking. What do you want to do?"

Which was the big question. The bar was a two-story affair full of people. Booth knew us all on sight and would probably run when we closed in, which would mean a nasty little fight in a public area. We might get bouncers on us, then have to take them out, causing someone to call 911, which would mean police flooding the place.

All I needed was about two minutes and Booth's thumb. But the repercussions might be significant.

I said, "Stage out front. When I call, we enter from both sides. Decoy and I will come in from the back. Koko will lock down our exit. You come in from the front. Leave Blood locking down that exit. But don't do anything until I get clearance. Calling Kurt now."

He said, "Roger. This is going to be great fun. I hope the prisons here are better than in Thailand."

I said, "Yeah, me too, since I won't be available to break our asses out. Stand by."

I dialed, getting Kurt immediately.

"Sir, we're staged to go in, but it's a bad, bad place for a takedown. I just want to make sure I'm covered for domestic operations."

I heard a bunch of voices in the background and realized what was going on. I said, "Am I on speaker?"

"Yeah, Pike, you are. What's the situation? We have about five minutes."

I went into politically correct mode. "Sir, we are about to enter an establishment and locate the man using the identified computer. If he is the target, we will not get out clean."

I'd made the call to go after the MAC address and ignore Peter Scarborough. It would be a defining moment in my life, either good or bad. If I was right, I would be a hero. If I was wrong, I would be the scapegoat of the year. Something I was used to, honestly. I'd learned early that it was easy to second-guess decisions but damn hard to make them.

I heard a crescendo of voices, then Kurt saying, "Hang on, damn it! Let him speak. Pike, we need to know the odds of success. We're in the window for abort. We don't make the call in the next five minutes, and we won't have the ability to do so. Can you stop it?"

What the hell? What kind of question is that? I have no idea.

"Sir, I can't predict that. I'm calling to ask for domestic authority. I'm about to enter a crowded establishment, and I'm going to do some damage. I don't have time for surgical. It'll be caveman. I'll get it done, but I want to make sure that's what you want. What the Oversight Council wants."

Someone from the back said, "Yes, yes. Tell him to go." That was followed by someone else saying, "Wait, he's going to compromise the Taskforce and we don't even know if it's worth it. What the hell are the odds of success?"

I thought the place sounded like a junior high dance, with about as much intelligent conversation coming out. I said, "Colonel Hale, this is Pike. What is the call?"

The sounds evaporated, and his voice came on. "You're off speaker. Pike, we have three minutes. I'm recommending abort. Don't assault. We'll live with the repercussions."

I said, "Sir, three minutes means those pilots are already in the envelope. Already in danger. And the repercussions are much, much greater than some strike against Syria. We lose GPS, and the whole country falls into chaos."

"Pike, that's going to happen regardless. We don't need to throw good money after bad. Compromising you will only cause the problem to be worse."

I looked at Jennifer, thinking of what I was sacrificing if the call was a mistake. I decided Kurt was right. There was no way I was going to trash my life based on some wish that the guy was inside and could stop the clock. If I were wrong—which I probably was—I might be going to jail at the same time our economy collapsed. Why throw gasoline on the fire?

Jennifer was staring intently at me, reading the hesitation in my voice. She said, "Pike, the Taskforce can burn. It's just an organization. Do it. The guy is here. You have an instinct for this. I know it. I *believe* it. Don't worry about us. Don't worry about the repercussions of this operation. Worry about the repercussions to America. You can stop it, right here and right now. Do what's right. Like in Mexico."

I locked eyes with her for an instant. She nodded at me, and I committed, wondering if she had some ESP that I was lacking. Praying it was true.

I said, "Execute. Tell them to execute. I'll stop the clock."

Kurt said, "What? Pike, are you sure?"

I said, "Fucking execute. I'm out."

I ended the call and said, "You'd better hope your instincts are better than mine, because my instincts are saying we're going to separate prisons."

She said, "Two minutes. Go."

I left the car with Decoy, saying, "Lock down this exit."

74

The Ghost watched Pelón's car driving away and debated whether to enter the house. There was some reason he'd gone inside, and it might give him an edge. He'd been there for more than an hour, but the Ghost had no idea why. Maybe he should enter and find out what the man had done. At the end of the day, he had Pelón's beddown location and could always return to the parking garage, waiting for his chance again should he lose the man. But Pelón might not return to the garage, which meant he needed to stick to him and ignore the house.

Choices, choices.

Hours earlier, in Mexico City, he'd planned a route of escape, going to several banks and withdrawing as much cash as he could on the three credit cards he still maintained. He'd checked the balance and seen one of them was fresh, with over ten thousand dollars in credit. The others had about two thousand each, after the cash withdrawals.

He'd used them to pepper the American radar with plane tickets, buying as many as he could to destinations in South America, the Far East, and, of course, the Middle East. One was to Hamburg, Germany, which was the ticket he had intended to use.

Out of curiosity, he'd checked Pelón's bank account and had seen three new transactions: one for a hotel called the Antlers Hilton in Colorado Springs, one for a rental car at the Colorado Springs airport, and one he didn't understand, with something called Manny Aviation Services.

After thirty seconds of research, he'd learned it was a private aviation company, and it dawned on him what Pelón had done.

He's spending my money on private jets. But why Colorado Springs? What's there?

His flight to Hamburg wasn't for three days. Three days and he'd be on his own, severed from the American's trail but also incapable of traveling anywhere else because that bastard Pelón had taken his money.

He'd stared at the bank transactions, then decided. He had nothing here. A new passport and a few credit cards he could never use once he left Mexico. Pelón had the money. Money that was rightfully his.

He'd used the card with ten grand to charter his own flight, right into Colorado Springs. Right to the man who had his money. The Americans would be watching the transactions he'd made today but wouldn't be able to react in time, since they had no idea of the name he was using and the air charter wouldn't reflect his destination. Only a purchase.

It was a risk, flying into the belly of the beast, but he knew from past operations that FBOs, even in America, were fairly lax. The charter, while expensive, was much, much safer than trying to trick the Americans with multiple tickets.

He'd landed two hours ago and had leveraged the charter service to rent a car for him, using cash to pay for it, then drove straight to the Antlers Hilton. Knowing that Pelón had a rental as well, he circled around back, positioning himself in a spot where he could watch the exits from the multipurpose parking garage. He'd conducted a reconnaissance of the garage, determining where hotel guests parked and liking what he saw. If he cornered Pelón in here, he could kill him without alert. Get the electronic token and be on his way. Provided Pelón had actually parked inside.

He'd waited, as he had on any number of operations, and his patience had been rewarded. Pelón had driven out of the garage, surprising the Ghost. In his heart he had only been half convinced that the man would appear, and here he was. The Ghost had leaned his face against the glass to be sure, then had followed through the streets. He'd shadowed Pelón to the small house, then waited outside for him to return to his car, wondering who the killer was meeting. Wondering what had happened inside.

Watching Pelón's taillights receding down the street, he put the car in drive, ignoring his curiosity about the house and deciding to follow. At the end of the day

Pelón's plans in Colorado mattered little. The only important thing was the electronic token he owned that accessed the bank account. A token the Ghost was sure was on his person.

Pelón traveled down Platte Avenue, going toward the city center. Once again acting as if he had a destination in mind. Making the Ghost wonder anew at what he was doing. He had the money, so why not simply flee? Why did he come here?

Pelón passed a large park, then turned left into an alley between two buildings. The Ghost followed. He traveled down the narrow gap, crossing one street, then another, the alley opening up into a parking area. Pelón's car slowed. A block behind, the Ghost waited in the alley, not wanting to reveal that he was there. Pelón drove a short distance through the parking area, then stopped, right next to an exit leading back to the east. Another alley. Seeing two other cars pull into the lot, the Ghost followed, keeping his eyes on the killer's car.

He pulled up short, giving him the ability to flee the way he had come but also circle around and intersect Pelón on Tejon Street, should he use the alley exit to the east.

He watched the car, waiting on something to happen. Curious as to what Pelón was doing here, in a back-alley parking lot in Colorado Springs.

Eventually, he saw a light come on inside Pelón's car, then recognized him exiting. He was only fifty meters away; even at night the Ghost could identify his shattered visage, the scars on his forehead glowing in the interior light of the car.

Pelón shut his door and crouched, moving through the other cars as if he were trying to hide. As if he were hunting something.

The Ghost followed his line of march with his eyes. And saw his target, twenty meters away.

75

I entered the back of the bar with Decoy, feeling the pressure of my decision. Not liking the weight on my shoulders. We ran into a room full of pool tables, the bar packed to the gills. I started swiveling my head, immediately realizing the stupidity of my bravado on the phone.

There is no way we're going to find this guy inside here. Not in under two minutes. Damn it. I should have aborted Operation Gimlet.

I called Knuckles. "We're in. Status?"

"I have the computer with me, and it's got about ten minutes of battery left."

No issue. Two minutes from now it won't matter.

He continued. "I came in the front, but there's a stairwell on the other side that leads into the bar to the south. I've got Blood positioned there. Pike, we're out of time. I'm tracking two minutes and counting."

"I know, I know. Find him. He's here." *I hope.*

Decoy and I pushed our way into the main bar area

and I saw a circular stairway leading up. *Holy shit. Another exit. That makes four. We are screwed.*

I pulled Decoy's sleeve. "I'm headed up. Keep going forward. You find him, lock him down. I don't give a damn about the repercussions. He resists, knock him the fuck out. Call and we'll handle the bouncers."

He said, "Wow. I'm getting paid to get in a bar fight. Where were you ten years ago?"

I would have laughed, but the impact of my decision to continue took away all humor. Beyond the fact that the US grid was going to grind to a halt, there were a lot of civilians in Syria who were going to be incinerated by American airpower. And I'd made the decision to execute.

I sprinted up the circular staircase, exploding onto the second floor and drawing stares. This floor had another bar running lengthwise from the staircase exit, and it was full of people. I started bulling my way through, now drawing glares. That was fine by me. I needed a reaction. Girls were talking and pointing, and guys were bowing up. I saw another staircase to the right and hoped that was the one Blood was tracking.

To my front was a balcony with a fire pit. No Arthur Booth. To my right was another room. I could see tables inside. I started moving that way when a lumberjack-looking guy said, "Hey, you got any manners?"

I said, "I'm sorry, I'm looking for my daughter. She's underage and she's here with a guy." The excuse was just the first thing I could come up with. His answer was the worst thing he could have said.

He glanced at the man behind him and said, "Maybe she's here with me."

My sweet daughter's face flashed in my head, forever six years old, and I punched his throat as hard as I could, watching him collapse on the ground. His buddy looked at me in shock, and blackness began to flow. The pressure causing the beast to appear.

I said, "You seen my daughter?"

He shook his head like he was a dog wringing water.

"Then move the fuck out of my way."

He piled into the people behind him as if he were fleeing a fire. I marched through the gap, everyone now focused on the turmoil. I reached the room and saw a man with a computer. He looked up, and I recognized Arthur Booth.

He slammed the lid down and took off running, straight toward the stairs on the far side. I started flinging people out of the way, but my rage did no good. The sheer physics of the bodies prevented me from intercepting him. I made it to the top of the stairs as he was reaching the bottom. Reaching the exit to the bar next door.

I bounded down the steps three at a time. He turned in the landing and I lost sight of him. For one second. He was gone, then he appeared again, flying into the wall and collapsing. Blood whirled around the corner, his fists raised. He saw me and turned back to the target.

I said, "Knuckles, Knuckles, jackpot. I say again, jackpot. Eastern stairwell leading to the other bar. Need the computer. Need it right now!"

Booth rolled around on the filthy floor, finally focusing. He said, "I have rights. I want a lawyer."

I pulled out a serrated knife and said, "All I want is your fucking thumb."

76

The *sicario* strained his eyes, trying to penetrate the glare from the streetlight. He'd passed the car and seen the person inside, the brief instant shocking him. It was the female from Mexico City. The same one from Tepito. The one who'd interrupted the meeting in the museum. But how? Why was she here?

And it dawned on him. She was still tracking Arthur Booth. She was trying to capture him for his computer skills. The *sicario* no longer cared about that, but he cared a great deal about what Booth would say. He would give up the *sicario*'s true name. And for that, she would have to die.

He sat in the darkness and thought of the intertwining of events. It was always a mixture of circumstances. On the surface, none seemed to matter, but all were intertwined. Random events that shaped future events, but there wasn't any overarching purpose. Like the fox in his youth. An animal following his nature had caused the loss of their livelihood and had driven his sister to prostitution. She had become a favorite of his Kaibil battalion commander, and because of it, his village had been targeted by rebels. He in turn had exacted his revenge. Had started on his path.

Nothing but random events.

Throughout all of the brutality he had searched for meaning. Searched to find some fingerprint from the hand of God, but had failed. And the woman here was but one more piece of evidence. He would kill her, and nothing would stop that.

He had worried about his soul. Worried that he would burn in hell for his actions, but there was no hell. No greater being that would punish him. The journalist had been wrong and he had been right. There was no such thing as good or evil. Only interconnected events. God couldn't punish him for actions that He could prevent. And He had never once prevented anything the *sicario* had done.

He slid out of the car, crouching between it and the one next to him, and began to stalk, his thoughts saddening him.

He wanted to believe in destiny. Wanted to believe, like the journalist, that there was good and evil in the world, and that following one path led to salvation. Even if it meant he would burn in hell for eternity. That one moment of truth would be worth the price.

But it wasn't to be. The girl would die at his hand, whether she was good or evil. Then Booth would die.

Then he would die, years from now, probably in a bathroom, much like Peter, after slipping on a bar of soap.

There was no such thing as justice. It was all random events.

He slid between the cars, staying out of the rearview mirrors of his target. He approached at a crouch, slinking along the ground. Moving forward one step at a time, he kept his eyes on the driver's-side door. He reached the rear quarter panel of the car and paused. He slowly rose up and saw the girl leaning forward, as if she were listening to the radio. Focusing on something else besides her immediate surroundings.

He pulled his knife and scooted forward. He took one breath and flung the door open. She turned in surprise. He grabbed her shoulder and jerked her out of the car, intent on stabbing her in the heart. From the ground, she kicked his leg, breaking his balance, then began to scramble away on her back like a crab.

He fell on top of her, surprised at her reaction. He grabbed her hair and twisted her head. She screamed and brought her knee up, hammering his inner thigh. He grunted and brought the knife down. She parried the blow with her forearm, the blade slicing her flesh.

Fighting like a banshee, she hammered his face with the same forearm, causing his vision to explode in stars. Still holding her hair, he slammed her head into the pavement, then felt a blinding pain in his right arm. He tried to raise it and couldn't. He felt another searing pain in his lower back, burrowing into his kidney, and rolled over, seeking the source.

He saw the Arab from the museum above him. The killer now taking his payment. He rose to his knees, the Arab crouching over him with a blade dripping blood. He felt the warmth of his body leaking around his waist, spreading on the ground. And he was finally at peace. Finally understood.

He said, "Of course. It's you. So there is no bar of soap."

The killer stared at him through his thick glasses, slight of build but breathtaking in his destruction. The *sicario* staggered backward, slapping a bloody hand against the car for support.

He looked up and said, "Tell me, please, do you fear what you have done? Do you believe in judgment?"

The Arab remained still and said, "I fear what I have done now. I fear that I have prevented my freedom. Because of you."

The *sicario* smiled. "Destiny. Not random. The fist of God."

His hand slipped in his own blood, causing him to slide against the car. He struggled for purchase, sagging forward. He looked his killer in the eye and said, "Thank you."

He began to fade, the vision of the killer replaced by one of his mother, cooking in the kitchen of their little hovel in Guatemala. The smells as vivid as the day they'd happened.

He fell onto his face, his body hitting the pavement and splashing the blood rupturing out of his vital organs.

He heard his sister outside, calling him. Telling him it wasn't his fault. Beckoning. His body left the hut and he found her, sitting in a yard full of chickens, petting a fox on the head.

77

With Decoy, Knuckles, and Blood surrounding us, I dragged Booth back up the stairs and into the light. The clock was at one minute and counting. I threw him into a chair and shoved the computer in his face.

"Turn that shit off. Right now."

He made another comment about a lawyer, and I slammed his hand onto the table, running my knife against the back of his knuckle. The people in the bar went crazy at that scene, but my little protective security detail kept everyone at bay, and Booth saw the light. With sweat dripping from his greasy, traitorous head, he decided that admitting he could stop the attack would be better than losing his thumb.

He accessed the computer.

With forty seconds left, he made one dumb comment about not being responsible for what "we" had put on his computer, since it had been outside of his control. I placed the knife against his neck. Not sure whether I was serious, he looked at me with dishpan eyes and began typing, disabling all the little software booby traps. Which was a good call, because I was way, way serious.

The clock kept ticking. I said, "What the hell are you doing? Shut it down."

He said, "I'm trying to. I have to get through my security."

At five seconds I said, "Just so you know, your life is tied to this. It doesn't go down, and you do. Permanently. Right here and right now."

His fingers trembling, he tapped a few more keys, and the clock stopped.

I sagged against the bench, drawing deep breaths. Booth said, "Can I go now?" I popped him in the face hard enough to bounce his head into the wall.

SEVEN THOUSAND MILES away, Bricktop hit his release point. His headset chattering incessantly now, he talked to both his wingman and his copilot in a robotic monotone, maintaining the myth of calm over a military net, like every pilot before him. He opened the bay doors. The two MOABs sat silently, dumb pieces of metal holding more destructive power than anything on earth outside of a nuclear bomb.

He hit the release, and they fell to earth, now alive and seeking information to guide them to their target. They locked on to the GPS signal and began to glide, shifting left and right, furiously attempting to please their master by destroying themselves precisely where they had been ordered.

*   *   *

ABDUL HAKIM CRACKED the door to his house, peeking out at the cloistered confines of Palmyra. To the east he saw the glow of the infamous Tadmor prison, where President Assad's father had imprisoned many, many members of the Muslim Brotherhood for daring to defy him in a fight before Abdul had been born. Farther out he saw the lights of the Palmyra airfield, a military enclave that the regime apparently would do anything to protect.

Seeing nothing outside the door, Abdul touched his brother's arm and began walking down the alley, the houses so close together there was nowhere to hide should trouble appear.

A flash over toward the airfield caught his eye. He held up, pushing his brother into a wall, straining to see what had caused the light. A second later the earth split apart as if the Devil himself were escaping, the violent action muted solely by the distance.

Two seconds later the shock wave hit, and he and his brother were flattened on the sidewalk, buffeted with debris from a strike nearly a mile away. Abdul sat up and stared uncomprehendingly, watching a mushroom cloud rise exactly like in an old TV show, wondering if Israel had struck with nuclear weapons.

Unaware of how close he had come to dying because of a fragile radio signal.

*   *   *

BRICKTOP LOOKED OUT the window of his B-2 and saw the impact, feeling immense pride. A round-trip mission of national importance, from the heart of the United States. Just like the doctrine that had led to the creation of his aircraft during the Cold War. There *was* a reason for his weapon system. For the money spent on his capability.

After all, no snake eater had done a damn thing for this operation.

JENNIFER FELT LIKE her head had been smothered in cotton. She fought the fog, some internal instinct telling her it was vital but not consciously knowing why. Her brain began to clear, and she saw the man who had attacked her slip against the car, then slam face-first into the pavement, his body across her legs.

She began to rise and heard, "Don't! Don't move."

She turned and saw the Ghost. Standing above her with a knife.

She pulled her legs out from underneath the body and he shouted again, "No, no, no. Stay down. Please."

She stopped her movement and looked into his eyes. She knew what he had done. Knew he had saved her life. She rose into a crouch, saying, "I can't."

He said, "I know."

And attacked.

78

I exited the bar out the back, dragging Booth with me and letting Knuckles, Decoy, and Blood handle the repercussions. It was a mess, but we knew what would happen going in. They had the cover story down, which was to act like a bunch of drunk service members here on temporary duty to NORTHCOM, at Peterson Air Force Base. With Booth out of the way, there was nobody who would contradict the story.

They'd either talk their way out of it or spend a night in jail. Either way, the Taskforce would back them up, and they'd get turned over to the "military" pretty quickly. Since I was out of the military and a full-fledged owner of a company that the Taskforce was worried would be exposed in twenty-four hours, I decided to take charge. Fleeing, as it were.

We came out the back patio and crossed the parking lot, me dragging Booth by the elbow. He kept complaining, moaning about how his rights had been abused, and I was considering just punching his lights out. The only question was whether carrying his dead weight would be worse than listening to his bullshit.

We crossed the alley and for the first time I noticed a scuffle near my car. Near Jennifer. I released Booth's elbow and began to run, seeing it wasn't a scuffle but a full-fledged fight to the death.

The battle spilled into the glow of a streetlamp, and I saw the Ghost trying to kill Jennifer. The image was completely surreal, like a nightmare come to life.

What the hell is he doing here? He hates me so much he gave up freedom to find me?

I reached the fight and hammered him in the small of his back, bringing him to his knees. I kicked the knife out of his hand and jerked his head up by the hair, causing his glasses to fly off. I raised my hand for a killing blow and heard, "*Stop!*"

I paused, seeing Jennifer with her hands on her knees, gasping for air. She looked up and said, "Don't hurt him. Leave him alone."

"What the hell are you talking about? He's trying to kill us."

The Ghost began to flex in my hands, and I lowered my grip, placing his head between my arms. I whispered in his ear, "Don't move."

He complied with the command, going limp.

I dragged him past Jennifer, to our car, and saw a body.

Jennifer rose up. Her face was pummeled and I saw a wicked slash on her forearm, bringing forth the rage again. I flung the Ghost against the door and he sagged to the ground, staring up at me.

I thought about killing him outright, and Jennifer said, "Pike. Don't."

Staring into his eyes, I said, "Why not?"

"He saved my life. He killed the man on the ground. If he hadn't intervened, I'd be dead."

For the first time, I looked closely at the body. It was the strange kidnapper from Mexico, which confused me even more. As is my nature, I decided force was the answer. I leaned into the Ghost, taking his hair into my hand and banging his head against the car door.

"What the fuck are you doing here? What's going on?"

Jennifer grabbed my arm, stopping the assault, and the Ghost spoke. "I was trying to escape. But I guess you can never escape your destiny."

He smiled at some inside joke and I turned to Jennifer. She said, "I don't understand it any more than you. He saved my life, Pike. He really did."

I felt movement over my shoulder and saw Booth doing a shuffling, rambling run. Like something out of a zombie apocalypse movie.

What the hell? Now this?

"Jennifer," I said, "would you mind keeping that asshole from getting away while I have a conversation here?"

She took off, and I turned back to the Ghost. He looked up at me serenely. No fear and no regrets.

"What happened here? What's she talking about?"

"She saved my life in Mexico. I made the mistake of returning the favor."

His words sank in, but I was having a hard time assimilating them. It made no sense. The guy was a master terrorist who killed without remorse. Why the hell would he protect Jennifer?

"Are you telling me you saved Jennifer's life here? Tonight? Interceded on her behalf?"

He smiled without any humor and said, "Unfortunately, yes."

If what he said was true, he was putting me in a very awkward position. I couldn't very well pummel the man who had saved Jennifer's life. There had to be some ulterior motive. "But why? Why would you do that?"

I saw Jennifer coming across the parking lot, dragging that waste of flesh we knew as Arthur Booth. The Ghost said, "Because she helped me once, at great risk to herself. You give up what you are, and you are lost."

"But you were trying to kill her just now. I don't get it."

His eyes closed and he said, "I don't understand either. I'm sure you'll get my answer in due time, inside my cell."

79

I watched the Dulles runway lights approach and wondered what news was waiting on me about my team. I'd talked to Kurt immediately after leaving Blondie's, and the decision had been made for me to pack up what I could and get Grolier Recovery Services out of the blast radius in Colorado Springs. We were still working to stop the Anonymous leak, which was set to fire in a little under twenty-four hours. If we couldn't, the Oversight Council had decided that CNN's making a link to the mess in Colorado Springs would be enough to cause further digging. Jennifer and I had bundled Booth, the Ghost, and the computer cell onto the Gulfstream with orders to get to Taskforce headquarters in DC, leaving the rest of the team behind.

The Oversight Council had been ecstatic at our success, of course. Initial reports from Operation Gimlet were positive, and the GPS constellation had held. No Wall Street collapse. No collapse of our cellular network or power grid. No collapse of our military capability. Three hundred million citizens of America went about their daily lives not realizing how close they'd come to Armageddon, but it was par for the course for the Taskforce. The public's not knowing was the definition of success.

On the other hand, the Oversight Council did know, and I thought they were cheering a little bit early. On the phone call I had reminded Kurt the mission wasn't over until extraction was complete. We still had some cleanup with Knuckles and the rest of the team. He was working it, and I wondered what had transpired during my flight.

We touched down and I dialed my phone. Kurt answered, saying he was in the Dulles FBO with a support package and was ready to receive. While I waited inside the plane, babysitting our detainees, the support package traveled out as if they were a maintenance crew, bringing all sorts of containers and tools to the aircraft. They entered and I pointed to Booth, saying, "Him first." They went to work.

As they stuck a needle in his arm, sedating him, the last image I had of Arthur Booth was him blubbering in hitches, tears running down his cheeks. He was shoved in a container and wheeled away. I had no idea what they'd do with him, since he was an American citizen, but honestly, I didn't really care.

The Ghost had sat silently, waiting on them to return for him. Stoic. Understanding his fate. Certainly no tears.

I could tell Jennifer was conflicted about the whole thing, but it was what it was. He was a terrorist who had killed Americans. Had tried to kill both Jennifer and me on different occasions. Had almost blown up Knuckles with an IED. Had come close to killing a ruling citizen of the United Arab Emirates and our own envoy in an attempt to destroy peace in the Middle East. If it hadn't been for the Taskforce he would have succeeded, cheering about the deaths.

And yet he'd saved Jennifer from the Mexican hit man. Something that mattered greatly to me.

Americans liked a black-and-white world, with everything clean. Some men wore the black hats, and some wore the white. Black was pure evil and needed to be eradicated. White was the shining knight and could only do good. The problem was I knew the truth. I wore a white hat, and I had seen and done things that couldn't even charitably be considered worthy of the color. And now I was looking at a man on the other side who had done something that was.

I said, "I want to thank you for what you did. Unfortunately, that's all you're going to get."

He looked at me, remaining silent.

I waited, and when he didn't respond I said, "You and I both know you didn't help in Mexico. But you did in Colorado, and that means something."

The Ghost barked a short laugh. He paused a moment, then spoke. "Means what, exactly? I get your gratitude? The truth is I saved your lover in a moment of weakness. It was a mistake, and I'll now pay for it."

Lover? Now a damn terrorist can see through me?

I ignored that comment and said, "You mean that? What you did was a mistake?"

The support team appeared inside the aircraft and the Ghost extended his shackled arms, giving them an easy vein. A man stuck in the needle and he flinched.

He turned from the man and looked me in the eye. "You and I are closer than you think. You are closer to the man I killed to save her than the man standing above me right now. You know it. I know it."

I said, "I don't kill people for an outcome. I kill people to *prevent* an outcome."

He said, "Maybe. Maybe you do. But it's only because of where you were born. Sheer luck. If you were in Mexico, the killing would be different. You'd still do it."

"Bullshit. Don't justify your pathetic attacks as part of a system of fate. You don't even believe that. If you did, you would have let Jennifer die. It's more than circumstances, more than a series of events, and you know it. You told me that you had to be yourself or risk losing everything. And in so doing you *did* lose everything. Why did you save Jennifer?"

His eyes began to fade from the medication. He said, "I honestly don't know. Right now, I believe it was a mistake, but if I had to do it over again, I'm not sure I wouldn't still be sitting here."

I watched his eyes close and said, "That's good enough."

I let the support team finish their work, then motioned

for the computer hacking cell to exit. Jennifer and I went last, meeting Kurt in the FBO lobby.

He shook my hand, then saw Jennifer and said, "Jesus. You really did get the shit kicked out of you."

She had a black eye, butterfly bandages on her forehead, and a large gauze pad covering stitches on her right forearm. She said, "I'll live."

He shook her hand and smiled. "Sorry about the damage, but it looks like I don't have to fire you now. Come on. I have a room down the hall."

We entered a deserted pilot's lounge with a row of La-Z-Boy chairs and a dining room table in the corner. He motioned to the table and took a seat. Before he could start I said, "I want to talk to you about the Ghost. I promised him a better cell if he helped with the mission. I'd like to honor that."

"Why? He didn't help at all. In fact, his premature alert almost caused a total meltdown."

"He saved Jennifer's life. That's the only reason we have him in custody. He could have let her get sliced up by that nut job from Mexico, but he didn't."

"He's still a terrorist."

"I know that. I'm not saying let him go free. I'm just saying give him some amenities in his cell. That's all. Make his time a little easier."

He leaned back and remained silent. I said, "Look at Jennifer. He saved her life. The least you should do is give her a vote."

He glanced over at her, taking in the damage again. He said, "He tried to kill you. You think he deserves a reward?"

She said, "He's going to be locked up forever for that, but only because he saved my life in the first place. He's going to die in that jail, when he could have gone free."

He said, "We haven't seen it in the Taskforce yet, but the budget crunch is coming and I'm not going to spend my money making a terrorist comfortable."

I pulled out the digital token we'd taken off the hit man from Mexico and slid it across the table. "How about making al-Qaeda pay for it?"

After I explained about the bank account from the hit man and more prodding from Jennifer, Kurt said, "Okay, okay. You guys are relentless. Dumbest damn thing I've ever heard."

I smiled and said, "It'll only be dumb if the Ghost's jail cell is better than the team's. What's the story with them?"

"They'll be coming home today. Should be here by late afternoon. We hit a snag with NORTHCOM, but the SECDEF is sorting it out. We couldn't get to the command before the police, and their first answer was 'Never heard of those guys.' The police held them a little longer until we could get someone on the phone who backed up the story."

"So we're clean? What about the dead hit man?"

"He's causing issues. Luckily, he was killed while you guys were inside, so we have a pretty solid alibi, but the coincidence is there. The police have demanded names and addresses for follow-up questions, so those guys won't be operational for a while. Especially with this You-Tube thing coming."

Great. So I'd left a dead man who was now causing my team to stop operations.

While we were getting both the Ghost and Booth secured in our car, another car had entered the lot. I'd left Jennifer guarding the two men and was dragging the hit man to the trunk when I saw the lights flash as it hit the speed bump at the entrance to the alley. I didn't know if it was police responding to the Blondie's disturbance or just another car full of patrons, but either one witnessing me dragging a dead body was bad. I stuffed it next to a pickup, and we'd left. Wasn't anything else I could do, but the repercussions were now harming my team. Made worse by this YouTube video coming out.

I said, "Where do we stand with the video thing?"

"Nowhere. We'll get Booth behind a computer and see what we can find, but it probably won't help unless he personally knows the guy, which he won't. It'll take too long to go through all of the leads. Right now the hacking cell is spending their time covering Taskforce tracks, including connections to Grolier Recovery Services. I feel like Ollie North ordering Fawn Hall to start shredding documents. Destroying evidence, and trying to keep this thing to a twenty-four-hour crackpot story."

"What about Creed? All that shit he located? None of that panned out?"

"Creed? You mean Bartholomew Creedwater? He's been helping you?"

"Yeah, and while Jennifer and I were running around trying to find Booth, he was rooting through Booth's home computer. By the time we picked him up for the flight he'd been at it for four hours. He's already done the homework, and he brought the computer with him."

80

I drove past McLean Central Park to the Dolley Madison Library, my designated linkup point. Ironically, our target's house was about two miles as the crow flies from the headquarters of the CIA, in McLean, Virginia, home of the rich and powerful. The library was close enough to the target to allow the team to penetrate without delay, but far enough away that the meeting would never be correlated with the follow-on break-in. My only complaint was that Kurt wouldn't let me do the high adventure.

Earlier, after hearing about Creed and his research, Kurt had practically flung him out of the building, taking him to Taskforce headquarters, leaving Jennifer and me at the Dulles FBO. Ordering us to stand by until he returned. Since Grolier Recovery Services already had plenty of nefarious digital connections to the headquarters, there was no way we were going to make matters worse by going there in the flesh. I decided to stay right in the comfortable pilot's lounge until we had an answer.

Jennifer had watched him leave and said, "Well, what do you want to do now?"

I curled up in a La-Z-Boy and said, "Get some sleep. I'm bushed."

She got in the chair next to me. "Looks like we get the same room together for once."

I laughed and said, "I don't think our secret is much of a secret. I think everyone on the team knows. Kurt is probably the only one still in the dark. Well, him and Creed."

She absently picked at the bandage on her arm. "You think that's a bad thing? Are you still wondering about me being in the Taskforce? On your team?"

I put my arms behind my head and said, "No. It's not a bad thing. I've thought about it a lot, and I'm good with you on the team. More than good. Mission-wise, we click, regardless of how we feel about each other. Or maybe *because* of how we feel about each other. I don't know. I have to get over some protective caveman stuff, but we work well together. We'll see what the team thinks of our relationship, but I'm more concerned about the command. If Kurt finds out about us, he might hammer me just because of the implications. This sort of thing is illegal in the military."

She smiled, liking the answer. "Then I guess we'd better not let him find out."

"Does that mean we're not doing anything in our first Taskforce single room?"

The smile melted into a frown. *No sense of humor.* I pushed her buttons some more.

I said, "Kurt won't be back for hours, and these chairs are comfy."

She threw her water bottle at me, barely missing my head. I batted it away and said, "Okay, okay. I get it. No single rooms on the Taskforce paycheck. Let's get some sleep."

She gave me her disapproving-teacher look and said, "You're working on no single rooms period."

I closed my eyes and thought maybe a minute had passed when I felt someone prodding my shoulder. I said, "Jennifer, you had your chance."

I heard, "Chance for what?"

I looked up and saw Kurt Hale. *Way to go, bumble brain.*

My watch told me I'd been out for five hours, which amazed me. I said, "Chance to get some sleep. What's up?"

"We've found the guy, but it's not pretty. The Oversight Council is working through options to mitigate the impact of the YouTube video given the information we now have. I need you and Jennifer to get back to Charleston and start doing normal things. Act like normal citizens in case someone comes around with questions. We think we can stop the bleeding fairly quickly, but not with you in Washington. Too many questions to answer."

"Who is it?"

"It's the son of an influential lobbyist here in DC. Unfortunately, a lobbyist working for the other party, against the administration. He made a career as a political aide, then took his skills to K Street. His son is the one doing the hack. A twenty-five-year-old loser. Apparently a genius who went to MIT and dropped out. Now he spends his time aggravating his dad by being a social leper, running around with Occupy Whatever Street and protesting economic summits. Lives in the basement of his father's house in McLean."

"He's here? Right here in DC? Shit, sir, let me go after him. We still have time."

"How? You think you're going to kidnap the son of one of the most powerful lobbyists in DC? Then what? Throw him in the Cloud? If it was some lone-wolf loser living in a trailer somewhere, maybe I'd let you kick his ass for a lesson, but not here. We'll leverage the folks inside the Oversight Council to mitigate the damage. Get the father to play ball using what he knows well—political capital."

"Sir, that's crazy. He'll smell blood in the water and get the very investigation we don't want. He'll use the video as a weapon. We need to do it preemptively. Like the congressman from Egypt. Remember him?"

"Yeah. Of course. He had a hand in my father's death."

"We do the same thing here. He went to prison for child porn instead of taking the heat for treason. Took the jail time instead of the death penalty."

"That's just it. The kid hasn't *done* anything, other than help Booth dig into our digital signature. He's posted a video saying he's going to expose an illegal government spy operation. Which is exactly what we are.

We're the ones breaking the law. We've got nothing to pin on him. The council isn't too keen on a domestic operation like that. I tried earlier. They said I was acting like Los Zetas."

Now *they get skittish.*

My mind working at ninety miles an hour, I said, "He's a hacker, right? He's hacked more than just our systems. Surely he's done something illegal."

"Yeah, Creed's found a ton of stuff, but we can't very well charge him without exposing how we got the information. We might as well put up our own YouTube video."

"The father's political?"

"Political as they come."

"Okay. Get me into his house. The senator agreed to the child-porn thing so we wouldn't give him the death penalty. Let me do the same thing here. I'll put child porn on his computer. Then we send a tip to the police through Anonymous."

"What?"

I began to pace, saying, "This will work. One of the things Anonymous does is expose child pornographers by hacking their systems and sending it to the police. About the only good thing they do. I'll get porn on his computer, and our hacking cell will alert the police, posing as Anonymous. They take him down."

"Did you hear what I said earlier? The Oversight Council isn't going to approve a frame like that. The congressman was a traitor and responsible for American deaths. This guy isn't. They want to work it from the inside, using politics. Anyway, that's only half the battle. That video is still going up."

"Wait, I'm not finished. You—or someone on the Oversight Council—engage the father. Somehow, get it in the father's head or his lawyer's head that his son was working with Anonymous to expose a child porn ring, and *that's* why the evidence is there. He'll jump on that like a hobo on a ham sandwich. He'll go for the lesser charge of hacking over the child porn, and he'll owe us big-time. We can get him to manage the video. Keep it from being a weapon. The kid gets a slap on the wrist and we get political control of the fight."

Jennifer was looking at me in awe. She said, "You mean you're going to plant child porn on his computer, then alert the police *posing* as Anonymous, then have him get out of the child-porn charges by admitting he was attempting to expose *other* child pornographers by breaking the law working for Anonymous?"

I said, "Yeah. That's about the size of it. He gets charged with what he actually did—illegal hacking. We provide help to the lobbyist through the administration, and that video goes nowhere. No follow-on evidence. Surely the Oversight Council will agree to that."

She said, "Where has that been hiding? Have you always been that devious?"

"Oh yeah. I got you to agree to Grolier Recovery Services, didn't I?"

It was a joke, but she scrunched her eyes, now wondering. I said, "Sir, let's do it. All I need is Creedwater. Jennifer and I can handle the B and E. He can handle the computers."

Kurt looked at me much like Jennifer, probably reviewing every past decision he'd made involving my team and wondering if I had manipulated him. He said, "I have to get sanction for that. Obviously. But I like it."

I said, "Hell, it's only ten in the morning. We can't get in until nightfall anyway. You do your work, and I'll do the reconnaissance. Just tell me if it's a go."

81

Apparently, the Oversight Council liked my deviousness, because twelve hours later I was sitting in a library parking lot about to pass the intel from our reconnaissance to the inbound team. Well, the council liked the plan but had really hated the idea of me doing the B & E. Too close to the flame for them. I guess it made sense. No matter how good I thought I was, every operation has a chance to go sideways. We were trying to defuse the YouTube video, and having the owner of Grolier Recovery Services arrested breaking into the house of someone who was about to post an exposé on Grolier Recovery Services wouldn't do much to shorten the news cycle.

Didn't mean I had to like it.

I saw the flash of headlights, and a car pulled in right next to us, killing the engine. I recognized the driver but went through the stupid dance of bona fides required by some Taskforce James Bond regulation. Eventually, the driver entered our car.

I said, "Hey, Spanky. Long time no see."

His face broke into a grin. "They told me you had done the recce, but I thought for *sure* they were full of shit. Since when do you pull support? Why aren't you going in?"

"Oversight Council. Jennifer, give him the data."

For the first time, Spanky noticed who was sitting next to me. Well, noticed she was female. Honestly, I was unsure how this would go, as Jennifer was still a little bit of a novelty due to the cellular structure of the Taskforce. Most members had never seen her, much less operated with her, and I knew that plenty of people despised her because of her gender alone.

He said, "Wow. So I'm getting briefed by a celebrity. Jennifer Cahill. Aka Koko. In the flesh."

I saw hesitation flit across her face and knew she was unclear on how to proceed. I felt the same way, wondering if he was paying her a compliment or about to piss me off. I opened my mouth to clear the air when he continued. "I heard about that call in Mexico. Gutsy shit."

That was it. Not much in the way of words, but all he had to say. The Taskforce was like a high school in many ways, with rumor and innuendo flying through its ranks due to the secrecy embedded in its construction. Made up of humans—very, very smart humans—who didn't like to be kept in the dark, it was tribal, with tales passed by word of mouth at the shooting range or on the combatives mat. He'd just told me that Jennifer's word of mouth was better than good.

She nodded tentatively, then said, "You want the rest of the team to hear this? It's a little complicated."

"Yeah. It's just two of us, with a computer geek as a snap link. Bring the laptop to my car."

Twenty minutes later and she was done, back in my vehicle. I waved to Spanky and pulled away, hating the fact that we weren't playing.

Jennifer said, "He's pretty nice. I thought that would be harder."

"Why? You had all the information they'd need. Did they agree with your plan?"

"Well, yeah, I guess they had to. I didn't have another idea. He asked a couple of questions like he didn't want to execute a climb, but that's what I'd do. I guess I should have made a plan based on no skill."

I broke into a grin, wondering if I'd ever get the chance to stab Spanky in the eye with that comment.

Earlier, waiting on approval from Kurt, I'd kicked Jennifer from the car to play the "lady out for a stroll" while I took video from our vehicle on the target house. Since all I had done was take pictures, I'd tasked Jennifer with coming up with a plan. She'd briefed me her idea, basically sneaking in from the back deck using a caving ladder, but she hadn't wanted to be responsible for telling the team. She wanted me to do so because of my referent firepower in the Taskforce, an idea I'd automatically shit-canned. There was nothing worse than someone else briefing your plan. I mean *nothing*.

I said, "Did he think your course of action was weak? Or was it because you'd come up with the plan?"

She thought for a moment, then said, "Neither. I think he was afraid of making the computer guy climb. But there was no other way."

I laughed, started the car, and said, "He's just pissed that he didn't prepare for contingencies. Good to go. Get Kurt on the phone."

She dug through her purse, and in the overhead glow from a streetlight I saw blood on her forearm, seeping through the bandage. Much worse than should have been happening. Reminding me how this wasn't all fun and games. I said, "What's up with your wound?"

"Nothing." She dialed, then passed me the cell. "The butterfly bandages aren't holding, that's all."

I started to respond, then heard a voice on the line. I scowled at her, knowing she'd handed the phone over precisely to prevent the conversation.

It was Kurt. I gave him a SITREP, then asked how the timing was going for my brilliant plan.

"Police are alerted. Shouldn't be too long now. Oversight Council has the ball. They've already prepped the groundwork. Just waiting on the trigger."

"How long before the video is released?"

"We don't really know. Supposedly in the next few hours. We might actually get the arrest before it goes out, but even if we don't we're okay."

"Sounds good. I have to get Jennifer to an emergency

room. Her cut has busted open. I'll be on my cell. Let me know."

Kurt said, "I'll do better than that. Your team is in town. The Colorado thing is blowing over. The fingerprints from the dead guy are tracing back to Mexico, tied into a bunch of drug cartel killings. Nothing to do with the team. The police are on a totally different trail now and spun up about the cartels being in Colorado. It was significant enough to bring in the DEA. They couldn't care less about a bar fight. The worst of it is going to be a large fine for public drunkenness and disorderly conduct."

I leaned back in the seat, thinking about the circumstances. About how the dead hit man was going to provide cover for our team. About how I had been prevented from bringing out his body, and now that was going to draw attention away from our mission. About the random events that had caused the outcome.

I said, "That's probably the best news I've heard in days."

"After your last SITREP, I'm sure it is. Decoy's waiting with a full med bag. Skip the emergency room."

I put the car in gear, saying, "Where are they?"

"Twenty-second Street Embassy Suites. They're waiting on you at the bar. They've already reserved a couple of rooms for you and Jennifer. I'm going to need you in town for a few days, just in case."

I looked at Jennifer and said, "I can deal with that. No problem."

*   *   *

WE ARRIVED AT the Embassy Suites and moved straight to the restaurant in the back. It was closing in on one in the morning, but I wanted to see the team before crashing. We entered and they were all there, drinking around a table and telling lies. They saw us and waved. Decoy stood up and took Jennifer's hand, stretching out her arm and checking out her bandaged wound. He was surprisingly tender, given his reputation as a man-whore.

"I understand you could use my skills again."

She smiled and said, "Yeah. I guess so. I'm not as indestructible as you guys."

From the table, Knuckles grinned back, saying, "Nobody is. In our own minds."

She and Decoy walked away, and I got the skinny on what had happened after I'd flown out. In between talking, we watched the television like we were tallying precinct votes on an election night, waiting on the story.

I waited for a break in the conversation, then leaned into Knuckles and said, "You didn't tell anyone, did you? Nobody knows about Jennifer and me, right?"

He said, "Pike, I haven't said a word. Honestly, if you can make the right decisions, like you did in Mexico, I'm good with it."

"What about the team? You didn't say anything to them?"

"No. Not a word. Unlike you, when I say I won't do something, I don't."

I grimaced and said, "Knuckles, it wasn't like that. It just happened. I didn't ask for it."

He smiled and said, "Yes, you did."

Before I could answer, Blood said, "Here it is."

On the screen was a local newsman talking about an arrest for child pornography. The story would have been small, but it involved a very, very influential member of the political establishment, and in Washington, DC, that's all it took. The newscaster made a point of saying that it wasn't clear whether the computers in question had been from the father or the son.

A twist I hadn't even considered, but one that would definitely work in our favor.

Jennifer returned with Decoy, her arm in a new bandage. She had a smile on her face like she'd just heard a good joke. Given that she'd been with Decoy for thirty minutes, it raised my alert status.

I said, "Good to go? He didn't carve you up like a SEAL?"

She said, "No. He was gentle." She winked at me and said, "I swear all we did was talk about you."

For no reason whatsoever the words caused a spasm of jealousy. *What the hell does that mean?*

Decoy said, "You two must be smoked. No rest for the wicked."

I said, "Yeah, actually, I could use some sleep. You guys have our rooms, or do we need to check in?"

Blood said, "We checked you in."

He slid across a key-card envelope. I opened it and saw a single key.

Confused, I said, "Is this my room or Jennifer's?"

I looked up to find all of them smirking. Next to Decoy, with a grin on her face, Jennifer said, "I don't know about Kurt, but I think that answers your question about the team."

ACKNOWLEDGMENTS

Originally, in outline form, this manuscript was tracking to be a personal Taskforce action to rescue Jennifer's brother, period, with little in the way of global stakes. Even so, I needed something to get the Taskforce involved and chose our unmanned aerial vehicle usage on the border as a sort of throwaway linkage to the drug cartels. I studied weaknesses and homed in on the GPS controls, specifically for the UAV. It would have stayed that way, but the more I researched our GPS constellation, the more astonished I was at how many things in our lives are controlled by it. So much so that Arthur Booth was born and the manuscript took a decidedly different tack.

The Architecture Evolution Plan for our GPS is real, as is the fact that Boeing is building it. Selective availability is a real thing, and President Clinton did order it turned off in 2000, for good reason. GPS does, in fact, provide a single point of failure for a ton of things you don't even think about, such as most of the cellular phone networks in the United States, a majority of banking transactions, power grids, stop lights, and a host of other things, but the reader can rest easy at night. The GPS constellation is a very important part of our daily lives, but it's also one of the most secure and robust assets that we have, from the ground systems to the satellites themselves. How do I know? Because I had the honor of seeing it in action.

I'm indebted to LTC Tom "Steamer" Ste. Marie and public affairs officer Jennifer Thibault, who both graciously facilitated my visit to Schriever Air Force Base. Steamer, the commander of the 2nd SOPS that controls the GPS constellation, took time out of his busy schedule to explain how it functions and fix some of my pretty boneheaded technical details (proving once again, just because it's on the Internet doesn't mean it's accurate). In my previous life, I had to give informational briefings to numerous people, and it was always a pain, as it took me away from something more important—namely national defense. We used to call it Touching the Magic, and this time I was on the receiving end from the 2nd SOPS squadron commander. For that, I am grateful. More important, we're all indebted more than we know to the men and women of the 2nd SOPS who keep the GPS constellation flying. They do a tremendous amount of work that goes unsung by the average public, but not by those who study such things. In 2011, the International Astronautical Federation gave a one-time sixtieth anniversary award, picking the single thing in the annals of space exploration that demonstrated measurable benefit to humanity as a whole. The Global Positioning System was chosen out of everything else that's ever been done in space. After my research, I'm surprised it took so long. Rest assured, while the 2nd SOPS is allowed to chuckle, any mistakes with reference to the constellation are mine and mine alone.

As for Mexico, I was once again lucky. When I mentioned to a buddy that I was going to write about Mexico, I found out that a Navy SEAL I know was working in the embassy. I contacted him, and he took time out of his schedule to give me a helping hand peeling back the onion in that part of the world. He was in the process of moving back to the United States, but like SOFs everywhere, he laid out the red carpet upon my arrival, giving me a granular feel that I couldn't get from books. More important, he introduced me to Dudley A., a journalist who has lived in and reported on Mexico for major news outlets across the world for more than twenty-two years. When you read about Tepito in the book, that isn't my imagination at work. That's me being naive enough to allow Dudley to take me through it. I'll tell you, the pucker factor got pretty high when the cabdriver said—in Spanish—"Please lock your doors now." We made it out okay, but it probably wasn't the smartest thing I've done. Beyond Tepito, Dudley gave me invaluable advice on where to go and what to look for to ensure the accuracy of various scenes. All I had to say was "I need a location that does XXX" and he'd say, "I know *just* the place." One scene that ended up in the book will make him cringe, because it's so touristy. We did indeed have a margarita underneath the bullet hole fired by Pancho Villa in La Opera. I had no intention of using that bar, but given the scenario the *sicario* was dealing with, it worked.

As for the Cloud, I'm indebted to Mike, an old 1/75 Ranger that I met under bad circumstances at Arlington, during a funeral for a mutual friend. He's now fighting the increasing number of marijuana growers in our national forests—no small chore, and possibly another book—and was more than willing to give me a town that could potentially host the Cloud in Utah. I gave him my parameters, and he gave me a name (by text while he was out in the woods on an operation, no less), but make no mistake, everything involved with the Cloud is pure Brad Taylor. The sheriff, the jail, the holding of terrorists, and the *Cloud* are all fiction. Pretty believable fiction, though, huh? Look over your shoulder the next time you're arrested. Just kidding.

Once again, the Barrier Island Free Medical Clinic hosted a charity auction for the naming of an individual in the book. The BIFMC provides continuing primary health care to uninsured adults living at or below 200 percent of the federal poverty level. All of its doctors are volunteers, and all of its operating costs are donated or generated through fund-raisers. When they asked me if I would be willing to auction a character again, I said, "Well, yeah, but I've only got a bad guy this time." They thought that was great, and the bidding went high because people wanted to name someone besides themselves, in secret. In the end, Arthur Booth, the man who founded the clinic, won the "honor," due to the generosity of some anonymous bidders. He didn't know it at the time, but he will when he reads the book.

I'm slowly weaning myself from working in the security world in order to become a "real writer," and I'm indebted to my publisher, Dutton, for sticking with me. To my editors, Ben Sevier and Jessica Renheim, thanks for your keen eyes and necessary tweaks, which always make my manuscripts better—even if it means killing a fifteen-year-old boy at the beginning of the book. Also, I would be remiss if I didn't thank my publicity guru, Liza Cassity, for her superb work on my behalf, as well as the entire marketing team who is always there at the drop of a hat, regardless of my requests—and sometimes those requests seem a little strange, I'm sure.

I wouldn't be where I am without the friendship and advice of my agent, John Talbot, who goes above and beyond on my behalf regularly. I truly appreciate all you do. Last but not least, a huge thank-you to my amazing wife, Elaine, without whom I couldn't do my job. Thanks for keeping all the balls in the air and doing it all with grace and style. She told me she would rather I get to the Honey-Do list than be mentioned in the book. Oh well, I did manage to milk that for a few years. I promise I'll get the list knocked out soon. I swear.

Pike Logan and his team are tracking an American arms dealer in Tel Aviv who may—or may not—be attempting to sell sensitive nuclear weapons components to the highest bidder. When Pike's team breaks up an attempt to kill a friend and former Mossad direct action team member, they stumble upon much more than they expected—a concerted conspiracy to topple a democratic African country.

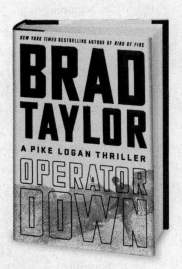

 Penguin
Random
House

1

Being a spy is a lot like being a bank robber. In espionage—as in crime—it's always the little things that get you. You can plan for an entire operation, allowing for one contingency after another, foreseeing when and where things might go wrong, but you inevitably miss the little things. A drop of sweat on a doorknob, drywall shavings left behind after the installation of a bug, a nick in the brass plate of a lock from a tension wrench. Small things with huge impacts.

In this case, the little thing happened before Aaron Bergmann had even left Israel, when a travel voucher routed through Mossad headquarters included a man who had been specifically excluded from the mission read-on. For a specific reason. And that little thing would prove devastating for Aaron and his neophyte apprentice.

Casually tapping the tablet in front of him, Aaron said, "Alex, turn just a tad bit to the right. I'm missing the man on the left side of the table."

Across the table from him Alexandra Levy shifted

slightly, her face aglow. She said, "This is so exciting! Straight out of a James Bond movie."

He chuckled, then said, "Right there. Good." He hit record on the tablet.

Alex stiffened a little bit, as if she were posing for a photographer, holding her angle. She whispered, "That thing will really read their lips? Tell us what they're saying?"

Aaron said, "Yep. If you can keep the camera on them, but don't look so rigid. Relax a little. I'll tell you if it shifts off."

Aaron continued manipulating a piece of software in his tablet, something that was highly classified and usually reserved for active Mossad agents. A simple button camera in Alexandra's blouse was tied by Bluetooth to his tablet and seemed to be something out of a 007 movie, but in truth, both were commercially available to anyone who wanted one. The secret was the software churning through what the camera sent it.

Artificial intelligence for facial recognition had grown by leaps and bounds in recent years, and the Mossad had taken that in a different direction, focusing on the spoken word. They'd replicated the human act of lip reading into the cyber world, designing a software suite that could decipher what was being said without hearing sound.

Alex relaxed her body a bit, contrition floating across her face. "Sorry. This isn't my expertise. You should be doing the camera work."

He laid the tablet on the table and took a sip of beer, saying, "You're doing fine. This beats working in the diamond exchange, right? Keep up the talent and I might recruit you for my firm."

She grinned and said, "No, no, this is enough excitement. I enjoy being able to help—I've never even been to Africa—but I'll stick with my boring job."

There was no fear in the statement. No realization of the risk. It was like she thought they were executing a high school senior prank. She had no idea of the threat level.

That would come later.

She glanced over the balcony toward their target and said, "Besides, I don't think your partner would agree to that. I think she hates me."

Three people sat at the table they were filming: two white and one black. Their target was a man of about thirty-five and, unlike the rest of the patrons in the restaurant, was dressed in a suit as if he were still working in his office in Israel. The other white man looked like he was about to head out on a safari, wearing cargo pants and a shirt that had more pockets than a photographer's vest. He had shaggy blond hair, ice blue eyes, and a feral quality. Aaron had seen his type plenty of times before, but only in a war zone. It intrigued him.

The final man was tall, with a thin mustache and coal black skin. He was dressed like a local but didn't act like one. Ramrod straight, he showed not a whit of humor. Had they held the meeting at a café in downtown Johannesburg—where the target was staying—they would have attracted attention by their very disparate appearances, but they didn't here. Which explained why Aaron's target had chosen this restaurant. The one thing remaining was to find out why the meeting was occurring.

The only man Aaron recognized was the one the Mossad had asked him to track—an employee of a diamond broker in Tel Aviv. The other two were a mystery, but he'd know about them soon enough when they reviewed the footage later.

The primary problem with the lipreading software was choosing a language—try to lipread German when the target was speaking Chinese and you'd get gibberish. Here, in the township of Soweto, just outside the city center of Johannesburg, South Africa, he was sure they were speaking English. There was no way the black man spoke Hebrew, and he would be astounded if his target from Israel spoke something like Swahili or Afrikaans. No, they'd be speaking English, and the fact that his method of recording the conversation came through in visual rather than auditory means was a plus in the current environment.

The outdoor balcony they were on belonged to a restaurant called Sakhumzi, as did the patio holding the target's table. Just a stone's throw from the historical houses of Nelson Mandela and Bishop Tutu, in the section of Soweto known as Orlando West, the restaurant hosted a smorgasbord of local food and native performers and was a permanent stop for tour groups large and small traveling to see the ghetto made famous in the uprising against apartheid. Because of it, there was a constant drumbeat of laughter and clapping—something that had no effect on the lipreading software. As long as Aaron could keep a line of sight with whoever was talking.

Aaron focused on the computer, tapping icons and ensuring three computer-generated squares remained over the mouths. He said, "Position is good. Keep that." When he hadn't responded to Alex's statement, she repeated, "Your partner doesn't care for me at all. I thought she was going to throw me out of your house."

Aaron looked up from the tablet and said, "Shoshana? She doesn't hate you. She's just mad because I brought you instead of her. She was aggravated at me for the decision. It's nothing personal."

Making sure not to disrupt the camera angle, she said, "I don't think so. When you left the room, she was . . . a little scary."

Aaron laughed and returned to the tablet, offhandedly saying, "You need to get to know her. She's not all knives and death threats. She just acts that way. She understands that she didn't have the knowledge base for this mission. When we fly back tomorrow, I'll take you to dinner. The three of us."

Alex smiled and said, "I'd like that. I think she thought . . ."

Aaron looked up from the tablet and said, "Thought what?"

"That we . . . I mean, you and me . . . might . . ."

Aaron scoffed and said, "You're twenty years younger than me."

She said, "Yeah, but it was the Mossad that asked me . . . *you* asked me . . . I mean, they wouldn't do that unless it was for a reason."

Aaron realized she thought she really *was* in a movie. And realized she was hitting on him. A twenty-something *sabra* that worked inside the Israeli diamond exchange, she was no doubt attractive. Brown hair, brown eyes, liquid skin, and a quiet intelligence surrounded by an innocence he no longer possessed, he would have hunted her like a wolf a decade ago, but no longer. She deserved to live in her innocence. His entire existence was ensuring people like her could do so. He decided to put an end to the fantasy.

"Alex, I picked you because you understand the diamond market. Yes, you're attractive, which meant I could use you to blend in, but I need your knowledge. Period. You listen to the tape, you tell me what they're talking about within the diamond world, and I write an assessment. That's it. This isn't a complex thing. We're not here to save Israel from Blofeld. We're here to save Israel from embarrassment. That's all. It's a simple mission."

Turning red, she tilted forward and whispered, "What does that mean? I wasn't suggesting anything."

He said, "You're screwing with the camera angle. Lean back."

The target at the table answered a cell phone.

Aaron said, "Shit. Lean back—now."

Alex did so abruptly, causing the camera to sway wildly. Aaron said, "Stay still."

The man turned away from them, still on the phone.

Aaron said, "We need to move. *You* need to move. Stand up and go to the bathroom. Walk by the table and get me a shot of his face as long as you can. Stop and ask the table for directions, but not to him. Let him keep talking on the phone."

Hesitantly, Alex stood. More forcefully than he wanted, Aaron said, "Go."

She did, sidling between the throngs of tour bus patrons and locals, threading between the tables and down the stairs, the picture on Aaron's tablet jumping left and right. She reached the patio and it stabilized. She walked toward the restrooms, then stopped at the table, asking directions. He recorded about a fifteen-second snippet of the phone conversation, unsure if the software would be able to utilize the footage because the target's face was partially obscured by his smartphone.

He glanced over the balcony to see the interaction, and she broke contact, doing a passable job of being a tourist. He saw no outward interest in the interruption.

Aaron ignored the rest of the feed, wondering if Alex would be smart enough to cut it off if she really chose to use the bathroom. She did. Or maybe the Bluetooth simply lost contact because of distance. He grinned and took a sip of his beer, surreptitiously giving the target table a side-eye.

The target was asking a waitress for the check. He immediately picked up his phone and called Alex, telling her to return.

The men tossed some rand on the table, preparing to leave, and he saw her coming across the patio. She mounted the stairs to the balcony and he stood, saying, "Hopefully they take the same car. If they split up, we'll stick to the target."

Hidden by the balcony railing, they let the group exit the restaurant, then followed, getting to the parking lot just as they were loading a single car. While he had made the comment earlier about one vehicle, a part of him spiked at the action, since they'd arrived in two separate cars.

He should have listened to his sixth sense. Lulled by the minimal threat of his mission, he thought he had his bases covered but had forgotten a hard truth he had learned in the past: In warfare, the enemy gets a vote.

2

Crossing the lobby to the Las Vegas Venetian casino, another gaggle of bearded men went by, all wearing cargo pants and baseball caps with Velcro patches. Half of them toted some form of corduroy nylon backpack, which also sported a variety of gun-porn patches, like *ISIS Hunter* or a *Punisher* skull.

I said, "I have never seen this many super-commando 'operators' in one place in my life."

Knuckles laughed and said, "Yeah, this event brings 'em out of the woodwork, no doubt. But make no mistake, the real deal's running around in here as well. In fact, keep your eyes peeled. The odds of us running into someone we know are pretty high, so be prepared to run the cover story."

Working in cover was the worst when you did it in an area where the locals potentially knew you. Whenever that happened, the nastiest thing that could occur—besides getting your fingernails pulled out by the enemy—was running into someone who knows who you are in real life. It was the surest way to blow the hell out of what you were pretending. An FBI agent infiltrating an outlaw motorcycle gang would be in dire straights if he bumped into a friend from law school.

In this case, Knuckles was still active duty Navy and I was retired Army. In the world of the Taskforce, when we were out in the Badlands earning our *ISIS Hunter* patches for real, he was a civilian employee of my company, but if another SEAL from his past saw him here, they'd know that was bullshit, so we'd created a story that was plausible should that happen to either of us.

It was my first trip to the fabled SHOT Show in Las Vegas, the largest gun show on earth, and the interior of the Sands convention center was literally stuffed with booth after booth selling various weapons, accessories, and outdoor gear. It was Mecca to people like me, and the Taskforce sent a contingent every year to prowl the halls looking for anything new that we could incorporate into our mission. Back when I was on active duty, as the team leader, I'd always let a junior member of the team make the trip, and Knuckles, my 2IC, had been a few times before.

Given how he was dressed, I'm surprised they let him in.

In contrast to the bearded ones, he looked like he had come to protest the convention, with his long hippy hair, Che Guevara T-shirt, and lack of any tacticool paraphernalia. He was even wearing a leather necklace with a bronze peace sign the size of a fifty-cent piece—either as irony or a challenge. With him it was hard to tell, but if someone took it as a challenge, they'd be sorely wishing they hadn't. Unlike a lot of the posers at the convention, he was most definitely an Operator.

While the trip *was* a little bit of a boondoggle, we did have a specific mission. We'd just come from a booth manned by a company called ZEV Technologies—a maker of high-end aftermarket components and custom frame/slide work for Glock pistols—and had sealed a deal to test some pistols for our specific applications.

Although we already had our own armorer support that we used to hone our combat weapons, Kurt Hale—the commander of the Taskforce—was wondering if we weren't just reinventing the wheel and wanted to see if it would be better to simply farm out the work. After talking to ZEV, I was beginning to believe he was right, only our wheels were something from a Conestoga wagon while ZEV was racing around on run-flats.

We pushed through the crowd and entered the cavernous Venetian casino, working our way to Las Vegas Boulevard. We exited into the sunshine, leaving the commandos and gamblers only to be hit by Guatemalan refugees trying to hand me cards with hookers offering their services. One of the strangest things about Vegas.

Knuckles said, "What did you think?"

"Seriously? I think we should have flown here with the entire team's Glocks. No question they can do better than our internal armorers. Nothing against them, but did you work the one they had on display? Better trigger than ours by far."

Knuckles took a left toward Caesars Palace, passing the

gigantic Venetian hotel, saying, "So forget about any other vendors?"

He had a point. While we didn't fall under any official DoD rules about contracts, it would be stupid to latch on to the first one we found. We had a list of potential companies that could meet our goals, and it wouldn't be right not to at least check them out. But I was pretty sure where I would end up on my recommendation to Kurt.

I said, "Naw, we should hit 'em up as well, but we only get two days out here, and I want some Vegas time. I'll send Retro and Jennifer to go hunt them down."

"Retro isn't going to like that, and Jennifer's not exactly an expert."

Retro had been a teammate of mine since Jesus was wearing diapers, but all things come to a close sooner or later. He was set to retire from the military at the end of the month and had truly come out here as a complete vacation. Kurt knew he wasn't needed but had let him come along as a little retirement gift. Unbeknownst to me, in all our time together, I learned he absolutely loved playing craps, and his wife frowned on gambling. He had planned on spending his entire time in the casinos betting away his per diem like a drunken sailor.

As we were planning to leave for the trip, he'd begged to come along, getting a seat through Kurt, then had turned around and told his wife he was desperately needed for national security, which she bought. As they say, "What happens in Vegas . . ."

I said, "It's not going to kill him to take a break for a

few hours, and as far as Jennifer goes, she could learn something."

Jennifer was my partner in Grolier Recovery Services—our company—and, outside of some serious weapons training I'd given her, had no military experience. She wasn't qualified to judge whether a vendor was worthy, and wasn't needed on this trip either, but I'd paid for her to come along out of my own pocket because, well, she was a partner in more ways than one. She'd planned on spending her time at the pool—or if the weather was too cold, in the spa.

I felt my phone vibrate and saw it was her. I said, "Speak of the devil."

I answered, "Hey, we're on Vegas Boulevard headed home. What's up?"

"Kurt wants to talk on the VPN. Secure."

"About what?"

"Apparently, about a mission. In Vegas."

BRAD TAYLOR

"Readers of novels set in the world
of Special Forces have many choices,
but Taylor is one of the best."
—*Booklist*

For a complete list of titles,
please visit prh.com/bradtaylor.